DRAGON FIRE

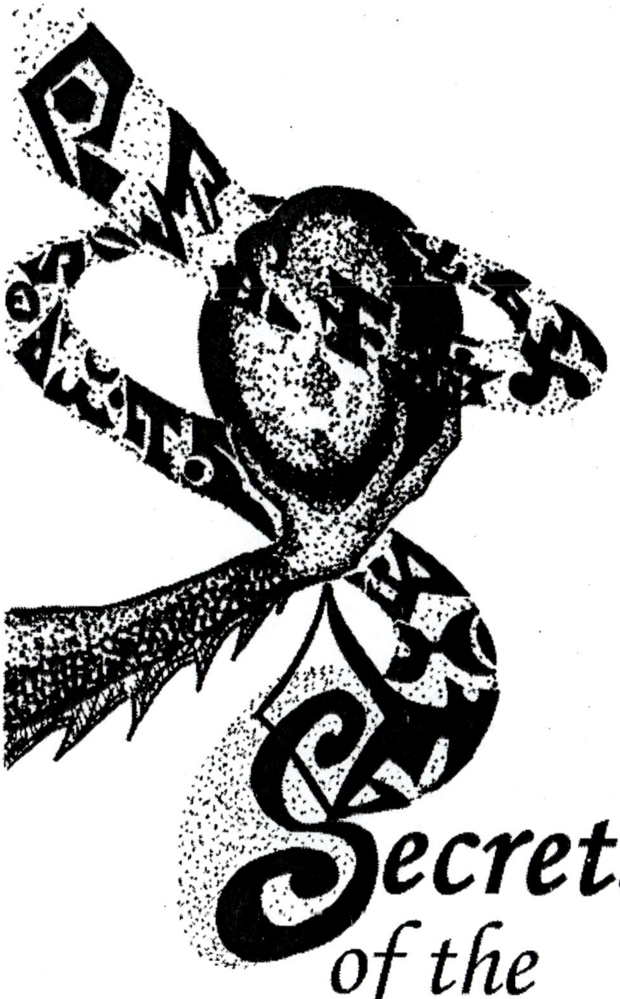

Secrets of the Last Dragons

by
E. Miriandra Rota

Illustrations by E. Diane Coleman
Cover art by Joan Critz Limbrick

Copyright © 2003 by Miriandra Rota

Front Cover Art
"Dragon Fire" by Joan Critz Limbrick
To order a print of "Dragon Fire"
and to view additional artwork:
www.joanlimbrick.com

Illustrations
by E. Diane Coleman
For prints of the illustrations in Dragon Fire,
contact Diane at P. O. Box 81,
Troutdale, VA 24378

Interior and cover layout by Masha Shubin.

This is a work of fiction. The events described here are imaginary. The settings and characters are fictitious and do not represent specific places or living or dead people. Any resemblance is entirely coincidental.

All rights reserved. No part of this book may be reproduced or transmitted in any form or by any means whatsoever, including photocopying, recording or by any information storage and retrieval system, without written permission from the publisher. Contact Inkwater Press at 6750 SW Franklin Street, Suite A, Portland, OR 97223.

www.inkwaterpress.com
ISBN 1-59299-035-5
Publisher: Inkwater Press

Printed in the U.S.A.

DEDICATION

For the Dragons

"One day we will be called upon. In that day we will be asking ourselves to leave everything that is familiar. It is then that each one must drink of the more-of-that-which-we-are. It is then that we must turn from all that we have been and face that which we are becoming. It is then that the Ancient Ones will weep at our splendor!"

— **Zog,** Winzoarian of all Dragons

CONTENTS

THOSE BEASTS OF FIRE CALLED DRAGONS 1
IN SEARCH OF WIZARDS 11
ZOANNA'S CALL 25
THE MOMENT IN STRETCHED TIME BEGINS 34
THE FIRST SECTOR OF LEARNING 44
WHAT IS THAT CLANGING?? 54
FALLING INTO THE DREAM STATE 67
IF YOU DON'T MIND MY ASKING – PROVE IT! 79
THE OLD DRAGON'S CHAMBER WALLS CURVED INWARD 87
MENTARD WAITED FOR THE EASY 98
I AM THE ONE. I AM THE ONLY ONE. 113
YOU WILL YIELD!! 123
FAIRIES! 133
ILLUSIONARY PEAKS AND GNOMES 144
THEY ARE WATER DRAGONS!! 157
MENTARD'S JOURNEY INTO THE UNKNOWN 172
REMEMBER, WE ARE ALWAYS WITH YOU 186
THE ELDER WAS RIGHT. THEY WOULD NEVER BE THE SAME. 200
THE TIME IS NOW! 214
ONE YOU WILL NEVER SUSPECT WILL TURN EVENTS! 223
WE MUST DRINK THE MORE-OF-THAT-WHICH-WE-ARE! 234
FOLLOW MEEEEE! 246
THE OLDEST DRAGON CALLED 256
EPILOGUE 267

LIST OF ILLUSTRATIONS

MAP, LAND OF THE DRAGONS

TIME-STREAM, ONE OF TWELVE STREAMS

SECRETS AND SYMBOLS

DRAGON WINGS

KLEEANA'S GOSSAMER WINGS

SYMBOLS THROUGH THE PORTAL

WIZARD ON MENTARD'S SHOULDER

THE CHALLENGE

ACKNOWLEDGMENTS

There are many people who have contributed to the journey during which this book was written.

My gratitude goes especially to Grayson Howell for believing in me. Thank you for all your support and encouragement, for listening to each emerging chapter, and for loving these dragons as much as I do.

Thank you Cynthia McTyre for volunteering your expert editing talents without knowing that twelve chapters would grow into twenty-three, and for holding the story in the highest light.

Thank you Joan Limbrick for gifting your glorious painting, Dragon Fire. Your art always takes my breath away.

Thank you Diane Coleman for enthusiastically drawing our illustrations over and over again until "we got it right," for being such a good friend, and for sharing Zippy.

Thank you Donnie Coleman for your dedicated computer expertise, for the many hours devoted to illustration corrections and revisions, and for your genuine caring. You are a gem!

Thank you Arthur Hilt for generously giving your loving support in so many ways without asking, "What's going on?" and for being a trusted, good friend.

Thank you Skip and Faye Atwater especially for your love and spiritual guidance, for always encouraging me to explore more of who I am, and for welcoming me home when I most needed it.

Thank you Richard Jennette for our many spiritual talks, for your unhesitating encouragement and support, for your very funny sense of humor, and for being my friend of friends.

Thank you Donna Adams for being there during the most difficult times. You have always been the best. You are the best.

Thank you dear dragons for the life-changing gift of writing your story.

Land of the Dragons

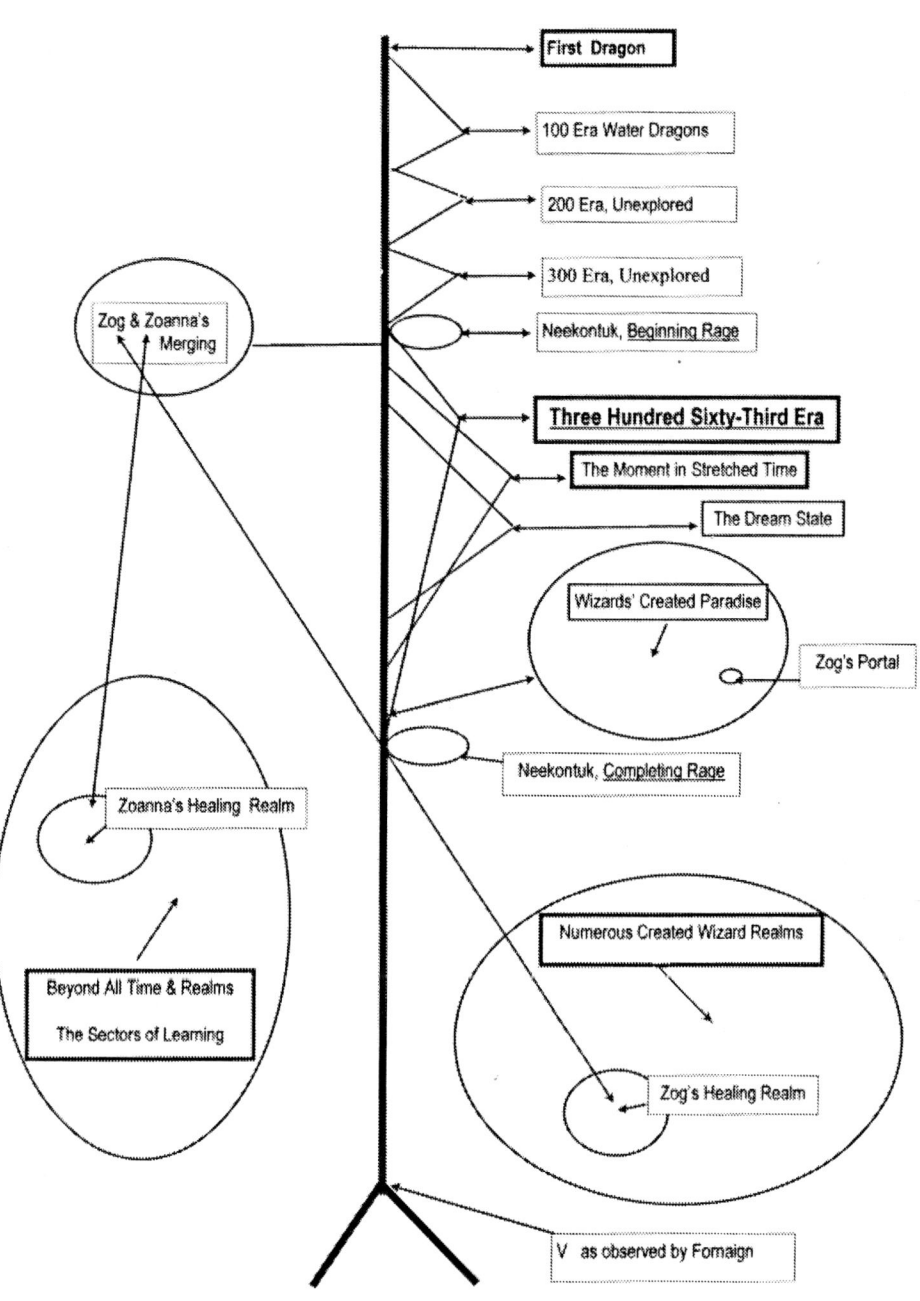

Time Stram, One of Twelve

CHAPTER ONE

THOSE BEASTS OF FIRE CALLED DRAGONS

Long ago, when the land was populated with fairies, gnomes and wizards, there lived with much grace and dignity, those beasts of fire and hearts of love called dragons.

Together they resided not only in the mountains, but also on the grassy plains where they brought their young to bask in the warmth of the sun, to play and to spread their wings in the open air. Until their wings are fully-grown, dragon inglets[1] cannot fly alone or lift off the mountain.

Zoanna had been such an inglet and during her youth held great impatience for the growth of her wings. She was continually spreading them to gaze upon the size of her fan, knowing for certain with her fully developed eye gauging that they were growing — just not fast enough. Her frequent examination developed her wing muscles to such a degree that she later became the Grand Damme of the entire Dragon Floggen[2] as she could soar to great heights for greater lengths of time. Often she flew alone. None others were capable of flying with her. It was during such a flight that she met Zog, her future mate, who also was quite accustomed to flying alone for similar reasons.

As she and her two young ones now basked in the sun, she remembered those times with

---

1 Inglets: newly birthed and young ones.

2 Floggen: family and community.

fondness. The mating ritual of dragons being one of flight and fire, strength and surrender, and merging while in flight, Zog and Zoanna had flown together in such manners with an intensity never before felt among any Floggen. Their ritual had lasted for twice the usual fifty years.

While they had rested their depleted beings in the caverns of the great mountain, the fairies and gnomes had come about them to breathe a breath upon their hides, to caress their folded wings and to place drops of golden elixir into their mouths. Cared for in this manner, they had slept for thirty years.

The birthing rhythm of their inglets had nudged them to awakened states of stretching, yawning, breathing fire and thunderous releasing of the remnants of their passions.

Zoanna basked in such a memory as she watched her two inglets. Kleeana, her first born, examined her opened golden wings; while Mothan breathed his fiery breath into the wind. Her life was full, and the land supported that richness with its abundant food and deep clear waters. In truth, never had the land and its inhabitants resided in a better flowing. It was near the time of Sleecha[3], when the first leaves and flowers burst forth upon the valley land before the mountain trees even awakened, that she rested upon the sweet grasses and that the Golden Era began to lose its glow.

A dark cloud rumbled overhead and when Zoanna lifted her long neck to bring her head in view of the cloud, she was stunned by the sight of not a rumbling cloud but that of her beloved Zog, efforting to fly, struggling with tattered wings and plundered body. Dark smoke flowed from his nostrils where raging fire familiarly called her name as he approached.

Not to the field, although it seemed to be the easiest journey's end, but to the mountain did he go. With groaning effort, he lifted his wings again and again until he was at the entryway of their home.

Zoanna whistled her anxious breath to her two young ones, and they climbed upon her great strong back. Once they had

---

3 Sleecha: the first breath of spring.

attached their claws into the grooves grown during the last seventeen years as the two did develop, she unfolded her great wings, wafted them once and lifted her graceful body into the sky. With swift strong movements, she flew toward the mountain and the great puffs of dark smoke.

The fairies gathered the inglets, while Zoanna breathed her fiery breath into the green covered nostrils of Zog. His body fluids were depleting even as she worked to save him. The gnomes carried containers of oil and ginseng root to place upon his wounds and torn secondary, gossamer wings.

Zog lay quietly still, not exerting dwindling energies in an effort to spill forth the tale of his injuries and more so, the onslaught of darkness only four dragon-flying days away. Yet what was the need to even quickly compute in his mind how soon or how much longer their paradise would remain undisturbed? He had barely flown the last farthem[4] and now here he lay, forcing himself to replenish his strength that he might lead his family and their Floggen either in battle or in flight. Such decisions would require his full abilities to future journey within the realm of possibilities....

Zoanna waited until Zog's breathing became regular and unlabored before releasing her focus upon his life force. Her keen but loving gaze flowed over his wounds, some deep into his flesh beneath the thick armor-like layer. She remembered his journey to the Neterlund, where he remained with the wizards until together they had transformed his hide into thick platelets, denser than the mountain's inner core. Zog, however, had insisted on remaining longer with the wizards to form the fluid underbase upon which the platelets rested, giving him the ability to change form in mid-flight. It was the fluid underbase now that Zoanna breathed her soft breath upon, inviting the memory of its creation to take form once again and allowing herself to wonder what force could have found its mark beneath the platelets and prevented her beloved's transforming. She wondered

---

4 Farthem: 1,000 miles.

5 Fleecia: section or block of time outside the realms of cause and effect.

DRAGON FIRE: SECRETS OF THE LAST DRAGONS

why Zog hadn't used his symbols to remove himself from sight or detection.

Invisibility incantations had held Zog with the wizards an additional Fleecia[5]. It had been his undetected return home that had introduced such abilities firstly to his family as he quietly took form before their startled eyes; and secondly, when he appeared at the Kloan Gathering[6], much to the pleasure and astonishment of the elders who had never been able to call forth the portal to the wizards. Indeed, Zog had been the first dragon to venture into those realms which were not of their usual elder-gifted capabilities.

The memories of those times seemed to settle themselves into the past and even Zoanna's expert calling could not maintain them within the present. She reluctantly relinquished such attempts and turned her full attention to the outer platelets which had begun to solidify and change in color from deep luminescent green to dark bluish gray, the signal of future journey. She quickly spoke softly, trying to disguise her alarm, "Your wounds must heal first.... Your strength must be restored...."

Zog heard. His body stirred a little and the familiar green returned. Zoanna's love encircled the great form of her beloved and there they did reside within the Chamber of Replenishment[7], each merging with the other, flowing golden essence giving and receiving in one breath, each being the injuries, each being the strength, each being the peace, each being the concern. It was during the merging that Zoanna became aware of the approaching darkness. She had never known Zog to carry such concerns, yet as they flowed through her and she became them, a new

---

[6] Kloan Gathering: a gathering during which the Floggen introduces their young and where the elders demonstrate practices integrated from other realms not accessible to the entire Floggen. Also, when within the cavern of Mutchiat, a decision-making gathering of the Elders and/or Representatives of each Floggen.

[7] Chamber of Replenishment: once adult dragons have become mates, their merging together creates patterns of wholeness, love, and the celebration of their union. From that time forward, any merging automatically creates a chamber comprised of the patterns, and functions to re-establish those patterns within both dragons. In this instance, Zog's physical health is restored. Within the merging, each dragon can then release into the wholeness, experiences and adventures, discoveries and beauty. All that is released is merged to become part of both dragons.

frequency began to take form and before she could choose, there resided between them that called fear.

She didn't allow it to fill her; neither did Zog allow the fullness of his own fear to be released for merging. He knew the Floggen would need the strength of Zoanna's innocence. His decision to maintain his fear and not dispel it through merging within their chamber changed the way Zog experienced the upcoming times. Some would say that it sharpened his senses and abilities, while others would say that his inability to further access the portal of the wizards placed a thin barrier around portions of his heart. A few would speculate that it was there that Zog maintained the treasure of his past journeys to a realm none had since neither searched for nor even spoken about during late night whisperings when the elders gathered. And some would barely remember the colors of the paradise that shivered and trembled as the darkness flowed into the Nacha[8].

Zog and Zoanna had continued merging until at last the flowing between them released the chamber. Even though Zog was restored and his wounds healed, he remained with Zoanna, basking in the rosy radiance of her glow. He called the fairies to bring his two inglets so that they might be together once more before he spoke of his experiences to the Kloan gathering.

He gazed upon the two young ones and allowed a trickle of joy to fill his heart. He breathed a blue flame toward them and their delight in his presence filled their home. Even though there would never again be a *usual* to their home, Zog breathed it all into his senses, as did Zoanna. She too allowed the knowing to remain unspoken. It was this treasure of their family joy that would sustain them during their speaking to the Kloan.

For Zog, it was this joy, too, and the viewing in his first future journey that filled him with a strength he had never felt before. Such strength had only been hinted at during his timeless forming with the wizards. It flowed as a red river through every form and within all manners of his great dragon being.

---

8 <u>Nacha</u>: a mountain range two distances from their home.

DRAGON FIRE: SECRETS OF THE LAST DRAGONS

· · · · ·

Even before Zog had vibrated forth the trumpeting of his urgent call, the elders of each Floggen had begun to gather. Some journeyed from the Great Lac[9] while others who had felt the shift in their mountain range itself had simultaneously placed a trumpeting call into the Glarian[10].

The Great Cavern within Mutchiat[11] had opened its portal wide to allow the trafficking of so many large beasts, and it was now that all fires were placed in suspension as they recognized Zog's position of Winzoarian[12].

It seemed long ago that the Glarian had whispered among themselves that they might be gifted with an actual Winzoarian. The news had quickly spread that young Zog had demonstrated not only invisibility fazings but those of changing form in mid-flight. In fact, he had mastered form-changing at such an early age that many had become so accustomed to his playful manner of delighting them with such colorful displays that they almost took his abilities for granted.

Gifting them in the same manner, Zog now appeared before them, first as the reflective form of themselves and then as the flow of his home mountain when Treiga[13] had settled upon its crests and radiated more colors than any of the other mountain homes. Such demonstration favored the elders with a joyful tickle around their piercing eyes, and all present remembered the deep honor they had felt when they named him Winzoarian, the first

---

9 Great Lac: a body of water used by the elders for traveling to those realms wherein the gatherings of Floggen Elders from other mountain ranges meet. Also a body of water used by parents and their young during times of seasonal transformation and the shedding of the previous journey's experiences, a merging experience for the young, similar to the adult replenishment merging chamber.

10 Glarian: the entire population of dragons residing physically in One Realm, even though they might journey to and participate within other realms not designated as their home.

11 Mutchiat: the largest mountain range and location of the Floggen and Glarian gatherings.

12 Winzoarian: one who is adept at producing abilities written of only within the symbols each dragon contains encoded within the portal of his or her heart.

13 Treiga: the deepest of winter.

THOSE BEASTS OF FIRE CALLED DRAGONS

any could remember 'cept where such abilities were carried within their histories.

Zog settled his great glistening being before them and without the usual greeting, began to speak of the oncoming rage.

"I have been to the outer rim of our furthest realm." Many had traveled there and knew the exact journey and the stark nature of the outer rim. "It has changed." Without pausing for them to assimilate the colors he projected upon their knowing, he continued, "What was once our familiar gray and stone is now orange and fire." The three who maintained the stories of all realms leaned their great bodies forward. They knew what Zog was speaking of. "The only time fire did fill the outer rim was during the height of the Great Change. None of us were in form during that time, yet I have past-traveled and seen for myself what did occur during the dwindling of our number to less than one-half and then to none."

Zog did not display for them what he had seen during the past-travel. Instead he spoke of the current orange fire. "Though I, as well as many of you, can breathe a fire registering in metaclores[14], I could not match the fire at the rim." He waved their rumblings aside. "The flatlands are boiling and the wave of darkness has already reached within the home of Kilchek[15] twenty farthings from our first range."

Kilchek and his Floggen had all but vanished and as the elders glanced around, they knew that none of Kilchek's Floggen were present at this Kloan. Yet Zog would not allow them to enter one tone or vibration in support of the possible reforming of Kilchek. Even as he had struggled home, Zog had toned the sounds that would have located Kilchek or any of the others. There had been no response.

---

14 <u>Metaclores</u>: the highest measurements of dragon fire.

15 <u>Kilchek</u>: a leader of his own Floggen who perished in the onslaught of the Great Fire.

16 <u>Neekontuk</u>: written of in Glarian histories as an onslaught of raging fire and power, which disintegrates everything in its path. Thus far, in known histories, the Neekontuk has endured through three endings and beginnings of Dragon existence.

7

DRAGON FIRE: SECRETS OF THE LAST DRAGONS

Instead, he continued, knowing that the oncoming cloud raged toward them. "Even as I speak, a great wave of the Neekontuk[16] comes upon us." Not one sound could be heard as the three hundred and fifty-seven dragons waited for his next words. "We have never spoken openly of the Neekontuk before this day," he passed his benevolent gaze over them, "nor of its disintegrating powers." He allowed a deep breath to slowly pass through his recently healed nostrils. "Indeed we have never spoken among us of the histories of Neekontuk as it endured the three endings and beginnings of our existence."

He wished he didn't have to continue to use the word or to speak of the close-by onslaught. He wished for one brief second that he might speak with them of the many celebrations they had enjoyed together. The color of the smoke of his breath demonstrated that momentary wish as he continued speaking at an alarming pace. In truth, as he rendered the description of the powerful onslaught and the ranges that were no more, it was that slight color within the smoke flowing from his nostrils that also gave the Kloan a slight moment to breathe a breath and still the growing growl that began deep in their own inner rumblings as they prepared for possible battle.

As Zog sensed their rumblings he shocked them by stating loudly, "The best solution might be to flee!" He looked back into their wide-open stare. "I will future-travel three times before I speak with you upon our best action." He pointed to three of his fellow leaders. "Come," he said, "we will future-travel now. There is no time to prepare the fires, or need to speak the rhythm of words. I know the way well!"

Each future journey required three fellow leaders to maintain focus as anchors for Zog while he dissolved his great body before their eyes and traveled into a realm they called the future. Each anchoring leader would then maintain his focus on the

---

17 <u>Structure, Blue</u>: Created by the wizards, blue lines racing upon themselves to form an energetic structure in the shape of the two of Mutchiat's peaks, one upright and one inverted, each residing within the other. Created for Zog the first time he, as an inglet, began to phase out of the wizard's realm. As Winzoarian, Zog continued to use the blue structure for future-travel purposes.

THOSE BEASTS OF FIRE CALLED DRAGONS

patterns of Zog, as they knew him. Sparkling blue lines raced upon themselves as Zog's familiar structure[17] continued to form itself in the place where his body stood before dissolving. It would be into the structure that Zog would return.

The three he had chosen had anchored several times before, which should have relieved them of concerns. Yet this time Zog was gone for twice the usual stretch of time and each one felt the pull on his own body integrity as he waited for Zog to take form once again.

· · · · ·

Zog entered his first future-travel without hesitation. Great wings unfurled to their fullest degree, each layer supporting the one above it, until he felt the strength of the replenished merging with his beloved Zoanna tested to its capacity. His first destination was the Timeline overview — the same overview to which the wizards had treated him resulting from their pleasure in discovering the depth of his abilities even at the young age of seven hundred and fifty-two. Then, he had gazed upon all realms and, as a moving living story, beneath his intent gaze formed the histories of not only his Floggen but also all Floggen over all time.

The wizards had waited for his gaze to settle on the depicting of the present moment in the Timeline, but instead he had raced to the future. They had quickly joined their wizardry and blocked from his young curious sight the exact moment of the current onslaught. Together the wizards had created another realm which depicted the flowing of a dragon future in a most beautiful land, promising a flourishing continuing of Zog's family and all future Floggens. His young heart had swelled with joy and comfort at the future sighting.

Even though it had been their immediate bandaid creation, it was only after Zog had returned home that the wizards met to discuss what they had just created. It was different, they had agreed, when they had created a realm for themselves to journey into. Then they had delighted in their own mastery and had played for the sheer joy of discovering just what had been created to surprise even themselves. After such play, they had simply dissolved their playground.

However, now that someone other than a wizard had actually seen and recorded a created future realm, it was decided — after much deliberation — that the realm must be maintained. It was also agreed that, in Zog's absence, they would necessarily remove the block they had momentarily placed before his apt gaze. Such removal did then allow the viewing — by any who were capable — of the long-time rhythm of the Neekontuk's devouring of all physical realms, including the dragons and their land. Although it was a quick decision, as they would never disturb the Natural Time Continuum, it was not an easy decision. Even then their wizard gaze had demonstrated to their heart-felt knowing just the present onslaught which now brought Zog to the very same observation point where he unleashed his piercing laser vision to investigate the flowing of the future.

It was there that he saw himself as an inglet, searching in a similar manner. Just as he was following the route once journeyed with his wizard teachers, a jump in the continuum knocked him back; and before he could determine to remain, he unwillingly continued to fall into the blue light structure maintained by his three anchors. At the last moment, however, it was his stretched sighting that turned his fiery blood to burn with hope. Located at the juncture of his future-traveling destination was an unexplained portal and a glimpse of a realm, a beautiful realm! Now he knew why he had scheduled three stretchings of time. His dragons might be saved! Their entire existence might be saved!

As he allowed his great physical body to take form once again, he felt the strain his journey had placed upon his anchors. When he was fully assimilated, their helpers without hesitation began merging to replenish them so that they would be ready to anchor Zog's next future journey.

CHAPTER TWO

IN SEARCH OF WIZARDS

The wizards lived in the twenty-fourth realm, though they had access to all realms including the physical. However, it was the dragon physical realm that presented limitations to them, and again and again they had tried to take physical form only to dissolve before they had completed. There were three who continued to enjoy that physical realm by placing their awareness there. Such practices had led them to develop certain manners of affecting the dragon physical more directly than they cared to admit. However, even these manners were limited to a partnership with nature and the fairies and gnomes, which lead the three wizards to assume a similar smallish form quite different from the twenty-fourth realm wizards.

Their partnership delightedly led the wizards to observe certain dragons; and it was during just such an observation that the inglet Zog had startled them with his abilities not only to see them, but to follow them back through their portal between realms.

"Wait!" he had shouted, his inglet nostrils flaring smoke and fire, "Who are you?"

His exuberance singed the entryway to their homeland and rather than spend the next few timesects repairing such distortions, they stopped and met his laser gaze. Perhaps it was Zog's innocence combined with astounding focused strength

DRAGON FIRE: SECRETS OF THE LAST DRAGONS

that nudged them to invite him to their realm. Then again....

They thought-spoke to each other, *He **saw** us*, exclaimed Winjut.

Well that's not all, chimed Plienze, *let's just admit it! He followed us here! Now that's the living end!*

Clorfothian, the elder of the three, hushed the rising thought-speaking, *Now, now. Let's not be rude...and besides, I'm not sure he can't hear us....*

"Of course I can hear you!" Zog moved his big dragon inglet body closer, his scales glistening and his wings just a little unfurled from the excitement of such an adventure.

Plienze coded his words and thought-spoke again, *Bet he can't pick this up.*

"C'mon, fellas," Zog reached out a big clawed hand toward them.

The three wizards had tried every encoding they knew and even invented some on the spot, but nothing seemed to maintain their attempts at secret communications. It was then that Clorfothian invited Zog to join them in the soft green meadow so that they could get to know each other.

Zog, Winjut, Plienze, and Clorfothian made a handsome team right from the moment they all gave up trying to figure out how everything could have possibly happened. The three wizards gleefully demonstrated their magical transformations; and when Zog decided that he too should be able to change form, the three wizards hurried to discourage such an attempt — to no avail, of course. It was after they had reformed the meadow not twelve but thirteen times that they promised they would teach Zog how to change form. And even though he had insisted on learning *right now*, his fazing in and out of form alerted all four to a new fact: Zog had limited time access to their realm.

"Quick!" It was Winjut who was the first to take action with the other two following his lead in the next breath. They created a structure in which Zog could easily return and take form. It was the least they could do, all three had agreed.

Blue. It was the most magnificent blue Zog had ever seen. He watched his three new friends form lines around him, up

IN SEARCH OF WIZARDS

above and down to his tail. The blue light encased him and before he knew it, he was back in his homeland, taking form — right in the middle of an elder gathering.

"Good Grief!" Meran[18] was the only elder who *could* speak. The other eleven stared in disbelief at the forming body of Zog. It was the first, but certainly not the last, time the inglet of Meran would extinguish their nostril fires and re-ignite them before they could actually realize it was occurring at all. In fact, it was in the second after his full forming that the taste on their long tongues let them know that such an extinguishing and re-igniting had occurred. In truth, if it weren't for the engaging enthusiasm of Zog's rendering of his adventure to the realm of the wizards, the eleven might have singed his young nostrils with their angry snorts.

Even though dragons carried the reputation of quick full-fired response, elders weren't prone to impulsive breathings. And the demonstration before their eyes was something none of them had ever mastered and indeed all of their Glarian had only read about in their histories of those times before the first great Neekontuk.

Zog's words tumbled over themselves, "Three of them," he began, "and they were just as surprised as you are right now!" He looked into the piercing eyes of the circle of elders. "And they didn't think I could hear them either!" Zog laughed an inglet laugh, slapping his claw against his hide, now completely formed but still holding a blue glow. "Why, they tried everything to fool me, but I just decided that I'd hear what they had to say — and I did!"

He took a deep breath and continued. Like his father, Zog enjoyed telling of his adventures, a talent that alerted the Floggen to his leader possibilities. Even though he was Meran's son, the leader of a Floggen was determined by abilities naturally demonstrated during inglet development.

It was during Zog's telling of his fazing that Meran interrupted with fatherly concern and, assuring the eleven elders that

---

18 <u>Meran</u>: Floggen elder, leader, and father of Zog.

they would hear the entire tale, he gathered his son to him and together they flew to their cavernous home.

Although Meran had not only seen the wizards but also consulted with them on a number of occasions during times of major Glarian decision-making, he had never been able to enter the wizard's realms. It was the wizards themselves who had brought his awareness within the histories to those who had been able to journey to not only within their created realms but to the twenty-fourth and beyond. None but those few, they had assured him, had ever been able to reside with them on the twenty-fourth.

"Why, there we're just a breath of the ethers..." one of them had exclaimed, but another had whistled and they disappeared. After that one-time speaking of the twenty-fourth, they never referred to it again. Yet Meran's keen mind held everything clearly, and it was now as he gazed with pride at his napping inglet son that he recalled the entire speaking, even to the tone and pitch of their whistle. It was rumored in all lands that dragons could reproduce any sound or tonal vibration with such accuracy that even the original emitter might authenticate it as his or her own. It was only the fairies who were able to sing non-replicatable songs, much to the joyful delight of all dragons.

· · · · ·

There had been a few who questioned the origin of the wizards, firstly within their own mind-wanderings, and then secondly together, as their curiosities and vibrations attracted each other until they met in those wanderings. It was within the Neecha between the two mountain ranges connecting their Floggen that those few met to discuss their interests and their discoveries about wizards.

Meteranke had the most experience, and although he could certainly speak with limited authority to the group who gathered, he was the first to openly admit that his experiences with the wizards neither approached the depth of Winzoarian requirements nor did he seem to be able to begin such feats.

Although Meteranke had been invited to train for anchoring of one who would future-travel, his true passion lay within those stories of the wizards and his hopes of participating directly with them. He had whispered his hopes and curiosities to a few of his dragon friends, who had wasted little time assuring him that Winzoarians such as Zog were written of only in the histories long before the forming of this, the Third Realm of Dragons. His friend Fornaign had been quick to remind him, "Even Zog's *father* didn't travel to those realms! For the life of the fire within you, Meteranke, you have been invited to be an anchor!" Fornaign had been invited at the same time and that they studied together was one of their great joys.

Even though Fornaign knew of his friend's pleasure at being chosen for such training, he continued to chide until Meteranke stopped gazing beyond the familiar mountain silhouette and admitted his hopes to be close to folly.

"You have to admit, Fornaign, you too have wondered about the wizards." A small puff of smoke seeped its way out of Meteranke's snout.

"Wondering is one thing! But to actually entertain the possibility of not only locating their portal, but having the ability to enter and to actually meet with them is... is... well it's putting everything that calls for your focus here in timelessness." He leaned his dragon body forward and placed his intent directly at his friend. "We all know what that does! And if you can't concentrate on the training...."

"I can concentrate. I can concentrate." Meteranke began pacing the floor of the great cavern they had discovered together during an adventure flight the previous decade. "I don't believe that wondering about the wizards and even attempting to contact them will jeopardize anything that is going on in my training. In fact, it might enhance it!" He side-glanced back at Fornaign and waited for his words *contact them* to find a thought pathway past Fornaign's efforts at practicality.

Fornaign stopped another barrage of reasonings in mid-ignition and felt the intent of the words awaken possibilities. A slight smile found its way to the corner of his jaw.

It was what he loved about Meteranke, who never felt threatened by even a full-fledged fiery exchange, and who had become his friend as a very young inglet when he refused to give away their secret hiding place to the other inglets.

Now his whole demeanor changed. "Contact them... Contact them?"

Meteranke grinned a wait-until-you-hear-this grin. Fornaign huddled his shining body beside Meteranke's and, expanding his outer awareness lest any other be attracted to the vibrations of their speaking, whispered, "So, tell me! What has transpired?" His excitement was matched by the changing colors of Meteranke's slightly unfurled wings as the first sharing of the delight of his youthful dragon adventures began. Although he had repeated it again and again with Fornaign, each telling brought to their realm of knowing a little more of the experiences, until they both began to have interchanges with the wizards.

It was the vibrations of those tellings that had drawn the attention of the other three, and as the five now met in the sworn-to-secrecy cavern, it was with his first long-ago rendering to his friend that Meteranke began their meeting. They had already waved aside his protestations of having any expertise in wizard communication, and it was with stilled fires and as slight as possible smoke breathing that they waited for his story to begin.

"You see," he began in the middle of a thought, "I think you just have to decide...."

"We know! We know that part," they had interrupted him. "Just begin your story!" They had beseeched him in such a fashion that their radiating colors reminded him of the exact moment that he had decided, decided to contact the wizards and similarly refused to take no for an answer.

"I was flying over Mutchiat when I saw the first glimmer of what I thought was a distortion." He looked to them; "I take it you've all discerned a distortion before?" They all nodded except for Brianna, the youngest of the group.

"I'm not sure," she unhesitatingly spoke. "Would you take a moment to describe...."

Meteranke held a fondness for Brianna and spoke a unanimous feeling, "Of course! That's what we're all here for — to speak, or should I say *finally* tell, what we know." The others nodded in agreement.

"A distortion is a wave in visual perception." He knew the statement wasn't enough for Brianna, yet he also wanted the speaking to be clear and uncomplicated. "It's my opinion that there really is no such thing as distortion." He continued before she could bring up her recent studies of the ancient histories. "I know what we've been taught about distortions, and I also know that the histories contain references to them. However, my experiences have led me to different conclusions."

Brianna could hardly contain herself and began to cite those historical facts that had excited her curiosities and had actually led her to searching out the wizards for further understanding.

"Hear him out, Brianna," stilled Karthentonen.

"But Kar," she breathed a sigh of greyish smoke, "it's a topic that brought me here!"

"I know," he smiled softly, "you'll have your chance to speak on your topics. Remember? This isn't a Glarian meeting after all. It's the five of us...."

Brianna felt the comfort of the fifth member of their group as he nuzzled beside her. Treiga had been born during the deepest of winter and because he held the record for bringing his large body to such low temperatures, his parents had named him after the season itself. Although Treiga never efforted in stilling his fires, he also held the Flame Intensity Magnitude record for his age.

It was such balance that brought him to the wizards at their invitation. He was in no hurry to tell his own particular story — which was the balance they all admired. In truth, they all admired each other and had from the first time each had met, and especially now as they gathered together.

"As I was saying," Meteranke continued, "by its very definition, distortion leads us to believe that one manner of being, one taking form, is more valid than another." He began to get lost in his theories when Fornaign breathed a smoke stream.

Meteranke recognized the stay-on-course signal and continued, "When I first saw a wave, an actual wave go through our mountain, I didn't know what to think. No one else had seen it and everyone, even the elders, refused to discuss the possibilities of a distortion in or of the mountain.

"I decided to make my own studies and that's how I eventually came to some conclusions," he made a small bow to Brianna, "that I'm open to change." Brianna breathed a blushed fire. He smiled at her innocence; "I look forward to further discussions." Although inexperienced in the pleasures of round-table comradery and inwardly thrilled at the encompassing welcome of the others, Brianna's hunger for the truth held her youthful attention on the remainder of Meteranke's explanation of recognizing a distortion.

"Each time I saw, physically saw, a wave ripple though the mountain, I made note of it. One early morning I saw it just as I stepped out of my cavern. It was so close that I decided to jump into it!" Brianna involuntarily gasped. "Wait!" He tried to catch her thought-flowing. "I rode it like flying on a vibrational current!" His pleasure in the telling brought Brianna into the moment of his ride. Meteranke's discernment with thought-flowings was well celebrated even amongst the elders.

Meteranke projected his experience of riding the wave of distortion. Colors flowed into each other and returned to their own integrity. Songs of the fairies filled the cavern. They all felt the nearly alarming dissolving of their form and the returning to form in one quick breath. None had suspected Meteranke of such projection abilities. He whispered to Fornaign, "Just learned that one last week!"

"So you see," he continued while enjoying their astonished looks, "what we call distortion is... well, perhaps requires us to redefine distortion itself." He gazed at Brianna's beaming glow. "Now, sweet Brianna, you know how to identify a realm wave. But! For the sake of communication, we'll call it distortion."

"OK, OK!" Brianna agreed. "I can wait until another time to discuss this. I'll have to research the histories under different names and experiences. I'll bet there's more than one reference to this. That's probably why I couldn't find more – I was looking through the standard definition." She stressed the word *standard* and settled back to hear the story Meteranke was about to tell.

"Well," he continued, "after I experienced the ride in the realm wave, ...er distortion, and after I found that it seemed no one had any actual experience -- as it has always been judged as something negative or something to avoid — I decided it would be my own adventure. I decided that I'd be the one to know all about it.

"That's what led me to deciding, as I was saying in the beginning. I had a feeling that the wizards would know about distortion and what it really was." He paused to remember the exact moment. "I determined that I would contact them and ask." The other four sat waiting for him to continue. He emphatically stated, "I DETERMINED that I would contact them and ask!"

"But how did you know that you would?" asked Kar. "I can decide something but that doesn't mean that it will happen!"

"On the contrary," replied Meteranke, "that is when I learned my first lesson with the wizards." The thought patterns of the four came into total alignment, partly because they could hardly wait for the lesson, and mostly because it was their manner of gleaning the fullness of communication. By aligning thought patterns, each dragon assisted layered information and awarenesses to become part of their mutually supportive experience. Such alignment was also a first-level preparation for merging, which later became part of the celebration into full-grown dragonhood.

"I gathered all my force, as if I were in front of the Glarian and demonstrating Flame Intensity. Then I DETERMINED that I would talk with the wizards." The four seemed to lean forward to hear more of what he was saying. Even though they had each had their own experience with the wizards to varying degrees, they knew that Meteranke had been communicating with them for a long time -- at least they hoped that the underground rumors were true.

"A portal opened up right before my eyes!"

"Where were you?" asked Kar.

"I'd followed what I thought was a distortion to the third peak of Mutchiat. You know, the peak that hides behind the gathering chamber." Kar nodded. "Well, I hovered as close to the peak as I could without disturbing the flowing."

"What did the portal look like?" asked Brianna.

"Like the colors of the flowing I shared with you a moment ago, only they moved within a design."

"What was the design like?" she asked again.

"Well," he brought his experience forward, "let me show you." Meteranke breathed a fiery breath toward the back of the cavern. In the very center of the fire there appeared a blue form within a form.

"Hey!" Fornaign moved closer. "That looks like one of the forms we're studying in anchoring class!"

"Exactly," exclaimed Meteranke. "And that's what I saw. That's what the portal looked like and continues to look like every time I ask to speak with them."

Treiga reached his claw forward, pausing the interchange. Calmly but with raised eyebrows he spoke, "*Every time* you speak with them?" His deep resonate voice rumbled the cavern. "What do you mean *every* time? How many times have you spoken with them?" He paused and then added, "And how often, Meteranke, how often?"

"And on what topics?" added Brianna.

Meteranke knew there would be questions, but he continued with the telling of the first time he spoke with the wizards. It was his favorite story, as the other stories built upon it and the surprise of it all liked to be rekindled inside his great green being.

"After I saw the portal, I moved closer to have a better look. It opened. It just turned and opened. I tried to enter, but the energy was so great that I couldn't."

Kar interjected, "Some of the Ancient Ones spoke of a different kind of alignment...."

"I know of that," responded Meteranke, "but at the time I hadn't even researched the opening of a portal, never mind how to go through it."

He felt them wait for the words. "I might as well tell you right now that I have not been able to go through the portal. Not yet, that is." He waited to see the disappointment on them as he had carried such a feeling inside himself ever since his unsuccessful first try to enter the portal.

He didn't find it. Instead, he saw admiration and love. Treiga was the first to speak. "I might as well tell you that I have not been able to go into the wizard realm either. And I too have stories to tell about my own attempts." He spoke in his gentle manner, "Perhaps that's why we're all here, Meteranke. Perhaps that's why we're all here."

"Please! Go on with your story," chimed in Brianna. "Tell of what happened next! I can hardly wait!"

Meteranke smiled at her youthful impatience. Somehow the disappointment he'd felt seemed to lessen with their encouragement to continue. In truth, he thought to himself, he had only shared his wizard stories with Fornaign, and even then only a few of them. This was a new experience and one that seemed to be filled with surprises, much to his delight.

"When the portal opened and I finally realized I would not be able to enter, I stood back and looked through the opening. It was like looking through the end of the great cavern where the fairies and gnomes go, like a tunnel. After a few moments, my eyes adjusted to the light that kept flickering. That's when I saw him. The first wizard."

Brianna began to ask, "What did he look..."

Meteranke continued, "I wasn't sure what to say after all of my deciding. I've never seen such golden light, not even in the Glarian celebrations. I think he adjusted his light so that I could see him better. I'm not sure about that though. He just began to take form before my eyes."

All four leaned forward, speaking in unison, "And??"

"Well, I'm not sure about all of this..."

"You?" questioned Fornaign. "You aren't sure?"

"Well, Fornaign," continued Meteranke hesitantly, "the form kept changing."

"From what to what???" entreated Karthentonen.

DRAGON FIRE: SECRETS OF THE LAST DRAGONS

"Well, first I saw a great golden light."

"Yes..." replied all four in unison again.

"And then the light began to take form. That's the part I'm not sure about. The light began to take the form of a golden dragon." There, I've said it, he thought to himself.

No one spoke a word. He waited. Still no word.

"Well, I suppose you're as stunned as I was." He looked from one to the other. "You see, I'm not sure the wizard took form as himself, or if he took a form that was easy for me to see, or if he never really took form and I projected my wanting to see something and it was interpreted as a form of myself." He looked to his long-time friend. "Fornaign, what do you think?"

"All these times you've spoken of this story and I don't ever remember you mentioning those possibilities." Fornaign reflected a moment and then added, "In fact, I think you always said the wizards were golden light...."

"For'... you know what happens when thought patterns come into alignment. More comes into view, awarenesses deepen. I even wondered right before this gathering if the form might change, but it didn't."

"All that really doesn't matter," interrupted Treiga. "Let's be as clear as we possibly can be. You said that the form, the golden light became a golden dragon?? And that's the form of a wizard?"

"I know there's a question...."

"Meteranke, just answer me. Is the form of the wizard a golden dragon?"

"Yes, if that's actually who or what I've been seeing."

Treiga continued with piercing intent, "And every time, however many times you've spoken with them, the form you speak with is a golden dragon?"

"Well... sometimes the form changes from gold to different colors, depending on the topic of the teaching. But for the most part, the wizard always comes forth as a golden dragon."

Treiga sucked in a huge breath.

"What is it?" asked Kar. "Does that have a special meaning to you?"

Treiga responded softly, "Yes. It is the image that has been coming to me in my night journeys."

"Wow!" Brianna was up and breathing fire before the others could caution her about her excitement. "Wow! That's right in the ancient histories! It's a little hidden, but I've always wondered about the referring to the Golden Shadow Being! But I thought it was more about some kind *of Ancient One* rather than a wizard, and...."

It was both Treiga and Karthentonen who breathed a cooling breath just as Brianna realized the results of her excitement. "Oh... I didn't realize what I was doing..." She brought her thoughts back into focus and looked to Meteranke. "I just can't help but be excited about what you're telling us...."

"I understand," said Meteranke. "I've had a while to think about all of this. And then there's the teachings themselves."

Karthentonen brought them back to the present moment, "I don't like to be the one to mention that we've been here for quite a while.... I wouldn't want to arouse curiosity right at the start."

"Kar is right," Meteranke sighed, "we'd better end this telling. I suppose that will let everything align itself and perhaps more will come into our awareness."

He looked to them and now saw the friends he sensed long ago would one day gather together. They didn't know it yet, but he hoped they would be the ones who would journey through the portal with him. *It's perfect*, he thought to himself, *it's perfect that we are five. Now just one more to make the number complete, the number the wizards talked about....*

"I hope you'll be ready to tell us of the first teaching when next we meet," said Treiga as he began balancing the cavern's energies so that there would be no trace of their presence or of the topics they discussed when they departed. Balancing energies was more an act of respect for any others who might use the cavern than an act of secrecy. Yet none could deny that they'd decided to continue with their secret meetings. Only Meteranke knew there would be one more to join their group.

Dragon Wings

CHAPTER THREE

ZOANNA'S CALL

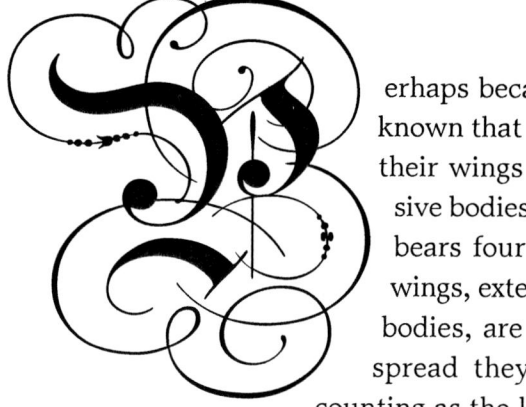

Perhaps because of their size, it is little known that dragons reside more within their wings than in their fiercely massive bodies. Each fully developed adult bears four sets of wings. The middle wings, extending from the back of their bodies, are the largest.[19] Indeed, fully spread they span in width the same counting as the length of their grand bodies from fiery nostrils to the tip of their whip-like tails.

Within the adventure-formed abilities to fully merge with other dragons and other realms, is also developed infinite subtle demonstrations of the beauty of all that has been merged. Not the least of these demonstrations is the rippling kaleidoscope of colors the middle wings can evidence

---

19 <u>Dragon Wings</u>: Dragons have four sets of wings, the largest being the middle pair attached at the middle of their back. These wings, as do the other three sets, contain a communication system. Unique to the middle wings, across the top edge runs an energy within which resides the DNA, cellular patterning. The smallest set of wings has been misinterpreted in some histories as gills, but they are not. Set right at the throat, directly under the jaw, they fan outward upon command. Signaling dragon presence, such fanning sends vibrations and frequencies from the face of the fan, catapulting forth a flash of light with force similar to that of a bolt of lightening. The third set of wings is located under the large middle wings and is set forward so that the middle wings overlap a little. The top part of these seemingly small wings is exposed of themselves. Very thin and translucent and at times the palest of light blue or green, they have the capabilities of activating crystalline structures. (See illustration, Kleeana's Gossamer Wings) The fourth set of wings is seemingly part of the very large ones in the center of the body, but shaped differently. They reside only on the edge of the center wings and are about one-fourth or one-fifth the size of the large wings. Like a very slick wedge, the large part is attached and then shapes itself to a point. Such wings enable their large bodies to be extremely capable of refined, determined movement.

before any viewer lucky enough to receive such a gift.

Though gossamer in appearance, the middle wings are more powerful than fragile and are indeed the strongest part of a dragon's structure. As if that were not magnificent enough, woven within the fabric of the middle wings resides a unique communication system. Such a system is their most developed and natural way of collectively participating within the physical realm in which they currently reside.

This having been said, it was with determined flair and unfurling of the most majestic middle wings of the Kloan, that Zoanna announced her presence. The magnificent spectrum of prismatic colors only a fully developed Grand Damme *could* demonstrate flowed forth and not only filled the great cavern, but touched the hearts of all three hundred and fifty-seven dragon Representatives.

Each Representative had been chosen by his own Floggen for his ability to thought-merge. Even a dragon who attends a Kloan for the first time, thought-merges and having done so, activates the patterning within wing encodings, allowing him[20] to participate with their sophisticated communicating as one entire unit.

Such Kloan communications caused a rumbling within physicality, and it was this rumbling that began to subside as the fullness of Zoanna's gift filled them with a richness of strength and freedom of flight they hadn't realized had become depleted.

A Grand Damme was able to easily detect the imbalances such a gathering might place upon each Representative. The flutter of her heart center filled them with a sweetness remembered from the youthful comfort of early nesting and beginnings of

---

20 Representatives of Floggen are always male. The females, who are the balancers of the energies and thought-formings of their Floggen, remain in their home location while the male Representative attends each Kloan Gathering. Each female dragon also receives the transmittings of the Representative concerning the topics of the Kloan Gathering. From her, the families access such transmissions for full integration and understanding of the entire dragon population.

21 Zoanna's Love: Being Grand Damme and the oldest of all female dragons, she has loved them all for the length of their lives, and that love has provided the platform upon which she has stood many times, calling them to be all that they can be.

first journeys. Resting within her familiar loving embrace[21], the Kloan gave her their full attention.

Like Zog, Zoanna wasted little time in formalities and began speaking directly upon the topic of their rumblings. Continuing to reside with the radiating color display, she spoke strongly and clearly, as if she were guiding her own fully-grown children.

"It is a great temptation to prepare for battle and to flee home to our Floggen and incite them to prepare for battle. Even now some of our Floggen are feeling our concerns and are preparing for battle.

*"What do we believe we are going to battle? How do we believe we will approach an oncoming rage so great that in our histories it has **totally** destroyed any trace of us?"*

She looked directly at some of the youngest members, inexperienced in restraining their natural, determined exuberance. *"And some might be thinking that you are the ones who will hide from the oncoming rage and be the new Floggen to begin the fourth realm of our existence. The histories, however, have spoken, and those of you who are able to delve into the histories know.* **None have survived.**

"Then, let us firstly honor our histories..." Zoanna expanded her wings to their fullest and spilled forth the depth of her understanding of their histories. Her pause was brief. *"...and then recognize that a different solution MUST present itself.*

"We are the carriers of great strength. By our very nature, we are capable of changing our form; though some have not accomplished this manner, it does not make them lesser than. It makes them adept at something else."

She allowed her loving gaze to capture each intently concentrating Representative. As she turned, her still fully opened wings radiating in all directions, they felt the force of all that she was telepathing.

"As you are aware, I have been speaking for a time within the knowing that we are a whole... that the Floggen of each of us is a wholeness, within which each one contributes... and together we form our Floggen, our whole. And, many of you are aware that I have spoken of our Kloan as a whole and that each of us brings a piece, a part of a whole."

Each certainly did remember the many times Zoanna spoke with them, firstly in a manner that felt strangely known, yet unknown. Each time she called them to gather, her speakings had filled them in such a way that they began to view not only each other but also all of their own Floggen as a whole entity, as a living entity. Even now they remembered how she had helped them to discover more of their own fulfillment, more of their own understanding of the magnificence of who they were and are.

"We could discuss many of your concepts, yet the truth remains: we are alike, and we are quite different. Each one of us can do something the other cannot.

"Then, together, as one, it seems we MUST be able to do something that we could not do individually. Then, my journeys have been within those realms and I have wondered, wondered of what it is that as a whole we can accomplish.

"Now... that which was in our histories, the Neekontuk, is approaching. Then I say, while our leader is journeying to our future, to our possibilities, let us begin the solution. Even before he enters his second viewing, let US begin OUR participation by maintaining who we are and by maintaining that unique quality which each of us bears."

Her words called forth the strength within their great dragon spirit. Even though some held back their participation until they might hear her entire proposal, the majority of the Kloan had already agreed to follow her call to action. She felt their support and their hesitations, their joining and their staid clutching to a manner that had fulfilled past purposes.

Their Grand Damme stood before them and embraced their support *and* their hesitations. Within each and every way of their decidings, she breathed her loving dragon breath and spoke the words that would call them all, even to the last hesitating one, to be more than they had ever been before.

"And while maintaining our uniqueness, let us bring our thoughts and our manner into one. Let us bring our thoughts and our manner into the oneness of the Kloan. The entirety, a

Representative from each Floggen, is here at this Kloan, here, gathering together. Let us begin OUR participation into the solution, even though we do not know where it will lead us.

"By our very own histories we know that a battle will not serve us but be the end of us! Perhaps the histories are incomplete in that they have not borne the description of how we did perish. Perhaps we did, in a blaze of fighting, in trying to stop the oncoming onslaught of dissolving flames and energies...."

"*Now, now we can begin.*" She refused to allow herself a thought-merge with her beloved Zog, but remained the focal support of the gathering. "*Our leader, even as I speak, prepares to step within the center of the blue structure and journey forth to discover perhaps what we can do, what course we can choose.*

"When we unite as one, we place at his access another possibility. We know that the battle is not the answer, even though we want it to be. When we unite as one and decide to, we give our leader another avenue to explore within his future journey.

"*For, we all know and are quite aware that what we choose in the moment affects the possible future.*" She allowed her words to echo through their knowing. Her great wings radiated the light of the truth she spoke in words and in thought-merging.

"Then let us choose now and assist our leader by offering another possibility. That perhaps together, in so doing, does our union offer to him a piece of the solution — perhaps something that would not be evident without our union. Then as he goes forth, let us now choose to unite!"

Zoanna felt her last words fill the cavern.

Unexpected. The vision was unexpected. For one fleeting second she thought it inappropriate to be visioning... yet, it appeared before her:

A golden essence flowed from the vibrating of her expanded wings. It floated about her until it formed a broad circle around her great dragon being. She commanded the smallest wings to fan fully open at her throat. Though a vision, she felt the force within her fans building. Fully opened, they began to quiver.

She was unable to detect if the quivering was physical. The vision consumed her attention as bolts of golden light charged forth from her open fans into the golden circle, increasing its size until it became a gigantic undulating wave. Vibrating. Toning. Touching all three hundred and fifty-seven dragons.

Zoanna forced herself to peer though the vision. The Kloan, her dragon family, remained still, unmoving as if suspended in time. She wanted to wonder what was occurring. It was then that she heard the whispering. Softly, directly it came, *"Continue. Your vision is real. We are with you."*

Peace. Strength. Something beyond what she had felt before…. Questioning fell away. Wondering fell away. She allowed the vision to fill her. It did….

She breathed her fiery breath forcing the golden wave to spin around her. One waft of her wings sent the undulating gold outward to her Kloan. Deep within her knowing there rose a sound, slight and gentle at first, and then gaining in volume until its trumpeting resonated through her heart. She raised her long neck upward as the sound traveled its way up and out, resonating against the walls of the cavern.

Through a veil, as if from another realm she viewed the Kloan. They remained still, unmoving….

In the stillness there were three who felt something, something calling, waking them from a long sleep. Their dragon bodies remained unmoving, frozen in the position of listening to their Grand Damme. Yet, no sound.

Instead, they felt the force of her grand knowing, they felt the call to unite. It was as if the core inside their very beings were spinning in gold. It wasn't that each of the three decided anything, but more that they became that which they had always been.

Only once before had their wedge-like wings activated. It had been during the Kloan's grand celebration of the naming of Zog as their Winzoarian. Even then there was a feeling, as if a magnetic pull to move toward each other. None had experienced such a pull before, and even though it lasted but a few moments, the event remained with them and not only confirmed their choice of leader, but alerted them to the possibility of the beginning of a new era.

Within the awakened state of the three, the tingling within their wedge-like wings brought forth the remembrance, kissing their thought-merging. Though their bodies remained still, in the light their middle wings unfurled and wedge-like spears raised. It was then that they saw her behind a veil, peering at them. She called to them and in the next moment they too were behind the veil, moving forward with precision and grace. The gold that was within them also surrounded Zoanna. They felt the pull. The remembrance stretched beyond the past.

Each of the three inserted the tip of one wedge into the flux. In it went until the entire wedge was buried, seated in the gold. They joined with their Grand Damme. They had never participated in such a full manner before, feeling themselves flowing as the river. Within the swelling they became each other.

Alert. Their thoughts wanted to question what was occurring. Before even the budding of fear could enter their union, Zoanna's love filled them to the brim and overflowing.

For one, it was as if he existed as One and then did not exist at all! Two basked within the love they had yearned for since the beginning of taking form.

The vision changed. Zoanna felt the intensity shift. Together they saw: The entire Kloan, led by the elders, raised their wedge-like spears and moved toward the river of light. Each dragon inserted the tip and then the entirety of one wedge into the flux. It was a procession that could be written in their histories. One of bravery, strength, and surrender. A celebration of who they would become together as One.

It was Zoanna who wondered. The three flowed within her wondering. Could the vision become real? Could the entire Kloan turn from their debating and dare to unite in such a full manner? Could they even now feel the wondrous golden flowing? She breathed it into herself and allowed herself to revel in the timelessness of One.

• • • • •

It was within that basking that Zog called forth the three compatriots who would maintain the blue form while he traveled for the second time into the future. Even though each moment brought the raging onslaught closer, Zog paused to speak with them, to honor their strength and their unfailing dedication to him and to the entire Kloan. It was upon such strength that his entire future-travel would rest.

Mentard had been the first to step forward when Zog was named Winzoarian. Without hesitation, Mentard offered his loyalty. Although pleased, Zog wasn't surprised. He had felt a kinship with his friend since their first meeting. And even though Mentard had journeyed from his own Floggen and joined them at the time of deciding, in truth, it was Mentard who many thought would be the one named to lead their Kloan.

Zog breathed a fiery breath toward his friend. "Now together we do what we have not done before." He turned to the other two, remembering their beseeching him to allow them to train, to learn what was a second nature to Mentard. Niara and Connock had both quickly proven themselves with a repatterning now used by all students who prepared to maintain the blue structure for a future-travel.[22]

"I am convinced," Zog began, "that there is a way we can escape the Neekontuk." The intensity of his speaking riveted their attention to him, even while they began transforming before his eyes. "It is not possible to combat its oncoming momentum. It is too great." He saw the blue begin to phase, firstly about them. It was time.

Still he stayed with them. "I have seen a glimmer of something... of a portal. It is there that I plan to travel." He looked to his three compatriots. "I will travel for as long as you can maintain. I have already called an additional three to begin repatterning for a possible participation."

To their ripples of protest he spoke, "We have not done this before, it is true. You will remain in your positions. When you become depleted — and you will, I know. This will be a long

---

[22] Maintain structure for future-travel: It had been discovered that some could maintain for what seemed like an unlimited number of future-journeys, while others were limited to as few as two. For this reason, the training program had been developed. As a secondary purpose though not lesser, those who trained also became quite familiar with the patterns involved in future-travel.

journey. When you become depleted, they will join with you. They will give their strength not to the structure as they have been trained, but to you.

"You are the most experienced. I need you now more than ever before. The Kloan needs you now more than ever before."

He stepped into the blue structure just as it formed in full strength and vitality. "The entire Kloan needs this journey now more than ever before. Our existence depends...." They saw his glistening body dissolve before their eyes. Their test of endurance had begun.

CHAPTER FOUR

THE MOMENT IN STRETCHED TIME BEGINS

For his second future-travel, Zog's destination had been the moment before the portal appeared in the Timeline. He was certain of it. Yet as he took form the flames and rolling rage of dissemination licked at his wings and enveloped his form. Turning and lashing out, forming and reforming his shields, he fought valiantly, breathing his highest metaclores into the furnace of flames. To his surprise they had hesitated for a brief second, which was all he needed to waft badly singed wings and lift from the unyielding biting, torrent.

The overview was not where he wanted to be using valuable time, yet from there he could see exactly what was occurring. At least that is what he planned. Without his wizard friends, viewing was limited to his abilities alone. Just beyond the raging furnace lay the green beauty of his homeland and the majesty of the mountains within which his Floggen resided.

The Timeline beyond was one that he had traveled often for the sheer joy of being in the spirit of his wizard friends and for the satiating of his unquenchable curiosity. His body integrity called for attention and he drew on the strength of his three compatriots, hoping they would be able to maintain and certain that they would not expect such a drain on their abilities so early in his journey.

Their strength filled him and he felt his wings restore and vision sharpen. Just beyond his homeland sparked a flashing light. He hadn't seen it before, yet as a beacon, it called him.

Without hesitation he placed his intent and there he did appear. Yet when he arrived at the location, the light was nowhere to be seen! He thrashed his awarenesses around, searching for the smallest ripple. He found it. Initially it appeared as a distortion, yet the blink of light called again.

Refusing to wait for the portal to open, he dashed forward and, as he had in his youthful exuberance long ago, singed not only the portal but the beginnings of what looked like his homeland but more vibrant. Resonating a bellowing sound, he called for his wizards. Again and again he called for them. He heard no response.

It appeared to be paradise, lush in its greenery, vibrating with unexplored mountain ranges. Although something... something felt just a little wrong — so subtle was the wrong that his perceptions placed it within the interpretations of the residue of the recent battle and raging torrent — he thrilled at the sight of such beauty. It was perfect for the entire Glarian. Wafting his wings, he raised and soared over the lands. Lakes abundant, waterfalls, caverns, beauty sparkling before him confirmed the answer to his search.

With the exception of his bout within the fires, this discovery was easy. It should have been too easy, but Zog wished such a paradise for his dragons. He gathered the vibrations and intonations of their to-be new home so that he might project his viewings and they might see for themselves. He longed for the Neecha[23] that he might reflect on the slight hesitations, that he might be certain of his choosings. Yet the immediacy of what placed itself just at the doorway of his homeland pressed him to delve deeper into the lands laid so easily open to him.

---

23 Neecha: an inner sanctum between two major mountain ranges, wherein dragons entered alone or together to explore without the automatic merging with their Floggen or with the Glarian.

There had to be another portal, one more established, one whose entry would not require experience or expertise. One that would open wide so that his entire Glarian might easily enter. Not allowing his thoughts to enter the next hurdle of transporting the entire dragon population, he stretched his journey further and further into the new land.

It was in the meadows that he remembered. It was this same discovery long ago! As a youth he had been Timeline viewing with his wizard friends and decided to look into the future. All of a sudden there he was, in a paradise beyond his belief. In truth, even then he had seen his beloved dragons residing there. It had filled him with youthful joy. And even though the wizards had encouraged his exploration of the land, there had been a certain uneasiness about their play. He had felt it and just as he was going to ask about it, Winjut had called an end to his journey. The others had agreed and before he could protest, he was forming back on his homeland.

As the remembrance filled him, also did the remembrance of Winjut, Plienze, and Clorfothian. He allowed himself to long for their company even though he would never trade his sacrifice of their presence for the allowance of fear to fill Zoanna during their last full merging. Certainly that would have disabled her abilities to lead the Kloan into the journey she was now inviting them to dare to participate within.

Zoanna had spoken briefly with Zog while he recovered from his first future-journey and he was aware of the topic of her speaking. He had full confidence in her abilities and within the moment of remembrance allowed himself to wish that they were able to return to those sweet times of peace and joyful celebration.

That he had played here in this very meadow with the three wizards gave Zog hope that a portal existed and that his dragons would be able to meet the next challenge. There in the meadow he perceived a ripple! His reverie ended abruptly, and his entire attention focused on the location of the ripple.

None knew that he had played with distortions before, using the wavelengths to assist him in creating experiments. Initially such attempts had brought Winjut, Plienze, and

Clorfothian to their knees with laughter. Yet he had persisted and after many such laughable attempts, he began to demonstrate results that were not only a credit to his title as Winzoarian, but were challenges for the three to replicate. It had been their enjoyment together, and finally they had celebrated his abilities by aligning his frequencies with those that they used for creating their own realms and residing places.

Now his radar perceptions extended into the fabric of this paradise. He felt his three compatriots weakening and paused to allow the joining of the others he had requested to remain waiting for such an occasion. The ripple occurred again! Simultaneously he felt the surge enter his being. They had done it. He had no time to celebrate their success, but dove his awareness into the ripple.

It pulled him. It turned him round and round, toppling all that he knew end over end into a magnetic flux that stretched his abilities at maintaining consciousness.

"Noooooo!" he commanded. "NOT NOW!!!" He formed himself within the distortion. "I WILL MAINTAIN! I CLAIM MY RIGHT TO MAINTAIN IN ALL REALMS!!!" The words bellowed forth from his anguished efforts. Those compatriots who anchored also began to lose consciousness.

Zog knew he had to return, and still he forced himself to remain. He pierced his concentration within the distortion and commanded the frequencies to vibrate together. He called upon the encodings the wizards had bestowed. Slowly, more slowly than his agony could bear, a portal began to form. Placing the last reserve of strength, Zog empowered the portal with life force. Even as his consciousness dimmed, he saw it sparkle. It was real. He had done it.

Darkness. Pain. The flames ripped at his wings and bit into his flesh. Gasping for breath and finding none, Zog struggled beyond what could be called the supreme struggle. Twisting and turning, he called to the wizards, he called to his long-passed-on father, and he called finally to Zoanna. He was without form, he was with form, each pulsebeat ripping a raging furnace through the fabric of his very being.

• • • • •

Even within the Kloan visioning, Zoanna felt his call. It was immediate. As gently as she could, Zoanna released the vision and the merging with the three. Tuning the frequencies of her wings, time reestablished itself just as she phased out of view. The Kloan barely saw her disappear. They knew. They too had felt the pull, heard the anguished call.

At the portal of the Timeline she waited, reaching her love into the violent confusion. Even though she didn't enter, it pulled at her, inviting her to toss and turn into its rage. She searched for a feeling, a glimpse, a slight recognizable vibration of her beloved Zog.

It came after what felt like an eternity. A tiny thread of his love for her floated through the storm. She grasped onto the thread and united it with her beaming heart. The compatriots had already fallen and lay, still efforting to maintain the blue structure. It flickered and quivered with each pulsebeat pulling on their dwindling life force.

Only Zoanna recognized the pile of singed flesh and battered wings to be that of Zog. Two of the three compatriots had perished in their efforts to maintain, and it was their teachers who were assisting the inexperienced ones to release from the pull Zog had placed on them.

Even as she rushed to his gasping body, she heard the whispering. *"We will help you. The vision is real."* She wanted to push the speaking aside, to focus totally on her beloved. Instead she whispered with her thoughts, "Help me. Help me. Help me." As she lay beside him she whispered, "Make him whole."

Zoanna knew. Those who were adept at maintaining knew. The Kloan knew. Zoanna's merging with Zog would either restore him to a form that could be healed or it would release her from physical form as well. Without hesitation the Kloan thought-merged, sending all their intent of strength to Zoanna. Indeed, the Floggen of each Representative had become aware of what was occurring; and within each village and mountain, dragons thought-merged. Even the inexperienced placed themselves in

THE MOMENT IN STRETCHED TIME BEGINS

the frequencies that would allow them to send their love and comfort to Zoanna and Zog.

Without hesitation she began the merging. Through her heart first, riding upon the flowing of her love.... Finding the thread of him, the tiny thread of love that had reached her like a leaf on the winds of Cantoon....[24] She breathed her flowing, her life force into the thread. It was gray, still. Further she merged, finding movement. Anguish, pain. She took it to herself and breathed the softness of the meadows into that before her. The pain filled her, riveted her focus within the anguish. She allowed it; she embraced it.

Tumbling, end over end, confusion filled her. She embraced it and breathed the song of Sleecha into it. She felt her flesh burning and placed her wings into the fire, merging again and again within those brave sufferings of her beloved.

As if in the distance she heard the whispering again. *"We will help you...."* It was a surge of color and song, it was a golden river flowing. The help came even at the last breath of the two. It wrapped them in a cocoon of relief. Two merged as one.

She felt his presence take form. She had no strength to elate but only to recognize his presence. Zog felt. He felt his reconstruction. Who was doing that...? Into oblivion dove his consciousness only to awaken again in the torture of his journey. Zoanna breathed in the torture and replaced it with her soft songs. Again and again the colors shifted within and upon the cocoon. None dared divert their attention beyond the consequences of their two leaders. It was the moment their universe seemingly stood still.

In all their merging over the hundreds of years, Zog and Zoanna had never been gifted with such a cocoon. Though vision had not been restored, the warmth and vibration fed them nectar of sunsets, spring sweet essence kissing glorious mountain ranges, and the pulsebeat of a mother's breast.

It was as if the mother of the Universe held them in her arms and kissed the brow of a union so light-filled that none had

---

24 <u>Cantoon</u>: The time of year when summer's end brings the harvest and falling of leaves from the trees.

observed equaled splendor throughout any timeline. The fullness of their embrace rolled and merged, transforming pain into song and love into two-as-one. Indeed, their complete surrendering within and of each other radiated outward an exalted love previously unknown to any.

• • • • •

Choices. Choices beyond choices. It was in the middle of contemplating the myriad of avenues to explore that she began to awaken. *But how could it be? She was within the cocoon, and she was here at the same time. Deciding where to reside? What to learn? What kind of decisions were these? And who were these ones tending to her, assisting, as did the fairies in her own lair...* Zoanna stretched and yawned her awarenesses. Slowly. It came to her slowly. She was awake and then again, she was not awake. Her body was... where was her body? Her thought-mind searched for familiarity.

Where am I? What is this place? Whispering to herself, she turned her viewing only to catch glimpses of changing light. She was whole, without pain. Even though she could feel her body, she could not move one tip of one wing, nor one eyelid.

Different from visioning, she thought, *different perception*. She felt their presence but couldn't make out a form, and straining to do so caused the journey back to sleep, to comfort, to being held and loved, to postponing decisions. Within the moment before total surrender, her mind reached, *Zog... Where is Zog...?* Then, blessed rest.

• • • • •

Zog saw them atop the crest of the closest ridge. His big heart leaped with a joy he hadn't felt since... since long before the rage. The avenue, to which his consciousness would have immediately sped in order to access that roaring rage, was closed. He could neither see his charred body nor feel the pain. In truth, as a gift, the entire heroic battle was blocked from his knowing, as was the cocooning with its multi-leveled forming and dispersing, integrating and disseminating, healing and loving, and merging beyond merging, two-as-one.

Instead, his vision caressed the three beloved wizards as they beamed their encodings, inviting him at last to join. Not even questioning how he arrived through their portal and by their side, Zog reveled at the sight of them. The moment before he spoke, a tiny thought flickered and left before his consciousness could attach itself.

It did, however, cause him to pause and in that pause, the flash imprinted its image: *A fire? A battle? Somewhere.* Making note to perhaps explore the image some day, he brushed it aside and beamed his youthful, exuberant love to the three.

Winjut, Clorfothian and Plienze had been watching the effects of the flash and Zog's pause, and weren't quite prepared for the usual jolt of energy that flowed from his heart to theirs. It was with enjoyed humor that they felt themselves catapulted back and unable to right themselves until their forms had actually landed on the green grasses of the meadow they had created for this moment.

"It'll probably always be this way," grunted Clorfothian, brushing himself off even though there was nothing to brush off. The habit of brushing residue from his being had been formed long ago. When he first left the physical realm, he was more able to perceive flowing patterns that seemed to magnetize themselves to him. Deciding such magnetized patterns were but clutter, he had created an energetic to automatically divert them. However, the physical habit of brushing an invisible residue seemed to remain — a habit that misleadingly made his appearance to be a bungling wizard instead of the master that he was.

"***Some*** of us have habits that we never change," hummed Plienze as he, too, righted himself and straightened his apparel. Plienze had always presented himself with a certain dignity that made his joking quite unexpected and all the more amusing.

"Now now," chimed Winjut, who had been the first to leap to his feet and was watching the other two regain their positions at his side. "Just take a gander at who we have before us!"

If there had been such a saying as "a sight for sore eyes," surely Zog would have used it to exclaim his pleasure at drinking in the mannerisms and comfortable familiarity that he felt as he stood before his three wizard friends. "For the first time," he choked through emotions, "I appear to be without words!"

"Indeed, for the first time," exclaimed Winjut as he breached the space between them and warmly embraced the one he would always think of as his young, brilliant student.

Without hesitation Zog embraced not only Winjut but also Clorfothian and Plienze with one huge long sigh of relief. "I have never been more happy to see you."

"Now don't choke out your fires," Clorfothian patted Zog's warm vibrant body, "we have a whole day of play ahead of us and I don't want you claiming a handicap right off!"

From that moment the familiar four were bounding into their own adventures of creating, laughing, and any sort of play they could invent in the moment. The three wizards expertly maintained the atmosphere to be one of celebration at being together. Later, much later, they would speak of what had occurred and the form Zog was currently enjoying. For now, they too soaked in his manner of uninhibited demonstrations of love and mischief, the combination that had endeared him to them right from the first moment he burst into their realm.

• • • • •

As the entire Glarian remained thought-merged and focused upon the cocooning of Zog and Zoanna, the other-realm experiences of both leaders began to flow outward and trickle into the consciousness of all dragons. The Glarian, too, felt the shift in their own inner awarenesses, and before long a deep sigh of relief was breathed into the hearts of each dragon. The relief rippled through their many interpretations of a yearning fulfilled, and acted as healing balm. Gently it eased their focused

---

25 Kah-na Tro-Linaht: only recognized in the histories, a name given to the Moment in Stretched Time. A seeming moment within which the causes and effects reside outside of the ongoing Timeline, and therefore separate from any preceding moment in history.

intent from the two beloved leaders who had always swelled their hearts and tickled their curiosities toward the most expansive explorations that many had never dreamed existed, much less participated within. Each dragon passionately cherished the bond with Zog and Zoanna.

Perhaps it was that deep bond that held them all in a suspended state of being. It was, however, within that suspended-from-the-regular-rhythm-of-living state that Zog, Zoanna, and the Glarian entered into what has been called *The Moment in Stretched Time*. Only the Ancient Ones were conscious of its beginning. Only the Ancient Ones knew that the entire Glarian and its leaders had been transported beyond time. In truth, only those who had released physical residing *could* recognize the initiating of the Moment that had the potential of changing the entire rhythm of all that had ever been and would be.

The Ancient Ones baptized the moment, Kah-na Tro-Linaht[25]. The New Beginning.

Like a bridge from the Nothingness to the All That Is, Kah-na Tro-Linaht enveloped all that resided within its timeless realm and further, into that which had been and would be created in all realms. It was but a breath... yet without question, it did exist.

CHAPTER FIVE

THE FIRST SECTOR OF LEARNING

They didn't know why Zoanna's request was a surprise. It shouldn't have been. After all, they were the Light Beings and always aware of the causes and effects surrounding anyone whom they were tending. Yet their focus upon Zoanna's well being was so intent that none had remembered the simple truth that the great leader was a mother.

In the midst of assimilating and healing, her answer to their question, "How can we assist you?" was clear and their reaction spoke an additional underlining. The fact that it was a surprise to them caused Zoanna to wonder if indeed she was the only one who actually realized that a great change had occurred.

They were residing within Timelessness. Yet for the Light Beings the occurrence seemed to be merely hinted at during the lighthearted relief each assistant felt ripple through themselves and their manner of caring for Zoanna.

Such rippling might have signaled the Kloan that something strange, something wonderful had occurred. However, they too had been so concentrated — on the onslaught of fire and on the well-being of their two leaders — that they had not only entered the Timelessness unaware, but it seemed not one maintained even an inkling of the emergency that existed one breath before the Moment in Stretched

Time. It was as if the Kloan had simply gathered and were celebrating the union and merging of their two leaders.

If not the Kloan, thought Zoanna, *then perhaps these Light Beings can certainly recognize the change from being in the wake of the consuming rage to this peaceful rhythm here with me.*

Yet it appeared that neither could they remember from what she was healing nor why or how she had entered their realm. It was as if days upon days of joyful tending had existed and as if they had and would always be as they were, Light Beings caring for Zoanna.

Zoanna didn't know why she was awake to the Timelessness while the Kloan and all the others seemed to be living as if their recent histories together hadn't changed — or more so, didn't exist at all. To her, timelessness and the full awareness felt as easy and familiar as breathing. *Perhaps there are some, those who have traveled beyond,* she thought. Yet she couldn't bring to mind any who had accomplished such travels.

It was within these thoughts that the Light Beings asked how they could assist her, and the two names filled her heart and mind. Initially Zoanna believed that they came to mind because she missed them.

"Bring me Kleeana and Mothan," she smiled, "bring me my inglets."

The Light Beings pulled to themselves their formed disguise simulating physical bodies, and beckoned the two inglets who had grown in size and capabilities beyond most. They resembled their parents more than any cared to mention aloud.

Zoanna breathed her love into the place where her two inglets would sit. And in the very next moment, it was with the exuberance of youth that they entered her green encoded healing chamber and stepped into her love-breathings. Hesitating briefly until Zoanna's open invitation called them, both Kleeana and Mothan bounded forward and embraced her light-emanating form with joyful shrill whistles, subtle fire licks, and the caressing only the young can give and receive from their mother.

The Light Beings watched and tended the integrity of Zoanna's large heart as she listened to the journeys and discoveries of Kleeana and Mothan. Though their first question came without warning, it was then that Zoanna realized why Mothan and Kleeana came to mind during her reflection on the Timelessness and who might actually be aware.

"What has been happening?" they asked in unison.

Zoanna's delight in their question radiated outward filling the chamber and caused the attending Light Beings to come to full alerted attention. It seemed to them that such a question was the natural interacting of inglets and their mother. Yet the radiating light spoke otherwise. This mother and two inglets were everything but usual.

The full alerted attention combined with the delight of the three opened a portal that incidentally hinted to Zoanna that the Light Beings might be more aware than she had originally assessed. Perhaps they too knew that these were neither ordinary circumstances nor ordinary times. She made a note to herself to speak with them later.

Though none could fully realize the implication of such a simple question and the fullness of the radiating patterns, the Light Beings prepared to soften the effects of such an interchange and, if need be, end the visit should any sign of strain signal itself from Zoanna. It was to this purpose their attending continued.

Of course Mothan and Kleeana's question intimated that they were aware that something had occurred. In order for such an awareness to exist, they necessarily would have stepped beyond the all-encompassing effect of The Moment in Stretched Time wherein all knowing of previous Timeline occurrences had been suspended.

The thought-merging flowed quickly between the two inglets and their mother. Before the Light Beings could further estimate the ramifications of such communication, Zoanna began her story, the same story that would be written in the histories under the name Kah-na Tro-Linaht.

"You are perhaps the only two who have asked such a question, my dear ones." Zoanna's knowing swelled with pride for their abilities to perceive the changed dips and nuances within their dragon realm. "Though you cannot remember now, one day you will remember **all** of what has occurred within our realm."

Alert. More than alert. Kleeana merged her thoughts with Mothan's and quickly questioned, *Have you felt the absence of knowing? Have you...* Before his mother could begin the telling neither of them would ever forget, Mothan replied, *I have not felt one ripple.* Neither Kleeana nor Mothan spoke again. In all their imaginings never would they have expected the words Zoanna spoke next.

"It is little known in the Kloan or for that matter within the Glarian that your father and I have journeyed to other realms and within manners of being far beyond that in which we reside." She smiled at the two intently focused beings before her. "Far beyond even where you have dared to explore seemingly without my knowing." An inner blush washed over the two inglet thought-mergings.

"Where your father journeyed with the wizards and learned methods of creating and forming not only his own form but other realms and portals, I journeyed beyond our Timeline.

"It wasn't a journey that I determined, but more one that I found myself exploring during a speaking with the Kloan. While my body remained at the center of the encircling Kloan and my voice and mouth continued to speak exactly what I had intended, I found myself lifting out of not only my body but out of the cavern within our mountain and indeed out of our entire realm!" She waited for the full meaning of her words to fill them. "It was as if I were in more than one place at the same time."

• • • • •

She remembered it well. It was the first of many journeys beyond her usual explorations. Initially she had been anxious to speak with Zog of the adventures; but as her experiences grew, she found herself able to simultaneously reside in more than one place nearly all of the time and it had become cumbersome to speak of each encounter. Consequently, it was during their mergings that she released to Zog the manner in which she had been enriched by her adventures.

The first journey introduced her to the Light Beings and began The First Sector of Learning. They encircled her with their golden essence until she seemed to dissolve and take form in the same moment. It took her breath away and at first she thought she would lose consciousness.

But they spun the circle faster and faster which, contrary to what one might think, made her experience easier and easier. At the very last moment, Zoanna had released any thoughts of maintaining form and felt herself spinning. The realization that she was inside the golden circle brought her to a fully awakened state, which elicited cheers and applause from the Golden Beings who then appeared before her eyes.

The Golden Beings took form in one breath as golden dragons and then in the next breath they flowed as the golden circle about her. Lastly, the gold rolled in a rhythm — over, around and back into itself. She had learned how to fix her gaze, which allowed their changes to be maintained in the element of form. It was a learning that became the primary foundation for all her further experiences within The First Sector of Learning: the illusion of form.

Again and again she had traveled to their realm. Initially such traveling occurred at unexpected moments when she was totally involved with an activity in her regular rhythm of living: once during a speaking with other mothers of the Floggen, and another during a flight to the Neecha. At the Neecha, she met representatives from other Floggen and not only spoke of journeys to other realms, but guided them to experience the beginning of their own possible expansion. She often wondered how she could be maintaining such activities in her dragon realm, while simultaneously spinning inside a golden circle and taking form with her Light Beings.

It wasn't until the tenth lesson within the First Sector that she decided to place her physical body at rest while she journeyed to the golden realm, as she affectionately called it to herself. It was this manner in which she experienced the next forty or so lessons within the First Sector.

THE FIRST SECTOR OF LEARNING

· · · · ·

"Please mother, speak of the lessons themselves." It was Mothan who called her from the reverie of memories.

Without hesitation, Zoanna responded. "The lessons within the First Sector weren't really lessons, but experiences. And it was only in looking back at the experience that I realized what I had learned." She looked from Mothan to Kleeana, "Just like when you both began thought-merging long ago. You played with the distance between your physical locations until you realized that you could thought-merge any time and in any location."

Both nodded their agreement as they too remembered the play they had enjoyed. Zoanna continued, "And, it was just recently that you both realized that such unlimited thought-merging abilities were not the automatic experience of all dragons your age. Your father then spoke with you of the capabilities of the Representatives within the Kloan. You heard of how those capabilities enhanced every individual within the represented Floggen."

Kleeana spoke excitedly, "That was when we began practicing thought-merging while gathering with our friends."

"That's right," exclaimed Mothan, "and we began to realize that our friends were able to thought-merge with us." He reflected for a moment. "Sometimes I don't think they realized they were thought-merging, Mother."

"Sometimes," continued Kleeana, "they were talking with each other and thought merging with me at the same time. Yet, when I tried to speak with them of the thought-merging, they didn't know what I was speaking about."

"That was confusing for a while," Mothan remembered, "but then we realized that the Representatives probably went through the same thing when they returned to their Floggen." He smiled, his exuberance taking over the restrained nature he placed upon himself while listening to his mother's story. "I asked Kilchek once if that bothered him.... You know... if it bothered him that none of his Floggen realized the topics of their thought-merging."

Zoanna remembered Kilchek with fondness, "How did he respond?"

"I was there," Kleeana interjected, "I remember. He looked at the two of us with disbelief!"

"Well, yes he did." Mothan smiled. "It took a moment. He started to ask us how we could be asking such a question and then changed his response to something like, "You might know such a question would come from Zog and Zoanna's inglets!"

"But did he ever answer your question?" asked Zoanna.

"Yes. Yes he did. Kilchek said that it only *appeared* that they didn't remember or understand."

Kleeana recalled, "He said that everything is not always as it appears. In one moment it may seem as though our friends don't know what we spoke of during thought-merging and in the next moment they may have total recall. He said that maybe when they were in their own homes a knowing might fill them." Zoanna smiled inwardly at Kilchek's wisdom. He had been one of their best teachers.

"That's when I began to look at what **I** was becoming aware of." Mothan's excitement at what he had learned filled the healing chamber. "If I could see my friends being unaware in the moment and perhaps later they realized all of our conversations, then I asked myself what I was not aware of in the moment. I asked myself what I was becoming aware of...."

"And didn't that lead you," interrupted Zoanna, "to the realizing that there is nothing that you don't know? Didn't it bring you to the knowing that if you could step out of time, there would be no *later*, no *not aware of*?

Both Kleeana and Mothan sat back, stunned. They hadn't thought of that before. Zoanna smiled. "This, right now, is the kind of lesson I had in the First Sector."

She continued, "After I learned how to access the golden realm, I simply went there for my own enjoyment. I played with how to form and reform my body, how to journey within and without the Timeline, and how to influence other realms.

"Eventually I learned how to dissolve my entire beingness and...."

"What do you mean by that, Mother?" asked Kleeana. "What do you mean by *dissolve your entire beingness*?"

THE FIRST SECTOR OF LEARNING

"I was sitting with the Golden Beings. Together we had created a realm where we could experience color and sound. I loved that realm because I could feel the colors resonate through me. And I could allow the vibration of the sounds to affect not only my consciousness but also my physical form.

"But I thought your physical form was here in this realm while you were there with the Light Beings?" Mothan continued, "What form did you have there while you were with them?"

"I maintained my dragon form in both locations. In my last lesson of the First Sector I learned more about bi-locating."

"Wow! *Bi*-locating!" Mothan looked from Zoanna to Kleeana.

"Well, the lesson wasn't entirely about bi-locating. It was about letting go of the need to have a form at all..." Zoanna projected the picture of the lesson before their eyes.

She had been delighted with the Light Beings' encouragement of her taking form not only in their realm but also in two others, all while she maintained a physical form within her dragon realm. She was just about to attempt an additional location when all of her forms dissolved!

She had smiled to herself even then. It was all play. Next, without warning, all of her forms appeared again — right inside of her! She felt them. All of them. Yet there she was, one dragon. And there they were, all inside of her.

They had laughed at her puzzlement and sent a wave of love throughout her wondering. Without thinking, she placed her consciousness as an observer. That's when it happened.

She did not exist in any form. She saw that she was not a dragon in her dragon realm, she was not a light-being dragon in this realm, nor was she a light dragon in any realm. If it weren't for her consciousness, it would appear that she did not exist at all!

Such realization brought the Light Beings to cheering and applauding once again.

"Firstly," continued Zoanna, "I had learned how to dissolve my body. Well, it came as a secondary learning when I became an observer in order to figure out what was going on.

"Becoming an observer was the last lesson of the First Sector. Anyone who has passed from First Sector to Second knows that from the place of an observer, you can create or dissolve anything that is of you!"

She saw their puzzled look. "That's probably enough for one sitting," she said.

"But mother..." Mothan pleaded. His piercing eyes commanded more. He emptied himself in order to be filled.

Zoanna felt his hunger. "This is what you want to know dear Mothan: when you place yourself determinedly as an observer of your own self, you place your entire self there.

"Then, unless you decide otherwise, you do not exist in any other realm while you maintain observing. Only a conscious choice, a conscious decision will create you to be somewhere or, for that matter, will create you to be back where you were the moment before observation.

"It's not really complicated. It's more deciding and then maintaining that deciding."

That was it. That was what he had to know. Mothan breathed deeply, giving a thankful nod to his mother.

"But how do you maintain the deciding," asked Kleeana.

"That, my dear young inglet, is part of Sector Two!"

Both sat back. Even in her jesting, Zoanna began to evidence fatigue. The Light Beings moved closer and Kleeana and Mothan quickly released their deep focus. Their mother needed rest... and it would take time to digest all that she had spoken of with them.

The Light Beings registered among themselves the delightful abilities of Zoanna's inglets. They again cloaked their speakings with each other. Neither of the two inglets would benefit from hearing such speculation, nor would Zoanna's joy be augmented. For the moment they would allow her the enjoyment of the presence of her young ones. Yet, it was agreed that Mothan and Kleeana's capabilities would perhaps lead the Kloan during the releasing of The Moment in Stretched Time.

When the two left her side, the Light Beings eased Zoanna into a deep sleep, the same sleep that held her in stasis while she healed from all that had occurred within the Timeline. Still, the last words whispered before she slipped into unconsciousness were *"Zog, what of Zog?"*

• • • • •

Zoanna's speaking not only affected her two inglets in a manner that would change their lives from that point onward. Unknown within her deep resting sleep, because of her thought-merging abilities, she also affected the Glarian. Her speaking of the Timeline, her speaking of dissolving, and her speaking of being an observer trickled an expectation of knowing among a few. The few delighted in the trickle. Such delighting brought the gift of a slight awakening. The few turned and danced within their awakening until their numbers became more and then many. And it was the awakening of the many that showered upon each Floggen a calling to know... something.... In a gigantic sigh, the entirety of the Glarian came to a realization. Together. Together as One.

It might have been a difficult realization, a heart-wrenching realization if it hadn't come within The Moment in Stretched Time. In gatherings-to-come there would be much respectful speculation about the nature of the realization.

Yet within The Moment, it became evident to the entire Glarian that the merging of Zoanna and Zog was so all-encompassing that they might not see either of their leaders again. Many found themselves actually saying, "Perhaps this merging is the completing of their leadership."

None connected such merging with its purpose, the purpose of healing Zog as he had returned from the inferno. And none could even remember — in the state of Stretched Time — the inferno, its onslaught, or any of what had occurred just the moment previous to the Moment in Stretched Time.

There was no panic. No deep sorrow. Neither was there a conclusion of loss. Only the tiny beginning of realization birthed itself, a realization that would grow with Zoanna's telling of her story to her two beloved inglets. Indeed, none but the Light Beings knew of and considered the significance of the inglets' abilities to hear the story and integrate its meaning.

CHAPTER SIX

WHAT IS THAT CLANGING??

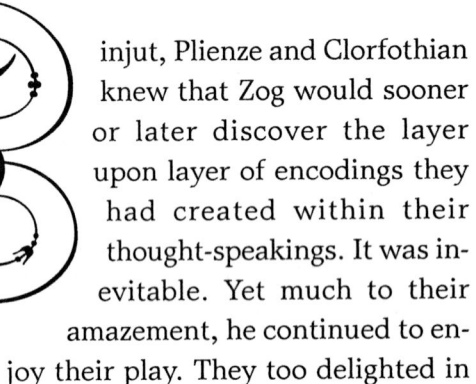

injut, Plienze and Clorfothian knew that Zog would sooner or later discover the layer upon layer of encodings they had created within their thought-speakings. It was inevitable. Yet much to their amazement, he continued to enjoy their play. They too delighted in his manner of celebrating a freedom as yet not recognized; neither did he sense any need of freedom from anything. He basked in their presence as they radiated their encasement of love about him and within their created realm.

Although he had continually surprised them with his youthful, and then later mature, awarenesses and discoveries, because of their mutual enjoyment of each other's company, they had not quite been prepared for the casual asking that he breathed upon them. They lay relaxing at the bottom of the mountain range –- just a slight rearrangement of encodings away from the realm within which he had sacrificingly created the portal for his Glarian.

Zog's robust life force thrived within the form they had expertly created. Even their reaching into his charred, lifeless form, calling him to come, to follow them, had been blocked from his knowing. They had emanated his patternings precisely and it was within that

WHAT IS THAT CLANGING??

cocoon-like vibration that the wisp of battered spirit lifted up and out of that which he had been and began the releasing of struggle and intensified battle that had so quickly and completely laid him to rest.

Within those precise patternings, Zog's dashed broken spirit, his last anguished beseechings for assistance to his Glarian, and the strands of wholeness twisted and contorted as such extreme efforting bends and gnaws until distortion seems to be relief, began to release and lay itself open for the love of the three wizards to heal. They had woven together memories of their beginnings and even most recent enjoyable adventures along with the expanded patternings of unlimited possibilities, intending the weaving to strengthen an avenue through which Zog could journey and recognize that which he was becoming – one of them.

They had all three known the taste of the flames of Neekontuk and it was their compassion for this beloved leader that determined them to maintain the integrity of the healing realm for as long as they did. Perhaps they would have chuckled as they had in the past, when Zog reached through their attempts at maintaining secret creations, if it weren't for the consequence such a discovery would bring.

"Well," he leaned his glistening, green, glowing body back against the hill. His wings had easily folded in upon themselves and only intensified the fullness of that which he was.

"Well," he repeated, signaling them that they had been caught at their own acting, "when did you plan on telling me what this is all about?"

Once before he had actually been able to irritate them with his abilities to conceal his own thoughts, and now again they wondered how much he actually knew. It was Clorfothian who spoke first.

"Now Zog, you can't blame us for having a little fun, old boy. After all, the old times rarely have given up of themselves to allow us such reverie...."

Zog snorted a blue puff of well-meaning indignation. "Do you actually believe I am that naïve," he stressed the next two words, *"old boy?"*

Plienze jumped to the rescue. "Now Zog...."

Zog's magnificence emanated before the three old friends, reminding them of other times and other realms. "I haven't felt this alive since..." he thought for a brief moment, "since the building of our chambers and the experimenting with wing-purposes!"

Winjut took advantage of the brief moment to expertly insert an assuaging balm. Zog was barely able to finish the sentence. His eyes blinked slowly and then with the light sigh of a carefree nap, he drifted off to sleep.

Clorfothian whispered even though there wasn't a need to do so. The sleeping giant before them must remain just that – a sleeping giant, at least until they could plan the next unfolding awarenesses. "Were either of you able to discern how much he knew?" He brushed at the empty space around him, muttering to himself, "Each time something has occurred he seems to have developed beyond what I can expect. I've never known one like him..."

"Of course you haven't," also whispering Plienze. "He is who he is."

Clorfothian interjected, "Last time...."

"This is not last time or the time before!" exclaimed Winjut, putting a stop to the speculation of Zog's capabilities. "This is *this* time and we'd better get busy. My balm may have been a little stronger than I intended, but I'm not sure how long it will last. With Zog, everything's a guess!"

While the three wizards huddled together, creating and discreating plans and encodings within which they might lead Zog to an understanding and eventual awakening to all that had occurred, Zog's mind searched for the topic he'd set aside.

It had been during his studies with them that he had developed his abilities to sleep and still explore, and it was within this familiar skill that he now not only searched for but found the flash and its imprinted image: fire and battle... somewhere.... The three felt his discovery and before they could place another barrier to his awareness, Zog had journeyed into the flash with the curiosity of an adventurer. The magnificent form before their wizardly gaze dissolved.

WHAT IS THAT CLANGING??

The journey carried him back, away from them, and into the realm he'd forgotten existed. It was the merging with Zoanna that caught and lessened his fall into the charred, lifeless body. She drank into herself the possibility of shock even before his awareness could grasp at what was actually happening. And it was through the suspended merging within the deep love and oneness with Zoanna that Zog saw not only his body but all that had occurred during the battle.

Zog's knowing riveted through Zoanna as she reached to maintain their merging. Her healing chamber filled with Light Beings, encircling her form and embracing her spirit lest she, too, release physicality all together.

Such encircling gave the semblance of separation within the merging of Zog and Zoanna and each filled their breathings with determined union. It was exactly what the Light Beings had hoped for, and soon the encasing of the two reestablished itself stronger with renewed intent.

The Glarian felt the fall of Zog in a way that shook the entire Moment in Stretched Time. *It waved within itself and that which would be the future folded in upon that which was the past.* Such folding disturbed the peaceful experience of the Glarian and brought to the entire consciousness the awareness of not only their two leaders merging, but also the extreme intensities of such merging. Where one began to remember, all began to remember.

It was Mentard, the only surviving original maintainer of the blue structure, who remembered more, remembered the strain upon the very fabric of his entire being. In such remembering and through the smoke breathing itself into the structure, they had struggled to maintain even with the added strength of those assistants who united with them. He remembered the charred form.

Horror. Disbelief caught him as the other two, Niara and Connock, dissolved in their strivings to maintain. It was Mentard who now remembered drifting into the numb sleep even as his thought-merging reached toward his beloved leader. It was Mentard who now felt and integrated the thoughts that had been held in the Timeline. He had failed. He choked on the memory of Zog's charred body.

The Glarian felt the knowing trickle and then flood through them like the Sleecha rivers in their great valleys. They remembered their gathering and the maintained focus. Zog and Zoanna were merging in a manner that had never been experienced within their realm. Zog and Zoanna were.... They couldn't bear to speak of the departing of Zog and consequently the eventual departing of Zoanna. They wept the sadness of knowing from their hearts. The wrenching sound of such weeping from so many great giant beings vibrated through the fabric of the Kah-na Tro-Linate. The stretching of the fabric and the wailing lament called out to the Golden Beings, who gathered the sadness into their great light and absorbed the heartache lest it return to the Glarian and cause another fold, perhaps prematurely ending the Kah-na Tro-Linaht.

Even though the dragon population was unknowingly residing within the Moment of Stretched Time, their enjoyment of the peaceful rhythm had been interrupted to such a degree that it was as if every movement and proceeding slowed nearly to a stop. The Golden Beings took advantage of the slowing and continued to breathe their love upon the Glarian. Consequently, the merging of the remembering of the extreme occurrences within the Timeline and the peace of the Moment in Stretched Time fell prey to the slowing. Such infinitesimal movement laid itself bare to possible influences by any who could maintain a consciousness of both the continuing Timeline and the Moment in Stretched Time.

· · · · ·

The Golden Beings watched the five who had long ago begun to seek their realm. It was upon them that the hope of a new page in history rested. Upon their adventuresome spirit rested the possibility that the cycle of destruction and sleep might finally be laid to rest. To know the immensity of their participation within their own unfolding story would perhaps have choked the natural flowing of their manner of discovery. Thusly, it was to their benefit that they met in their usual manner of friendly determination to simply solve the next puzzle that presented itself to their curiosity.

The Golden Beings knew them well, perhaps better than they knew themselves. Meteranke, Fornaign, Brianna, Karthentonen, and Treiga felt the effects of the folding but were not consumed by it. They heard the wailing, but did not wail. They knew of the great sadness but did not take it into their young dragon beings.

Their combined abilities led them to expanded scanning and swift discovery of the absorbing of the great Glarian heartache. The Golden Beings veiled their identity within their absorbing but allowed the awarenesses to remain with the five. Those who veiled also remained as observers even as the five thought-merged and agreed to meet at the Neecha.

It was Brianna who was the first to arrive, and without hesitation, she began setting the purpose of their gathering. Stilling the alarm that wanted to well up within her dragon skills at remaining objective, it was to her great relief that Treiga appeared shortly after. Even the presence of Treiga radiated a balance to the energies within the Neecha, making it be quite different from the rolling effects within the Glarian as the folding and absorbing attempted to balance itself from possible extremes. And though Brianna wanted to ask the obvious questions, Treiga's love radiated outward and she breathed it into herself. There would be time for questions *and* answers.

Meteranke and Fornaign arrived together with Karthentonen landing on the ledge behind them. The three entered one behind the other, with Kar sealing the entryway as he simultaneously folded his wings and glanced around to receive an affirming nod from the others.

They had matured in their gatherings, and while they had not achieved all the goals such an adventurous five-some would set for themselves, the automatic thought-merging began even as they settled their great dragon bodies against the walls of the Neecha.

Now well-practiced in presenting the facts as the histories revealed, Brianna began releasing her knowing of Timeline changes, Glarian wailing, and -- reluctantly -- the passing of leaders. Within Brianna's knowing, Treiga wove his strands of balance, non-interpreted awareness, and his realizations concerning the stretching of balance required for Zog and Zoanna to maintain merging while still residing within their functions as leaders of the Glarian.

Kar surrounded the merging with the depth of peace with which he had been gifted during his first visit to the realms of wizards, even though he frustratingly had not been able to see or speak directly with them. The encasement of peace allowed their gathering to release all sense of immediacy.

Meteranke and Fornaign, who had already begun merging as they were meeting together when the fold in the Moment in Stretched Time occurred, easily uplifted the frequencies of the gathering. Discovered quite by accident as an incidental to their traveling with intent to the portal of the wizards, the uplifting of group frequencies had served them well, as it seemed to belay the cause and effect of Timeline participation.[26] The five's merging and shared information having been completed, Meteranke spoke first.

"Unless our access to information has been unknowingly stinted," he nodded to Brianna as he stressed the word *unknowingly*, "we have entered a new page in our own histories!

"And I find it hard to believe," he continued, relaxing into the comfort of their familiarity with each other, "that we are the only ones who seem to have these awarenesses. Yet I, for one, cannot find any others who are remaining objective and who have the capabilities of residing simultaneously outside the Timeline *and* within whatever this barely moving dreamlike state is."

He turned his gaze: "Kar, what is this state anyway? I was floating in it for a while, but then something happened and I seemed to snap out of it...."

"And then you go back into it?" asked Fornaign. "I've been doing that. I wasn't aware of it initially, but during one of the fluxes I seemed to really wake up." He looked at them all. "In

---

26 Timeline Participation: Although the wizards hadn't communicated with the five at this point of development, they had been pleased to celebrate such abilities in ways that only wizards can. Needless to say, such celebrations had piqued curiosities as the pulsating colors and rolling waves of light flowed over the mountain ranges and into many a Floggen's evening gathering.

WHAT IS THAT CLANGING??

fact, I don't think I've ever been this awake!" Fornaign too looked toward Karthentonen. "Tell us, Kar, if you can."

Kar leaked out a tiny fiery breath, which brought a smile only to Treiga, who had become best friends with Karthentonen and was quite accustomed to balancing the exuberance that remained even when maturity eased its way into the resistant, rebellious youth and produced the magnificently wise member of their group.

"As far as I can tell," Karthentonen began, raising his dragon body so that he could walk while he spoke with them. "As far as I can tell, there has been a forgetting." He looked to each of them. "I know we're here to speak of our awarenesses and I am prepared to also speak of what I know. However, more importantly, I believe we can discern together that the entire Glarian has forgotten something."

Fornaign stirred from his relaxed position. "Not only the Glarian.... Well, I know we're part of the Glarian, of course," he smiled, "but in a way we are not. What I want to mention is that I too feel as though I've forgotten something... something important."

Meteranke looked from one to the other. "Have we all felt the absence of knowing?"

"I never thought of it that way," said Brianna. "I suppose I'm so used to searching for information that the absence of knowing is part of my everyday life!"

"But this is different," continued Kar. "This is from my own past, from my own history. There's something I just can't seem to remember...."

"Yeah," agreed Treiga, "and it's important. Something major is missing."

It was Meteranke who steered their attention back. "Kar, then speak about what you are aware of. Maybe between all of us we will piece this together."

"But wouldn't we have already done this in our thought-merging?" asked Brianna. "I mean, if we could have discovered this together, wouldn't we have already?"

"Not necessarily, Brianna." Kar knew what she was referring to. "Thought-merging is more a merging of all that we are, not necessarily our speculations or absences."

Meteranke continued the statement, "We merge together all that we have integrated within our own selves. If there's something that doesn't quite fit with our understanding, then we haven't integrated it."

"Oh, I see. Then, please, Kar, continue with what you have discovered," she pleaded. Brianna too had matured, yet her youthful impatience seemed to linger, a trait the others had eventually viewed as an attribute to their gatherings as it seemed to spur their momentum.

"It's more of an experience than my reflected knowing. I haven't come to any conclusions yet." Kar resumed his pacing of the expanse of the Neecha. "I was relaxing in the glow of a journey to the portal. I'd entered through the portal and actually ventured further into the wizard's realm than I ever had." He quickly responded to their surprised looks, "That's when I realized something was going on. You know," his stride took on an extended measure, "it seemed as though I should have been quite pleased, more than pleased in fact. But I wasn't. I was just... relaxed... as if nothing were really too important.

"I tried to make myself be on alert and I could not. That's when I started retracing my actions during the day and then the day before, and the day before that.

"I couldn't bring my thinking to a time when I wasn't so... so relaxed!"

"But did you have a feeling... a *passive* feeling of emergency?" asked Treiga. "Did you have a feeling that something had happened but you couldn't quite connect with it?"

"Exactly! Tre, exactly!" Kar was about to continue when Meteranke interrupted.

"I have had the very same feeling. I still do. Even right now," he continued, nodding to Kar, "I feel it right now. I just can't seem to access that information though."

"But wait a minute!" Brianna breathed a larger than usual puff of blue smoke but kept on with her excitement. "I know

WHAT IS THAT CLANGING??

when that happened before! I know when such an unknowing happened before!"

They all focused intently on her next words. "It was written in the histories of the Neekontuk."

The word *Neekontuk* caused them to freeze. It shattered their concentration. The union and interweaving let go of itself and they fell into a sluggish consciousness of near sleep. It was thick. In slow motion, they reached for each other, trying to thought-merge, to uplift their awareness. Through the seeming lazy efforting, they heard.

It was a banging as if from far away. Persistent, it was. Banging. Shouting. What was that shouting? What was that light piercing into the thick sleep? Again, banging. Calling out.

Meteranke reached through the dense drowsiness. His mind slowly flowed to the portal and peered through. *Two. There were two of them. Small.* His thoughts sluggishly registered. *Small dragons.* He saw the two dragons merge their intent and breathe a fiery breath through the portal. It entered the Neecha like the clanging of a bell and shook their dream state. The two breathed their intent again. The dream state began to let go of its hold upon the five. The two breathed once more and the clanging became an irritation. It was Fornaign whose drowsy speaking turned to a resonating bellow, "WHAT IS THAT CLANGING!!!" He covered his ears.

"Wait!" Meteranke shook himself awake, still a little foggy, but awake enough to realize the identity of the two who were just outside the portal of their gathering. "Wake up!" he shouted. He merged his thoughts with them, pushing his way through the thick residue. "Wake up!" his mind shouted.

The combination of clanging and Meteranke's shouting brought the others to attention. Simultaneously they were all about to ask what had happened when Meteranke interrupted even the beginnings of such asking.

"We have to decide what to do here!"

"What do you mean," Brianna adjusted her dragon body to a more attentive position. "Decide about what?"

"There are two dragons outside the portal!" Meteranke's excitement was a puzzle to the others. The standard policy when the Neecha was being used insisted that any dragons who approached honor the use and remove themselves from the portal. Meteranke emphasized, "It was their banging on the portal that woke me up, that woke us all up!"

"Banging?" Karthentonen's face demonstrated the contradiction. "Banging?" he repeated. "How could anyone *bang* on the portal?? We sealed it...."

"It's not the banging that I'm pointing out," said Meteranke. "It's that the banging is what woke us up!"

It was Treiga who asked the final question, the question that changed their experiences together within that Neecha gathering and within the many more gatherings to come. "Who? Who could do that?" He paused briefly and then, "With the entire rest of the Glarian seemingly asleep to all of this, WHO could not only approach the Neecha, but WHO could actually reach through our seal and bang on the portal..." his mind reached for an explanation. "...and cause the banging to enter here... here among us... and wake us up from a sleep?" His questioning exposed a child-like look upon his adult face, "And, what was that sleep?"

Neither Treiga nor the others had had such questions since the first meetings they enjoyed so long ago.

Meteranke peered out the portal again and saw the two. "There are two young dragons outside the portal. They have merged their intent and are quite" — he stressed the word *quite* — "QUITE capable of more than I think we would suspect."

"Well," urged Brianna, "who are they?"

"That's what I've been so surprised about." Meteranke looked at the other four. "The two are Zog and Zoanna's inglets."

Silence. Dragon bodies frozen in place. Clanging, irritating clanging.

Finally the four moved and spoke in unison, "Who?? Who is outside the portal?"

Meteranke spoke distinctly, "Kleeana and Mothan. Zog and Zoanna's inglets."

WHAT IS THAT CLANGING??

The four spoke, again simultaneously, "WHAT???"

Fornaign stepped beyond the shock and spoke emphatically, "We'd better open the portal before that clanging drives me to flames!"

"I agree," shouted Brianna over the disturbing noise. "My head can't take that another moment!"

Meteranke asked, "Then it's agreed? We open the portal? And let them in?" The others nodded, cringing at the increasing volume of the annoying sound.

In unison, they turned their thought-merging to release the seal upon the portal and watched the two young dragons tumble into the Neecha.

• • • • •

"It's about time!" exclaimed Mothan as he tried to control the red-orange flames that involuntarily flicked out through his words.

Brianna helped Kleeana up from her tangled tumble. "Are you all right?"

Kleeana's bright eyes sparkled at them. "Of course I am all right. The question is, what happened to *you* all?"

Mothan joined, "Yeah. What happened to you all?" He turned his young face toward each of them. "One moment you were getting to the good part...,"

Kleeana finished his statement. "...and the next you were fast asleep. Like the others!"

"We couldn't let that happen!" Mothan jumped up.

"No, we didn't want to be the only ones..." Kleeana's words trailed off into silence. The four felt her sadness.

Kar smiled at the two. "Let's all sit back here," he said calmly. "We'll close the portal again...."

But it was Meteranke who interrupted. "You could hear what we were discussing?" He looked from Mothan to Kleeana. "You could hear what we were discussing," he repeated, "and you saw when the sleep overtook us?"

All five glistening dragons focused their gaze upon the two.

Mothan and Kleeana looked sheepishly at each other and finally shrugged their shoulders. "Well. Yes."

Mothan added, "If you must know, we have been... for quite a while."

It was Kleeana who spoke the words they would discuss for many a Neecha gathering. "Without you five, we're goners!"

CHAPTER SEVEN

FALLING INTO THE DREAM STATE

The five compatriots embraced Zog and Zoanna's two inglets with warmth and with curiosity. And as they again closed the portal and Treiga balanced the energies of such exuberance and all-knowingness, the group began to unite in ways that neither the five nor the two had expected. It wasn't as if the seven deliberately decided to enter a merging that would establish a manner of openhearted all-embracing which none other had experienced while living upon the land as it changed and transformed. They simply, in the desire to celebrate their alikeness, began to thought-merge and in so doing lifted out of the cause and effect which seemingly held the remaining population of dragons spellbound.

Their thought-merging carried them far beyond their physical bodies, far beyond the cavern where they continued to meet in secret. Indeed, as each individual's experiences and adventures became the joy and delight of the others, it was as if the walls of the great cavern fell away and the Neecha no longer existed. Time and timelessness too fell away as they embraced and united deeply, completely, beyond the oncoming rage, beyond the Glarian's realm of cause and effect, beyond the dream-like Moment in Stretched Time, beyond the realms of the wizards, and beyond the questions and answers. Each one had certainly experienced traveling without the huge body, yet this was past traveling. Their bodies existed... somewhere, their

Neecha existed... somewhere, and their purpose for gathering existed... somewhere, but not here, not now. This was different.

There was a spinning, but they were not spinning. There were symbols, floating, forming and disforming, their meanings easily known without words and without concern — or attachment when the knowing released from their awareness. There was the continual soft speaking of the story, of all stories and the absence of the need to listen.

Each of the now seven held his and her own experiences, yet felt those experiences flow outward and into the others. Each felt themselves flow out, in, and through what appeared to be the others, as if they were individuals and they were not. Each had separate thoughts and then there were no thoughts at all. There was no striving. Before a possible question arose, the knowing filled all seven simultaneously.

Meteranke's possible question began to swirl, as somewhere some time, perhaps back in his home, he had once wondered who would be the one, the last one to join their group. Somewhere a wondering began about the two young dragons and how they fit in with.... Yet, even the plans, so carefully laid within his expanded awarenesses, dissolved into... into nothingness.

The speaking came without words, yet with words. It was spoken and not spoken. Known. *"There will always be one. There will always be one last one. That one is the only one."*

Perhaps if they were back in the Neecha, the many possible questions would have been excitedly explored and indeed carried with them as they left their gathering and reentered their own lives within their Floggens. However, within the enveloping flowing there was only knowing, only truth.

The opening hadn't actually appeared before them, but more that its pulsating glow had always been and always would be. And along with the flowing, without hesitation they entered together as one... and then... they were no more. Nothingness. There was no absence of. Just... nothing.

The Golden Beings watched and loved. Each Golden Being had long ago entered through the portal into the Nothingness. It was the same journey all the Ancient Ones had either discovered or dissolved into when their bodies had completed their usefulness and their journeys upon the land were at an end. It was the same Nothingness to which the Golden Beings returned for replenishment. And, except for the fairies and gnomes, none others who still resided upon the land, none others who still maintained a physical body had ever entered the Nothingness and returned to the land.

Yet, as the pulsebeat of the portal breathed itself outward once again, the seven returned from the Nothingness and into their thought-merging. The pulsebeat breathed each one forth — an individual yet a part of the others — into the realm where they sat together in the cavern. So well had they sealed the Neecha that none 'cept the Golden Beings knew of their leaving or their return to their physical bodies.

The vague pleasure of becoming tapped itself on the shoulders of seven dragons as they lay against the walls of the Neecha. Deep, full peace became the patternings through which they took form and in the taking form, somehow knew that they always had been... in form.

It was Mothan who spoke the first words. His speaking was neither expected nor unexpected. And listening to his words seemed like what they had been doing all along.

"There are a number of locations that I find myself in, that Kleeana and I find ourselves in. Each location seems to be related to the others." Mothan spoke with certainty and, quite like the habit of each of the five, began walking the width of the Neecha as he spoke. "It also appears to me that the Timeline expresses itself differently within each location. Thus far I have discerned three locations, and I'm not certain if any or all are actually located within or out of the Timeline itself."

Meteranke, as well as the other four, smiled a soft smile and allowed himself the enjoyment of Mothan's speaking. He was, in fact, describing some of their conclusions. Upon his speaking the last remnants of that which had been nothing flowed forth, took form and filled their wondrous dragon beings. An awareness trickled in with their taking form. The awareness, each one determined, would be explored at some other time.

For now, though, they simply felt themselves to be more of who they really were, fuller than ever before. Stronger. More certain.

The fullness and strength rippled through the outer edge of their middle wings, changing the encodings and adjusting the levels of expansion and inclusion. While the Golden Beings observed such formings, they continued to breathe their breath of love within the Neecha and especially upon Mothan as he spoke the words that seemed to nourish all that they were becoming.

"I have confidence that I can speak of each of the locations *and* that we can maintain our awakened state as I speak." He paused his pacing and looked to each questioning dragon. Shrugging his shoulders, "Well, the last time you were speaking about a concept that resided in another location, you fell into the thick Dream State[27]."

Before Brianna could arouse herself to question, Mothan continued. "Kleeana and I have observed this in a number of instances with other dragons. Whenever information about another location is expressed, a sleep state occurs." He sat down again, next to Kleeana. She added, "That is, unless we are in the location that's moving so slowly that it *is* almost the sleep state. It's like everyone is dreaming. Seems impossible to even speak of another location there."

Kleeana leaned forward as she remembered a recent experience. "In fact, the last time Mothan and I were at that dream location, we HAD to thought-merge or I believe we too would have been unable to even discuss objectively what was going on! It's quite consuming."

Of the five who were listening, it was Meteranke who spoke. "Describe the locations, if you would. I want to compare my own experiences," he looked to his compatriots, "as I'm sure we all would." Each nodded in agreement.

"Well," said Mothan, "when I became aware that something was going on — something BIG was going on — was when

---

27 <u>Dream State</u>: or sleep state, both referring to that consciousness which resides within the Moment in Stretched Time, the Kah-na Tro-Linaht. The Dream State began when the Moment in Stretched Time folded in upon itself and slowed to near stop.

Kleeana and I were at home with the fairies. It's what we are calling the Dream State. Initially, I didn't remember why we were with the fairies."

Kleeana added, "In the past, when we were inglets, we stayed with the fairies when Mom or Dad were addressing the Glarian. Because we were still young, the fairies protected us from the intense outpouring of vibrations that emanated from the Glarian gathering."

"But this was recent." Mothan smiled at his own statement, "Well, whatever *recent* means, depending on the location you're in!"

"Let's not get too complicated, Mothan," chided Kleeana. We don't even know what will happen with all of us speaking about these things."

"You're right," he agreed and continued. "Anyway, when we left the Circle of Fairies[28], it was like we were flying into thick air. And everything seemed to be moving slower, much slower."

"Where was that?" asked Fornaign.

"Right in our own mountain range." Mothan looked directly at Fornaign. "Have you had the same experience?"

"First, tell me what the others of your Floggen were doing, what was that like?" continued Fornaign.

"They were moving slower. In fact, we were wondering what they were doing there with the Glarian gathering going on."

Kleeana interjected, "I remember asking someone if the gathering was over and the response was 'what gathering?'. That's when we knew we had some exploring to do."

"How was it to move around in all of that?" asked Karthentonen.

"We could move OK, but it took a little more effort, a little more concentration." Mothan paused. "I'm not sure if we could overcome that by changing our focus. I haven't tried that yet."

---

28 Circle of Fairies: an enveloping circle of love created by the fairies who attended inglets. The purpose of the circle was primarily to protect the innocence of inglets from any expanded vibrations from Kloan Gatherings; from non-physical exploration, as inglets continued to take form and develop; and from any physical, non-physical, or vibrational threat that might prematurely end inglet innocence.

"I have felt the same," said Fornaign. "However, I had been thought-merging with the Glarian Gathering and then it seemed something changed." He thought back to the experience. "It was almost like a distortion, but not quite. You know," he gestured to the group, "a distortion is external, but this felt like... well, like it went through me!" He gestured again, "That's it! It felt like it went through me."

Brianna studied what they were saying and then, "You mean a distortion rippled through you?" She looked at each one, "Or, a portal opened and you inadvertently stepped through it?"

"No," said Treiga, "It was more like I was thought-merged with the Gathering in one moment and then not something, but *everything* shifted. And," he remembered, "I was no longer thought-merged. In fact, I couldn't reestablish contact."

"That's what happened to us," Mothan looked to Kleeana, who agreed. "It was as if everything and everybody was part of something together, but we were on the outside. We could move around, we could talk with anyone, but we couldn't feel anything in their talking. We were separate."

"And we have been separate since then," added Kleeana. She thought for a moment, then, "We found if we thought-merged and moved as fast as we could, that most of the time no one could see us."

"Yeah," smiled Mothan, "It was like we were invisible." His smile broadened, "In fact, if there wasn't so much to figure out, I would have liked to play with that a little more..."

His words reminded the five that although Mothan and Kleeana were grown dragons, they were still young and still the inglets of their leaders. When Mothan continued with his rendering of other locations, his maturity surprised them once again. It seemed they were all more alike than any cared to admit or dared to celebrate.

"That was the location where we began to realize that something was going on. Then we went to the realms that the wizards had created for us to play in, hoping that they'd speak with us and maybe answer some questions. Which, as you know, isn't what they like to do.

"But no one was there. We could feel it when we entered...."

Brianna was the one who interrupted this time. "You're both able to travel to the wizards' realms? And you've spoken with them?"

"Sure," smiled Kleeana, "hundred of times." She blushed a little at her own bragging as her delight in what she and Mothan had been doing spilled over and out. "We started going to visit them when we were quite young. You, of course, know that our dad used to visit them?"

Meteranke nodded. It was a given that everyone knew of Zog's adventures. No one really knew the exact content of those adventures, but it was common dragon knowledge that his relationship with the wizards was what brought him to the abilities of Winzoarian.

"Well," Kleeana continued excitedly, this time she too walking the width of the chamber, "one day when he returned from the wizards, I saw the portal. I'd never seen one before, but the colors were so bright I could hardly miss it."

"The fairies had just released their Circle," remembered Mothan, "and there was the portal!"

"I just decided to jump in!" Kleeana involuntarily jumped her dragon body. "I never really thought about it. I don't even think I knew how to discern the difference between the portal and my chamber. I just jumped in – and Mothan came in right behind me."

She radiated colors into the chamber and projected their initial entrance into the realms of the wizards. The five didn't know whether to applaud the brilliance of the colors, or to question Kleeana on how long she had been able to project colors the way her mother did. They were too stunned by her expertise and she so involved in her sharing that their surprise went unnoticed.

"They stayed right there in front of us. Three of them." Mothan also stood, and his merging with his sister filled the chamber with sounds and vibrations none of the five had experienced before. "I knew they were the wizards my dad usually

Kleeana's gossamer wings radiated colors into their chamber.

spoke to because I heard him tell Mom about them." He looked sheepishly at the five, "Well, I wasn't listening in. I was sitting right there with Mom when Dad returned."

The five thought-merged and collectively expressed heartfelt honor at hearing the intimacies of their leaders' family life. Dragons were nearly always automatically thought-merging; however, the cause and effect of their lives within their homes was kept to the family itself and rarely shared, not for the purpose of exclusion but more for the purpose of honoring their own family vibrations.

Mothan and Kleeana felt the group's gratitude. Kleeana surprised them atop the wonder of the fullness that was being communicated. "Let's face it. You're more like family to us now...." A slight flicker of sadness changed the radiating colors emanating from her middle wings, which slowly folded in upon themselves.

"Everything has changed," explained Mothan. "Everything." He too felt Kleeana's sadness and remembered the location he hadn't yet spoken of.

He looked at the floor of the chamber and continued, "I might as well tell you of the location... the location that the speaking of usually causes everyone to go to sleep." He looked up and at each one of the five compatriots. "Oh, I don't mean that everyone is less adept. They're residing in their location, and it won't allow any influence from another location to exist." He regained his strength of speaking.

"I think it's a natural protection included in the fabric of the location," added Kleeana.

"How can we be certain we won't have the same experience when you speak of it here?" asked Brianna.

"I'm confident of our abilities to merge," responded Mothan. It felt a little strange to him that he would be speaking with such certainty to these five dragons he had come upon seemingly by accident. He had been extending his awarenesses just for play, just to see if there were any other place he could explore, and he had heard them talking. Initially he turned away, not wanting to hear any conversations and determined to find a place he could surprise Kleeana with. It was the two words, *wizards* and *portals*, which caught his attention, however. And it was without hesitation that he shielded his thought-merging with them and reveled in the pleasure of hearing other dragons speak about his own treasured joy: realm jumping.

And here he was now, not only gathering and speaking with them, but actually participating in the discerning of the whole puzzle as it had unfolded before each dragon in the chamber. Those thoughts and memories traveled through him like a quick flash, yet unshielded, and filled the five. It wasn't the time for explanations or even discussions about Mothan's and then Kleeana's participation with the Neecha of the five. In fact, as the events of the upcoming adventures presented themselves, there never would be time for such discussions. However, the abilities of all seven to merge easily did benefit their experiences immeasurably, and it was within this exact benefit that Mothan invited them to merge as he spoke of the location that, until now, had caused all other dragons to sleep.

The five thought-merged and embraced the two new members of their Neecha. Together they formed a golden circle that flowed in and about them and the chamber. It was within that circle that Mothan spoke.

"We seem to be in a different time. Now. Here." He breathed deeply and allowed the strength of who he had become to flow out of his young heart and into the circle. Like an undulating river, the circle flowed around them, over and under, in all directions as the seven continued to merge in the center.

"In addition to the Dream State where everyone is moving so slowly, there is another location with another time going on. It is a time and location we all used to live in. I think we are still living there... and here.

"In that time, the entire Glarian is united and focused. They are focused on the union of our parents, of Zog and Zoanna."

The flowing of the gold increased in speed and undulated in all directions about them. The humming and ringing of such flowing filled the chamber, and had it not been for the seal they had united in creating, certainly the portal would have opened wide and allowed the golden flowing to spill forth into the realms of which they had been speaking. Yet the chamber portal did maintain itself and their Neecha continued. It was the first of its kind in the entire history of dragon existence.

"The reason the entire Glarian is focused on our parent's merging," Mothan continued, "is because Zog had returned from his second future-travel... not..." He forced himself to continue. He had to. He had to tell them. "Zog returned... dead.

"My mom was speaking with the Glarian and merging in nearly the manner we are right now, and that's when Zog fell back from his travel." It felt funny to speak of his father by his name, Zog. It helped him maintain his objectivity. There would be time for other thoughts later.

"She merged with him immediately. Mom has great capabilities of manifesting her body in many locations, but this time she didn't. She dissolved her body from the gathering and merged with Zog.

"They have been in that merging since then.... It's as if time there has stood still. It's as if the entire Glarian is frozen there, focused on the two of them. And there's something else going on, something everyone had become fearful of."

Mothan breathed deeply and continued, "And like I said, they are frozen there *and* they are all also present in the Dream State... the one that is slower. If we're in the Dream State, we can't speak of the frozen location where Zog and Zoanna are merged, where Zog returned... without the listener falling asleep.

"But there's another location — the one I most want to know about." The spinning increased its momentum as Mothan spoke with all his strength. "Just one moment, one second, one breath before the merging of Mom and Dad, and the Glarian's focused state. There is something unbelievable. Something waiting for us."

He felt their attention heighten. "In the Timeline, the Neekontuk of our histories is once again upon us. That is what everyone has become fearful of." He waited. They remained united. They remained focused. They remained awake. He quickly continued.

"The great raging fire, the great power disintegrating everything in its path, as we have read in our histories, destroying that which we are together, is upon us.

"It is why Zog future-traveled. He wanted to find a way to help the Glarian, to save the Glarian. I don't know what happened when he traveled. I don't know what happened to the Timeline.

"He was supposed to pick the realm on the Timeline. He's done it hundreds of times before. But this time, something happened.

"He stayed there, even when the flames caught up to him. He stayed there to still try to save the Glarian. What I don't understand," Mothan's voice became small, as it was when he was an inglet, "is how could anything catch up with Zog when he was outside of the Timeline? He was dipping into a part of it... and I'm certain he wouldn't deliberately enter the Neekontuk! So... how did it catch up with him?"

The five felt the ache in the hearts of both Mothan and Kleeana. Treiga called them back. Slowly, gently, he called them to release the merging, the intensity, the golden flowing. "It won't benefit any of us," he thought-transferred softly to his compatriots, "if something happens to the two of them."

Even though Mothan and Kleeana wanted to tell more and even though they heard the thought-transfer, they allowed the caring of the five to fill them. It felt comforting. Finally, they were not alone.

Mothan and Kleeana slept in the comfort of the love and caring of the five. Quietly the others spoke of all that Mothan and Kleeana had shared. And even though Mothan could hear their whisperings, he did not merge but allowed himself to drift into his normal sleep breathings. As he released his intensities, one thought placed itself at the edge of his consciousness. He still wanted to tell them.... "Oh well," his mind surrendered to sleep, "Kleeana will remember...."

CHAPTER EIGHT

IF YOU DON'T MIND MY ASKING – PROVE IT!

The wizards saw and felt the memory of Mentard return. They saw the ripple of its effect upon the Glarian. Even though it brought to their Kahna Tro-Linate a knowing that changed the nature of the peace and ease of living the dragons had been experiencing, the fact that Mentard's remembering had such power was more than the wizards could have hoped for.

Swimming in the hopelessness of guilt and failure, Mentard wept for the loss of his two co-maintainers, Niara and Connock, but more so for the lasting vision of Zog's charred body. It was into that state that the wizards entered and without his knowing, gathered Mentard and brought him to their healing realm — the very same realm they had created for Zog.

There, they cleared the patterns of those painful experiences and created a temporary memory for Mentard so that he would heal. Heal, so that they could gradually open his awarenesses to more, to what they had hoped they could have given to Zog.

The agony in Mentard's heart began to release its hold and finally his dragon body began to turn from ashen gray to a slight green hue. Slowly his breathing became less labored. His wings, folded so tightly against his great dragon body, began to relax and unfold ever so slightly. The wizards continued their building and mending, as the realm itself held the intent for which it was created. Though gradual, Mentard's healing filled him, and even the temporary memory block eased itself more completely into his thought-mergings.

It was within the wizard's playful creating of imagery and sounds that he awakened as if from a long sleep. Stretching his dragon body, unfurling all but the wings at his jaw, he allowed the sound rising from within his heart to be released. Such vibration filled the realm and caused the wizards to applaud at his presence, as they attempted to give the impression that he had been there with them many more times than this first. His testing of fire singed the hills, which quickly reappeared as the adept wizard encodings fulfilled their purpose.

"Ha!" It was Clorfothian who bound toward him. "At last you have awakened!" Quickly responding to Mentard's building confusion he added, "Oh, I know you don't remember us. After all," he brushed at the air around himself, "we haven't really seen each other in..."

"Never." said Mentard. "I've never seen you before."

"Well..." Clorfothian was unprepared for the statement and stopped right in his forward bounding, suspended in mid-air.

"You are right!" exclaimed Plienze. "Absolutely right! I don't suppose we can fool you."

"And why would you want to?" asked Mentard, settling his great dragon body upon the base of the hill. "Who are you three characters, anyway?" he asked with a casualness that told the three wizards that the memory block was holding just fine.

Winjut stepped right up to the dragon and spoke clearly and as honestly as he dared considering the circumstances. "We are wizards."

"Ha!" exclaimed Mentard. "And how do I deserve to be in the presence of wizards? Tell me that!" He snorted a short puff of blue smoke. "If you don't mind my asking," he smiled, "prove it."

The challenge was all the three wizards needed. It was an open invitation to supply Mentard with as much joy and pleasure, as much knee-slapping laughter, and as much light-hearted play as they could muster and not give themselves away — just yet.

IF YOU DON'T MIND MY ASKING - PROVE IT!

• • • • •

Zog felt his beloved Zoanna's embrace, heard her whisperings, and felt his own awakening. He couldn't quite remember ever awakening within their merging. And it seemed, as his lazy thoughts barely strived for any interaction, neither could he remember anything at all. It wasn't a disturbing awakening, but more a casual glance as he might have given himself during an all-too-infrequent stroll about the Great Lac.

Zoanna's love glowed a greeting into Zog's consciousness. "Hello my darling," she spoke softly, her words caressing Zog's brow. "Don't try to do anything just yet." She breathed a soothing calm within their embrace. "We have the gift of unhurried time, dearest one. We have forever."

Zoanna waited to see what effect her first words had on Zog. It was his awakening, and she wanted to introduce him to his new realm in the easiest, most comfortable manner.

"Sweet Zoanna," Zog's love returned her breathings, "you have ever been the easer of my mind, the igniter of my strength, and the whisper within the wisdom of my spirit. Which will you be now?" He smiled upon the fullness of who she had become, the fullness so many enjoyed. Yet to Zog, Zoanna was the beloved of his heart and the intimacies they had shared were theirs and theirs alone.

She began his story by treating him softly and gently to an ability she'd learned long ago. Her thoughts, lazy too, reached back: *Ah, yes, it was in Sector Two that I learned Manifesting of Being within Merging.*[29] While maintaining their flowing within each other, a slight adjustment within her intent of form gave Zoanna the familiar option of calling forth her golden form.

The Golden Beings had invited her into their Cavern of Learning and Forming[30] at the very beginning of her Sector Two adventures. It had been their intention to gift her focus with certain refining of form-within-form and with a celebration of the abilities she had demonstrated during Sector One. And it had been a

---

[29] Manifesting of Being within Merging: learned within the Cavern of Learning and Forming. See next footnote.

dipping of their own awarenesses within the Timeline that birthed a further realization even within their Ancient Selves: One day their star pupil would, more easily than any could dream or create to be, pass on her reflected awarenesses and expanded abilities to her two inglets. They also realized — within their momentary Timeline dip — that such passing on of their shared wisdom could be the ending or the beginning of all they had hoped for; the beginning of the fulfillment of the purposes for which they all had maintained themselves, instead of completing their journey and returning directly to dissolving into the Nothingness.

With a single thought, Zoanna called her form to be that of a Golden Being. Shimmering warmth fell from her as if unused essence.

Zog watched the golden flowing of their merging swirl and unite within itself. At first he thought an Ancient One was taking form, against all possibilities, right within their merging! Yet the form grew more familiar and in the next moment he recognized her.

"My dear!" Zog's joy filled him to overflowing. "I don't remember you telling me about this!" Even though they remained merged, he could feel himself looking at his beautiful Zoanna — in golden form. "And how is it that *I* can be so learned as to maintain *and* view?" he asked. His thoughts raced ahead; *does that mean I too can maintain form in more than one location? I've always admired your ability....* He interrupted his own ques-

---

30 <u>Cavern of Learning and Forming</u>: an invitation to enter the Cavern of Learning and Forming has been extended to few dragons who continued to remain in physical form. In truth, Zoanna was the second; her great-grandmother, during the end times of the first great dragon existence, had been the first. The cavern itself resides within a realm that contains the encodings of both physical and nonphysical. It is necessary for any who enter to have the ability to maintain a knowing that, although they appear to be residing in physical form, in truth their form is not staid but is a pulsebeat of form and non-form. Within that knowing then, those who enter this particular chamber would necessarily also be aware that their physical nature was the smallest — though not insignificant by any means – part of who they were. Zoanna, as well as her great-grandmother, questioned what comprised the totality of all that she was, even when she was an inglet. Few could speak with her upon the topic and it was then her great-grandmother, in nonphysical form, who whispered to her within her inglet wonderings. Her speakings with her great-grandmother had begun her search into the realms beyond physical while she was still considered an inglet. The Cavern of Learning and Forming pulsated itself into many different forms and patterns, demonstrating the lessons and adventures that can be experienced within its vast boundaries.

tioning with further speculation. *Why, we could merge with the Representatives....*

Zoanna drank into her heart Zog's familiar manner of jumping into action before she soothed with, "There will be time for everything, my dear." Zog hadn't realized yet that he had released his physical form, hadn't realized yet that his manner of relating to his Glarian would be in some instances more direct and in other instances from afar. Perhaps one day, he would be able to allow them their journey without seeing and knowing the best direction they could take for a fuller manner of residing. For the moment, though, Zoanna wisely allowed Zog's speculations to weave themselves back around to her and her form, and to their union. Then, she would begin the speaking of his story. There was no timekeeper here, no cause and effect to consider, and no raging onslaught. For Zog, that was over. Her job was to guide him toward the full knowing of all that he was.

The Golden Beings knew she was more than capable of the telling, of guiding Zog, of extending the invitation to be an Ancient One. Like them, he was, and there wasn't even the slightest consideration that Zog might choose the Nothingness... yet.

• • • • •

Having more than proved themselves, the wizards also began a gradual introduction of Mentard's possible role within the unfolding events as the dragon realms maintained the pulsebeat of the Timeline.

"Now **that** magic is something I'd like to latch my claws onto!" Mentard pointed one wedge wing toward the portal Clorfothian had just created. In unabashed play, Mentard sent a patterned charge through the portal. Though he had practiced and developed selecting patterns and discharging them through both wedge wings, he had never done so in the company of wizards, neither had he discharged the patterns into wizardry!

Clorfothian's portal radiated such brilliant colors, sounds, and ancient patterns that Plienze shielded himself in automatic reaction – something he hadn't done since his first entry into wizardry. It was Winjut's quick action, however, that created the cloak on both sides of the portal.

Mentard beamed a chest full of success at surprising what he'd called to himself, the entertaining three.

"And WHAT did you think you were doing?" Winjut took a deep breath in an attempt to tone down his alerted focus.

Mentard shrugged his shoulders and maintained beaming, "Just playing!"

"Now Winjut," calmed Clorfothian, "we did ask for it."

"Yes, yes we did," echoed Plienze, righting himself from the unnerving position of shielding from the unexpected.

Their words succeeded. Winjut sighed and plopped himself down on a stool he simultaneously formed under his own body. "I suppose we'd better get to talking… talking about why you're here."

"Yeah," boasted Mentard one more time, "before I…." Something flashed before him, in his mind. *What was that?* He looked to the three who were studying his stopped-in-mid-sentence pause. "Did you guys see a flash?"

Winjut didn't want to protect Mentard with sleep and, refraining from any fix-it balm, jumped right into the bold truth.

"The flash is sometimes experienced during healing. It can be a signal of integrating memories…."

"Or," continued Plienze, "it can be a reaction of your consciousness to the words *why you are here.*

"It's obvious," finished Clorfothian, "that you've wondered why you were here." He paused a moment and, before anyone could speak, added, "You did begin right off with asking how it was that you were in the company of wizards… deserve to be! That's it!" Clorfothian snapped his fingers, which sent a spray of patterns much like those Mentard had fired into the portal. "I believe you said, 'How do I deserve to be in the presence of wizards?'" He smiled a big smile at Mentard. "Isn't that right?"

Winjut shook his head. "Let's get on with it! Who knows what'll happen now? Remember what happened with Zo…."

Plienze jumped atop the nearly spoken name. "So, my friend. Sit yourself down and we'll do our best to fill in the blanks!"

"And then there's more, of course," Clorfothian chimed, in the hopes of distracting Mentard's curiosity about Winjut's nearly spoken name.

"Do sit with us here," invited Winjut, who, having recovered from the near slip, waved his arm to create a comfortable resting-place. A place where all four might relax a little, breathe deeply, and enjoy each other's company before diving right into a rendering of facts that could possibly reverse the healing Mentard had successfully achieved. He sent a reinforcing force to the fabric of the healing chamber and turned his focus totally on Mentard.

Mentard's greatest strength had always been his ability to allow circumstances and even the most intense adventures to unfold at their own pace. Some called it an ability to remain in the moment, while others recognized a deep resonance they felt when in Mentard's presence. And a few recognized the resonance to be an attribute of an Ancient One; yet none of the few spoke of their knowing to each other, or for that matter, to anyone at all.

Mentard's original question had changed a little from *deserve to be in the presence of* to more of a statement: "Something's going on. I'm here... wherever *here* is... and I've been playing with wizards!"

Mentard wasn't fooled or distracted from the nearly spoken word. There was just something that led him to believe that at the end of it all, he'd know the word – and much more. He settled back into the lush, green meadow Winjut had created, stretched his wings a little, and waited. He knew he was about to hear something he'd never heard before, and from wizards! This was going to be good – better than good – this was going to be *quite* an adventure!

Little did Mentard know what rested not only upon the telling, but also on his ability to remain in the moment while his recent past caught up with him.

The three wizards focused so totally that it was without their conscious knowing that the Golden Beings encircled the healing chamber and merged with the very encoded fabric of light.

• • • • •

Zoanna's taking form invited Zog to do the same. Although he hadn't studied such abilities, Zoanna expertly and easily released her knowing into their merging. It was with one full movement that Zog determined his entire being to also become a light form.

The essence of that which Zog was, who he had been, who he would always be, began to swirl and form. Different events flashed within his mind: the first time he met his wizard friends, the first time he took form in the blue structure, the surprised look on his father's face, the sound of his inglets' laughter, the fullness of a Glarian meeting, and the peace of their home. Zoanna maintained their merging and continued to release those shared memories, memories that could augment the strength Zog was experiencing in taking form.

Basking in the merged love of two-as-one, Zog fully and completely took form: a Golden Light Being. His magnificence radiated outward. In truth, there was not one being who did not feel the effect of his powerful forming. Zog, of course, didn't recognize his own magnificence. He simply knew he had taken form, that he and Zoanna were merged, and now they *both* were in form. Golden Form. Nothing had ever felt better. It would be a while before *all* of his awarenesses were integrated. And it would be a while before he recognized himself as an Ancient One.

CHAPTER NINE

THE OLD DRAGON'S CHAMBER WALLS CURVED INWARD

The Timeline was of itself, created to flow and sequence events. There was no stated speed to the Timeline's movement; it simply continued to flow. The Neekontuk raged itself upon all that resided within its path; and although its forward movement had slowed to nearly a stop, it still did move and devour.

Impersonal as it was, the purpose of the Neekontuk mirrored the journey to the eventual resting-place of all beings, of all Ancient Ones: the Nothingness.

Within the patterns of the dissolving of that which is, there birthed the rhythm of taking form and releasing form. Within the patterns of releasing form, there birthed that called fire. And it was within those patterns of fire, of releasing form, that the Neekontuk did become.

Of its own self, it was not destruction; but was the means for the releasing of form. Of its own self, it was not a raging torrent of devouring force; but was the very impersonal movement of that which resides within the moment before releasing form. The Ancient Ones knew it well. The Moment resonated a continuing invitation, impersonal too: All that resides within form, will and does release form, to take form, to birth again and again — the pulsebeat of All That Is. Yet, the Neekontuk only knew itself and the purpose of itself.

Within the Timeline, there exist portals, realms, and avenues – the traveling through which could result in a temporary residing separate from the Timeline. The writings within Glarian histories neither addressed how the portals, realms and avenues came to be, nor who established their intent. And, researching those particular answers required certain consciousness-expanding abilities and, therefore, was an avenue into which not many entered. Until now.

So it was with exaggerated innocence, cloaked determination, and cautious wording that Brianna asked first the librarian of the ancient texts and then her favorite teacher of her favorite studies: the Histories of Dragon Realms, of course.

Although both had freely offered the young studious dragon all they knew on the topic, for Brianna the results had been less than fruitful. The librarian had delightedly opened the locked section of ancient texts and invited her most frequent library visitor to enter and explore.

Brianna had pretended surprise and thanked her friend. Had it not been for her determined search, she might have felt a slight regret not only at pretending but also at having sneaked past the same librarian just the previous week, as she had opened the same lock and left it open while cleaning and dusting the old volumes. Brianna had spent the entire day, to no avail, searching those ancient texts.

Her teacher had most willingly spoken of dragon realms and even touched on the Timeline briefly, but the answers Brianna sought were not to be found with her teacher. She had left the great halls of learning with her questions unanswered. Her questions were actually the ones Mothan innocently asked: "How could the Neekontuk catch up with Zog if he was outside the Timeline? And, if Zog was observing, how could the Neekontuk affect him at all?"

She barely heard the voice of the Old Dragon. He'd seen her dejectedly sitting outside the school grounds. He'd heard her deep sigh. He was about to continue onward when a glance back at the young dragon stopped him in his tracks. He'd only seen one other demonstrate such colors as the ones spewing out of the top of Brianna's head. It was then that he had decided that he'd better see if he could help the inglet.

"Nice colors," he said as he approached the slouched dragon. "I say, nice colors!" he repeated a little louder.

Brianna looked toward the voice and then upward to where the Old Dragon was pointing. She hadn't realized her intent thinking had released the colors he was pointing to. "Oh, excuse me," she said, and aligned herself the way Treiga had taught her.

The Old Dragon watched. *Pretty impressive*, he thought to himself. "You look rather discouraged," he said to the still slumped-shouldered dragon.

"Oh," sighed Brianna again, "I can't seem to find much information on the creation and intent of Timeline portals." She'd surprised herself with the sound of her own voice stating her actual question aloud. Perhaps it was that she was despondent that she didn't even try to disguise the full intent of her question.

"Oh," said the Old Dragon so matter-of-factly that Brianna relaxed again. "There was only one dragon I knew who could speak on that topic with any kind of experience. The Old Dragon began to walk away. "Don't know if he's still around," he tossed over his shoulder and then added, "I think his name was Kilchek."

Brianna watched him walk around the hill and out of sight.

• • • • •

The Old Dragon felt the ripple within the fabric of Zoanna's personal healing chamber, and his visioning abilities gifted him with the sight of Mothan and Kleeana asking rather insistently, "Why can't we see our mother??"

Although Zoanna could successfully reside in many locations at one time, her full attention remained devoted to Zog's awakening.

So many questions, the Old Dragon thought to himself, *these young ones have so many questions*. He shifted his focus and determined his presence to be directly behind the two inglets. Quietly he took form as Kleeana stressed again the importance of visiting with her mother. The Golden Being saw the Old Dragon take form and, breathing a sigh of relief, smiled knowingly to his old friend.

Just as Mothan was about to ask rather pointedly, "What was so amusing?", the unexpected voice behind him caused a startled jump.

"I believe I can help you." The Old Dragon smiled at the quick pivoting around of both Mothan and Kleeana.

"Who are you?" asked Mothan, the first to recover from the surprise.

"And how can you help us?" asked Kleeana. "Do you know where our mother is?" she asked hopefully.

"And why we can't see her?" Mothan turned to glance at the dissolving Golden Being. "Or more accurately, why is she unavailable to *anyone*?" He stressed the word *anyone*.

Kleeana spoke softly, "I've never known our mother to be unavailable to us... to me." Even though she had matured and developed many of her dragon abilities, Kleeana's inglet mannerisms and then feelings rose to the surface. A tear traced itself down her face and onto the blue tinted shoulder.

Mothan too felt the effects of not only this frustrated attempt to meet with his mother, but also the culmination of the most recent intensely powerful events. He wrapped his dragon arm around Kleeana. His welcome hold brought a needed comfort, and she allowed herself a few brief moments of quiet sobbing into Mothan's embrace.

Mothan's breath of soft, rosy smoke upon her face spoke the knowing that they had been, were now, and always would be, together. It brought a trickle of joy to Kleeana's heart, and soon she was smiling shyly while simultaneously turning to the Old Dragon, who had been watching the interaction between the two inglets of Zoanna and Zog.

"*Can* you help us?" Brianna asked.

The Old Dragon smiled, "Well, I believe I can," he said looking from Kleeana to Mothan. "Let's go to my chamber where we can explore all that needs exploring!" He pointed his wedge-like wing to the side of where they were standing. The portal turned silently, opening without the sometime fanfare of sounds and

THE OLD DRAGON'S CHAMBER WALLS CURVED INWARD

colors. "Follow me," he said as he moved his old but agile dragon body through the oval opening and into his personal chamber.

Mothan motioned for Kleeana to follow the Old One; and while she did, Mothan scanned the adjoining chambers. His mother was not there, not in any of them. He extended his scan to and through all the healing chambers and still could find not even a residue of a former residing of his mother. He too stepped through the portal, and at the last moment registered two healing chambers that he was not only unable to scan, but also unable to locate exactly. He'd only felt their slight existence.

The Old Dragon's chamber was simple and uncluttered, yet invitingly comfortable, and it was with ease that the three rested against the living walls. Soft sunset colors relaxed the two inglets, which was the intent of the patterns the Old Dragon had breathed into the walls as he led the way, inviting the two to follow.

"Now, I suppose some information about your mother would be a good place to begin?"

"Yes! Please!" Both Mothan and Kleeana leaned forward a little, even though there remained only a slight dissipating residue of the immediate and building anxiety that had previously, nearly frantically, been spurring them on.

"Now you tell me," he looked to both of them, "if I'm wrong about anything... or if I'm assuming too much."

Kleeana and Mothan nodded. The Old Dragon held their full attention.

"Firstly, there have been times when your mother -- and father, for that matter -- have been unavailable to you." He continued without interruption. "Now if you remember, the Glarian gatherings were something Zoanna... er, your mother was directly involved with."

"Well, that's true," agreed Kleeana. "We were maintained in the Fairy Circle."

"Now that you mention it," added Mothan, "both our parents in those kinds of instances were unavailable to us." He paused briefly and then added, "But this is different -- *very* different. There's a lot going on now!"

"That's just what I'm getting to." The Old Dragon decided that his speaking should be all the more to the point. It was necessary. "You are absolutely correct, Mothan. As you are obviously both well aware, this is a very full time.

"In one sector your mother and father are merged," he hesitated briefly and then decided to continue, "while in another realm the Neekontuk rages at the heels of our entire existence."

"Yes, yes," interrupted Mothan, "and then there's the sector — as you call it — where everyone is blissfully living as if... well, as if there's nothing to be concerned about."

Mothan stood and began pacing the length of the chamber, which accommodated his movement by automatically elongating — an accommodating that momentarily distracted his intent speaking of the three timeline sectors with which he was familiar. "Hey!" he beamed, looking from one end of the chamber to the other, "That's pretty neat!"

The Old Dragon smiled. "Do you think you are the *only* dragon who paces?"

All three dragons chuckled.

The Old Dragon continued in the middle of Mothan's "*I know all of that*" speaking. "Then let's get further to the point. Right now Zog and Zoanna are merging..." he raised his outstretched arm to pause Mothan's imminent interruption. "Their merging is NOT the same merging that's occurring in the sector you've called the Dream State or in any sector in any time. This merging is different. *Quite* different.

"As you both know, Zog fell from the battle within the flames. When he returned, there was barely..." he looked at the wide eyes of the two inglets, "... well...."

"We know," said Mothan. "He was... dead."

"Well," repeated the Old Dragon, "That's not completely correct. His physical form was no longer useful to him."

The Old Dragon remembered well the scene of Zog's continued attempts to reside within the charred body, his continued attempts to bear the pain in order to help his dragons. The Old Dragon didn't allow himself to bring the images for viewing.

These inglets knew enough. Such images would serve no good purpose — not at this speaking.

It was Kleeana who asked the question that continued their Sector of Learning, the one that had begun with Zoanna so many experiences ago. "Then, what form is my father in right now?"

The Old Dragon knew that his speaking with the inglets of the two most amazing leaders all of Dragondom had ever had the gift to be guided by, would be involved and perhaps flow in ways that might be unexpected even to the Oldest Dragon. And, he supposed their questioning would eventually lead to the topic of his being *the oldest dragon* and consequently, because of their capabilities to integrate the truths, would carry their knowing beyond all sectors.

The Old Dragon had taken, he thought, all of the most expanded options into consideration — even if it had been in a quick flash. Yet, nothing could have prepared him for the journey into which the two inglets before him would embark and explore — all in seemingly one breath.

The Old Dragon would have liked to take them through the portal to the Timelessness, where it was easier to integrate awarenesses. But he knew that he would never be able to contain their youthful exuberance — nor would he want to. The Timelessness, by its very nature, invited explorations within explorations, and usually the teacher or guide remained with the first-time traveler for several reasons — the primary reason being the assuring of a pathway back through the exact portal and into the Timeline where they had begun. It wasn't the kind of experience any teacher would choose to "reign-in" a student. "No," the Old Dragon said to himself, "*we won't go there this time, not yet anyway.*" But even as he firmly decided, he felt a shift in the vibrations of his chamber. This was going to be anything but usual.

Mothan and Kleeana watched the changing expressions ripple through the Old Dragon's face and then, though quite subtle, ripple again through the tips of his middle wings. Mothan thought-spoke to Kleeana, "*Have you ever seen this Old Dragon before?*" "*No,*" she responded, "*But I've been wondering if he's the one*

Dad's father spoke of...." She paused and flashed to Mothan the memory of Zog and his father, Meran, talking and laughing together. Mothan integrated the scene with his own memory of the same event. "*You could be right. He fits the description.*"

Mothan and Kleeana, from the very first moment, had not been *invited* to listen to their parents' conversations and discussions; but as their huddled curiosity was detected, they were lovingly *allowed* to continue listening. Consequently, they grew and matured through what might have been deemed topics too expanded for most inglets. Skills learned in advanced classes had become their play and adventure long before they were of an age to attend even the beginning classes of dragon abilities.

The Old Dragon felt and heard their brief questioning and, although he reminded himself that any talents these two inglets demonstrated shouldn't surprise him, nonetheless, their refined mergings and memory accessing impressed him. Without thinking, he rubbed his clawed hands together and whispered nearly aloud, "*This is going to be some adventure!*"

"Exactly!" voiced Mothan, his hungry attention waiting to be fed.

It was Kleeana who brought them again to the focus of their first journey: "So... where **is** my father?" She paused briefly and then added, "And mother? Where is Zoanna?"

"That's easy," smiled the Old Dragon, while thinking to himself that the topic *Taking Form while Merging* was a little advanced to begin with... but here we go! "Zog and Zoanna are together — right now, right this instant — in all realms within *and* without the Timeline." He paused long enough for the full awareness to fill the two and then continued before the inevitable flood of questions could be spoken aloud.

"You are both aware of their merging in the Timeline where Zog's body returned from his second future travel." He wove soft embracings within the words he spoke, and expertly shielded from the two the image of Zog's charred body and his attempts to continue to reside within it.

"Yes," they nodded. Mothan and Kleeana leaned into each other, taking comfort in each other's physical presence.

THE OLD DRAGON'S CHAMBER WALLS CURVED INWARD

"You have experienced the Glarian's awareness of that merging as the Glarian resides in what you are now hearing as the Kah-na Tro-Linaht or The Moment in Stretched Time." He felt their attention pique.

"You have assumed — and rightly so — that a semblance of Zog and Zoanna's merging resides in what you have been calling the Dream State. And you are right," he continued, "in wondering how real anything is in that state."

The Old Dragon moved closer to his two apt students; and as he did, the walls of his chamber curved inward, embracing the three with predetermined comfort, clarity, and a shielding from the knowing of any others.

• • • • •

It was the moment before the Old One moved closer, the moment before the shielding became tighter-meshed and solidly fulfilling its purpose, that a tiny vibration was recognized by the five. Even though they were all in different physical locations, each felt the vibration and affectionately recognized the familiar patterns of Mothan and Kleeana. That the two inglets' patterns were demonstrating vibrant colors which the five easily recognized as the *uninhibited youthful expanding to receive* caught their attention.

What could be so inviting that they would open so wide... so completely? Meteranke allowed his wondering to thought-merge with the other four. *And who are they with?* joined in Brianna. Without further discussion, it was decided the five would meet — first in the Neecha. From there they could decide where to go. Surely together they could discern the location of Mothan and Kleeana.

I wonder if they're talking with the wizards? Fornaign speculated to himself. He nodded to Treiga and Karthentonen as they arrived, one close behind the other. Brianna, with fully unfurled wings, came into view moments later; and although it was unlike him, Meteranke was the last to enter and combine to seal the portal. The energies swirled about them; and just as they were setting the intent of their portal, the Old Dragon saw. *Now the fun really begins,* he smiled to himself.

• • • • •

The Golden Beings felt the rippling of Truth, the celebrating of Knowing, and the alerted opening of Mothan and Kleeana. As well, the Golden Beings saw the meeting of the five whom they had been observing since the first gathering at the Neecha.

• • • • •

The wizards — even as they began the cautious speaking with Mentard — recognized the familiar but infrequent vibrations throughout their created realm. It had been during the last phase of the first Neekontuk that such vibrations of clear truth had birthed. The first Ancient Ones had united together, merging all the wisdom and histories of dragons residing in all realms and then — with full intent — breathed their full knowing into the Golden Essence they would become. Some would deliver the knowing into the portal to the Nothingness, their dissolving serving the whole as the patterns of all-that-was took form as the Living Word, forever residing and changing within the portal.

• • • • •

Zog, celebrating his Golden Essence Being, swelled into the joy of freedom, unhampered by physical form. And it was the slight beginnings of Zoanna's speaking to Zog the story of who he was — and who he was becoming — that caused the vibrations the wizards had more than noticed. Zoanna's clarity and fullness of being wholly expanded. Although in the past, in the Timeline, it might have been a risk to expand in such a manner, here with Zog there could be no holding back, no encoded releasings. Here, now, was the moment, the eternal moment of total all-knowing truth.

Zoanna began gently, lovingly. "Darling, there once was born into the dragon realm, a brilliant light. Though the brilliant light didn't know the effect his life would have upon all dragons, he did realize that he was, above all else, a brilliant light. His parents, who were leaders of the dragons, saw the bright light of their inglet and named him after the light. They bestowed upon him the name, Zog. And it was then that he fully took form."

CHAPTER TEN

MENTARD WAITED FOR THE EASY

The speaking of Truth in the three realms, Zoanna to Zog, the Old Dragon to Mothan and Kleeana, and the wizards to Mentard, affected not only the participants, but also the manner in which the entire Timeline experienced its own self. The encodings residing within the spoken truths entwined within each of the three chambers and tingled within the wedge-like wings of all dragons.

Some who resided within the Dream State of The Moment of Stretched Time began to wonder at the gentle awakening within which they found themselves; while others, becoming more conscious of the cause and effect of the recent releasing of their leaders, began to send the call for a gathering. Their call was quite different from the usual call, however, as it didn't carry the familiar vibrations of Zog or Zoanna. There was no leader calling them together; yet first a few, and then more, responded until all the Representatives prepared for a Glarian gathering.

Some of the elder dragons speculated among themselves about the correctness of a Glarian gathering without Zog or Zoanna. And some decided they would not attend such a gathering. "After all," they reasoned, "there has been no formal passing, no ceremony to honor Zog and Zoanna — if in truth they have released from physical form. Why, it would be disrespectful!" Other elder dragons decided they would attend to observe what would occur at such a seemingly unstructured gathering. And a few elder dragons prepared to attend in order to guide when necessary and also to encourage when needed.

The beginnings of such gathering and action within an awakening state of consciousness caused a ripple to fluctuate ever so slightly through the Timeline. It was known, of course, that *always* such mass awakenings affected not only the present, but had an indirect way of changing not the actual occurrences of the past, but the manner in which the occurrences where experienced, interpreted and then either integrated or released.

In that part of the Timeline where movement had slowed to a near stop, the ripple undulated over and through the barely moving cause and effect. Where there had been less than a snail's breath, now began a slight — barely slight, barely perceptible — increase in movement. Where before, any objective viewer would have perhaps believed that the Neekontuk was frozen in its own ever-so-slow movement, now such a viewer could, with maintained focus, perceive the forward rolling of the Neekontuk.

The raging flames raised themselves slowly, yet certainly, and licked and bit at whatever lay in their path. Impersonal in its own self, the Neekontuk continued its destruction of all of the dragon world and of all the dragons who resided there, just as it had done twice before in their known histories.[31]

• • • • •

The three wizards were well aware of not only the beginning of the awakening of the Glarian within the Moment of Stretched Time, but also of the increased movement — slight as it was — of the Neekontuk. And — even though less experienced wizards would possibly have been tempted to hurry their indoctrination of Mentard with his own story and the facts of the

---

31 <u>Known Histories</u>: Actually, the dissolving had occurred in the number of three hundred and sixty-two times. However, the development of dragon consciousness had not reached a level that could either contain the truth or understand its implications until the three hundred and sixty-first time.

most recent events — Winjut, Plienze, and Clorfothian continued in the cautious play with the hope of their purposes, Mentard.

"What you've told me," said Mentard casually as he leaned back against the same hill Zog had leaned against not so long ago, "is all quite interesting -- about the state of the Timeline and the Moment in Stretched Time...." He looked to the three, "But I don't see the point! Why is this information so carefully doled out to me?"

Mentard chuckled a little. "Did you think I'd gasp at hearing about Timeline change?"

For the first time since they began to bring Mentard's knowing to current events, while assuring he would maintain focus and not fold back into the grief from which they had so lovingly lifted him, the three wizards were momentarily speechless. Mentard enjoyed the moment and took the opportunity to further push his point.

"After all," Mentard continued, "I did study Timeline fluctuation...." Another flash caught his attention. "Hey! Did you see that one?"

"We felt it," responded Plienze as calmly as he could. "Most likely it was caused by your dipping into your own past."

It was Winjut who made the decision to release a little more objective information. He knew it was a risk, yet if Mentard continued in the same manner of uninhibited cajoling, he would more than likely boast his way right into a full memory of concentrated past events -- within the very part of the Timeline that had increased its forward movement -- right into the Neekontuk.

"Look, Mentard," Winjut began. The other two knew *this was it* and called forth, from the fabric of their created healing realm, the wholeness of the love they felt for all dragons and the peaceful resonance from the core of the all knowing, to help counteract any flared reaction Mentard might experience within his remembering — or if the optimum were served, within his own awakening.

Winjut continued, "It's obvious that something is going on here, of course. And by your extraordinary ability to allow the unfolding of what *is* going on, as you've called it, you have given yourself a chance...."

Mentard leaned forward, prepared to ask *A chance for what?* but Winjut only took the opportunity to lean forward also. Without complicating the moment with further wizardry, it took him two boundings to leap up directly onto Mentard's great dragon knee and look directly into his compelling yellow eyes.[32] "A chance to play one of the most important parts in the history of all dragons...," he had Mentard's full, undivided attention, "and to live through it!"

The dragon's piercing gaze would have dissolved any other; however, Winjut and his compatriots were much more than wizards.

"All right," Mentard stretched his wedge wings outward, "Let me have it. I won't interrupt or boast my knowing." He looked from Plienze to Clorfothian, who were both smiling broadly. "Yes," Mentard admitted, "Yes, I know that I boast. Why, it's been part of who I am! And boasting has been a useful tool...."

"You don't have to explain to us!" Clorfothian stood up and walked toward the still-sitting dragon. "Everything, ev-ry-thing about you has combined to be you!"

"And you're extraordinary!" chimed in Plienze. "Let's face it, how could any dragon less than extraordinary be here with us — and for this long?"

Winjut pointed to where he stood on Mentard's knee; "Do you mind?"

Mentard smiled an I'm-glad-we're-friends smile. "No, go ahead."

Winjut patted the huge knee and sat himself down. "Now where were we?" He let his thoughts align themselves and then continued.

"Mentard, speaking about all of this has been a risk, a gamble that perhaps you'd be unable to maintain the consciousness you are currently enjoying.

---

[32] <u>Dragon's Eyes</u>: yellow in color, as the golden essence of all Ancient Ones, contain in their very center, a mirror image of the encodings of the Living Word residing within the portal to the Nothingness.

"And now that we'll speak more directly, you **must** use your abilities to remain focused in the moment." Winjut continued to weave love and peace within his words. "During some of our speaking, we'll be mentioning some difficult information to hear...."

Another flash. Mentard noticed the flash, but remained focused on Winjut's words.

"Good, that's good," applauded Plienze. "Keep focusing just like that, *old boy*." He stressed the words *old boy* and a sigh of relief escaped Mentard's mouth. The blue smoke covered Winjut, who coughed and waved his hands until it dissipated toward the green hills.

Mentard shrugged his shoulders and smiled sheepishly, "Sorry. It's not one of my strengths."

It was Clorfothian who stepped up to Mentard's immense clawed foot, raised the hill just high enough so that he wouldn't have to keep straining to look upward, and began with the delicate subject of the recent past.

"Mentard, we're all aware that something quite different is going on. It's not only going on here. It's everywhere!" Clorfothian began pacing atop the raised hill and, with his usual way, brushed the area to both sides as he walked. "This is an amazing time." He stopped, jerking himself around to be directly facing the huge dragon face. "Now Mentard, when I speak the next words, you just stay focused, you hear?"

Mentard nodded. At times they had all four laughed and joked, and at other times they had been serious. Neither Clorfothian's mannerism of brushing nothing aside nor his quick jerk to attention brought a smile to anyone's face.

"Twice before in the known histories of dragon living, all that was and all of the dragons were destroyed. Each time, the cause of the destruction has been a raging, devouring fire." Clorfothian paused and registered that Mentard was doing quite well. "The name of that fire has been called Neekontuk."

Another flash... and another... and another. Mentard's focus wavered a little. He felt a thickness form about him, about his mind. It felt like sleep. Without further help from the three

MENTARD WAITED FOR THE EASY

wizards, he shook it off –- taking care not to toss Winjut to the green grasses below. Mentard spread his small green, glistening, gossamer wings. Their beauty filled the meadow, and the sweet music accompanying their opening[33] cleared Mentard's mind. He nodded to Clorfothian to continue.

Without hesitation, Clorfothian did continue. "In a section of the Timeline, the Neekontuk's flames are licking at your home, at the homes of all dragons."

It was Plienze who stated more of the truth as the three wizards crossed their wizard fingers. The Golden Beings breathed a breath upon the wizard's realm.

"Your leader, Zoanna, was speaking to the Kloan Gathering while..." he hesitated for a moment, "...while you prepared to do something you had done hundreds of times."

A giant breath expelled from Mentard's nostrils. He himself choked out the words, "I was preparing to anchor...." His memory wasn't quite complete. *What was it that was so hard to remember?*

Winjut relieved his wondering with, "Yes, you were preparing to anchor. And now you want to force that memory to give itself to you. But it doesn't work that way, Mentard. You can't force your defenses to let go." Winjut patted the huge knee. "We can do this together. It's easy."

Mentard sighed a calming breath –- no blue smoke –- and waited for the easy.

Winjut smiled. He loved this big guy, trying so hard. Sincerely trying. "What we do is skip over what you're trying to force and talk about the end of the story... well, the near end. You see, sometimes a difficult experience remains difficult because we can't see the bigger picture. Our vision is stuck on the difficulty."

Clorfothian sat down on the still raised hill; but before he could speak, Plienze startled him with a quick leap, landing atop the hill beside him. Mimicking Mentard's innocence as best he could, Plienze shrugged his shoulders, "Well, we all have to be

---

33 Music at the Opening of Gossamer Wings: light, delicate, flowing melody. The sound of gossamer wings opening were a gift from the fairies to soften the apparent need.

able to see eye-to-eye, if you know what I mean!" Clorfothian smiled too. It was a good pause, a relieving pause.

"Mentard," began Clorfothian, "I'd like to skip to a topic about someone you, we all for that matter, love and admire." Without hesitation he said, "Zog!"

All three looked at Mentard. No flash. No disturbance. The memory remained deep, very deep. And for the moment, that was good, very good.

Mentard's smiled broadened. "Now that's a topic we'll need a little respect for!" His chest swelled once again with the allegiance he felt for Zog.

• • • • •

The five settled quickly into their familiar way of meeting: sealed portal, merged consciousness, and focused intent for their use of the Neecha. It was easier than breathing and, had it not been for the absence of Mothan and Kleeana, it would have been a regular "hold on to your middle wings we're in for another amazing adventure" meeting. However, perhaps because of the innocence still nestled within the wisdom of the two inglets, all five expressed concern. It was with the intent, then, to discern not only the level of welfare both inglets resided within, but also exactly where they were located and with whom they were opening so wide. It was an unspoken but clearly understood conclusion that after their discerning, all five would then, without further delay or hesitation, go to the exact location.

"Actually, now that we are all together," began Brianna, "I don't feel worried about either of them." She looked to Treiga, who had become her dearest friend. "I, for one, question our concern." She didn't wait for a response from the others, but continued with, "I must honestly admit that my first reaction was one of curiosity and then wanting to journey with them." She looked to Karthentonen. "Kar, you yourself have said that Mothan and Kleeana together have provided us with explorations we would either have never dreamed of, or at the least would have taken... well, a long time no matter how you look at it!"

It was Meteranke who responded to Brianna's honesty. "I, too, have felt no cause for alarm. However, I also know that our two inglets have a tendency to jump into circumstances and then later need a helping lift out."

All four smiled at Meteranke's reference to a recent event when both Kleeana and Mothan journeyed into one of the wizard's realms and became so involved with the adventure that they forgot how to access the avenue home. The five had extended their searching, vibratory patterns as a group into several realms until the wizards appeared and actually questioned what they were doing.

Rather than point a wedged wing at Kleeana and Mothan's undisciplined play, they had replied with general statements about exploring realms. Even though the statements were exactly true, they had not been a complete response concerning the present purpose for journeying within the wizard realms.

Of course the wizards had easily discerned their attempts at the slight disguising of their actions. The consequences of such filtering had been quite disconcerting as the wizards placed additional encodings within the fabric of all of their portals.

At the time, because Mothan and Kleeana were already residing within a wizard realm, they automatically became aware not only of the new encodings, but also of the exact portal home. And as they appeared before the five, their look of innocent surprise reminded the five of what it might really be like to be parents!

In the end, the results were quite positive: rather than ask Kleeana or Mothan, the five worked together to decode the portal encodings and eventually won their beloved wizards' praise and invitation to many as-yet-unexplored realms.

The shared memory and consequences flashed through all five simultaneously, to which Meteranke responded, "Well... I'm not so sure of the *lifting out* part of what I was saying!"

Fornaign slapped the side of his great dragon leg and laughed loudly and heartily, filling the Neecha with a myriad of blending colors and loudly trumpeting sounds finishing in a beautiful symphonic tone.

Karthentonen applauded, sending sparks in every direction. "Thank you, Fornaign! Thank you!" he applauded again. "I enjoyed that."

It was Treiga, of course, who gathered their energies, synchronized the purposes, and fed them back to the group. "We may as well accept the fact that at times we all are like overbearing parents..." he paused for a brief moment's slight reflection and then admitted, "and at other times we are more inglet-like than any of our group!"

Meteranke joined in with, "All that we're saying," he nodded (as in the beginning times) to Brianna, who still blushed against her will, and then continued, "is that what you began with, Brianna, is true. However, we all have felt — and if I'm correct, still feel — that our attention has been sparked by something; that our awarenesses are standing at attention; that something major is in the making; AND the avenue through which it all has journeyed to us is our not only beloved, but quite capable: two non-present group members.

"Here, here!" Brianna smiled broadly. "So, let's get to the facts!"

"Actually," said Karthentonen, "I felt a shift somewhat before I caught a glimpse of Mothan and Kleeana's wide-open receiving...." The others felt his thoughts align and allowed the pause. "And, even before that moment, I experienced flashes of occurrences in the Timeline. I'm just realizing that right now!"

Without hesitation, the group thought-merged to a deeper level and awaited Karthentonen's sharing of the recent Timeline occurrences.

"The first was of the gathering in the Dream State." Even as Karthentonen's formed images of several Representatives arriving at the Mutchiat Cavern, Fornaign merged his own similar vision of the same gathering along with smaller flashes of the few elders who were refusing to respond to the call.

While the five easily maintained the first vision, Karthentonen released the second. "This one is quite incomplete. Maybe one of you has more to add." The colors exploded, and each fully received the hazy image of a lush green meadow with what appeared to be a distortion in the distance.

"Ah! What I find interesting," said Fornaign, as he adjusted the vision to demonstrate his discovery, "is that whereas in the call to the gathering, neither of our leaders' encodings are present, yet the Representatives *are* gathering; and here in the distortion at the far reaches of wherever this is, resides the quite unmistakable imprint of Zog!"

If it had been a casual gathering, perhaps all four would have commented on Fornaign's discovery. Instead, they held the images and continued.

Meteranke felt a thrill ripple through his dragon hide. "This is all more than we have experienced thus far. I'm not sure what it could be...."

"Continue, please," entreated Brianna. "I'm receiving something too!"

"The last, before Mothan and Kleeana's flash, was this one." Meteranke released his vision of the nearly stopped raging fire.

Treiga expertly added his own refined vision. The five held themselves, merged and knowing. They all saw. It was undeniable. Zog's patterns resided in the flames! They thought-merged the two visions: the green meadow with the distortion and the nearly stopped flames. Both could merge easily. Both contained Zog's patterns, the very same patterns that were missing from the call to gather.

The five felt the realizations of Truth ripple outward from their thought-merging, ripple through their entire physical dragon bodies. Zog's powerful, familiar-to-all-dragons, clear and unmistakable pattern, the call to come forth, the call to gather, Zog's call to *"gather here where I gather"* resided simultaneously in the distortion at the far reaches of the lush green meadow AND in the flames of the nearly stopped raging fire!

As if the awarenesses weren't full enough, Treiga released his vision with, "I'm not quite sure if I'm receiving or remembering this now." The barely perceptible increase in movement flowed into the flames. Together they all saw the previously nearly stopped flames gain speed. They saw the flames lick and bite at their familiar mountains.

It was Brianna who softly, strongly, and with great honor and respect, released the final vision. Barely audible, she whispered, "When we first began here today, I saw the vision I've been carrying for quite some time... since my last research... well, I believe it was since my conversation with the Old Dragon."

No one hurried her. Not one beseeched her to release her vision. They all held their thought-merging: knowing, with the wisdom of who they were, that every moment unfolds in perfect order and completeness; that nothing in the moment is ever missing; and that everything in the moment called eternity is as full as it is, as full as it possibly can be. Within that knowing, Brianna continued.

"From the histories of who we all are... dragons, that is... I receive this vision each time I delve into those histories, particularly the recording of the two previous known destructions.

"Actually," she continued, feeding into their merged vision her full knowing of all the records she had investigated, "the writings do NOT speak of the Neekontuk as *destruction*." She inserted into the merging, the text to which she was referring. "As you can see here, there is a speaking of the flames, of a raging fire. But nowhere is there the word *destruction*. The word that is used is more a phrase: *dissolving, dissolving into nothing*.

Knowing the capabilities of her friends, Brianna continued without pausing. "In both instances, after the *dissolving* of all of the dragon world and of all dragons, there is a new dragon world and new dragon gatherings, who eventually find each other and begin a Kloan.

"There is no exact record that I have been able to find that describes how the new dragon world forms, or where the new dragons come from for that matter! Now," she continued, "that having been said, this is the vision I receive *every time* I research this topic." As if floating above what appeared to be the Timeline, two undulating golden rivers flowed upward while wrapping around each other. Each of the five dragons recognized the undulating rivers as those same flowings that resided within their wedge-like wings. And even at the recognizing, those wings tingled and raised.

The golden weaving in Brianna's vision broadened and became larger and larger. Within their thought-merging, they saw the golden rivers flow and form. They saw the gold become two golden dragons, merged together, two-as-one.

In one breath there was one magnificent golden dragon, radiating essence and light. And in the next breath there were two magnificent golden dragons, intertwining and merging.

Again, softly and sweetly Brianna spoke, "This is what has come to me during our Neecha here today." She released living, moving patterns and symbols. They flowed of themselves as if suspended over the dragons' visioning.

For a time, in the seeming timelessness of their gathering, the living, moving symbols held them spellbound. And then, without warning or hint of reason, the symbols became easily and completely located within the two golden dragons, merging two-as-one. Within the dragons, the symbols continued to move and form, move and unform.

Brianna's nature called forth her wondering, questioning, and delving into the known. Even as the five maintained, even as the images spun within their merging, she asked – and received. They were impressed with her expertise, and later, much later, each would remember to congratulate her on the refinement of her talents. For the moment, though, they remained focused and open to receive simultaneously, as she did, her answer.

Her question had been concerning the symbols, of course, and whether they had resided anywhere before in dragon existence. The answer flowed forth in stages.

First came an image of two dragons, standing as flames enveloped them. Just at the moment of total fire, the symbols appeared and then disappeared.

The second vision came in the form of a portal. As the portal opened wide, a golden dragon could be seen. He was holding his great clawed hand outward, extending it toward the portal. As the vision sharpened, golden essence could be seen in his hand. The dragon then extended the essence he held, further

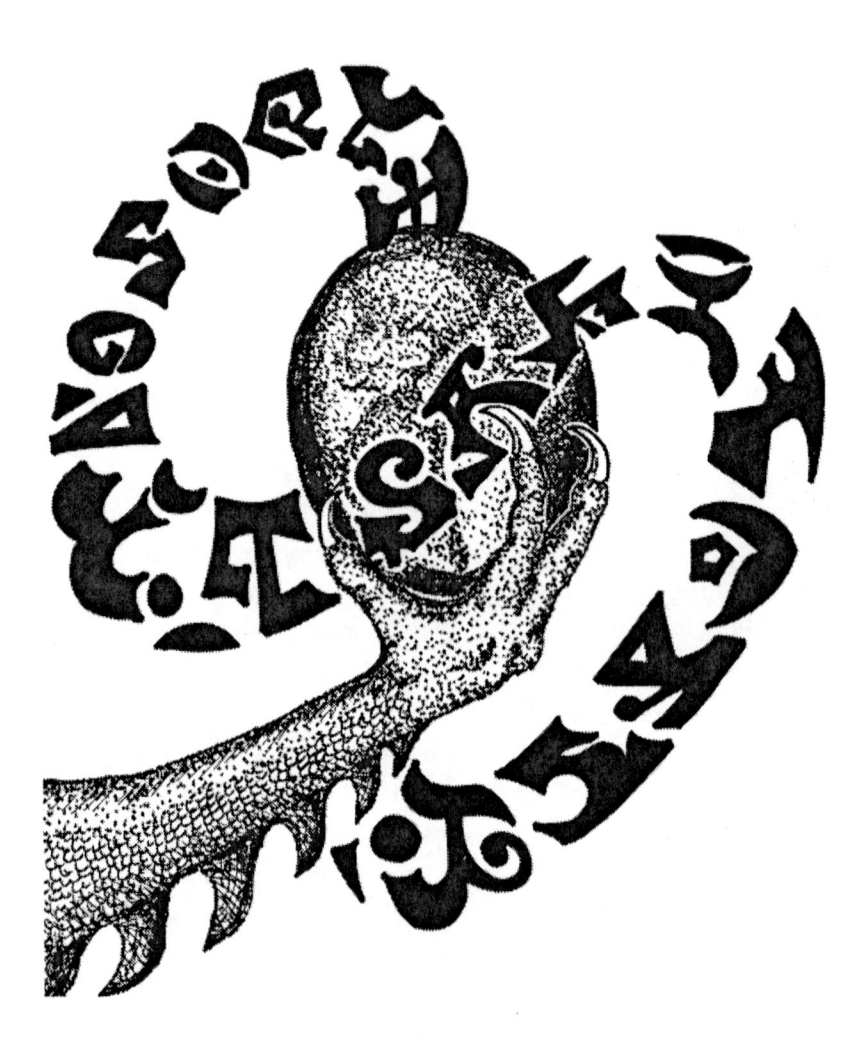

The dragon then extended the essence he held, further and further, until it was through the portal! They could be seen quite clearly: the same symbols flowed and formed within the held golden essence.

and further, until it was through the portal! They could be seen quite clearly: the same symbols flowed and formed within the held golden essence.

The third vision pictured Zoanna, leading a Kloan gathering. While the entire dragon population of Representatives was held as if in stopped movement, Zoanna spun a golden river of light about her great dragon being. Then she leaned forward and deliberately breathed her breath into the river.

Again, the living moving symbols resided within Zoanna's breath and then in the river. The river moved and in the next moment, became the same golden flowing as in the vision.

One of the dragons in the two-as-one carried the very same patterns as Zoanna. In truth, they saw that one of the golden dragons was indeed Zoanna.

The last vision demonstrated to the five their own discovery of the patterns of Zog's call. Again, the patterns flowed and moved. In one giant flash all five saw Zog's patterns reside within the second golden dragon.

In their vision, in their thought-merging, they saw, heard and felt the call: *gather, gather together where I am*. The visions flashed again and again: the fire, the distortion, the portal, the two golden dragons, and their identity revealed.

The five didn't know how long they held their united visions. It was like the nourishment for which they had been searching since… perhaps since they each first realized they were dragons.

The spinning slowed and gradually released each of them. As with the many experiences they had shared in the Neecha, the five didn't discuss or do anything to dissipate the visions or information gifted by their merging. Instead, they allowed their created intent to direct their conscious focus. It was Karthentonen who spoke first, quickly, "Did you all get a fix on their location? Mothan and Kleeana?" He looked to each of his compatriots. All nodded 'yes' with certainty. "Then we go?" he asked.

Even before the short question was completed, they were standing, preparing to fan their great wings. Merged intent opened the great portal, cleared the Neecha of any residue of their visioning, and lifted each dragon from the ledge of the mountain.

Five magnificent dragons, fully winged and filled with visions and purpose, directed their flight to the Old Dragon's chamber.

The Old Dragon sensed it. He felt their flight. He delightedly felt them coming. He had never turned from an adventure, especially one of this magnitude.

CHAPTER ELEVEN

I AM THE ONE. I AM THE *ONLY* ONE.

In the Moment in Stretched Time, Mutchiat and its great cavern remained untouched by the biting flames of the Neekontuk. In fact, none of the Representatives, who left their own communities to fly over the familiar ranges toward their meeting place, had as yet remembered the realm of their regular living. Each, as well as nearly the entire dragon population, believed the Kah-na Tro-Linaht was and always had been their natural rhythm. Such total absorption was the nature of the Kah-na Tro-Linaht. Little did they know that everything, even the fabric of that which they were calling home, was about to change.

The first Representatives who arrived at the cavern were actually those whose homes were the furthest away in distance from Mutchiat. Their entry into the grand cavern was a different gathering than in times of the past. There had been no call. No leader beckoned them. And as they entered, the absence of their leaders' intent and embrace left their movements to reside within the echoes of themselves. Even as their numbers increased, the cavern felt empty and their energies a little scattered. Still, they did arrive and gather, even though the usual greeting of long established friends wasn't filled with the also usual fires and smoke, or sparks and sounds. They greeted each other in such subdued manners that none need be reminded to be more contained. There was no calling to order. Each dragon had gone directly to his place and settled there, waiting... waiting for something.

The something took the form of three of the youngest Representatives who stepped nearly into the center of the encircling gathering. None would step up and onto the platformed ledge from which both of their leaders had addressed them all on so many occasions.

The youngest dragon, Kahlna, opened his middle wings and deliberately demonstrated his colors of innocence and inexperience. It was the best action he could have taken, as all the dragons present — even those few elders who kept themselves in the alcoves — carried within their own wings similar innocence. Thusly the youngest dragon began to speak with an almost unanimous support of the Kloan, as each dragon's wedge wings subtly raised in recognition of Kahlna's stepping forth to speak.

His voice was young, yet with his most focused strength of purpose he began:

"I am Kahlna from the mountain range of Nahlenchiat." He nodded to the young dragon standing to his right, "And this is Treinelyia from the mountain range of Treinelchiat. Nodding to his left, he introduced his second compatriot, "This is Breenkel from the mountain range Mitel-Kelchiat."

Within the silence of the Great Cavern of Mutchiat, Kahlna took a deep dragon breath and continued, "Forgive me for my boldness in standing here, in my own inexperience, to speak with your great wisdom and strength."

The gathering recognized Kahlna's sincerity and in some instances began to thought-merge with the young spokes-dragon, to assist his speaking. The elders waited and observed.

"Of all that we are together, I don't know why I am the one dragon who has been called to speak first. And although I have tried to bring forth in my mind exactly what I would say, I have been unable to. In truth," the young dragon swallowed which released a slight green stream of smoke from one nostril, "I do not know what I will say. I only know that I have been called to speak." He paused long enough to look around the gathering and into as many piercing eyes as his quick glance would allow.

I AM THE ONE. I AM THE *ONLY* ONE.

"Unless anyone here is led to speak," Kahlna displayed his colors of preparing to step aside, "I will continue." No one stepped forward. In fact, there was not one sound or one slight puff of smoke.

There was something in the way the youngest dragon began that reminded one of the elder dragons of Zog's first speaking before them as their leader. They had expected Zog's outgoing enthusiasm to spill forth from the platform. They had expected his speaking to be filled with fire and smoke, inspiring the Glarian with adventures and plans.

· · · · ·

It was not that Zog's first speaking had been a disappointment. Not at all. One could say, however, that his manner and words were a surprise.

It's true that Zog, from his inglet time, had continually surprised and delighted them all. The elder dragon had reflected many more times than once or twice upon why even he hadn't expected to be surprised. Even now, in the great chamber, he chuckled to himself about the nature of the unexpected and how they all might have been clearly astonished if they hadn't been held spellbound when Zog had begun speaking in a most subdued manner. In fact, they had all quieted their breathings in order to hear his words.

Zog had displayed neither majestic colors nor trumpeting sounds. Instead he had begun much like this youngest dragon. He had thought-merged with them all when he sent out the call to gather. His call had been different from his father's call. Where Meran had always been direct and informational even in the patterns of his call, Zog's call had been simply *"gather here where I am."* They had all eagerly responded.

In the stillness of the Glarian gathering, Zog's words had filled them easily. "Great dragons, you have heard my call and arrived here to *gather where I gather.*" Those first words had continued to be the words he had used at the beginning of every gathering thereafter.

Zog had continued with, "I have asked of the wizards and I have asked of the Ancient Ones what I would speak at this gathering." As he had turned to face all of them in turn, they had found themselves excitedly expecting to hear wizard wisdom or ancient guidings. Instead they had heard, "Neither the wizards nor the Ancient Ones would tell me what to say to you!"

Zog's smile had been the one familiar ingredient from his long-ago speaking. "I then asked myself what I would say to you and, although it may be hard to believe, I could not hear my own words." The Glarian had chuckled a little, each glancing briefly to the others a knowing familiarity of Zog's wonderfully long stories.

"Upon my flight above Mutchiat," he had continued, "it came to me that in truth, it is not *my* words at all that I have come here to speak, but that it is *your* words." He had helped them know and understand. "Inside of each of you lives all of what is called forth to speak at this Kloan."

Zog had invited them to be more of who they were as individuals. "Merge your thoughts, your knowing." He had stretched his thought-merging to encompass all of their strengths and seeming weaknesses. "Open your great dragon hearts and as Representatives call your Floggens to open their hearts."

Zog had then fanned his great wings, all sets in succession including those at either side of his jaw. Those two sparked and filled the chamber with great white light as if the Kloan gathering were a crystalline structure itself. Then Zog had gifted them with the radiating colors of all the realms he had explored, gifted them with the symphonic sounds of the universes he had played within, and showered them with the honor he felt in being named Winzoarian.

"Then together your words do flow forth to fill me," Zog had said, holding them in the near blissful state of merging. "Then it is actually you speaking these words at this gathering." He had paused and for a moment some thought they had seen Zog's great dragon body disappear, yet there he had remained.

"We are great dragon beings," the speaking had begun. "We are more than who we have been. We are more than the Ancient

I AM THE ONE. I AM THE *ONLY* ONE.

Ones to whom we look for guidance." None had previously heard or consciously thought of the spoken words, yet it was as if they were each saying the words as Zog spoke them.

"One day each of us will be called upon. One day each dragon will be called upon to demonstrate the truth that we are more than dragons." The words had felt foreign yet more familiar than their regular breathing. "In that day we will be asking ourselves to leave everything that is familiar." Zog's voice had resonated strongly then, vibrating within their great cavern. "The greatness of who we have been, the stories of our adventures, and the fulfilling of our hopes and dreams will call us to remain as we are. Our love of who we are together will beg us to remain seemingly unchanged."

The fullness of who they had been had filled Zog to overflowing as his final words had entered their open hearts. "It is then that each one must drink of the more-of-that-which-we-are. It is then that we must turn from all that we have been and face that which we are becoming. It is then that the Ancient Ones will weep at our splendor!"

They had wanted to applaud and, at the same time, to run away; to cheer what Zog had envisioned with them and at the same time to flee home to the familiar. It was then that Zoanna had stepped beside the greatness of Zog and sung to them their own song.

The song had filled them to weeping; it had filled them with peace, and it had filled them with the present moment. They had all returned to their Floggens with much more than words would ever express. The gathering had been nothing that any had expected.

• • • • •

The Elder chuckled again to himself: *wasn't that the nature of surprise? Now this young dragon has begun by saying he doesn't know what his words will be! During these times,* thought the Elder, *there is only the unexpected.*

Kahlna's voice called the Elder's reminiscing to an end, as he too merged to assist this daring young one in stepping into their current adventure.

Treinelyia and Breenkel, the two young dragons standing beside Kahlna, opened their wings and released the sweet colors of simplicity, of fearless adventure, and of their determination to fulfill a purpose -- such purpose as yet unrevealed even to them.

Kahlna felt the support of his two compatriots; they reminded him that he could only be himself, the youngest dragon, and no pretending would or, in fact, *could* change that fact. The realization was a relief to him, and his outward sigh demonstrated a peace more developed than could be expected from one his age. The Elder dragon's attention came to full alert.

"In fact," said Kahlna, almost casually, as if he had been speaking to them for hours, "I am even now just opening my mouth and letting these words be spoken." He smiled just a little and the Elder thought he perceived a slight shrugging of this youngest dragon's shoulders.

The slight shrugging changed to a more evident gesture of "I don't know what I'm doing" as the youngest dragon raised his two arms outward. "Unless I'm led to stop, I will continue doing what is beyond what I could have imagined even in my Beginning Visionings[34] at the Great Lac."

He continued without interruption, as the words came flowing out of his open mouth:

"Long ago, there came upon these lands, dragons of great fire, of great courage, and of great wisdom. When they breathed

---

34 Beginning Visionings: when inglets are brought to the Great Lac for the first time, their parents take the responsibility of thought-merging and form a link between themselves, their inglet, and the population of dragons present at the Lac. During the first visit, the inglet feels and experiences the effects of this also first thought-merging with more than his family. Within the mind-merge, the inglet calls forth from the patternings within his still-forming wedge wings. The patternings release the great gift of a vision and the inglet celebrates a knowing of the nature of the possibility of his adventures during the next phase of his maturing. Because the vision occurs within a mind-merge, the population of all dragons joyfully carry within their knowing, the first visionings of all inglets. When any dragon, inglet, or elder, refers to his or her first visioning at the Great Lac, those patterns are called forth within the dragon population. The effect of such calling forth establishes a deeper merging, which can be used to enhance whatever is currently occurring within the moment of the reference.

I AM THE ONE. I AM THE *ONLY* ONE.

upon the lands, the lands responded. The caverns opened to invite them to reside within the mountains. The waterfalls flowed and gathered to form great lacs where the dragons might bring their young to be celebrated. And the realms did hover close to the land so that portals might be created and journeyed through. So loved were the dragons by the lands and all that lived and resided thereupon, that the dragons decided that they would remain.

"From the deciding of the first dragons upon the lands, there came with great wafting wings and open hearts, more and more dragons until the lands were populated by a rhythm and breathing of those creatures who loved the lands in their warm celebrating embrace.

"The dragons resided upon the lands beyond the counting of time, for there was not reason to count the days, or months, or rhythms of being. They simply were."

Treinelyia and Breenkel fanned all sets of their wings, even those as yet not quite completely developed at either side of their jaws. Turning to face all directions, there came from their open wings a swirling of colors, which expanded and formed before the Kloan, a vision.

The vision depicted the arrival of the first dragons upon the lands. The Kloan saw and, without determining to do so, leaned forward to discern what they were seeing. Could it be true? Yes. It was. The first dragons were different. Their wings were greater, spread wider. Their scales were glistening. They seemed to be emanating a light, a light the color of their sunrise. Their bodies were less in size. In fact, it appeared that the first dragons' wings were the largest part of their bodies.

The scene within the vision shifted and changed. A ripple scaled up and down the back spine of every Representative as they saw, from the furthest mountain, something.... They forced their piercing gaze to sharpen. It was what appeared to be a dragon, different even from those within the vision. His scales were brown. There was no glistening color or light. Yet he flew with a precision more developed than even those they had recognized as elders.

As the dragon flew within the vision, he came closer and closer, over the mountain ranges and then, as if to deliberately astonish the gathering, he flew right into their chamber! Some wondered if the vision had actually become real! Others involuntarily blinked their eyes again and again in an effort to be sure of what they were seeing! Yet in their thought-merge, they saw and knew: what appeared before them was real, very real.

The dragon standing in the center of the vision taking form within their cavern of Mutchiat — was old, very old. Perhaps ancient. His eyes glared at them. Green. Then blue. Not yellow, like theirs. His gaze expanded and he filled their cavern with his presence.

Even while they struggled to believe what their senses assured was real; the very old dragon stepped up to Kahlna. In one deep breath, the oldest stood in the exact place the youngest had been standing. In truth, the Representatives could no longer see Kahlna nor hear his innocent voice. Before them stood the oldest dragon they had ever seen.

Some Representatives wanted to boldly ask, "Who are you?" and "Where is our youngest dragon?", but none uttered one word. Instead, they listened. The words flowed from the old dragon to them without his speaking. It seemed that his words became their thoughts... or was it that their thoughts became his words?

"Young dragons," he began, and even the elders knew that to this dragon, they too were young. "I am called the One." His voice was strong yet peaceful, embracing yet solitary. It moved through them like a river, a river of life.

"Yes," he responded to their unspoken thoughts and questions, "I am old. I am very old." What had been a vision now became their place of residing, and their references to what was real and what was vision left their grasp.

"In fact," he continued, "I am the Oldest Dragon." He paused to allow their questioning minds to settle, to return to undivided merging. Then his words entered directly into them:

"Before you came to exist, I already was. And," his speaking softened, "when you cease to be, I will remain.

I AM THE ONE. I AM THE *ONLY* ONE.

"I always have been. I always will be. I am the One. I am the *only* One." The Oldest Dragon knew that they couldn't quite comprehend all of what he was saying, yet he continued. His speaking wove patterns of love around and within them. Each Representative relaxed into the weaving; and when they did, each Floggen felt the love and heard the words of the Oldest Dragon:

"I have seen you in your gatherings, in your living upon the lands." His words invited to surface, memories of long-ago times. "I have come among you, to teach you and to help you.

"Whenever you have awakened a little, whenever you have allowed your curiosities to create a journey to venture within, I have placed myself within your journey to celebrate your awakening."

Some of the Representatives remembered meeting a stranger who was yet familiar — one who seemed to say the right word or look a certain way, a way that caused them to venture further into their discoveries.

The Oldest Dragon continued, "I have come among you because I love you. You are more than my children." He looked around the circle at each of them. "You *are* me."

He thought perhaps this time he would be able to speak the whole story to them, to open their minds and thoughts to more of who they were, but even with his speaking of these few words, they had begun to slip into a soft sleep.

They had done well, and it was not that he was waiting for them to awaken, but more that their awakening was *his* journey. The Oldest Dragon stopped speaking and gathered the weaving of his vision, gathered the patterns he had placed at the doorway of their minds. He gathered the essence of his presence and — in one quick movement — he lifted himself from the gathering.

In the blink of an eye, their youngest dragon, Kahlna, stood before them. The words had ceased pouring from his mouth. Some wondered... a little, while others allowed their wonderings to rest within tomorrow's dreams and sleep.

Kahlna spoke clearly, as if he had been continually speaking to them all along, "There are no more words. I must be finished." He and his compatriots stepped away from the center of the gathering. In fact, it had been their intention to simply step to the side. Yet their wings ached to feel the breath of the land beneath them and their bodies begged to be in flight. They continued moving until they had walked out of the chamber and onto the landing ledge. Without hesitation, the three — Kahlna, Treinelyia, and Breenkel — wafted their wings and began their journey home. They had been the first to arrive and the first to depart.

The others too began to leave. The gathering was complete. None spoke of it, but simply left to return to their home, to their Floggens.

There was one, however, who had heard all the words. The Elder. He neither flew home nor wondered. Instead, he stepped into the place where the oldest and the youngest dragon had stood. The Elder expanded his mind, his thoughts, and his heart.

The Oldest Dragon felt the Elder's expanding. At long last, it had begun: the beginning of the return to One. The Elder heard the words echo through his knowing again and again:

"Before you came to exist, I already was.
And, when you cease to be, I will remain.
I always have been. I always will be.
I am the One. I am the only One.
You are more than my children.
You are me."

CHAPTER TWELVE

YOU WILL YIELD!!

Zoanna's telling of Zog's story was more than a rendering of the highlights of his life from the moment of taking form. Also was her telling more than a Mehentuk[35], though Zog and Zoanna began within those memories. A Mehentuk holds its many purposes and can assist any dragon to begin to enjoy the realizations that come with an objective view, while allowing the dragon to also easily and gradually let go of any attachment to what might have been determined incomplete.

It had been written in the histories that without the assistance of a Mehentuknen[36], dragons had often floundered within the emotions that also rose within their visioning, and there had been those who tried to return to the physical to finish what they believed was left undone. Though well meaning, the attempts to influence the physical had caused such confusion that the Ancient Ones had consequently created a realm within which the particular patterns and encodings of the dragon who had just released his physical body

---

35 <u>Mehentuk</u>: At the time of passing from physical the dragon sends forth a call and in response to the call, waves of memories and the causes and effects of the now ending dragon life rise to the surface of the consciousness. The rising forth of the richness of the events and the viewing is called Mehentuk.

36 <u>Mehentuknen</u>: A guide, one who assists the dragon involved in the Mehentuk to maintain a balanced viewing.

would call forth a Mehentuknen. The Mehentuknen would assist that dragon through the next phase in developing a consciousness able to function without a physical body.

In the event that a dragon determined that he would choose Ala-kleeha[37], he would necessarily participate with his Mehentuknen in a Mehentuk dedicated to that purpose. Often, after such a Mehentuk, would the dragon choose to pulse between the freedom gained in his newly refined objectivity and the portal to the Nothingness. Such pulsating resides beyond the interpretations of purpose and fulfillment, and is simply the dragon's manner of experiencing the fullness of all that he is.

• • • • •

It had been Zog's insistence in his continued effort to use his charred body in order to save his dragons from the onslaught of the Neekontuk that alerted the Ancient Ones of his need for a Mehentuk. Yet it was also his expanding awareness — as he oscillated between releasing his physical form and an insistence in residing within his physical form — that had actually begun the change and would eventually help the Glarian more than any act of actually returning to and healing his well-used physical body.

During the many attempts to dive into his lifeless form, Zog was able to take a deep breath of something, something nurturing. Then, once filled, he had determined to live and bend the devastating pain into a strength he could harness — not against the Neekontuk as some would have had him do, but toward a pathway to the portal he had created. A pathway for his dragons.

It was, however, the intensity of yet another memory that called both Zog and Zoanna. Even though Zoanna would have preferred to weave more ease and comfort within the telling, the truth begged to be told. It was Zog who began his own telling, even though all of the speaking thus far had been delivered by Zoanna within her loving embrace.

---

37 Ala-kleeha: Chosen during the Mehentuk, a new life and return to a physical dragon body. Ala-kleeha is a process for male dragons. Within the process, the male dragon – having released his previous life and physical body — returns to be birthed within a new family and a new life. (See Myo-Neela in Glossary)

YOU WILL YIELD!!

As with his other experiences, Zog stood at the helm of his own journey and began with his usual intensity. He called forth his first sighting of the great flames as they rolled across the lands.

"It was the fires of the Neekontuk," he paused to allow the pictured memories to focus according to his direction. "Yes, those fires." They both saw the devouring of the ranges through Zog's long ago vision:

Flashes. Light. Flames. Fire. More questions. Even as he had hurried to warn his Glarian, Zog's curiosity had catapulted him closer.

"I had activated my armor and shielded when…." Before Zog could finish speaking, both of them saw. Zog had flown close to the devouring flames, skimming the surface of their licking, and then back out again. He had reformed his armor, activating the encodings within his wings.

"I wanted to have a closer look," Zog reflected, "and I wanted to test the momentum."

Through their merging, Zog and Zoanna became the unfolding story. Zog dipped deeper into the Neekontuk as it had rolled past the mountain rages of Kilchek — rolled unaffected by Zog's prying into its character, into its cause and effect.

Three times Zog had dipped into the flames, each effort bringing him a little deeper. At last he stood before the rolling wave. He stood ready to force the biting to turn upon itself. Although the actual event had happened so quickly that it nearly ended before it had begun, Zog deliberately slowed their viewing. He wanted to see exactly what had occurred.

Zoanna no longer felt concern for Zog's well-being within his Mehentuk. With his determining of the manner in which they would view the event, he had easily and completely stepped from his healing dragon self into the fullness of who he was, who he had always been: an Ancient One. Like any who reside within their own fullness, it would be a while before Zog would become aware of even a hint of his own grandness.

The Timeline once again formed itself to the determining of its viewer. It slowed. There, within the leaping of the largest flames, stood Zog, his small fans open and quivering, both sets of large wings unfurled to their widest reach, and his wedge wings activated and ready to insert. They did. Simultaneously, his small quivering fans had fired white charges while his wedge wings had inserted themselves into the hovering wave. From deep inside, Zog had felt the rumbling build until it became a thundering ball of fire as it rose to his great heart.

It was there that the vision slowed. Although they remained merged, Zoanna was but an observer as Zog continued to determine the unfolding of the Timeline:

As if a dance within light, Zog's tremendous wings reached back and then thrust their tremendous wafting breath into the flames; once, twice, and then with the third, Zog's fans again fired balls of white light. Rapidly. One after the other.

They both saw. Zog saw. The Neekontuk paused. It looked directly at Zog. He hadn't hesitated for one moment. Zog called for his heart's thundering ball of fire. It rose up his long neck, seeking the object of its expression. Zog had opened his great mouth and, leaning back his head, forced the thunder into one stream, one great stream, and without hesitation fired it into the paused Neekontuk.

Explosion. Fire biting fire. The Neekontuk's wave had built and built, carrying its momentum. It had loomed over Zog's intent-filled being. He didn't look upward at the deafening, raging firewall about to crash down upon him. As if oblivious to his inevitable plight, he had determinedly continued to aim his thick stream of thunderous flames into the wave. *If only it would bend back into itself. If only it would fold upon itself.*

Zoanna heard the words of Zog's intent. Even now he whispered them. *"Fold back! Give! Give a little and I'll have you!"* Though he knew the results of his efforts within the battle he had so valiantly fought, he still urged the event itself to deliver the results he had wanted then — and wanted now.

Zoanna allowed his wanting. It was her decision. Her option was to call forth the beauty of One and lift him to rest, or to allow. Zog was strong. Always had been strong. In fact, just when the Kloan had wondered on numerous occasions if Zog would be able to complete an intended journey, he treated them with reflections, waves of delight and never-before-viewed realms. It wasn't that they had ever doubted his capabilities, but more that they had been continually amazed at his accomplishments.... Zoanna knew. Knew that Zog was more than capable. He **was** his own strength.

Zog heard his own whispered words. Charged patterns had fired from his wedge wings into the wave. Zog's patterns. Clear. Strong. Strong with intent. He heard his own voice as he had growled out the command: "YOU WILL YIELD!"

More patterns had penetrated the wave. Fanned charges had ridden atop the patterns and pierced through the wall of fire. Again he had growled, had commanded, "YIELD!"

In one quick waft, his great wings had carried him directly into the wave. He had bellowed, "YOU ARE NO MORE!" With all the strength he could demand from all that he was, he had bellowed again: "ONLY I AM!!"

Zog saw. Zoanna saw. The raging, devouring wave had leaned itself back and back with each of Zog's commands, until it did lean itself back into its own movement, back into the second before it had raged upon Zog. The Neekontuk had folded back upon itself.

Zog could have left the Neekontuk to writhe within its own confused direction. He could have again wafted his great wings and lifted himself out of the flames. But he did not. Zog's great love for his Glarian had filled him with purpose, and he had continued to charge into the confused furnace, that was licking at itself and licking at him. Scorching his wings. Sucking the breath from him until his nostrils had been damaged and unable to breathe fire.

Zog looked along the Timeline, past the visioned struggle. He directed his piercing gaze. He looked closer, deeper. *"I want to see,"* he thought-spoke to Zoanna. *"I want to see what...."* He stretched his visioning, calling forth a clarity few had enjoyed. *"There! Look there!"*

He pulled the focus of their viewing to a speck in the Timeline. Something from the future reached and stretched itself. White. It was white. Reaching and stretching again, it had ignored other Timeline events and targeted one spot, one location, one being: Zog!

The white latched itself onto Zog as he had fought the folding of the fiery confusion and, like an elastic returning to its unstretched state, the white did also and, in so doing, had pulled Zog from the flames.

Zog wasn't interested in where the white had placed him. He wanted the identity of the white. *"Did you see that?? What was that?"* he thought-spoke to Zoanna. She was already following the white as it unstretched itself back to its point of origin.

Two golden dragons, united as one, saw. Refusing further examination, in a blur the white shot past them and into the future. Someone. Someone or something in the future had reached into its own past and pulled Zog from the flames. But who? What? His intent questioning released his focus.

Rest called him. He wanted to resist, to continue the Mehentuk. *"How could I need rest? Need anything?"* Zog's thoughts drifted over his wonderings. *"How could I need? I am an Ancient One...."* The essence that breathed itself into a golden dragon released its form, as did Zoanna, and merged. One being: Two as One.

Even as they remained merged, the Mehentuk continued delivering its overview of the natural rhythm of Zog's journeys. Zoanna's love continued to gently encourage the knowing of what had always occurred.

And Zog, reveling in his golden being, easily incorporated his inglet and adult adventures with a gradual but complete knowing: he had never only resided upon the land. Though his abilities and adventures into other realms had been magnificent, they were but a partial picture of what had actually, fully been occurring: Zog had always been continually oscillating within a pulsebeat between his residing upon the land and a near stepping into the portal to the Nothingness. Always.

Zog's awareness of such Truth activated the next phase of the Mehentuk. And it was within Zoanna's speaking of the portal itself that she began to also integrate the recent events as they had occurred within *each* expression of the Timeline.

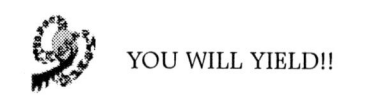

Zoanna's adept manner of stepping from one part of the Timeline to another not only initiated the anchoring of Zog within a new awareness of his identity of Ancient One, but also initiated the ever-so-slight but definite dissolving of the boundaries between one section of the Timeline and another.

It wasn't that Zoanna was unaware of the effects of her telling; it wasn't that she was so objectively beyond the story of the dragons who resided upon the land; and it wasn't that Zoanna cared so deeply for Zog and his birthing consciousness that she had left their beloved dragon world to fend for itself while the Neekontuk continued its devouring.

Zoanna was keenly aware of everything that was occurring in all realms, in all segments and their boundaries of the Timeline, and within the minds and hearts of all dragons. Her great love expanded to include all — especially did it expand to include the explorations of her two inglets, Mothan and Kleeana.

• • • • •

Even as he continued speaking with Mothan and Kleeana, the Oldest Dragon prepared the portal of his chamber to be able to accommodate the five who were swiftly following the slight patterns Mothan's scan of the healing chambers had produced. It was, however, Mothan who first spoke of the approaching dragons.

"They **will** demand entry, you know," he said matter-of-factly.

"I've been looking forward to their arrival," the Old One responded. He turned his smile toward Kleeana. "It appears you have five most adept friends!"

"We do," said Kleeana. "We probably should have told them we were coming to see Mother… but who would have known what would happen? Who would have known we'd be sitting here with you?"

"I suppose," said the Old Dragon, "that we should wait until they arrive, rather than continue with our speaking."

"Oh I don't think we have to wait," jumped in Mothan. "We all merge quite easily. They'll be able to know what we've spoken of right away."

"That is," questioned Kleeana, "if it's all right with you?"

The Old Dragon again smiled, this time at the sweet innocence of the amazingly developed young Kleeana. "My dear," he spoke as a father might to his inglet, "*everything* is all right with me." He stressed the word *everything*.

Yet before he could continue, the presence of a focused intent made itself known at the portal of the personal chamber of the Oldest Dragon. Just as the five prepared to summon their fullest request to enter, the portal opened. The chamber increased in size to accommodate five more dragons, filled with questions, searchings for Mothan and Kleeana, and with the delight of yet another amazing adventure.

Still, though the portal had opened, they waited. The Oldest Dragon, impressed with their respect for his chamber, rose and physically walked to the portal. Of course he could have simply projected the vibrations and colors of *inviting to enter*, but at times he relished the old ways and manners of being. Without effort, though, he reached the portal and stuck his old dragon head out — past the swirling — to be directly in front of the five!

Such a physical presence was a surprise to say the least, and all five jumped back into the alcove — the very same alcove that had held Kleeana and Mothan as they had insisted on seeing their mother.

His surprised effect on the five rippled a pleasure through the hide of the Oldest Dragon, and he augmented the unexpected with a very wide-mouthed, deep toned "Y – E – SSSSS?"

Brianna was the first to recover. "You!" She stepped forward — just a little — as the nostrils of the large dragon head before her began to fill the alcove with smoke.

"Why, it's you! Outside the library!"

Before she could send an explanatory image to the other four, the Oldest Dragon opened his mouth wide again. Brianna stopped in mid-word.

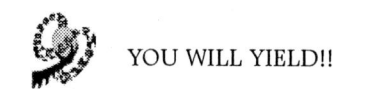

"Well," the Oldest Dragon's deep tones echoed around the alcove, "are you coming in?"

Meteranke stepped up without hesitation. "Yes sir, indeed we are!" He motioned to the others, giving the still-frozen Brianna a nudge. "Thank you sir, we would be delighted...."

The large dragon head disappeared from the portal and only his echoing words remained, "Well, you'd better come in. We have a lot to speak on...."

As all five, each after the other, stepped into the accommodating chamber, the Oldest Dragon finished his statement, "And, it appears you all — individually and collectively — have more than enough questions to..." he gazed at each of them, "well... to suspend time, I suppose!"

The Oldest Dragon motioned them to find a comfortable spot. Yet when each one saw the beaming faces of Mothan and Kleeana, the reunion sounds, colors, and as little smoke as possible filled the chamber, which had actually *again* expanded to accommodate the shrills and delights of the now seven.

The Oldest Dragon stood back and watched. It was a sight to behold. *A fine combination,* he thought to himself, *of youth and innocence, maturity and refined development of skills.* He didn't motion them to stop, or be calm. Neither did he determine the moment to get to the facts. There would be plenty of time for that. And for this delicious moment, he drank into his old spirit the young delight and love which filled his chamber.

It reminded him of long long, long ago, when the first dragons had stepped upon the land. Their innocence had danced before them, and wherever they explored, it was as if they were stepping into the essence of that very innocence. He had watched them grow and develop a manner of residing together which had allowed each the width, breadth and expansion of their own joys and discoveries. *Yes,* he recalled, *there had been some who had tried to establish a certain order, an order according to their own experiences. Yet even they provided a kind of framework through which the eventual Kloan could grow and emerge.*

The seven dragons had settled themselves against the embracing chamber walls and were intently watching the Oldest

Dragon they had ever seen. Perhaps they could have thought-merged to discover exactly what he was thinking. But of course they wouldn't. It would be too much like intruding. *"And,"* thought one of them, *"I just wouldn't want to get singed for trying!"*

The thought caught the attention of the Oldest Dragon and, as if he had forgotten they were all there (which of course he had not) he cleared his throat and said, "Well, yes, yes there… or rather **here** you all are!" He sat himself down in the space that was obviously his sitting place, as the colors and shaping of the wall fit him exactly.

*"I want to be able to create **that** one day,"* thought-spoke Mothan. To which the Oldest Dragon responded aloud, "And so you shall, my dear young dragon! So you shall. But first, we have other topics to address." He looked to the others who each held a question or two (or twenty) in their minds. "And questions! Yes, we have many –- perhaps **all** the questions to answer!"

The Oldest Dragon's demeanor changed to be more intent; and when it did, the seven felt the expanded energy and adjusted their manner of communication and reception so that nothing, absolutely nothing would slip by unnoticed. In one moment they had thought-merged and expanded, aligned their intent, and opened for the birthing adventure.

The Oldest Dragon was impressed –- again –- with their abilities and without speaking that fact, he expressed it through the vibrations within the chamber. They felt his admiration for who they were together. It was a good way to begin.

CHAPTER THIRTEEN

FAIRIES!

There were no formalities to observe — never had been. The Oldest Dragon[38] continued right where he had paused in his speaking with Kleeana and Mothan.

"Zog and Zoanna are residing separate from and also within several sections of the Timeline." The seven were more than ready to hear.

"I suppose I should tell you," the Old One paused a moment, "that in the telling we will change everything. Everything." He waited for a response. It came from Brianna.

"I've been studying...." The others smiled at her more-than-familiar opening words. Their familiarity with her manner of speaking felt good, felt comfortable. "Well I *have* been studying — about the beginnings of our Dragon Eras, and it seems to me that when the elder dragons spoke their stories before the Kloan, the Kloan changed. It appears that nearly everyone experienced increased abilities and awarenesses. It seems like they became...," she searched for the right word.

The Old One finished her statement, "They became more awake."

"Exactly what does that mean?" jumped in Treiga.

"Well," said the Old One, "that is exactly what we're getting to."

---

38 <u>Oldest Dragon</u>: Literally the oldest dragon. That fact unknown to the seven, they refer to him as Old One, Sir, or Mehentuknen.

Treiga was never anxious for an answer. He knew it would come just at the right moment. Not everyone in the Kloan appreciated Treiga's natural ability to let the moment unfold. Nonetheless, his long-time compatriots, Karthentonen, Meteranke, Brianna, and Fornaign not only admired what Treiga brought to any gathering, but they also depended upon and merged with his allowing. It seemed to enhance their abilities to receive and understand.

The Oldest Dragon began what was later called The Truth Telling in the written histories and within the stories all dragons spoke aloud to their inglets as they prepared to enter Nacta[39].

"In all times and living upon the land, dragons have gathered together and formed a Floggen and then a Kloan. We are beings who have, since more than one of us resided upon the land, not only enjoyed the camaraderie of each other, but more so, have reveled in the discoveries of all that we can experience when united in purpose and when thought-merged."

Karthentonen made a note to ask at the fitting moment about the *more than one of us. Was this old dragon the one, the only one who had always resided upon the land? The Oldest Dragon?*

The Old One felt Karthentonen's wondering. *This is moving along perfectly,* thought the Old One to himself.

"Each Floggen," he continued to the wide-open-ready-to-receive dragons leaning against his chamber walls, "lived and enjoyed their own natural rhythm, and during Kloan Gatherings, shared their adventures, learnings, and understandings.

"When they had become accustomed to their manner of living, of residing upon the land, there began to develop a settling into the comfort of such living." He looked to the adventurers who sat before him. "Even though journeys and further explorations awaited them, their contentment held them within it and, in a manner of speaking, lulled them to sleep."

It was Fornaign who sent the first thought-spoken question to the Old One: *Yet, sir, the sleep was a beneficial manner, wasn't it?*

---

39 <u>Nacta</u>: Adult dragon living.

The Old One continued, incorporating the answer to Fornaign's question. "Yes, within the comfort and seeming sleep, the dragons... er, **we** thrived. Our inglets grew healthy and strong, and their abilities to manage their physical realms developed until they were, as Nactas, masterfully skilled at creating within the physical and partnering with the land[40].

"And it was such partnering that caught the attention of first the fairies and then the gnomes, who both decided to not only make themselves known to us, but also began to participate in the partnering.

"Some of the dragons were intrigued with what partnering with especially the fairies could bring, and they sought out adventures and journeys. The fairies gladly introduced them to realms beyond the physical.

"When those dragons then returned from such adventures, their manner of relating to the physical necessarily had changed. They found that within their regular steppings upon the land, they perceived more than the physical — while the dragons who had not journeyed with the fairies beyond the physical, did not seem to see, to know, to perceive anything more than the physical."

The Old One directed his next statement toward Fornaign. "As they walked among their fellow dragons, among their beloved families, it appeared that many were asleep."

Mothan had never withheld his speaking or thought-mergings and his youthful exuberance spilled forth through both manners of communicating. "That's like the dragons in the Dream State! They don't seem to know what's going on — or even that something IS going on!"

"But Mothan," responded Kleeana, "our dragons in the Dream State *have* experienced non-physical awareness — at least in the past they have."

Fornaign spoke next, "What we're calling the Dream or Sleep State seems to be something a little different. From what I've

---

40 Partnering with the land: The land of itself fulfilled its own needs within its rhythm of flourishing and completing that flourishing to dissolve back into its own self. Through partnership, the dragons lived within the natural cycles of the land and that which grew from and returned to it.

discovered," he hesitated for a moment, wondering if it was appropriate to display his own discoveries during the Old One's speaking. Detecting no obstruction to what he wanted to show them, he flashed the image of his objective view of the dragons in the Dream State.

The other six welcomed Fornaign's well-developed abilities in objective viewing and easily received his images -- as they had so many times in their gatherings at the Neecha. *Now we're really cooking!* thought Brianna.

The Old One loved them. They were easy to love. *And their willingness to be open yet discerning might just be enough this time,* he thought.

"You see," said Fornaign, as he projected a soft light on the Dream State, "there they are -- going about their living in a seemingly regular way." Then he projected another soft light upon a gathering, the Kloan Gathering that appeared to be frozen in place. "Now here -- if you'll look closer, you'll see -- here the same dragons are again! And I could show you more."

"But my point is," said Treiga as he released the images, "I think what's going on now is more about Timeline."

Karthentonen joined in, "Even though within more than one of the Timeline locations it appears that there exists a Sleep State, a...," he paused just long enough for Brianna to interject, "An unknowing. That's what's similar to what... er," she looked to the Old One, "What are we to call you, Sir?"

"Whatever you call me would be appropriate," said the Old One." He liked the familiarity of their communications.

"Well," continued Brianna, "the unknowing is what's similar to what our... *Mehentuknen*" -- she liked the word as it came to her, and although it had never been used to describe this kind of telling, it did seem to fit after all. Brianna smiled at the Old One and then continued, "Similar to what our Mehentuknen is referring to. That is, the dragons who hadn't enjoyed the non-physical journeys with the fairies simply didn't know -- about any of that. Is that right, Sir?"

"You are absolutely correct," the Old One turned his benevolent gaze to all seven. "In truth, you are all correct. Mothan, you are right about recognizing the Dream State of your Kloan. And Fornaign, you are especially correct in recognizing a Timeline... well, we'll call it a *fold* for now." The word perked the seven's united interest, but the Old One stilled their mounting questions by continuing with, "You are especially correct, Fornaign, in discerning the different Timeline goings on -- the result of the fold -- AND" he emphasized the word *and*, "we will get to that and much more. We'll get to it all."

"But for now," chimed in Brianna, "we're talking about those beginning dragons."

The Old One heard Treiga's quiet thought to himself, *humm... if there's a fold in the Timeline, are the beginning dragons now also the current dragons?*

"We are, for the moment," continued the Old One, "speaking of the awarenesses of those dragons who had journeyed with the fairies beyond the physical. And we are speaking of how they began to realize that the general populace of their dragon community, their Floggen, was," he nodded to Brianna, "unknowing or asleep to such possibilities."

"Please continue, Mehent..." Kleeana stumbled just a little over the word, and when the entire seven embraced the title and extended the meaning, the word easily flowed from her, "Please continue, Mehentuknen."

The Old One did continue, while remarking to himself that all seven had accepted the format of a Mehentuk, with its telling, its objective viewing, and the possibilities of all the choices including Ala-Kleeha and Myo-Neela.

"The dragons went to the fairies," he gifted them with the vision of those times, "and asked what to do about the apparent sleep of their dragon families. Of course, fairies don't participate in such queries — not because of a choice not to, but more that they really don't see separation -- even within the difference between asleep and awake. Which, of course, also brought the dragons to the conclusion that it was neither correct nor incorrect to speak to their Floggen concerning their adventures. They did, then, decide to tell them."

"That's how it began," Brianna whispered her realization. She thought-spoke to her friend, Treiga, *This should be written in the histories.* To which he responded, *And maybe you'll be the one to write it there, to write all of this there!*

The Old One approved even without the need of approval.

"Then what did they do?" insisted Mothan.

"They called for a Kloan Gathering," replied the Old One.

"Wow! They didn't start small, did they?" Mothan expressed his delight in the dragons' choice.

"They wanted all the dragons to hear what they had to say — all at the same time, that is," the Old One confirmed.

"What happened?" Mothan's hunger for the telling actually spoke for all of them, and even Treiga could feel the Truth building not only within the chamber but within his own heart.

"Well, it's quite simple," said the Old One, adjusting the patterns of his chamber walls to accommodate not only this slight speaking but also the conclusions and awarenesses that would follow. "The Kloan did gather, as it was their usual response to a call." Again he projected the image of the long ago gathering, though this time the image formed in the center of the chamber.

There before them was a great chamber, different from the one Mutchiat contained in that the entire dome contained an uncountable amount of quite curious fairies who emanated a myriad of colors across the ceiling of the cavern.

The Dragon Representatives were seated in a circle on the edges of the great cavern's spacious room, and in the center stood several dragons. Brianna counted twelve, and thought-spoke, *Only twelve. There were only twelve of them.* A response floated to her, *And we are only seven.* Brianna added, *with a Mehentuknen!*

The Old One allowed the vision of the long-ago gathering to tell the story:

The Kloan settled and waited for the purpose of the gathering to be revealed. Although never before had a group called for a gathering, they weren't surprised or anxious. They simply waited as they always had.

One of the twelve moved forward and stepped up and onto the large platform the twelve had created specifically for the gathering. Again, the Kloan had noticed the platform and, although it had never before been in the center of their great cavern, they unsuspectingly agreed that it added to the décor and indeed one day might be quite useful.

From the platform, the one of the twelve began to speak to them, opening the gathering in their usual manner:

"Greetings all dragons! Greetings Representatives! And greetings to the Floggen of all Representatives. What a great gathering are we within this great cavern!" They all settled back against the cavern wall and waited to hear the next words.

That the dragon standing on the platform veered from their usual listing of Floggen talents didn't disturb or excite them. They had no reason to be anything but comfortably waiting.

"There are a few of us," the dragon turned to acknowledge the remaining eleven dragons who continued to stand in the center of the cavern rather than sit along the encircling wall. "There are a few of us," he continued, "who have been experiencing something a little different." He looked around the cavern at his wonderful Dragon Representatives. "Different from what we had been experiencing and different from anything you are as yet aware of."

Some of the Representatives stirred and sat more upright.

"We hadn't gathered together… yet," he nodded again at his eleven compatriots, "we all simply had a similar interest. And we individually followed that interest."

One of the Dragon Representatives who had sat more erect spoke out, "What was the similar interest?"

It was what the twelve had hoped would happen. Although a Representative had never informally spoken out at a Kloan Gathering, it seemed nothing could contain his question. The Gathering stirred again. Some were beginning to feel a little disturbed, while others felt their dormant curiosity sparked to take notice.

The dragon responded with such elation at speaking their secret aloud at a Kloan Gathering, that he had to repeat it twice.

"Fairies! We became interested in the fairies! And we began to meet with them!"

A rumble of words echoed within the cavern as Dragon Representatives speculated to each other what *meeting with the fairies* could mean.

"Wait," the excited dragon held up his clawed hand, "There's more — much more!"

The rumbling increased until first one, then two, and finally a third Dragon Representative stood and breathed their bright orange, fiery breath. The sight of their fire stilled the entire gathering — except for one. Another of the Representatives spoke out, staring at his three fellow Representatives, "What are you doing? What is going on?"

The three who had breathed their fire didn't pause for one moment, neither did they answer the questions. They not only walked to the center of the cavern, but also walked directly to the speaker. Without hesitation the three embraced him with their smoke-filled shrills. "We are like you!" one exclaimed. "We thought there were only three of us," spoke another. The third, looking at the eleven asked, "May we join you?" One of the eleven softly said, "It seems you already have!"

The twelve became fifteen, the rumbling increased and again the one Representative demanded, "What is going on!?" He bellowed his insistence, "I, for one, want to know!"

Silence. The cavern remained silent. Again they waited. They had no reason to believe that the answer would not come. It did come.

"That is exactly why we are here," spoke the dragon of the now fifteen, "to tell you what has been going on for us."

A second dragon from the original twelve stepped forth and motioned to the speaker, who returned to their small group. "We have a story to tell," he began, "and I will tell it right now."

Not even a trickle of smoke could be seen. They were ready to hear.

"We each individually went to the fairies who had been among us all." Although all might have nodded 'yes,' they were more intent on hearing what was being said. "As I spoke with them, they began to show me different things. I believe the first that they showed me were the lights in the hills." He looked around the cavern at them. "I know some of you have also seen the lights in the hills. The fairies took me to those lights. The lights swirled and turned as we came upon them. Then, without my expecting them to, the fairies surprised me by flying right toward the swirling!"

Not one word, rumble, whisper. They all continued to listen.

"Then they motioned me to follow them." He looked around the still cavern. "And I did!! Into the swirling!"

Dumfounded. The majority, if not all of the Representatives sat dumfounded.

"It felt great!" he continued.

One dragon from the astonished gathering spoke aloud, "What was it like?"

A Representative beside him chimed in, "And what was on the other side?"

First one of the fifteen and then another stepped forward to give his accounting of his adventure with the fairies:

"It felt almost like stepping through our great waterfall," said one.

"And the colors seemed to be around me and inside of me at the same time," exclaimed another.

"The sounds are now what I call 'Fairy Songs' and I always feel like... Well, like I've been made new –- if you know what I mean."

"On the other side, as you have asked, is nothing like our world here. It's... it's more like the clouds in the sky."

"That's true," another of the fifteen added, "until you ask a question and the answer appears before you." His enthusiasm spilled forth in his telling, "Like when I asked what I could do, where I could go from there -– what appeared was a picture, a view of here, where we all live. I could see our land and our living on the land. I could even see back to when we first came to the land."

Each one continued to spill forth descriptions of their experiences through what they began to call Fairy Portals. The fairies at the dome of the great cavern breathed love upon the still amazed Representatives. Although not really heard, the fairies also continued to softly sing their songs.

● ● ● ● ●

The Old One allowed the vision to dissipate. "Some of those Representatives became so enthralled with what they heard that they asked the fairies to come to them. And others remained stunned — as if what they heard couldn't find a place inside of their knowing. After a time, those ones hardly remembered the gathering at all."

Kleeana was the first to speak, "But some did hear. Some did wake up."

"But," asked Treiga, "was it really waking up? Were the others really asleep? Or were they simply maintaining their realm?"

"That's a good question," said Karthentonen as he adjusted his body to a more upright position. "When we've journeyed to other realms together, sometimes one of us remains totally focused on that realm, which frees the rest of us to explore within it. That doesn't mean that the one who is focused is asleep."

"Kar, not to dispute what you're saying," Meteranke was the first to stand and begin walking within the adjusting chamber, "but in a sense, the one focused *is* asleep to the discoveries of the others. I know I am when I'm the one to focus." He paused in this pacing. "It's only when we thought-merge later that I receive the information on the realm. And," he pointed one clawed finger upward, "that's why we unofficially take turns acting as focus."

The Old One stood, motioning Karthentonen to sit, "One pacing dragon is enough!" The Old One took long strides and then turned to set his piercing eyes on the seven. "Isn't it that we've decided that the sleep or Dream State is undesirable? Why?" He looked to each and then answered his own question, "Because we can't see the purpose it?"

"Well, if there's a purpose," spoke Mothan innocently, "then why are we here? Why did those fifteen speak to their Kloan? Like that one dragon asked, 'What's going on?'"

The Old One answered, "It happens when it's time for change. When the purposes are complete."

"But how do we know that?" insisted Mothan. "If you'll excuse the words, sir, it can't be just because you say so."

The Old One loved this young one. "Yes, it's true. Nothing is complete because I — or any one dragon — say so. Change happens when the number of awake dragons increases and the telling of the Truth can not only be heard but can be absorbed, integrated, and then becomes part of the manner of living. Then the Sleep or Dream State is released, is no more."

"But," said Brianna, "as someone said, we are only seven. That's hardly a majority."

"It doesn't take a majority to participate within the change," said the Old One, "And, we are not the only ones speaking the Truth. There are others."

Now he had their full awakened, give-me-more attention. They were right where he hoped they would be.

CHAPTER FOURTEEN

ILLUSIONARY PEAKS AND GNOMES

"There are others?" Brianna's feeling of relief spread through the group. "Like the three who thought they were the only ones learning with the fairies," she concluded, "I suppose we've all thought that we were the only ones — that is, until we meet the others."

"And," remembered Kleeana, "that's how Mothan and I felt until we discovered your gathering at the Neecha." She smiled shyly at the five. "Discovering that we weren't alone in being able to not only recognize the Dream State but be able to stay awake and not fall into it... well, that was the greatest!" She added, "And that's why we just had to keep listening in to your gatherings. We didn't want to be alone any more."

"Well," Mothan's honesty moved him to speak too, "it's true that we didn't want to be alone, but we also wanted to see what you would do about your discoveries."

They all remembered the effects of the Dream State and of the pounding on the portal to their Neecha. Mothan continued, "It seems that, for some reason, the Dream State is quite powerful." He turned to the Old One, "Why is that, Sir? Why is it so powerful?"

Brianna couldn't help but add to Mothan's questions. "It seems to me that the Truth, the total knowing would be... well, would be the *most* powerful," she concluded and asked all in the same breath, "and if it *is*, then why *is* the Dream Sate so powerful?" She looked to Mothan and then thought she would add just one more question, but instead it was as if a dam broke. "And IF all of that that is true, and the purposes ARE complete, as you said, well... what were the purposes of the Dream State? Of the state of comfort with the first dragons? And, what will happen to those dragons who are in the Dream State? And, what DID happen to those first dragons who couldn't hear even the adventures with the fairies? And, if they were the FIRST dragons, are we the second? Or third dragons — since this is the third era? And...."

When she looked up from the floor of the chamber and into the faces of her friends, she realized just how many questions had spilled out. She shrugged her shoulders, "Well, I want to know... I want to know it all!"

The Old One spoke softly, gathering the questions and the disseminating energies to him. He would feed that energy back to them transformed and whole. The answers would begin to satiate their search for the Truth, and then... *well, we'll see*, he thought to himself, *we'll see how they do*.

"I suppose," the Old One began, "that we could agree that one question leads to another and then yet another, AND the questions you have asked," he looked at Brianna and then Mothan, "are, for this moment, a good place to begin!"

All seven sat quietly, waiting for the answers. Like the first dragons, they had no reason to believe that the answers would not come. And, unlike the first dragons, the seven were awake and aware, and prepared to experience whatever might occur within the Telling of the Truth.

"I'll continue a little more with the telling of the first dragons," said the Old One, "and then we'll get to our present — *seeming* present — circumstances and the questions about power."

He didn't project a scene from long ago, but instead spoke simply, almost matter-of-factly. "As I have said, after the Kloan Gathering concerning what the fairy realms had to offer, there were a few — quite a few — dragons who decided to ask if they could participate with the fairies. Some waited a time, but eventually their curiosity led them, too, toward the unknown and eventually to those realms and portals.

"The manner of living upon the land changed — even for those dragons who could not or would not allow themselves to explore beyond the physical. How did it change for them? That's easy. The explorers began to carry within themselves and consequently around themselves, a certain energy, an excitement, an expectancy for more — more adventures, more discoveries, more delight in uncovering their own sleep and awakening to the known.

"Even those dragons who didn't enter the explorations experienced a surge in their energies and began to participate within their own lives in a way that eventually engendered a certain expectancy, a certain delight in a higher level of fulfillment. Oh, their days were filled with the same rhythms and participations of old, but their *manner* of experiencing those rhythms had changed.

"In that way, their Sleep State changed and the purposes became complete: there had been established a peaceful manner of living upon the land.

"And it was upon that peaceful, content fulfillment-of-purpose, upon the old manner of living that the new, awakened state for some, and awakening state for others *could* begin to become the next regular rhythm — a rhythm that would incorporate peace, fulfillment, *and* a delight in exploration and discovery. You see, exploration upon the foundation of peace gives the explorer a precious gift: an open mind. And that was the foundation that the first dragons then gifted to those who would follow — and eventually to you, my dear seven."

He let them absorb the first phase within their Sector of Learning. They knew to allow the knowing to fill them. Thought-merging enhanced their understanding of the Old One's speaking. As would every Mehentuknen, his speaking had begun gently, easing them toward the awarenesses that would change them beyond what they could possibly expect. *They are doing well*, he thought, *quite well*.

They didn't know how much time had transpired. They were, however, called from their thought-merging to receive the next telling – called by the word *time*.

"Now if you remember," continued the Old One, "one of the first dragons who spoke to the Kloan mentioned a viewing of their current living upon the land; and in fact, he said that he could see back to when they first arrived. That, of course, was the beginning of an objective viewing of the Timeline. And that's just what we'll continue with. Yet, rather than my telling you everything, we will travel the Timeline together."

He felt their excitement build and chuckled to himself that they were, without a doubt, explorers.

Brianna had explored the Timeline through her studies of their histories, but she had never positioned herself to be viewing the actual Timeline.

Karthentonen and Fornaign had been given glimpses of the Timeline when the wizards determined such a viewing would be helpful in understanding the current realm into which they had journeyed. And, although they had individually and together explored many realms, they too had not viewed the actual Timeline.

Meteranke had received flashes of the Timeline within his well-developed visioning capabilities. Those flashes had always left him hungry for more.

Treiga was the only one of the five who had actually been successful at not only journeying through numerous realms and portals, but who had been gifted by the wizards to view that portion of the Timeline as it related to the weaving together of those realms, and to that portion of the Timeline which held the Dream State.

They had all five viewed the oncoming Neekontuk in what they finally concluded to be a realm and, therefore, separate from Timeline cause and effect. However, even that viewing was not quite the expanse of the *entire* Timeline. It was that expanse that demanded to be seen.

Mothan could hardly contain his excitement with just hearing the word *Timeline* and *exploration* used in the description of their next event. He had a hidden, lingering agenda: he wanted to find his mother... and then there was Zog.

Kleeana, the least suspected to have had Timeline experience, had already thought-merged with her Mehentuknen, as she affectionately called the Old One, and flashed her viewing: that section of the Timeline where the Neekontuk raged, and where her father had all but disappeared. The Old One was surprised at Kleeana's experience and would have invited her to tell the others. Yet within her thought-merge was a fear of returning to that section again. She needed comfort more than praise. He embraced her within their thought-merge, and breathed within it a comforting breath of love and gentleness. *Don't worry*, he said to Kleeana, *we'll do this together*. The others didn't detect their shielded communication.

"Now," the Old One prepared them for their Experiential Learning Sector, "there's nothing difficult about all of this." Although each one of the seven had never shied away from the difficult, they liked the sound of this beginning. "We'll start with the same viewing that dragon of long ago began with." He could feel Mothan especially wanting to surge ahead, to view the entire picture, the *entire* Timeline. And, like his father had, he was already preparing to look into the future.

The Old One answered Mothan's wanting. "We're beginning with the past for a number of reasons. Mainly to gather an understanding of those times which have become the foundation of our living today. Perhaps," he continued in a casual manner, even though what he would say next would intimate anything but the casual, "Perhaps," he repeated, "we will have the opportunity to enter into the Timeline itself -- in several places -- and be able to change our understanding to knowing. Experience!" he emphasized the word. "Experience is the key, dear adventurers! The key to knowing!"

They were ready -- more than ready. Yet the Old One added the answer to Mothan's wanting. "I have placed a boundary, a block if you will, to assist you, to assist us in remaining within the selected section of time." He felt Mothan squirm a little, and responded to it, "Remember, the boundaries aren't meant to be constraints! They are definitely to assist you into the entire experience.

"Why, you didn't begin flying or using your wings by climbing to the top of Mutchiat and jumping off!!"

All seven dragons chuckled a little, as it was known that no one *could* climb to the top of Mutchiat, that it was *only* accessible by flight. And, only the most experienced in flight could maneuver through the crosscurrents and illusionary peaks placed there by the gnomes.[41]

The Old One stood, and at the same time motioned the seven to stand. "I'm certain," the twinkle in his piercing eyes danced at them, "that there will be enough surprises within this adventure — enough for even you, Mothan!" It was the first time that Mothan had ever blushed, much to his own surprise. The entire experience endeared him even more to the six — and especially to Brianna.

The Old One leaned back his big head and laughed loudly, fully. While he laughed, a swirling began to occur and as it increased in momentum, the seven became aware that the swirling was located at the top of the chamber. Before they could look upward to examine it, however, the Old One opened his fans with such swiftness that each of the seven was startled into heightened awareness.

Balls of white light charged at the swirling at the top of the chamber. Now they couldn't take their eyes off of the swirling as it spun itself open, open to the sky of their land.

"Well," said the Old One, as his chamber expanded to nearly the size of the cavern within Mutchiat, "What are we waiting for?" His amazing wings expanded and in one waft he had flown out of the opening. Without a moment's hesitation, each of the

---

41 <u>Illusionary Peaks around Mutchiat</u>: The gnomes, it was supposed – as not many had built an intimate relationship with the gnomes – were of the land itself and could, at their own deciding, summon the land to rise and take a particular form. In a like manner, they also could summon the image of a form, such as the illusionary peaks around Mutchiat.

It was assumed that the illusionary peaks were created to protect Mutchiat from curiosity-seekers, and would therefore only allow those who were ready for the other-realm adventures accessible only through the portals at the peak. Some also believed that the gnomes simply did not enjoy a lot of traffic near one of their favorite spots.

seven lifted their wings. Seven dragons, with the strength of who they were pulsating within their wings, and with the love of adventure filling their hearts, flew away from the chamber and toward the Oldest Dragon, their beloved Mehentuknen, as he led them to the peak of the great Mutchiat.

He was already proud of them, and as they began to come closer, to catch up to his flight, he turned and made a wide circle around them all. Swooping, turning and twisting, he flew with such precision that they all ached to be able to do the same.

As they flew with their full strength, he held himself as if in mid-flight, paused before them. No matter how hard they tried, they couldn't catch up to him. "Bravo!" he bellowed. Then in a flash he turned and flew. They heard his voice as it sang over the top of his amazing green gossamers, "Onward, dragons, onward!"

They felt a surge within their own strength, *perhaps because of his call*, they uniformly thought. Yet it was the adventure itself that spurred them to already use abilities they didn't know they had. It was a freedom greater than any adventure, this soaring and stretching of their wings, flying with the most agile, adept, oldest dragon they had ever seen. It was almost too good to be true! But it was true -- and very real.

When Mutchiat came into sight, the Old One flew higher and motioned them to follow. He waited as they came to him. Then he raised his great wings and, just as he was to waft them, leaned back a little and turned his gossamers to still the waft. When he brought down his great wings, the gossamers held the stroke of air. He remained paused in mid-air. Twice. He demonstrated the movement twice for them. Each one copied what he had done. It took a little more than twice to perfect the movement, but as first one and then another did, it was only a matter of thought-merging before all seven were also suspended in mid-air. It was easy, they thought, more than easy -- like floating without effort.

He didn't stop to praise them, but continued. "If we approach Mutchiat from up here, we can easily see the illusionary peaks." He looked to each of their eager dragon faces. "That's necessary. Dodging illusionary peaks can place you in the currents created to bring you down." Again he turned in such a swift manner that, if they had not been staring directly at him, they might have thought the Old One had disappeared from in front of them and reappeared a half a sector ahead of them. "Follow me," he called back to them. He didn't need to call twice.

There it was beneath them, the great peak of Mutchiat. Of all seven, Meteranke was the only one who had developed the strength to even approach the magnificent mountain. He had seen the illusionary peaks then, and now again here they were before him. Their illusion loomed and invited them to dip and swerve to avoid them. Again the Old One called out, "This way! Follow me!" He turned more slowly so that they could see, and placing their wings in the same position he held his, they followed one after the other. They wanted to swerve lest they hit their wings. "They're illusions! Don't look at them!" he ordered. "Look at me!"

The Old One raised his great wings — straight up and then back. He seemed to be falling — faster and faster! "Do it!" he bellowed. They did. All together at the same time. Seven magnificent, glowing dragons lifted their wings as far back as they could reach. They fell faster, faster, faster. "Hold on!" The Old One commanded, "Hold on!"

It was a quick drop, seeming to take place in one second. And it was a long drop, each one wondering just how long they could maintain. Yet they did. They fell into the opening at the peak. He was proud of them — more than proud. When the warmth of the mountain brushed against their extended bodies, each one began to relax a little. Mutchiat was like that. It always took care of those who entered its peak.

The way to the cavern in the peak was a gentle glide through a softly lit tunnel. As each one of the seven entered the tunnel, none of the others could be seen. Neither was the Old One in sight. Contrary to what might be supposed, such a solitary experience was comforting, and each one breathed in the loving embrace of the Peak of Mutchiat.

The glide led them to the upper chamber, where the Old One's beaming pride greeted them. Meteranke was the last to appear from the tunnel. The Old One gave him a knowing glance. Meteranke had waited to be sure they weren't followed. *The others needn't know for now*, the knowing glance said. Meteranke's barely discernable nod agreed.

"Bravo! Bravo to you!" applauded the Old One. "Now you each know how to enter the Great Peak of Mutchiat!" He allowed his gaze to rest briefly upon each one.

"Sir," Brianna asked the question all seven wondered, "does that mean we could come here on our own?" She hesitated for a moment and then added, "Could I come here on my own?"

The Old One smiled. "And what do you think? Of course you can!" His look shifted to brooding and in a quieter voice he continued, "But after our adventures, everything will be changed. I don't know if you'll even want to. Humm...." He slapped his leg and delivered his best flow of bright red flame. "Well! Best we get on with it, young ones, best we move on!" He glanced once more, quickly, at Meteranke.

The Old One motioned to the side of the chamber where Brianna and Kleeana were standing. The wall moved slowly, turning itself into a portal. Surprised, both dragons jumped back a little to allow the movement.

"Wow!" exclaimed Mothan, "how did you do that?"

The Old One again nodded to Meteranke, who surprised them all with, "It's known that the Peak of Mutchiat contains the patterns within all portals. Those patterns," he explained, "are of course also within our wedge wings." Brianna wondered how Meteranke knew. She'd never come across the Portals of Mutchiat in her research.

Meteranke felt her wondering and responded with, "Do you remember long ago when we first began to meet together? I spoke of the difference between *deciding* and *determining*. Well," he turned toward Brianna and bowed deeply. The gesture brought a smile to her face. The exchange between the two filled the entire chamber with light, and the entire group's delight in the occurrence only augmented the light. Their dragon bodies relaxed just a little more.

Meteranke continued, "I had determined, if you remember, to meet the wizards and to communicate with them. I directed my determining away from myself. I don't know why I did that," he reflected. "I just did it -- with great determination -- and the result was that a portal opened up before me, a portal to the wizards. It had worked!" Meteranke's dragon body glowed with the success of his determining.

"I eventually asked them if there could be another location where such determining might benefit me. They laughed and said unanimously that the Peak Chamber *required* such determining. I didn't know what they were laughing about at the time. I guess it was that I wasn't ready to come here, to make it here. Anyway, that's all I know about this chamber," he looked around the expanse, at his friends, "and about the calling forth of a portal."

"Quite right," said the Old One. "Quite right. And the portal we have determined to appear is the portal to Timeline viewing -- the beginnings."

He didn't explain further about the calling to appear of portals. Instead, he stepped right through the moving portal, saying as he disappeared, "Are you coming?" They did.

Each dragon, one after the other, stepped into the portal.

"It is like moving through a waterfall," said Brianna as she remembered the description given at the Fairy Kloan Gathering -- the name she would give the long-ago gathering when she wrote their histories.

Of the two remaining, Meteranke motioned Mothan to go. Without hesitation, Mothan too stepped into the portal. He thought this portal would be like the wizard portals he had so often journeyed through. But it was not. And just as he was thinking that it seemed to be taking quite a long time, a dragon arm extended itself into the whirling portal and a clawed hand grabbed onto him! Now the swirling rushed past him until finally, with a loud popping noise, he emerged from the portal.

"Wow!" Mothan adjusted himself to be standing right side up and asked, "Did, did that happen to all of you? Or, am I the only one who had to be pulled out?"

Before any could answer, Meteranke stepped out of the portal. Mothan saw and looked to the group, "I AM the only one, aren't I!"

It was Fornaign who stepped up to relieve Mothan of his misery. "No, I'm afraid you're wrong this time, Mothan. ALL of us," he stressed the word *all*, "had to be pulled from the portal."

"Oh," sighed Mothan, letting himself feel happy about the fact.

"Well," said Fornaign as he looked to his long-time friend. "All except Meteranke here!" He gave Meteranke a slight nudge. "How did you do that?"

Meteranke was about to respond when the Old One stepped forward. "It takes determining!" It felt good, thought Meteranke, to have his ability recognized. The Old One continued, "It's something you all would do well to learn."

"But sir," began Brianna, "how would I know that it would take determining to go through the portal?"

"Let's ask Meteranke," responded the Old One. "How did you know it would take determining to go through the Portal to the Timeline?"

Meteranke looked from his friends to the Old One, and then back to his friends again. "Actually, I didn't know."

"Exactly!" The Old One had surprised them again. "Determining is not something that is done on special occasions. It's, it's a way of living. Once you use your determining for one purpose, you will automatically use it for everything."

"You see," he waved a vision before them, "here you all are, ready to enter the portal." They all saw themselves. "It's true," he continued, "you entered with the air of adventurers. Yet, that's just it. You *entered*.

"No one — with the exception of Meteranke — **determined** to **go through** the Portal, through to the beginning of the Timeline.

"Now don't think you've done something wrong. You haven't. In fact," he added, "you can't do anything wrong! It's your adventure."

"But sir," insisted Brianna, "I still don't know what you mean by *determining as a way of living*.

"Of course you don't, my dear!" The Old One motioned to her. "Come over here to this portal. Brianna quickly stood in the exact spot she landed on when the Old One had pulled her out.

"Now," he said, "determine to yourself that you are going to go through this portal to the chamber in the Peak. **Determine that you will** and send that energy ahead of you."

Brianna determined with all her strength to do just that. The energy began to build.

"Good," said the Old One. "Send that energy ahead of you and go — go right now into the chamber!"

Like a flash, Brianna shot forward, through the portal. In the next moment she popped back to where they all were. "I did it!" she bragged, delighted in her own accomplishment. "Watch this!" She disappeared and then quickly reappeared — not once or twice, but many many times. The last time she returned and remained with them. The strange look on her face told the Old One what had happened.

"Gnomes!" Brianna whispered. "The gnomes appeared and asked me what I thought I was doing."

"And what did you tell them?" asked Karthentonen.

"I told them I was practicing determining," beamed Brianna.

"Then what happened," asked Treiga, even though he thought he could guess what had happened.

"Umm," Brianna hesitated and then admitted, "They told me I'd better determine myself right back through... that it appeared that I had it practiced well enough." She smiled again and then added, "They said..." she tried to make her dragon voice sound like the gnome's serious voice, "And stay there! There are others, you know, waiting to use this chamber!"

They all laughed loudly at Brianna's imitation. That is, until the head of a gnome poked it's way through the portal. "Very funny," he said. "Now are you all going to move, or are you planning to hold a meeting here?"

Lest they all burst out laughing at the gnome's references, the Old One stepped forward saying, "Now Garf, we'll be out of here before you can count to one hundred."

The gnome gave the Old One as mean a look as he could muster and then disappeared!

The Old One turned to the seven and whispered, "Gnomes can't count! Don't need to. They are always in the present moment." He chuckled to himself; "I've never seen anyone get so rattled as Garf when he has to wait. Throws him off kilter for only a few minutes." The Old One shook his head. "But because he's always in the moment, he thinks he's permanently off kilter — which of course he's not. Why, he's back to his old grumpy self right now. You can count on it!"

The seven enjoyed watching their Old One mutter to himself about the very strange gnome. "We'd better get on with our adventure," he said without a further mention of Garf. "We'll find another portal or circumstance for you all to practice determining. Once you've got it," he winked at Brianna, "then life without it is like... like sleep!"

CHAPTER FIFTEEN

THEY ARE WATER DRAGONS!!

Even as the Old One led the seven toward that section where the first dragons resided upon the land, a movement visibly rippled through the entire expanse of the Timeline just beneath their viewing. Although none of the seven knew quite what to expect in the Timeline journey, the ripple seemed unnatural, disturbing. Alarm brought them to full alert.

Without hesitation, Meteranke turned and, with Fornaign close behind, sped toward the ripple. The Old One would have called them back had not the second and then third ripple moved the Timeline like the waves on the sea. Astounded. He was more than astounded!

Through its causes and effects, the immensity of the Timeline had certainly surprised more than one dragon and Meteranke and Fornaign were no exception. It stretched beyond their sight with no beginning and no end. Rather than a line, though, they saw that the events of all time were actually streams of energy — flowing and winding around each other — yet flowing.

"Wow, what do you make of that?" asked Fornaign.

"Don't know." Meteranke studied the intertwining streams. Some were multi-colored while others were solid in color. Some brightly lit and some dark. "It's more like a Time-Stream than a Timeline, wouldn't you say?"

Fornaign couldn't take his eyes off of the Time-Stream. "I don't know what I expected, but this sure opens the portals for a whole lot of exploring!" He peered at the intertwining streams. "What IS all of that?"

Meteranke felt his Fornaign's curiosity heighten, as did his own. "I've never seen anything like it. And, For, I've been having a feeling something was about to happen," he confided. For the moment, it seemed the rippling had subsided, that everything was calm. Then a white flash in the distance caught his attention. "Did you see that?"

Fornaign was already charging toward the direction of the flash. The distance was further than where the flash first seemed to appear; and when Meteranke caught up with him, the bright light was no more.

"Where are we? Time-wise, that is?" Fornaign asked. He pointed in the direction of the flash, "Is that the future? Or are we still in the beginning of time?"

"Don't know," answered Meteranke. "Let's have a closer look." They thought they'd fly right down upon the flowing and do just that, but the energy radiating from the Time-Stream was too strong. Wanting a location that would allow an approach, they each flew in a different direction. They planned to meet back at the same location to discuss what their search had discovered.

Meteranke flew toward what he thought was the distant past, but when one of the Streams lit brightly, he took the opportunity to swoop closer. It invited him to descend and, in his turning, fly into the outer essence of the Stream. He would have wondered why this flowing allowed and the other did not, except that the movement within the Stream caught his attention.

He peered at the action and tried to discern exactly what he was seeing. His vision cleared. There were dragons — dragons flying in different directions, as if they were confused and... something.... The realization shot through him. It was fear! They were flying in fear and shouting to each other.

He tried to identify the location. The colors of the land were bright, seemed familiar. That's when he recognized it: the Dream

State, where everyone was usually moving slowly through the paradise-perfect world. *What's happened here?* he whispered to himself. *What happened to cause the Dream to change to... to panic!*

Meteranke flew down the Stream, back a little further in time. Again, the light of the Time-Stream invited a closer look. He saw something... something like a wall, a wall of energy. Unlike the stream, the wall was flowing up and down within itself. On one side of the wall was the disheveled Dream State, and on the other side was a giant wave of raging fire.

His dragon eyes pierced into the density of the wave. He recognized the very slow movement. It was the same wall of fire they'd viewed together in their last visioning at the Neecha. He quickly accessed their vision from his mind and aligned it with the giant wave he was peering into. They were a perfect match! And again! Without a doubt! He recognized Zog's patterns, Zog's call to "gather here."

If that weren't enough, something in the wall of energy was very clear. He didn't stay to examine it further, but turned and sped away. "The Old One has to know about this — right now!"

Meteranke would never leave his friend waiting at a planned rendezvous, but this information needed to be delivered. He pointed one wedge wing toward the location near the intertwined Time-Stream where he and Fornaign planned to meet, and fired a suspended charge of his own patterns. Hopefully Fornaign would interpret the charge and also return to the Old One and the others.

Meteranke's great strength sped him back to report his discovery. Even while his wings folded, he began to speak, "Old One! It's happening now!"

The Old One saw in his immediate thought-merge with Meteranke while he simultaneously heard the words charge forth, "Sir, the wall, the boundaries around the Dream State are dissolving! And the wave!"

The Old One held up one clawed hand. "No more time!" He looked to them all. "Where is Fornaign?"

Meteranke looked for a hint of his friend. "He went in the other direction, sir." He looked over his dragon shoulder again. "I guess that'd be the future, Sir!"

Just as the Old One sent forth a scan, he recognized another scan in place — with familiar encodings. Mothan thought-merged with the Old One. *When I didn't see Fornaign return, I thought I'd scan for him, Sir.* Though Mothan's explanation was true, the Old One knew that more was going on. Mothan didn't hesitate to confess, "Sir, I also sent out a scan for my mother, for Zoanna."

"Leave your scan active, Mothan. You've done nothing I wouldn't have done myself!" the Old One spoke aloud. He turned to the others who were thought-merging with Meteranke to view his experience at the Time-Stream.

"I see it," said Brianna. She gathered more than their focused viewing from the thought-merge with Meteranke, however. *The Streams...,* she tried to remember where she had read of the Streams..., *weren't they first called the breath*? Yet even that awareness surprised her. In truth, she couldn't remember *ever* reading the words *the breath*. Something was happening. Information not previously available to her was flowing into her awareness.

Even as the Old One called them to flight, Brianna looked down the long winding Streams in Meteranke's vision... back and back... into the past. One Neekontuk, two, three.... Three? A ripple delivered itself to her: one... hundred, two... hundred, three... over three hundred Neekontuks?? Over three hundred eras of dragons ending, perishing — and reappearing?!!

The Old One felt Brianna's knowing expand to include nearly the beginning, the appearance of the first dragon. He wafted his wings and called out, "Come with me NOW!" Glancing first at Mothan and then at Brianna, he commanded, "ALL of you! We can do more from another location." As if to stave off any plans to the contrary, he added, as he lifted and pointed his long neck away from the Time-Stream, "This will take all of us!"

• • • • •

Fornaign had searched the Time-Stream for any residue of the bright flash. Instead, he had found the source of the rippling. There, in what he guessed must be the future, the Time-Stream split: some flowed in one direction while other Streams flowed in another, making a V. The V was causing a pause in the flowing, a pause which rippled back through the Time-Stream. "But what is causing that separation?" he asked.

Fornaign might not have been as large a dragon as his friend Meteranke, but his great strength was well-known. As his reputation replayed itself in his mind, he declared aloud, "At least I used to be the strongest in... in *wherever* it was that I lived!" The sounds of his own voice startled him and he used the energy to build his strength. He aimed his determining at the V and fired his entire dragon being at that location. He sped toward the separating Time-Streams.

Hard. Impenetrable. Crashing. Unconscious. The energy emanating from the V would not allow entry.

Were it not for the wizards, Fornaign would have perished. It took a full order of thirteen wizards to gather such a determined dragon and bring him to their healing realm. So scattered was Fornaign's life force that they dared not use their forming and unforming incantations to transport him. Thirteen wizards carried his very large dragon body past the portals of thirty-seven realms and seventeen Sector of Learning Chambers before they arrived at the healing chamber already being prepared for Fornaign.

• • • • •

The Old One was leading the six dragons to a realm he had originally created for their relaxed reflections after Time-Stream viewing. *You just never know exactly why you are creating something*, he reminded himself.

Treiga flew up beside the Old One. "Sir...."

"I know," the Old One said, "I felt it, too, Fornaign."

"Do you think he'll make it, sir?"

"In one way or another..." the Old One looked into Treiga's questioning eyes, "he will."

"Sir?"

"They'll either be able to heal his body, or he'll be one of the youngest Ancient Ones in their realm." The Old One paused a moment to point the direction of their flight to the others. "There's no going back now."

"Sir, *their* realm?"

Treiga was very clear. The Old One appreciated the combination of clarity and balance within the dragon flying at his side. With so much going on, it was a relief to fly together.

"The wizards. Their realm. They've taken Fornaign to one of their healing realms."

"And, *Ancient One*, sir?"

They were nearly to their destination, yet the Old One couldn't avoid giving this sparkling young-but-mature dragon the answer he was seeking. "If they can't bring his body to a healed, whole state, he'll release it."

"But *Ancient*...."

"His consciousness is too expanded for an Ala-Kleeha during these times. He would become an Ancient One — with much... well, much to let go of."

Treiga thought the Old One was going to say, "with much to learn," which also told Treiga that he himself had much to learn. Even though the events were dramatically serious, he chuckled aloud at his awareness.

The Old One caught the wave of Treiga's self-realization and also laughed, and then added, "He has a good chance. His body was accustomed to different stresses and energy pulses — you know, from his anchoring training."

"Oh, right, sir." Treiga wondered if the others felt as he did — that their past together had just become their distant past — and the present... who knew what the next moment would bring? He couldn't help thinking about Fornaign.

The pulsating light ahead of them signaled the realm the Old One had created and was directing them toward. They had left the Time-Stream so swiftly and flown directly until they were actually beginning to feel their dragon strength wane a little. They'd lost all sense of where they were and how to return to the

Time-Stream. The events of the Floggen, the Kloan, the events within the Dream State all seemed to be unfolding without them. It had ever since they discovered that *something* was going on.

They had felt separate from their own dragon families ever since they discovered that the Dream State existed. Ever since they discovered that the home they'd known for their entire dragon lives was nearly frozen in place with their Representatives still at a Kloan meeting, where Zoanna had disappeared before their eyes. And also where the raging fires of the Neekontuk held its giant wave suspended over the mountain range where Mutchiat itself majestically rose. They didn't know how to put it all together or how to understand their part in it all, and not the least was the nagging question of the true identity of the Old One.

They had barely made it through the portal when, without hesitation, they dropped their tired bodies against the chamber walls. The encodings woven within the fabric of the walls embraced them and began to replenish their energies as they slept. It wouldn't be long before they were ready to go again.

The Old One and Treiga sat beside each other with Meteranke giving up trying to make his tired legs pace the length of the chamber. He, too, joined Treiga and the Old One.

Meteranke had his own awarenesses of the condition of his long-time friend, Fornaign, and determined — once his own strength had replenished — to send Fornaign a thought-merge bursting with life force. He hoped that would do it, would bring Fornaign's recovery to a level of maintaining his physical body.

Karthentonen thought-merged with Meteranke just in time to hear the plan to save Fornaign. "If you don't mind," he whispered a slight message to Meteranke, "I'll join you in that plan."

Meteranke smiled at his fellow adventurer. Great! Then either you or I WILL bring him back."

Karthentonen added, "Or both of us together!"

Meteranke felt their united plan slightly ease the tension in his dragon shoulders. *"Still...."* he thought to himself, and continued to go over his own plan. Soon rest called him and even the plan lay still, waiting for the opportunity to be reengaged.

Brianna remained awake just long enough to see that Mothan and Kleeana, who had become her adept flying partners, were settled comfortably. Their closing eyes invited Brianna's to do the same.

The Old One closed his eyes too and activated replenishing patterns within his own body. *There*, he thought as the patterns activated, *while all that is taken care of, I'll....* He sighed deeply as he stretched his scan to have an updated look at what was transpiring not only in the Time-Stream, but every where.

The realm they rested in was created beyond time and the Streams of energy flowing through time. Yet it was the nature of the seeming change that called the Old One to turn from his planned other-realm viewing, and to bring his consciousness to those Streams and the ripple they had all been affected by.

As his consciousness flowed over the Streams, it was at the pre-present Neekontuks that the Old One recognized Brianna's patterns and her determined journey toward what had been written as the past. While her body rested and replenished itself, Brianna's awarenesses journeyed toward the newly discovered histories as they had revealed themselves to her quick but most discerning glance. The Old One decided then that the young adventurer-historian had better have some guidance with integrating what she was about to discover.

The Old One stretched his presence to Brianna's and thought-spoke, "Well my dear, I see you were unable to refuse that magnificent pull to discover the Truth!"

"Oh hello, sir. I hope this isn't against the rules...."

"There are no rules," he assured her and then added, "except those that you make for yourself."

Brianna liked just about everything concerning the Old One. "Are you out and about too, Sir?" she asked. It was as if the two of them had paused, and were suspended in an undefined manner, in an undefined location, so that they might speak of the pull to the Truth.

He enjoyed her many questions and knew this journey together would be filled with many more questions and more answers for which questions could not even be created.

"Oh, I thought I'd see what was going on," he replied. Their thought-speaking was easy and comfortable. "That's when I detected your presence."

"I saw something, sir, as I looked down the Time-Stream." She didn't quite know how to sort out the three hundred eras she had seen, didn't know if she had correctly interpreted what she had seen.

He sent her relief with, "Why don't we travel there together and have a look?"

"Why sir, what a great idea!" She was ready to speed toward the location when she realized she knew neither which direction to go toward nor how to arrive exactly where she'd seen so much in one brief look through Meteranke's vision.

"Don't worry about how to get there," he said, and continued with, "in fact, there is no set of directions. The only *how* is determining -- deciding to arrive at a certain location, which you've already done...."

"Yes sir," interjected Brianna's enthusiasm, "I decided I would go have a look at what appeared to be more eras than our written histories contain."

"Of course that's where you want to go! And you can. Remember your determining?"

"Yes, I do!" Brianna was just about to determine herself to her desired location.

"Hold on, now." The Old One embraced her presence before she disappeared. "The next part of determining might be helpful to know."

"The next part?" Brianna felt his embrace and settled into its comfort.

"When traveling in this manner -- that is, through the histories, it's best to determine the kind of experience you would like to have."

"But I don't know that, sir."

And that was the whole point, it seemed. She didn't know anything about the experience she was entering.

"You do know." The Old One's words brought Brianna to a heightened awareness. "Don't you want to *easily* arrive in a consciousness that will give you a clear understanding of what you are viewing? Don't you want to remain objective and not be pulled into what you are viewing? And," the Old One was inwardly smiling at Brianna's surprise in the choices he was bringing to her awareness, "wouldn't you like to be able, if you choose, to dip into what you are viewing and *experience* it for yourself?"

"Sir!!!"

"I thought so," he replied. "That having been determined, let's place ourselves at the overview of your curiosity's discovery."

Brianna felt their merging. It was different, yet similar, to the merging she and the others were accustomed to experiencing in the Neecha. Merging with the Old One was... bigger, uncomplicated. She'd never really thought of the experiences with her friends at the Neecha as complicated, but more as adventures. Yet this was expanding.... She searched for the words, the description of what was happening. *Easy! That's what it is*, she decided. *Easy.*

Brianna was accustomed to journeying in that way: immersing herself into the experience and then objectively viewing what and how she was exploring. The pulsebeat between the two had always given her the uncanny ability to sense what was about to happen before it actually occurred. Such pulsating, of course, happened in less than a blink of her deep yellow, penetrating gaze.

They arrived at the exact location where Brianna had hurriedly calculated what she thought were over three hundred dragon eras. There they lay, stretched out for her viewing, one after the other. Three hundred and sixty-two!

"That's exactly correct," the Old One assured her astonished counting. "And that one over there," he directed her viewing in the opposite direction, is the Neekontuk that is about to devour yet another dragon existence."

Within the state of merging and objective viewing, the emotions that might pull them into an emergency reaction were missing. In fact, it wasn't that they didn't care, but more that they *could* care in a most unemotional and, consequently, effective way.

"It seems," began Brianna with what she did best — integrating the facts of history with a present unfolding event. "It seems," she repeated, "that, aside from the fact that none of this has been placed in our written histories, there must be a reason that the same event keeps on repeating itself."

The Old One allowed her the freedom to speculate, conclude, change her viewing, and much more. He was simply there to guide the flowing of the Truth, of the known, in a way that would allow every other event to have its own similar awakening. ...*And perhaps this time they'll do it*, he thought to himself, shielding his own purposes from Brianna lest she be distracted from the history-making discoveries with which she was involving herself.

Brianna inspected the manner in which the Neekontuk of the first one hundred eras dissolved the dragon worlds. The dragons who resided upon the land were many, many more than the dragons of her own era. Then she saw. The Neekontuk simply raised its great fiery wall and neither crashed down upon, nor devoured, the dragons and their land, but simply covered all that existed. Then the dragons and the land were no more. No dragons were panicking. It was as if they just didn't know what would happen. One hundred times and each time, they simply lived their lives until the fiery blanket covered them and they were no more. *Obviously*, she thought to herself and to the Old One, *they have no memory of the previous era!*

"Reflect upon It again," he suggested. "There's more."

Without hesitation, Brianna viewed each era. The dragons appeared on the land. She quickly thought to herself, *exactly how they appeared on the land is another mystery I'll have to research*. But right now she was focused — more than focused — on the events as they occurred. The dragons appeared on the land. Then, the fiery wave covered them... covered the dragons, living... innocently unsuspecting.... "I have it!"

"What is it that you've recognized?"

"They didn't even **see** it!" They didn't see it flow over their mountain? But... **why** didn't they see it coming?"

She waited for the Old One to speak. She knew he had the answer. He didn't speak. He allowed and waited — waited for the remainder of Brianna's awareness to fill her consciousness.

She viewed each era, paying closer attention to the rhythm of their daily living. She saw inglets and adults, and then gatherings.... What was she missing? Then she heard the Old One's words echoing through her, "Wouldn't you like to dip into what you are viewing and experience it for yourself?"

He knew she would more than dip into the era she was viewing. He knew she would take form right there. She did.

A slight wondering flew by her more-than-awake perceptions. It lasted just for a second -- long enough for Brianna to attach her intent to it, her intent to examine it later. The slight wondering was, *If I am in form here, am I still in form -- resting with the others? And if so, do I have two bodies?"*

She walked on the land. It was still. Something was missing. *There was no thought-merge*! She thought-spoke to the Old One, "During the first one hundred eras, the dragons didn't maintain a thought-merge. There were totally separate individuals."

"There's more," he said. "Keep going. You're doing very well."

Brianna drank in the Old One's encouragement. She began to walk beside some of the dragons. She tried to discern what they were saying to each other. Their language of speaking was different from hers; but when she thought-merged with them, she could understand the meaning of what they were saying. A gathering... they were going to a gathering... at their Great Lac.

"Old One!" Brianna excitedly reported, "They have a Great Lac, too!"

"Good," he said, "You've almost got it."

"I'm going to go with them...."

"Don't forget to determine – everything!"

Brianna determined her dragon body at the Great Lac with all the other dragons, but she remained nearly hidden behind some nearby bushes.

She heard the Old One again, "You can determine **everything** — even that you cannot be seen."

THEY ARE WATER DRAGONS!!

Brianna received the information and simultaneously took determined action. She became invisible. Another wondering with an attached intent flowed through her awareness: *If I am invisible to them, do I then still have a body?* She looked down at herself. Couldn't see her own body. Empirically she reminded herself that that only meant that *for the moment* she also could not see her own body.

Brianna watched. The dragons of the gathering rose together, with one waft, and then flew in a circle above the Great Lac. They flew slowly at first, until each one lifted and wafted their wings in unison. Their momentum increased and then, in one surprising movement, they all dove into the waters and disappeared!

"Stay with it," the Old One said. "You are very close."

Brianna peered into the waters. The dragons were *flying* in the water. She determined herself into the water. She flew with the dragons of old, felt the waters support her body, felt her wings move smoothly, gracefully. It was then that she recognized what she had been looking for. *It's here! In the water! Total thought-merging, total knowing of each other.*

One, an inglet, came up to Brianna and thought-spoke, *I know you're here. We all do.* Then Brianna felt herself surrounded by warm, embracing, dragon love -- Kloan love, Kloan merging. She had missed it. She also felt the Old One reminding her to remain objective.

In the next moment a rippled awareness flowed through the Kloan: *The Old One is here! The Old One is here!*

Brianna felt the Old One send a message to them -- in a different pattern of speaking. They formed a circle again and around and around they flew in the deep waters -- until again, all together as one movement, they lifted from their Great Lac.

Brianna followed them back to the land. Upon the land, there was again the absence of thought-merging... and the absence of something else... what was it? Brianna felt the Old One call her to return.

It was easy to return to the Old One. She had to know. Maybe he would tell her now.

Instead, he asked her to bring forward a memory of her own Floggen. She did. She placed it as an overlay upon the dragon land she had just visited. There it was. It was so clear that she could hardly believe it.

"There is no fire! These dragons DO NOT BREATHE FIRE!"

"And?"

"...And... they are of the water! THEY ARE WATER DRAGONS! The first one hundred dragons were water dragons! ...And...." It all came to her, all the awarenesses fit together. She knew. "They didn't know fire. They never saw the Neekontuk because they never knew fire — and they only thought-merged in water! Wow!"

"Very impressive," the Old One said. "Very impressive." Brianna heard the Old One's words. It was as if he was speaking in two locations. The swirling carried her back to....

Brianna was the first to open her eyes in the realm the Old One had created. Her friends were just recovering from their replenishment, a procedure that required stillness for but three dragon breaths. So much had occurred for her during those three breaths!

Brianna searched for the Old One's recognition of their journey. He nodded to her, "Very impressive!"

The others regained consciousness and each one had two questions: *How is Fornaign?* and *What do we do now?*

Brianna held the same two questions — and much more. The Old One sent her a message, *"Don't worry, you aren't withholding from the thought-merge with your friends. You cannot."* He paused and then added, *"They don't know of your discoveries because that knowing is held within you in a different manner."*

Brianna wondered if she would ever have the opportunity to reflect upon all of her wonderings. As they all stood for action, she attached an intent to the wondering of whether any others held a knowing in a different place? And, did the dragons of the first one hundred eras hold a knowing in a different place?

The Old One breathed a fiery breath and the top of the realm opened. One after the other, they followed his lead. Brianna hesitated for a moment — long enough for Karthentonen to notice. "Bri! C'mon!" That was all she needed. She was back. Back in the three hundred and sixty-third era!

CHAPTER SIXTEEN

MENTARD'S JOURNEY INTO THE UNKNOWN

Clorfothian, Winjut, and Plienze allowed Mentard's reminiscing of his love for Zog and the many times he had anchored during Zog's future journeys.

"Sometimes," Mentard lowered his voice, "we would be called to anchor when no one else was around. That's when he journeyed to other Universes." He fondly reflected upon those times. "I don't know if anyone else knew about those journeys. Each one seemed to take longer than the one before." Mentard looked to the three wizards, "But that never bothered us! In fact, I think it developed our abilities beyond most!"

The wizards knew that Mentard was quickly approaching the last time he anchored for Zog, and their plan was to temporarily ease him away from that memory and begin his training in Time-Stream journeying. The natural unfolding of Mentard's participation in the events they had arranged for him more than pleased them. It was, however, during his last relating of anchoring when no one else was around that a fluctuating simultaneously occurred not only in their created realm, but in all wizard realms. All three wizards maintained their interested participation with Mentard, while their shielded communications spelled more than surprise and bordered on an emergency alert.

It was Plienze who dosed Mentard with a slight pause-in-the-moment incantation, while Winjut adeptly scanned the other wizard realms for a cause for the fluctuating. Clorfothian slipped from the realm that was holding Mentard and determined his presence at the Time-Stream.

The ripples seemed to lift the Streams from their natural flowing. Clorfothian quickly followed the ripples to the same location Fornaign had discovered, the V. However, Clorfothian wasn't alarmed or puzzled by the V. He was more than familiar with the *coming together* of the ever-transforming Streams, as the continuing occurrences within them did unfold in all manners.

It was, however, Fornaign's interpretation of the V that caught Clorfothian's attention. Rather than seeing the V as a coming together, Fornaign had followed the Time-Streams as if he had been traveling within time itself, toward the future. When he came upon the V, to him, the Streams had seemed to split apart. And, with his consciousness of time and of separation, Fornaign had tried to penetrate the V. Clorfothian easily read the demise of Fornaign's charged attempt. The V would only allow, could only allow an entry into itself of timeless, eternal unity.

It was, of course, known within the wizard realms that both time and the concepts of beginning and ending were illusionary.[42] They do, however, understand how the concepts of *before* and *after* came to be, as the physical living upon the land and the seeming sequence of events had led all dragons to the uncon-

---

42 Illusionary, time & concepts of beginning and ending: Oo-Nah – a consciousness describing the all knowing of the Ancient Ones and any being who could maintain the expanded knowing of One; i.e., continual flowing, taking form and releasing form; while also taking form themselves and residing within the physical rhythms upon the land. Until the Great Change, only one could and has maintained Oo-Nah, that being the Oldest Dragon, or The One. There are others, the wizards in particular, who could maintain the consciousness of All Knowing; yet, they have not been able to maintain a physical presence upon the land. They have been able to create realms wherein a semblance of residing upon the land might occur. However, within those realms, they have never been able to create the cause and effect as it does naturally occur within physical form upon the land and within the belief-created boundaries of time. Consequently, the wizards are aware of the illusion of time, but have not been able to incarnate that knowing, or enjoy Oo-Nah.

scious conclusion of the existence of time and the constraints therein. In fact, it had been that exact compassionate understanding that had led the wizards to create additional portals and realms that would eventually lead adventuresome dragons to discover timeless journeys and other Universes, as had Zog. It was because of those kinds of journeys that Zog had been able to lead his dragons toward a more expanded daring to explore their own abilities.

It was hoped that such expanded daring had developed enough to fill the dragons with the courage they would need to make the necessary choices during the upheaval of their known existence. It was also hoped that the necessary choices, if made, would lead them through a transformation and resulting birthing similar to Ala-Kleeha — with one exception: the Ala-Kleeha would be participated in by ALL dragons *simultaneously*. It was more than a hope. It was the first time within the existence of all dragons that so many were awake to their innate ability to conceive of a profound existence greater than they were presently experiencing. With that exact consciousness, they could possibly dare to open their hearts and thought-merging to include the seeming unknown: the ALL KNOWING. And, in such a great occurrence, there could also be the conscious, totally awakened Return to One[43].

While examining the state of the V, a tiny awareness trickled into Clorfothian's concentration. He paused and called it forth. The awareness grew and responded to his call until it totally

---

[43] Return to One: In the histories of dragons residing upon the land, there had always been an experience that had led them to a type of union that would intimate the Grand Truth. The Grand Truth being that One Dragon did flow forth and step upon the land. His experiences were so plentiful that he breathed himself forth in forms of himself, dragons, so that all possible journeys might be explored. The last journey would then be the realizing of their dragon identity: all dragons are the breath of One Dragon. And thusly would be concluded that they were only One, One Dragon. Completing such a journey and Return to One, the One Dragon would then also return to the Portal to the Nothingness to release his form and all that had been created and experienced. The Nothingness then breathes itself into being again and another dragon becomes the One. Although all journeys and experiences appear to cover eras upon eras of dragon existence, within an illusionary time and its created Time-Streams, all that had been created from the One Dragon did and does occur in one breath, one moment. Such a Truth has not as yet been held within the physical nature. Neither has it been held within the vehicle for such knowing, thought-merging.

filled him: *Someone had journeyed to and participated within the first hundred eras! Someone had actually merged with the dragons of the first hundred eras!* Clorfothian ended his examination of the V. He had to tell them. *"Someone is carrying the true history,"* he whispered to himself. *"This could change everything!"* He couldn't seem to get back to Winjut and Plienze and of course, the on-pause Mentard, fast enough!

All three had discoveries to tell and, if there were such a phrase as *jumping out of their skin* in wizard realms, it would certainly have applied to these three wizards.

It was in the middle of Plienze's telling of the dissolving of the walls which contained the Dream State, and which bordered the Moment in Stretched Time, that Mentard's on-hold incantation let go of its constraints. Such liberating placed him directly into their discussion of more than they had been prepared to release into his knowing. The three wizards stopped speaking. Silence.

"When are you guys going to trust me enough to tell me what you hope I'll be able to successfully hear?" His dragon gaze intensified and the wizards knew that the time was now -- not necessarily because Mentard was challenging their protective unfoldment of his awarenesses. But more so because of the great magnitude of changes occurring in the Time-Stream, in the wizard realms, and in the exact consciousness of all dragons! The time, so to speak, was now -- for everything. And the synchronicity of the events holding the current awakening rested upon Mentard's ability to be more than who he knew himself to be.

"OK," began Winjut, "you're right! More right than you know!"

"That's exactly what I'm talking about!" declared Mentard. "I'm beginning to get a little..." he released a trickle of green smoke followed by more than a trickled snort of fire, "well, a little restless with all of this!" He stood and began pacing the green meadow they had been enjoying together.

Winjut let go of his restraints on unnecessary incantations and placed himself on Mentard's shoulder. Mentard glanced at his wizard friend and continued pacing, which tended to give Winjut a bumpy ride. Nonetheless, he remained on Mentard's shoulder and spoke directly to him.

"Much depends on your abilities, Mentard...."

Mentard stopped and stared his one golden eye at Winjut, waiting for the wizard to regain his balance.

"MUCH," Mentard emphasized the word *much*, "has always depended on my abilities. That's who I am! Who I've always been!"

Mentard began his pacing again, and said, "You're just going to have to take the risk.... If Zog could take the risk, then you should be able to!"

Rocking. Mentard's world rocked. Darkness began to close in. The wizards knew it was time -- whether they were ready or not, whether Mentard was ready or not -- for the memory of the results of Mentard's last anchoring and the memory of Zog's death. It was imperative that Mentard remain objective and not fall back into the darkness from which he was rescued.

Rather than try to control the manner in which Mentard's memories surfaced, the wizards surrounded him with their deep love and with allowing. Now it was their turn to remain focused within the intent of allowing, even though each held the hope of all Dragondom within his heart. They watched his great dragon body fall onto the meadow. Mentard's body remained asleep while his mind fought to stay awake.

Through the darkness and the rocking, Mentard maintained his strength of being. It had been part of his training and had been developed further during the secret times of anchoring for his beloved leader, Zog. When he had initially become concerned for Zog's longer-than-usual journey, and when Mentard had felt the pull on the integrity of his own strength, Zog had taught him, refining Mentard's training. It was those long-ago words that now echoed through Mentard's memories. *"Don't think about me!"* Zog had ordered. *"Just focus on the grandness of who you are! Focus on yourself, on maintaining your own strength, your strength of being who you are!"*

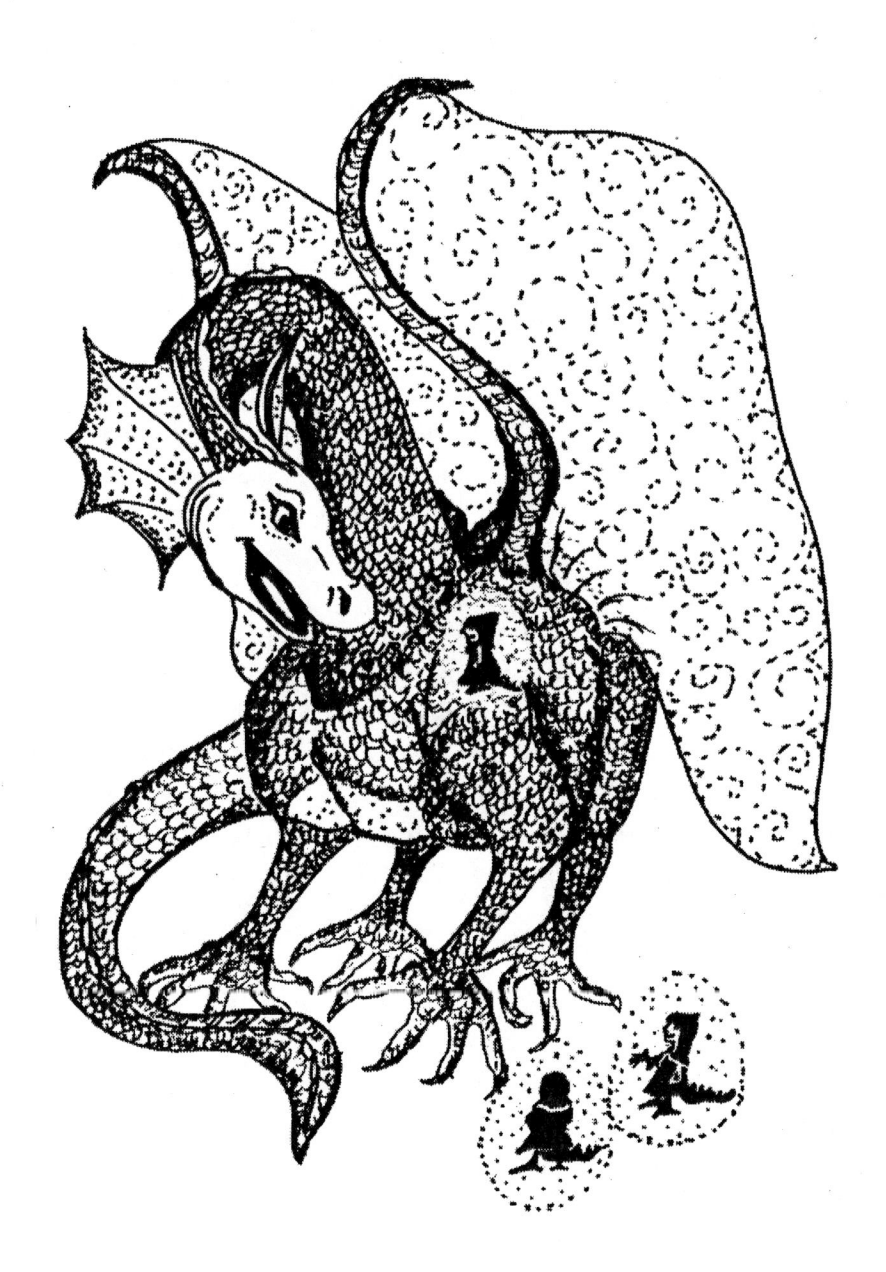

Winjut let go of his restraints on unnecessary incantations and placed himself on Mentard's shoulder. "Much depends on your abilities, Mentard."

With the waning of his strength, Mentard had been forced to release his concern for Zog and do exactly what had been ordered. Even with the first releasing of his focus on Zog and placing it on himself, Mentard had felt a surge of strength return. The experience had prepared him for many further anchorings, and it was during those times that Mentard had trained himself to maintain a knowing of his leader's journey while focusing fully on his own strength and his own identity. None other knew that he had become the primary anchor for Zog.

Neither did any know that Mentard held within his own heart a yearning to travel as Zog had, and a yearning to actually journey further — into the unknown. In truth, because of Mentard's gregarious nature, none would suspect him of wanting to do anything more than be the wonderful, strong and talented anchor that he was.

Mentard, however, had begun his own recording and further studying of the patterns Zog had laid within the blue structure as it had formed to receive his return to the land. And it was when Zog became aware of Mentard's particular attention upon those patterns that Zog delightedly began to place within the blue structure more and more patterns, mappings, and encoded portal entries for the sole purpose of nourishing Mentard's hungry curiosity.

As the darkness closed in around Mentard, any relating to the present realm with the wizards, any relating to his living upon the land, and any relating to anything familiar was beyond the grasp of his attempts at thought-merging. The swirling carried him into the depths of his own despair; and it was within that pain, that Mentard's training as anchor began to gift him with a tiny thread of the known.

The tiny thread tapped on his confused mind and distraught emotions. So refined was his ability to discern patterns that the tiny thread, easily and quickly recognized, became a lighted realm within which he could begin to regain his focus.

The darkness continued to swirl invitingly around, as Mentard sorted through the patterns within his tiny, lighted realm. He

MENTARD'S JOURNEY INTO THE UNKNOWN

accessed his records of the many realms within which Zog had journeyed, and he placed them as overlays atop the swirling. None matched. He overlaid the patterns of other Universes, patterns he had studied again and again. None matched. Rather than become frustrated or disheartened, Mentard's determined search for a way out of his own darkness fueled his focused intent.

Again he heard Zog's long-ago words and again began to focus on his own strength, his own knowing of who he was. It was through this focusing that he saw the patterns, blue like the anchoring structure he knew so well. *What patterns are these?* he asked himself. In response to his questioning, they appeared before him, dancing a blue dance. Mentard didn't have to overlay the patterns atop any of his recorded memories. Instead, he watched as they moved and situated themselves within the dark swirling and exactly atop their own match! "I never would have thought of it!" he exclaimed aloud.

The blue patterns matched the encodings Zog had used *between* realms, *between* Universes, and within his return to the blue structure[44]. Clear. More than clear. Mentard began his journey into the unknown. No one had taught him to thought-merge with patterns or encodings. It just came to him as the only way. In an instant he became the blue patterns. In an instant he became the knowing within the encodings. They were the journey itself! *What a discovery!* Mentard exclaimed to himself.

It was within the timeless, floating movement that Mentard maneuvered himself past numerous swirling portals, refusing invitations to explore the enticing unknown realms. Through his own blue flowing, he saw the Time-Stream and the vague movements within. He felt the vagueness remove itself to offer him a clear view of the great fiery wave and the patterns within the wave. Through the blue that contained all that he was, Mentard recognized the patterns of his leader, Zog.

The wizards refused to participate in even the slightest thought that Mentard might dive into the wave as Zog had. In-

---

[44] <u>Blue Structure</u>: blue lines racing upon themselves; created by the three wizards, a structure within which Zog could take form the first time he, as an inglet, began to phase out of their realm. As Winzoarian, Zog continued to use the blue structure for future-travel purposes.

stead, they continued to surround Mentard with deep love and their loyal allowing of the Truth to take form, their allowing of Mentard to become all of who he could be, the next leader of the Kloan – and much more.

Even against the magnetic pull of Zog's patterns, *"gather here where I am,"* Mentard held his focus. He viewed not only the metaclores of the Fire Wall, but also the barely moving Moment in Stretched Time. He observed the dissolving boundaries of the Dream State and the panicked activities of his dragon family. In truth, the more disturbing the information was that filled him, the easier it was for Mentard to focus as he had for the last three hundred years of his dragon living as an anchor.

Mentard felt the pull to return... to where? The blue patterns grew brighter, just as they had long ago — signaling that they would form themselves for the return of Zog. The difference was that this time Mentard was not an anchor. In fact, there were no dragons anchoring. This time Mentard was the one who was returning, taking form within the blue structure. It thrilled him.

The three wizards saw Mentard's great sleeping dragon body disappear. And in the next moment a blue structure began to form in their green meadow. It was large, powerful, blue within blue. It was the first time something had taken form within a realm they had created, something they had neither patterned nor intended. Yet, there it was, pulsating blue.

The green swirling within the structure looked vaguely familiar; and before they could nod their wizard heads or breathe an incantation, Mentard's green glistening dragon body stood before them. Magnificent. He looked magnificent. They all agreed.

Even as the blue structure continued to dissipate, Mentard stepped onto the meadow. "Hi, fellas!" He grinned his greeting and stood before them, spreading all giant wings to their full expanse. When his fans also opened, the three jumped back a little — a reaction that caused their great dragon friend to lean back his long neck and bellow a deep laughter that echoed around and through their realm. When the rumbling diminished to a soft thunder, Mentard shrugged his shoulders in his most endearing manner, and said, "Just kidding!"

MENTARD'S JOURNEY INTO THE UNKNOWN

Winjut, Clorfothian, and Plienze released their maintained intent with a giggle and then a rolling laughter. They flashed colored lights around the hills and sighed a relief from the "what ifs" they had deliberately hidden from their own thoughts. There was much more to do, to talk about, to teach. But for the moment they allowed themselves to enjoy Mentard's humor and look-what-I-did stance. It was a short moment.

Mentard lowered his glowing body against the hill and began. "Tell me about the patterns in the Neekontuk." He could have asked about the dissolving boundaries, the on-hold dragon existence, or the V in the Time-Stream flowing. He did not. It was as if he already knew his purpose and was ready for action.

"That's exactly where we need to begin," answered Winjut. "Those patterns are...."

"Zog's. I know." Mentard was without the emotions that had held him close to his own darkness. His objectivity and clarity shone through as he questioned further. "It seems to me that the only way those patterns could get into the fire would be with Zog's intent."

"Well...." Winjut was about to explain when Mentard interrupted with his already-formed conclusion.

"Even if Zog were consumed by the flames... even if he intentionally flew into the flames... his patterns would not be there unless he deliberately placed them there...." Mentard thought for a moment, allowing his studies and experience with patterns and forming to rise to the surface. "The only way he would intend his patterns there would be to deny... no, to challenge! To challenge the existence of the Neekontuk." Mentard stood and began pacing the meadow. It was a predictable movement.

"Such a challenge," he formulated his thoughts aloud, "would... perhaps... cause the wave to pause in its forward movement. It would have to...." He turned and faced the three beaming-with-pride wizards. "A challenge to existence caused a pause in the flowing of the Neekontuk!" He slapped his leg. "Brilliant!"

Mentard looked to the three, one after the other, "That's what took him down, isn't it." He sat back down against the hill. "That's what took his body." Deep realization filled the great dragon. "It wasn't anything I did wrong... it wasn't that I didn't maintain.... Zog returned so... so destroyed because he flew himself into the wave. Isn't that right." He looked to them again, "Isn't that right?"

Plienze leaped atop Mentard's knee. "Old boy, you have it right. All of it." He patted the slightly trembling knee. "Old boy, it was because of your maintaining, because of your strength and ability as his anchor that Zog could do what he did." They allowed the realization to fill Mentard.

"There's more," said Clorfothian softly.

Mentard turned his gaze toward his wizard friend, "More? What more can there be?"

"That's the whole point to all of this," Clorfothian waved his hand toward the created realm. "There is something left for you to do... with Zog... for Zog."

Mentard's youthful exuberance was gone. It had transformed into a tempered powerhouse of unlimited, focused force and intent. "I suppose that's why I AM here," he said calmly. "Just tell me what I have to do."

Winjut raised himself to float eye-level to Mentard's gaze, and this time it was Mentard who chuckled a little at the wizard's maneuvers. Mentard placed his large clawed hand under Winjut.

"Ah... thanks," smiled Winjut. "Actually," he began, "it seems you might not have to learn as much as we thought." Winjut paced a little back and forth across Mentard's hand. "You will have to learn how to maintain yourself here -- in full force, that is -- while you stretch yourself there...."

"That won't be so difficult," chimed in Plienze, as he also appeared on Mentard's outstretched hand. "If he can call forth the blue structure, I think it will follow a determined intent. I had a pretty good look at it while it was here."

"As did I," said Clorfothian, and he too made himself appear, next to Plienze. "I agree. And it seems our friend here," he smiled at Mentard, "has some talents of his own. Why, I believe he could maintain a focus through... well, through the greatest shaking and reforming of all time!" Clorfothian caught the glaring look from Winjut and quickly added, "Never mind about that...." Then he reconsidered and added, "No! I don't regret saying it. Now is not the time for secrets and protective speaking." He looked to his companions. "Don't we all agree on that?"

It was Winjut who was the first to agree — through the residue of his glare. "You're right, Clor, of course." He was about to tell Mentard about the grand picture of what was happening when Mentard himself cleared the air.

"How about we stay with this first task? There'll be a turn for the," he tried to imitate Clorfothian's voice, "greatest shaking and reforming of all time!" Clorfothian's love for the "old boy" grew even though he would have guessed that it couldn't become greater than it was. "However we look at it," said Mentard, "it seems that I have to learn how to maintain myself here and... what was that? Stretch myself to where?"

Winjut wove an incantation and swirled it around the realm so that a projection of the Time-Stream appeared, as if suspended, against the hills. "It's this way, Mentard," he began, "you're right. You will most necessarily need to maintain your physical self here. And while you are doing that, you will have to stretch your strength and intent beyond here.

"It's your choice, of course," assured Winjut.

"Get on with it! What am I to do???" demanded Mentard.

Winjut answered clearly and directly. "You are the only one who can maintain yourself here and stretch your strength and intent along the Time-Stream to where the Neekontuk and Zog battled." He pointed to the spot on the projected Time-Stream. "You'll have to grab onto Zog while he is in the Neekontuk. You need to pull him out."

"You don't have to ask...." Mentard answered, but was interrupted by Winjut.

"Wait! There's more." He had Mentard's full attention. "You have to grab onto Zog, pull him from the flames, carry him along the Time-Stream, and then deposit him back into the blue structure while you were maintaining as an anchor."

"But that will leave him with... with death!" exclaimed Mentard. "I'm confused," he admitted. "Why not deliver him right here? Why not deliver him to a location in the Time-Stream where he'll be whole?"

Plienze explained, "Mentard, Zog has completed his purpose here... er, on the land."

"Well, where is he?" asked Mentard, his innocence peeking through.

"Right now Zog is in total merging, beyond yet within his Mehentuk, with Zoanna. Right now Zog is an Ancient One."

"Oh." Mentard reflected a little on all that had occurred. The three wizards recognized what was happening and refrained from further explanations.

"I see," Mentard broke the silence. "You need me to pull Zog out of the Neekontuk so that he CAN fulfill the rest of his purpose, so that he can die -- in union with Zoanna." He looked to Winjut. "She gathered him up, didn't she?" The realization of the Moment in Stretched Time filled him. "That's where she went from the gathering, isn't it? That's what changed the way we were living on the land, isn't it. Making everything frozen in place. Isn't it?"

"Yes." All three wizards responded together. They waited. There was more. They felt it rising to the surface of his awakened state.

"AND! When I deposit Zog into the blue structure, everything will begin to speed up -- won't it!"

They continued to wait. The remaining awareness took barely a breath to surface.

"Then the boundaries around the Dream State will dissolve! What will happen then? How will the Dream State fit in with the... what do you call that? How will it fit in with our land as it returns to its usual way?"

"It won't," replied Clorfothian. "First of all, the Land of the Dragons will never return to its usual way. And secondly, the Dream State will always reside in the Time-Stream. It's just the boundaries that are dissolving. The boundaries only hold the dragons' consciousness within the Dream State. When their consciousness returns to what you are calling "usual way," everything and all dragons will be residing within the moment just before the Neekontuk devours the land."

"But...."

Winjut made a whistling sound nearly as shrill as those sounds made by the fairies during their dashing in and out of created realms. "Hold on here! Wait!" The sound caught Mentard's, Clorfothian's, and Plienze's attention. "Let's not get ahead of ourselves. We don't know exactly how everything will unfold. That's the greatness of it all!" He reminded them, "Remember! We can do anything with determined intent! And there are more of us than four!"

Mentard shook his big head, while streams of smoke flowed out and filled the entire valley. From past experiences, he knew that they would easily take care of the smoke, which Winjut did with a slight flick of an ear. "I just can't hear any more! Let's get started with what I am here to do. The rest will...."

"Good idea!" said Plienze.

"Yep, good idea," echoed Clorfothian. "Now, about that blue structure. Can you create it whenever you want to?"

CHAPTER SEVENTEEN

REMEMBER, WE ARE ALWAYS WITH YOU

Mentard discovered that indeed he could create the blue structure whenever he wanted simply by accessing the familiar patterns of an ending or beginning journey.

However, it took several practices before he could enter the blue structure and remain there fully intact. The first practice had begun fruitfully as Mentard had simply stepped over the pattern-filled, flowing blue lines, to stand in the center of the structure. However, none — including Mentard — expected his immediate, total and complete disappearance and just as quick reappearance.

To Mentard, his disappearance had flowed in a timelessness and had led him to a vast expanse of activated portals. Although another priority sat at the forefront of this adventure, he had made a record of the encodings within the expanse. Without hesitation, he had then called forth the exact patterns that had danced their dance before him in response to his efforts at lifting himself out of his dark despair. Again, they had easily appeared. It had been Mentard's decision to return to the structure that had activated the patterns, and in the next moment he stood in the very spot from which he had begun.

Again he had tried stepping into the blue structure and maintaining his physical presence. Again he had quickly disappeared. The second journey had led him to a white realm, as if he had flown into the side of a cloud. From a distance, several golden shimmering lights had begun to glide toward him. The white had parted with their movement, and the lights had approached closer. Mentard had seen something begin to take form.

He had heard of them, read of them. Yet this had been the first time he had actually seen Golden Dragons. Their light had been so brilliant that it had activated the automatic filter over Mentard's eyes. One Golden Dragon had stepped closer, and the distance between Mentard and the dragon had seemed non-existent. It was then that Mentard had not only heard the speaking but also felt the vibration of the words. They were soft and strong, deep and flowing.

"Mentard, we are with you always, during this task and all tasks that might follow. Though you might feel alone at times, remember that we are with you. When you return to your dragons, there will be but one other who will return with you. In that one will you find the strength you will need to lead them into their beginnings. Go now and do what you must do."

The Golden Dragon had begun to glide back into the white, but then had turned to gaze into Mentard's eyes. White light, a bright glistening light had charged between the two. It was then that Mentard knew how to do anything.

He hadn't remembered leaving the white. Their last words had echoed through him, *"Remember we are with you always."*

When Mentard had reappeared in the blue structure the second time, he was somehow different. Even as he had stepped onto the meadow and glanced back at the structure, the wizards noticed it right away; but through their thought-merged agreement, they hadn't mentioned it. Instead they had waited to hear and see what Mentard would say and do next. He didn't disappoint them.

"OK. After I maintain my presence within the blue structure, what would you like me to do next?"

Feeling the pride of a fatherly friend, Plienze responded first, "Well, we believe it would be a good practice to target a few specific locations...."

"Let's do it!" interrupted Mentard.

"It's not only maintaining your physical body here," interjected Winjut. "You'll have to stretch your life force, Mentard." He paused a moment and then added, "And to tell you the truth, I'm not sure how you'll be able to do that."

Clorfothian was more himself than any of them and demonstrated that fact by absent-mindedly brushing the air behind himself as he walked up to this amazing dragon. "I have a feeling our old boy has access to most anything!" He smiled up at Mentard, and added, "Er... don't you?"

Mentard breathed a deep sigh. "Hold on here! Let me think about this for a moment." He felt the presence of the Golden Dragons and then he saw an image of himself. It was as if they had thought-merged with him. Their vision gave him the answer he needed. He saw what he was to do.

"All right!" he said with such force that all three wizards instinctively jumped back. Mentard chuckled a little and then returned to his focused nature. "You pick the spot and I'll go there." He quickly held up his clawed hand to stop their redefining. "You pick the spot and I'll stretch my life force to that spot... AND latch onto something and bring it back here." He looked to all three. "How's that?"

The three wizards looked to each other. All this was quite new to them. Mentard appeared to be a great deal stronger in his intent, and they weren't entirely sure how well the encodings of their created realm would hold against Time-Stream juggling. In fact, they had only once been involved in a slight changing of the Time-Stream with the realm they had created long ago for Zog during his unfettered, inglet leap into the future of his dragon family.

Even then they had only inserted a created realm into the Time-Stream. Granted it had been an action they had never taken before and, because a dragon had resided within that realm, they had been forced to allow their created, inserted realm to remain in existence. Nonetheless, they had never removed something -- let alone some-*one* -- from one location and deposited it in another location. Now, they mutually wondered. Though the realm they had been currently using for Mentard was not part of the Time-Stream, how would the realm integrity be affected? And further, how would Mentard's practice affect the Time-Stream? Any change, they agreed, must be kept to an absolute minimum -- *and* none of them knew how to manage that!

Mentard also realized a difference in himself. Something had changed. He could hear everything the wizards were thinking -- individually and collectively. He shook his dragon head trying to be sure of what he was hearing.

It was Winjut who realized what was going on. "You heard us, didn't you, Mentard?"

"Well," began Mentard, "I suppose I did." He tried to reassure them, "I wasn't trying to listen...."

"Don't worry about that," continued Winjut, "but that you *can* hear our thoughts and thought-speaking tells me... tells us something."

"And what's that?" asked Mentard, quite interested in hearing information about himself.

"Basically," said Winjut, "it tells us that the time is now. That you're ready. Ready for anything."

"But how?" Mentard looked to Plienze.

"In order to hear our thoughts," said Plienze, "you have to be able to override our encodings."

"But I didn't."

"I know," said Plienze. "You didn't *try* to. That's the whole point. It just came to you."

"Not only that," said Clorfothian, trying to hold back his excitement, "but in order to have over-ridden our encodings, you'd have had to bring your thought-merging to the Ancient Ones!" He jumped up nearly half of his own height when he said, "That's what you did, isn't it?!"

Mentard neither smiled nor puffed out his chest. "I'm not sure exactly what happened, Chlor. I do know that I'm in some way different. Maybe in a lot of ways." He glanced at the projection of the Time-Stream. "I suppose I'll find out *how* different as all of this proceeds."

He had developed beyond their hopes. Now all that remained was the actual history-changing, Time-Stream-changing event.

"I still think you should have at least one or two practices," said Winjut. "After all, you will have to locate Zog exactly at his moment of diving into the wave — and then, you'll have to hold onto him until the blue structure takes form while you of your own past are anchoring. You'll have to do it, Zooooog...." Winjut couldn't believe he had actually called Mentard, Zog.

Mentard quickly chimed in, "Hey! It's a compliment!"

Winjut knew it was more than a slip of a word. It was a sign of danger. It was imperative that Mentard maintain his own identity while his life force latched onto Zog. And then, it was more than imperative that Mentard deposit Zog — and not himself — into the blue structure of old. Mentard could not succumb to saving Zog under any circumstances.

Winjut continued, but with more force and focus in his words. Mentard felt it. Plienze and Clorfothian felt it. Winjut was more serious than he had ever been. "You'll have to do it, Mentard. You'll have to allow Zog to be injured and in pain. He'll need that pain for his journey. I don't have time — we don't have time — to go into that now. You'll just have to trust me."

Mentard nodded. Winjut continued.

"You'll have to hold onto him — as he is — until the blue structure forms. And, Mentard, it'll feel like forever. It'll feel like it did when you were anchoring. But you must wait!"

Clorfothian added, "You'll see the other anchors dissolve, just as you did back then...."

"All right!" said Mentard. "Enough! Let's get these practices in. I'm going to have to be exact!" *More than exact*, he whispered to himself, *I'm going to have to be right on the mark.*

Winjut chose an easy location as the first mark. Pointing to a light on the Time-Stream, he said, "This is the moment when the three of us created a portal for inglets to explore."

"Inglets?!" Mentard raised one eye-lid.

"Well, none have used it as yet, Mentard," responded Winjut to Mentard's surprise, "but it's there."

"That's a good location, Winjut," said Plienze approvingly. "The encodings are gentle and uncomplicated."

"What would you like me to do there?" asked Mentard.

"Why not dip your force through the portal and bring back something," said Clorfothian, "that is, some-thing, not some-one."

"Wait a minute," said Winjut. "Not <u>here</u>!" he emphasized. Here is not the destination!"

"Oh," said Clorfothian. "Quite right."

Plienze had the solution. "There's a second portal further along. It's more complicated, but I think it'll do." He looked to the other two wizards. "You know, the portal at the Great Lac."

"Oh sure," said Winjut, "deposit something at the Great Lac with the entire gathering present!" He remembered the time they had created the portal so that they could observe the Beginning Visioning of Meran, knowing he would one day be the next dragon leader.

"Well, why not?" said Clorfothian. "Mentard is going to have to be exact and refined in movement."

"I'll do it," decided Mentard. "I'll do it." He peered at the projected Time-Stream. "Show me the two portals."

It had been decided. Winjut precisely pointed out the two portals and then watched as Mentard's laser vision centered in on first one and then the other. He read the encodings of each. If that weren't impressive enough, he then pierced his gaze through each portal and established an encoded pinpoint location for his practiced latching on and then depositing. When he was certain of his plan, he stepped back and refocused in their realm.

"Wow!" exclaimed Plienze.

"Must be something else I picked up." Mentard smiled at them even while he himself was surprised at his new abilities. It wasn't that he practiced them. It was more that he knew what he had to do, and then did it. He had never used his eye piercing like that before, and even as he realized that fact, he also wondered about what else he would be able to do *on command*. And then, of course, came the wondering if there were something that he would *not* be able to do *on command*.

Clorfothian heard Mentard's wondering and uplifted the thought with, "I believe you can do anything you determine, Mentard." He walked up closer to the dragon body and looked up directly into Mentard's yellow eyes. "You're radiating it! I've never seen you like this, old boy."

Mentard didn't say another word. Neither did the three. Mentard focused on the patterns of his blue structure. It felt a little strange considering it *his* blue structure. *But then again*, he thought, *that's exactly what it is*. It easily formed before him. Lighted, alive blue lines raced upon themselves to take form.

Mentard focused his gaze into the center of his blue structure and placed there the same encodings that lived within his wedge wings. The symbols danced before him, demonstrating their maintaining of Mentard's intended purpose: to continue to be in physical form within the structure.

Without hesitation, Mentard stepped through the blue flowing lines and into the center. He formed his body solidly. He placed his thought-merging within the encodings of his wings, within his great dragon body, and within the center of the structure.

Next he accessed the vision the Golden Dragons had given him. As the vision had demonstrated, he called forth a white force from the upper section of his heart. Without hesitation, the sparkling white flowed and formed outside of his body. He commanded it and at the same time he loved it. He filled his life force with his planned intent and sent it forth. It did go forth. It flowed and stretched itself along the Time-Stream until it arrived at its intended mark.

Mentard determined his life force through the portal and, as he had previously planned, latched on to something. Then, just as easily, he pulled it from the land. He was pleased with his own choice, knowing the wizards would never suspect such a refined selection.

He further intended his life force to unstretch itself slowly, smoothly, carefully until it arrived at its second destination.

Mentard's life force entered the portal and deposited what he had gathered from the first location: a sampling of all the colors from their dragon land. He released the colors into the sky above the Great Lac. They radiated and rippled forth, again and again. It had been a celebration written in the histories and had been the first sign that Meran would be the next leader.

Mentard, however, didn't hesitate there, but called his life force to return. It easily flowed back into his heart. He had done it. The first attempt was a success.

Mentard stepped out of his blue structure and looked up, as if expecting something, but nothing happened. The wizards too looked up to see what Mentard could possibly be searching or waiting for. Just as the blue dissolved into itself, Mentard's surprise arrived.

From the seeming sky of the Wizard's perfect realm spilled forth a short-lived torrent of water. All three — and Mentard — were more than wet!

Winjut shook the water from himself and whistled an incantation which dried them all — including the beaming Mentard.

"What!" queried Winjut, "What was that!?"

"Oh," sighed Mentard, "just a little of the Great Lac. Don't think they'll miss it."

The three wizards were without words. Who was this amazing dragon before them?

"C'mon fellas," said Mentard, "It was meant to be funny!"

• • • • •

If the wizards had had a way of figuring an expected effect, Mentard's actions would still have produced unexpected results — unexpected not only for the wizards, but for many. Though

Time-Stream studies had produced a great number of known facts, the truth remained that little, if anything, was known about what the Time-Stream was actually comprised of. The Oldest Dragon knew more than any, yet he would be the first to say that the Time-Stream was continually changing, even in its fundamental expression of its properties. *Any certainty of facts*, he was known to say, *was most likely based upon the false assumption that anything could remain staid — even in its own nature.*

Not only Mentard's gathering of the fabric of color from one location on the Time-Stream and depositing it in another, but also his gathering of the physical substance of water from one location and dropping it into a wizard's created realm — a realm separate from the Time-Stream — caused a change within the Time-Stream itself. With or without any knowing, within or without expectations, it changed. *The unspoken formula within the individual Streams automatically adjusted itself to accommodate the restructuring of its own substance.* As the newly formed Streams wound around each other, the adjusting also relieved the seeming unnatural effects of the V. Much to the amazement of those who were capable of objectively viewing the Time-Stream, the rippling simply ceased.

The stopping of the rippling was most felt in the Dream State, where fear and panic had begun initially to direct a chaotic struggle to discover what was going on, and had led finally to a desperate search for a way to survive the dissolving of their entire world. As the restructuring of the Streams completed its sigh into itself, the created intent of the Dream State was released easily. Consequently, some of the dragons began to have certain realizations about not only the state in which they had been living, but also they began to have realizations and flashes of memories that had been previously blocked from their access.

As the walls of the Dream State continued to dissolve, many more dragons began to awaken to the difference between the lulling comfort of the Dream State and the sharp, fresh knowing they had once possessed. Their choices were made easily, and the dragons they used to be filled those who found the lulling comfort to be distasteful.

Those who could objectively observe the goings-on within the Time-Stream were keenly aware and certain that they were watching the happenings of a never-before occurrence.

The Oldest Dragon had been guiding his six young dragons toward the dissolving boundaries of the Dream State when the Time-Stream adjusted itself and the extreme rippling stopped its wave right before their piercing gaze. Without the encouragement or any signal from the Old One, the six explorers split into two groups.

One waft of her fully developed wings lifted Brianna to view the Time-Stream from a greater distance in order to answer the immediate questions that quickly rose to the surface of her discerning thought forms. Had the rippling stopped along the entire Time-Stream? Were there any other boundaries around the Dream State? And, most important, how close and fast moving was the wall of fire?

A quick scan around the Dream State demonstrated but two boundaries. *Strange,* she thought to herself as she examined the boundaries, *that something as major to the Dream State's existence could only be recognized in their dissolving.* She flew around the still contained Dream State for one last look. *I've flown over this area — even through the thick substance itself — and never really noticed those two boundaries. Now that they're dissolving, I can see them clearly!* She determined to ask the Old One about that when and *if* there ever again was a relaxed moment together.

The gray cloud surrounding the Dream State had begun to change color. Another question rose to the surface. *Why wasn't the cloud cover also dissolving? And further, who determined it to be there at all? And, what was its stated intent?* The cloud color changed to contain a slight violet hue — the same violet that filled the depths of their Great Lac. Brianna placed a pause on the many more surfacing questions. Three of the others had flown closer to the Time-Stream and closer to the Dream State. Perhaps she could glean some answers from them during the thought-merge they would most certainly do when they met together after this journey. She determined to maintain the pause until then.

Mothan and Meteranke had flown close behind Brianna. They too, each for a similar reason, wanted to view the broad scan of the Time-Stream — and more. Each one was also scanning for a non-Time-Stream realm that might be holding the patterns of dragons.

Mothan expertly expanded his scan for any patterns that matched those of his mother's. There had been no response to this original scan and neither was there a response to the one he had confessed to the Old One. It was Mothan's plan to attach himself to any pattern that was clearly Zoanna's and then allow that pattern to pull him to it by the stated intent of his latching on. He had never attempted such an extension of himself before, and he hoped that it would deliver him directly into the dragon love he knew to be his mother's.

Mothan had also shrewdly reasoned to himself that, even with a determined intent, he might find himself in a location within which Zoanna had once resided. *And, he had thought, if that be the case, I will search again for her patterns and perform the same latching — until I find her!* He wasn't sure why he was so compelled to search for his Zoanna. He'd wondered, as his thoughts had drifted to rest during their last replenishment, if he were simply a grown dragon who wanted to see his mother again before she released her physical form. And, though unspoken even to himself, there was the earnest hope that he would merge with Zog.

When Mothan thought of his father, he continued to refer to him as Zog — Zog, the one who continued to inspire him in all the recent adventures. Even the name *Zog* helped Mothan to maintain clarity and objectivity in his scanning.

Light. There was a light pulse in the distance. It was close to the Time-Stream, yet separate from it. The patterns were slightly familiar. Mothan marked the location. This time he would ask. *I don't see how the Old One could refuse to allow me to at least make a deeper scan of that!*

Meteranke too saw the pulse and also marked the location. It was Fornaign he was searching for. He had heard Mothan's plan to ask the Old One for permission to leave their group's journey in order to explore the nature of the pulse. However, Meteranke had thus far marked three other pulses. He knew that when the time was right, he would venture outward in the hopes of reaching his long-time friend and deliver to him as full a dose of life force as any dragon could spare and still continue to maintain his own dragon body. *Maybe the Old One knows how to do that,* speculated Meteranke, *but in asking I'd leave myself open to his request that I **not** do it. And then there was Kar,* he thought. Meteranke hoped the opportunity to save Fornaign would come to him rather than to Karthentonen, even though they both shared the same intent. Meteranke wouldn't let himself think further in that direction.

Brianna thought-merged with Mothan and Meteranke. *Have you seen any other rippling?* The both flew to her side.

Meteranke was the first to speak aloud. It wasn't that he wanted to keep his plan a secret from Brianna, but more that he hadn't quite developed the intricacies and he didn't want to give Mothan any further independent ideas. "I think we'll have to fly along the Time-Stream expanse to be sure," Meteranke answered.

"We could each take a different route," offered Mothan. He couldn't help thinking of the flash and then his self-induced commitment to ask the Old One.

Brianna had understood Meteranke's reasoning for speaking aloud. In addition, she sensed the increasing intensities moving toward an unknown culmination of events. "I think it would be beneficial to stay together on this one." She looked to each of them. "We don't know what we'll find."

Mothan agreed before Meteranke could reinforce Brianna's suggestion; and without further discussion, they wafted their glorious wings and flew along the Time-Stream as it stretched itself toward what they would call the future.

"This should be familiar to me," said Meteranke. "Part of this is where I flew with Fornaign." His friend's name stayed a little longer on his long tongue.

Brianna knew that of their entire group, Meteranke and Fornaign had been explorers and friends together the longest. "It seems everything's changed," she said. "The entire Time-Stream seems to have... well, it's as if it has remade itself! If there is such a thing."

Mothan's thoughts leaped ahead. "We each have a pattern of a previous viewing, don't we?" His plan was evident. "Let's merge our previous patterns. It would give us a more complete picture and then it'd be easier to discern the changes!" Mothan's youthful enthusiasm spilled out of his fully developed dragon mouth, and he beamed his familiar I've-got-a-great-idea look.

It *was* a great idea, and in the next moment all three had thought-merged their individual viewings of the Time-Stream. Brianna's journey toward the first hundred eras merged with Meteranke's expert search for the cause of the rippling, and again merged with Mothan's journeys around the Dream State and further, along the Time-Stream's deliverance of his father from past struggles. The merging brought to them something they hadn't expected: a clear vision of an aspect of the Time-Stream. Without speaking, they uniformly focused. One of the Streams — of the multi-streamed Time-stream — seemed to be flowing in the opposite direction.

"Are you seeing what I'm seeing?" asked Brianna. She knew they did, but she couldn't help asking.

"Well, let's examine exactly what we are seeing," ventured Meteranke. The thought-merging following his discernment. "There they are. Twelve. Twelve Streams, all intertwined, loosely flowing as individual Streams...."

"Yet intertwined to be as one," interjected Mothan. "And the closer I look," he continued, "it seems to me that inside each Stream there's a flowing, like... like a river."

"And they're all flowing in the same direction," agreed Meteranke.

"Except for one!" Brianna couldn't contain their discovery. "That *one* is flowing in the opposite direction!" She paused. "Is that what you both are seeing too?"

"Yes... and no," said Meteranke, rephrasing his initial speculation. "I can't really see inside all twelve Streams. There might be others that are also flowing toward.... I guess we could say *flowing toward the past.*" The words felt strange as they trickled from his in-the-moment awareness.

"I don't understand," said Mothan. "How can that be?"

Neither Brianna nor Meteranke had an answer to Mothan's question. All three were quietly staring at the Streams.

Meteranke broke the silence. "Let's continue with our plan. Let's place our merged vision over the present Time-Stream. We may get some answers to our questions."

"Or have more questions," said Brianna. "My answers have routinely led me to many more questions." She shrugged her dragon shoulders, "I don't quite know what to do with them all."

The three dragons laid their merged vision of the Time-Stream as it had been before the recent change, atop the Time-Stream stretching itself below them.

The Oldest Dragon had remained at their meeting place. He felt the imminent discovery of the first three adventurers and breathed his ancient dragon breath to soften the realizations that would flood their knowing. They felt his familiar embrace, breathed it into their great dragon selves, and placed their unified, piercing vision toward the Truth as it revealed itself to them. Through habit, they registered the facts and laid all possible conclusions aside until they were complete with their viewing.

CHAPTER EIGHTEEN

THE ELDER WAS RIGHT.
THEY WOULD NEVER BE THE SAME.

The facts were clear. Externally the Streams appeared to be the same in size and in the manner they were intertwined.

Without emotion, Brianna empirically examined aloud. "I agree. They appear to be the same. However, I am only counting eleven Streams."

"That's the count I get, too," confirmed Meteranke.

"One could be resting behind another," suggested Mothan. "We could fly closer, maybe even in between the Streams if we're careful." He looked to the other two. "You know, to be absolutely sure."

Meteranke remembered the light he and Fornaign had initially flown toward. "I've found that deciding to fly close to a Stream and actually being able to are two separate issues. It wasn't that easy."

"I agree we need to be sure," said Brianna, "but we also have more to glean from here."

"Oh… yeah," smiled Mothan. "Thanks for the reminder."

"You could be right," added Brianna. "The twelfth Stream could be behind another."

While they were speaking Meteranke placed his gaze into the substance of the Streams… and then back out. "Wait!" He gazed

THE ELDER WAS RIGHT. THEY WOULD NEVER BE THE SAME.

in and then back out again. He looked to Brianna. "You'd better check this out!"

She followed Meteranke's patterns into the Streams. Meteranke motioned to Mothan, "Go ahead! You'll have to see this too!" Mothan quickly followed Brianna's probe.

It was undeniable. The entire inside of the Streams had changed! There was really nothing to compare. The Time-Stream and its individual Streams, as it lay below their viewing, contained within itself a substance that was totally different from that which all three had experienced in their recent past!

When Brianna and Mothan released their gaze and returned to Meteranke's stance, they were speechless. They heard the words of the Old One, "Remember, no conclusions. Not yet." His participation, even from afar, relieved the intensity of their discovery and rested the wanting-to-burst activity of their questions. Questions like, what did this mean for their entire dragon living, home, and families? Did their home still exist? And, would they ever be able to return to… home?

Brianna was the first to recover. "Let's go toward the past. I have a feeling that somewhere along the Time-Stream there will be a match — even if it's way back in the first one hundred eras."

Mothan and Meteranke's jaws both dropped simultaneously.

"I know," she responded to their stunned looks, "I have some explaining to do."

Mothan exaggerated the word *first* with, "*First* hundred eras?" And then, "*Hundred* eras? What?"

Meteranke was more accustomed to Brianna's discoveries and assumed she had delved into their dragon histories and uncovered some interesting and as yet unsubstantiated facts. "I didn't know our histories provided patterns we could use as overlays."

"They don't," smiled Brianna.

"But how will we access the patterns of… other eras?" Meteranke couldn't bring himself to say the words *the first hundred eras*.

"I have them," Brianna answered his disbelief.

"But how?"

"From my own journey." She knew it was a lot for both Mothan and Meteranke to believe. She motioned down the Time-Stream toward the past. "Follow me. I'll thought-merge with you while we go to…" she withheld her further knowing of what existed within the first one hundred eras, "…while we go toward the distant past."

Together they flew over the Time-Stream as it revealed itself to them. Brianna released visions of her journey, which opened the door for their awareness to follow. She didn't know how she accessed the ability to release some of her visions while maintaining the rest in her private inner knowing. Somehow she determined to do so and that's exactly what happened.

· · · · ·

While Brianna, Meteranke, and Mothan continued their search for the location in the Time-Stream that would match the patterns of their previous experiences, Treiga led the way toward the V. Kleeana and Karthentonen flew at his side. "It seems," said Treiga, "that the V was causing the rippling." He looked to Karthentonen. "Remember the flash Fornaign sent us before…."

It was Kleeana who responded. "It appeared that the V was causing the rippling, but we're really not sure about that."

Treiga admired the maturity that had been weaving itself into Kleeana's character. He'd been forced to change the way he related to her, as the inglet she was had given way to Nacta.

"You're right, Kleeana," Treiga responded.

Karthentonen had been feeling a pull toward something, he wasn't exactly sure what. "We could fly to the V, but I get the feeling that the answer lies somewhere else."

"What's the feeling, Kar?" Treiga trusted the solid reputation of Karthentonen's visioning skills.

"I'm not clear on it yet." Even as he said the words his feeling increased but would not define itself. "I just have the sense that we're closer to our answer -- or to something -- than we think."

THE ELDER WAS RIGHT. THEY WOULD NEVER BE THE SAME.

Treiga and Kleeana spoke the same words, "You lead the way, Kar." Kleeana added, "That's how Mothan and I discovered your Neecha.... I can't even remember how long ago that was!"

"That's it!" Said Karthentonen, his eyes ablaze with certainty. "We'll return to our Neecha."

"And then what?" asked Treiga.

"I'm not sure," said Karthentonen. "I only know that's the next step in this adventure. Something there will lead us further."

"But how will we actually get there?" asked Kleeana. "The entire Dream State is collapsing and...."

Both Treiga and Karthentonen felt a slight fear raise itself in Kleeana's concern. The fear was easily recognizable — it had been present in the Dream State. Kleeana's concern with their participation near the collapsing of the Dream State had activated her memories of her long-ago search for someone, anyone, who was not affected by the Dream State.

"Don't worry, Klee," Karthentonen said as he wrapped his big dragon arm around her. "We won't let you be lost." He gave her a gentle squeeze and then added, "Ever again."

"I suppose I'm acting like an inglet," she said. "But I, I just can't go back to that."

"Well," said Treiga, "you'll be happy to hear this!"

"What's that?" Kleeana took a deep breath and started feeling her balance and familiar surety return.

"The Dream State itself is no longer what it used to be."

"How do you know that?" asked Karthentonen.

Treiga's dragon face twisted one way and then another. It was an unusual look. Neither Karthentonen nor Kleeana could ever remember such unknowing showing itself on the face of their most balanced, steady, don't-say-anything-until-you're-sure-of-your-facts friend. It was the first time in a long time that they all laughed together.

"Well?" said Karthentonen through the broadest smile his face had stretched since, well, since Brianna had imitated the gnome.

"I, I suppose I have to say that I don't know *how* I know about the Dream State." Treiga looked to both of them. "It's a feeling."

"Maybe it's like Kar's feeling," suggested Kleeana.

"Perhaps," said Treiga. "I do know beyond a doubt that what we have known as the Dream State has changed. Everyone there is... is waking up!"

"I have a feeling," said Kleeana, "that we'd better get to our Neecha before the way is changed so much that we won't be able to find it!"

Karthentonen wanted to say that he doubted they would lose the way to the Neecha, but the truth was that Kleeana might be right. Instead he said, "Then let's get going!"

The Old One heard their conclusions and turned his gaze to the Neecha to set the patterns and intent. He wanted his three young ones to enter easily and obtain the next avenue through which their adventure would take them. It was imperative that they... but what was this? The patterns of the Neecha were not only already set, but contained the most expanded knowing of Truth. How could that be? Instead of delving deeper into the cause and effect that had resulted in the most perfect preparation of the Neecha, the Oldest Dragon rested himself in the absolute joy of watching the story unfold -- just as he had since his very first breath upon the land.

The three dragons sped toward their homeland, not sure what they would find, but certain that they would locate the Neecha that had served them so well on so many occasions. The Time-Stream laid itself beneath their journey. Even as they wafted their wings again and again, they maintained a scan of the Streams as they wound together as one.

Karthentonen recognized a light in the Time-Stream. It invited him to enter. Instead of swooping down and accepting the invitation however, he asked Kleeana and Treiga to wait while he inspected the location. The light flashed again. This time he recognized something. He flew toward the flash. As he approached closer, he saw that the flash originated from a portal separate from the Time-Stream itself. The patterns were undeniable. He raced back to Treiga and Kleeana.

"I'm going to have to do this. You'll have to go on without me." Karthentonen turned to race back to the portal again and was intercepted by Treiga who flew in front of him and paused -- the way the Old One had taught them.

"Where are you going, Kar?" Treiga fired the question. "And why?"

Karthentonen glanced ahead to be sure the light was still flashing. "Trei, I don't have time to explain. Fornaign. I think I've located Fornaign."

"What if it's not him?"

"Then I'll catch up with you." Karthentonen raised his great wings, ready to waft himself toward the light. "And Trei, if he's there, I'll be staying with him." His wings came down and off he flew. Treiga's words echoed over his shoulder as it bent toward what he hoped was true. "Be sure, Kar! Be sure the patterns are exact!"

Treiga watched his friend fly toward the flashing light. When Kleeana caught up to him, Treiga sent a thought-merge to answer her forming questions about Karthentonen. "It'll be the two of us," he said. Kleeana nodded. There was no need for further words. Together the two turned and flew toward that part of the Time-Stream called home. It was an odd feeling, they both agreed. So much had happened since they last entered their own skies and placed their dragon feet on their land.

Below, the Time-Stream laid itself easily and comfortably before them. As the two approached the Dream State and its dissolving boundaries, they also saw the ever-so-slowly-moving wall of fire, the Neekontuk.

"There," pointed Treiga. "It's there that we want to go."

"Not in the Dream State?" Kleeana had expected to enter through that supposedly changed time.

"It's been coming to me as we've been flying. We want to go to our Neecha."

"That's right."

"It doesn't exist in the Dream State. Remember? It exists right in between the Neekontuk and the dissolving wall."

Treiga's clarity was contagious and Kleeana understood exactly what he was referring to. He was more than accurate. He was exactly correct. Just as they prepared to enter that in-between place, a whispered reminder reached them. It was the voice of the Old One, replaying his instructions. *"Remember to determine! Don't just decide. Determine. Set your intent!"*

"Did you hear that?" asked Kleeana.

"Sure did." Treiga paused in his flight and Kleeana did the same. "We're going to be entering our homeland. Our previous experience was that the time was very slow — almost not moving," he said. "It may have changed, but we'll have to determine not to be affected. And to go directly to the Neecha."

"Done," said Kleeana.

They both engaged their gossamers and prepared for entry into the Time-Stream.

"And Klee," said Treiga, "it might be tempting to go somewhere else, but...."

"I said *done* didn't I?" Kleeana made her dragon self look as Nacta as she possibly could, and added, "I've been here before. Mothan and I came here looking for our parents."

"And?"

"They weren't here. The *in-between* is when my father... er, Zog had returned... and Zoanna left the Kloan to merge with him."

"Sorry you didn't find them."

"I did. Later. Well, I found Zoanna, that is, in her healing chamber. Mothan and I did. That's when she started telling us her story and about The Sectors of Learning."

"*You*'ve visited the Sectors of Learning?"

"No. Just heard about them in Zoanna's story."

Treiga felt the gift of Kleeana's still innocent honesty and at the same time hoped she would never mature out of it. Not many were able to maintain both innocence and honesty through the change to Nacta. His reflections were brought to a halt as

THE ELDER WAS RIGHT. THEY WOULD NEVER BE THE SAME.

they saw clearly their determined destination. Mutchiat never looked so good. Home.

One quick glance between them focused their energies and aligned their intent. The Time-Stream welcomed them as if they were long-lost children, now found. It opened its patterning and flowing.

It was easy. They flew into their world. Green. The hills were their usual lush green. And Mutchiat, majestic. Slower than slow. Any movement was barely perceptible. They noticed but didn't engage. Instead, they flew silently to the furthest peak, to their Neecha.

The ledge held itself open for their landing. One foot, another, closed wings, and they were both ready to enter through the more-than-familiar portal.

"Hold on!" Treiga stopped right before the portal. "How can it be?"

"What?" asked Kleeana as she folded her gossamers.

"Someone is using the Neecha!"

"How can that be? We left our encodings, didn't we?"

"No. We never did. Left it cleared, remember?"

"Oh." Kleeana peered into the portal. "Well, I say we knock."

"What? That's... that's just not done." He stepped further back from the portal. "If the Neecha is in use, you allow. You don't disturb."

Kleeana put her dragon claw hands on her dragon hips. "Treiga, how many times has this Neecha been in use when you've come here?"

"Well, none."

"Right. And, if you remember, Mothan and I didn't follow that rule." Kleeana continued before Treiga could interrupt. "And it's a good thing we didn't! Right?"

Treiga had to agree. "Right."

Kleeana sighed one of her inglet-like sighs, which always released an adult-sized puff of blue smoke. Treiga knew there would be no stopping Kleeana's decision to not only knock on the portal, but to enter — regardless of any inhabitant. He was right.

Kleeana focused her intent and breathed a vibration into the portal. Just as the vibration would have resounded, the portal opened. They heard the words, "Enter. Please."

Kleeana stepped forward and stretched her long neck through the portal and into the chamber. Treiga had just decided to grab onto Kleeana and pull her from the chamber, when she unstretched her neck and placed her dragon face right in front of Treiga's.

"There's only one," she reported.

"Who?"

"Don't know his name. I never did. I've always called him *the Elder*."

"The Elder?"

"Uh-huh." Kleeana smiled. "I think it's all right to go in now."

The voice from inside the Neecha spoke again. "How long would you like me to hold this portal open?"

Both Kleeana and Treiga jumped — just a little, but they did jump. It told them to refocus and call upon their clarity. They looked at each other and said in unison, "Done." Without further hesitation they stepped through the portal and into the Neecha.

It was different. Quite different. Treiga looked around at the swirling white. It filled the entire chamber, sparkling, rejuvenating, deliciously embracing him with the purest Truth he had ever experienced.

"Why didn't you tell me?" he asked Kleeana.

She glowed. "I wanted it to be a surprise."

"But how?"

"The Elder. He did it, I'm certain of it."

"In one sense you are quite right, my dear." The voice came from the white, and as the Elder moved his dragon body closer, the white parted to reveal a glistening, Golden Dragon.

"I remember you!" Treiga spoke without thinking — an action quite unlike him. He caught himself and continued with, "Er, Sir, I believe I remember you from the Kloan gatherings. Am I correct?"

"In a sense you *are* correct. Sir to you also!"

THE ELDER WAS RIGHT. THEY WOULD NEVER BE THE SAME.

"But...." Treiga had to admit that he neither knew what was occurring nor could he begin to figure it out. The energies of the Neecha were so perfectly aligned that it led him to an awareness that in actuality there was nothing to figure out.

Kleeana watched Treiga and felt his awareness expand to synchronize with the energies of the Neecha. She beamed her delight. Ever since she could fly and activate her gossamers, Kleeana had been able to match her frequencies with the most expanded. It had been easy. Easier than breathing fire, she'd always thought. It was in other circumstances that she had found difficulties, and mostly with the regular rhythm of dragon living and understandings. Now here she was in her favorite environment, the white essence. And Treiga, whom she had admired the most, was also easily able to be here. It thrilled her.

She'd met the Elder long ago when she'd been examining the vibrations left in Mutchiat after a Kloan gathering. The only female to attend the Kloan was Zoanna, and Kleeana knew that even when she was of Nacta, she would still not attend. However, that natural rhythm didn't stop her from examining after-gathering vibrations, and it was within that endeavor that she had met the Elder. He had been easy to talk with, and their meeting had been the first of many.

"Elder," she began, "this is my friend, Treiga." She turned to Treiga. "And Treiga, this is my friend, the Elder." She could hardly contain her joy, and then decided not to as she projected colors and delightfully transforming patterns into the white. It rippled and filled the chamber with sound, which lasted just long enough for each of the three to sit and lean their dragon bodies against the chamber walls.

The Elder began, "After the last gathering at Mutchiat," he paused and looked to Treiga, "you were not in the Time-Stream at that time."

Treiga maintained his focus. He knew that everything he was about to hear would be beyond... well, beyond anything he could expect.

The Elder continued, "At that gathering, from a great distance flew an old dragon. He was quite different than we were, yet he flew with precision and grace." He looked first to Kleeana and then to Treiga. "I know it might be strange to hear, but the truth is that he flew right into a vision that had appeared before the Kloan.

"I was standing in the alcove, as I usually did. There, before me, stood the oldest dragon I have ever seen. His presence was like a magnet to me.

"But before I could step closer, he began to speak." The Elder leaned his head back and drank the memory into his consciousness. "His words flowed forth into the Kloan. Some of the Representatives swooned at the words. I know now it was because the Truth was being spoken." He leaned his head back in reverie and again said, "Oh, pure Truth."

Then the Elder looked to the two dragons before him. "That's what you feel here. Pure Truth." He stood and began walking back and forth, his golden body sending forth sparks of creative essence as an emphasis to his words.

"After that Oldest Dragon had left and the chamber cleared, I went and stood where he had. His words had changed me. I... I couldn't be without them. And as I stood there, I heard them again, felt them."

He stopped walking for a moment and then continued, "That's when I came here. Been here ever since. I just can't bring myself to go back... back to the land.

"It feels to me that something else is going on, is calling me, calling all of us." He stopped right in the center of the Neecha. "Here, I'll project the speaking for you... so that you can hear it and feel it for yourselves."

The Elder opened his arms wide and from the center of his dragon body flowed a swirling gold. It formed a vision between his arms. There they saw the last Kloan gathering and heard the youngest dragon speak.

A vision within the vision appeared and there they saw the Oldest Dragon swoop and fly to stand exactly where the youngest had. Both Kleeana and Treiga bolted upright in their sitting. They recognized the precise flying. And, they recognized the Oldest Dragon.

THE ELDER WAS RIGHT. THEY WOULD NEVER BE THE SAME.

"That's our dragon!" exclaimed Kleeana.

The Elder held the visions in position. "*Your* dragon?" he asked.

"Yes! That dragon and our dragon are the same."

The Elder looked to Treiga.

"It's true," Treiga confirmed. "The dragon in the vision is undoubtedly the dragon we've been studying... er, traveling with."

The Elder looked solidly at the two. "Are you aware that this dragon, *your* dragon, is the Oldest Dragon in existence? Are you aware that he is the *First Dragon*?"

Treiga and Kleeana didn't know what to say.

The Elder continued, "If this is true — and it appears it is, as you would never be able to speak a distortion here — then you must hear these words, the words he spoke to the Kloan. You'll never be the same."

The Elder activated the visions and once again they saw the Oldest Dragon appear and begin to speak to the Kloan.

"Before you came to exist, I already was.
And, when you cease to be, I will remain.
I always have been. I always will be.
I am the One. I am the only One.
You are more than my children.
You are me."

His words filled them. The Truth filled them. The Elder was right. They would never be the same.

The Old One saw, felt his own words being called forth. It was confirmed. The time *was* now. It was indeed, the Return to One.

· · · · ·

Meteranke had sped toward the flashing light, the light with a slight hint of Fornaign's patterns. He wafted his great wings again and again, flying over the Time-Stream, giving it great breadth. The closer he came to the light, the more he was certain that it was the portal to a created realm. And if it was, then he was approaching a wizard's realm. The possibility spurred him on. Even as he approached, the portal opened to receive him.

It was soft, gentle. He recognized the healing chamber immediately and closed his wings. He tried to still his anxious wanting-to-know. That's when they appeared before him. Seven wizards. They were there to administer to *him*!

"Wait!" He put up both clawed hands to protest their attention. "This isn't why I am here! I'm...."

One of the wizards stepped up and raised himself to be facing Meteranke's confused dragon face. He said the word. "Fornaign. You're here to see Fornaign."

It was as if his long-time friend's name being spoken aloud pulled the breath right out of Meteranke. He sighed a great dragon breath. Green, then blue, then violet smoke poured out and filled the antechamber. One of the seven wizards easily cleared the smoke. They were quite accustomed to their dragons.

The wizard suspended in front of Meteranke continued, "We have him. He's still on the edge. We know why you're here." He waited for Meteranke to absorb what he was saying. Then he nodded to the six remaining wizards, who began to attend to Meteranke. Meteranke was beyond protesting.

"You can call me Neelak," said the suspended wizard.

"You probably don't realize how much repairing you, yourself need." Still suspended, he spun around twice, spinning in such a way that Meteranke could only watch. "You've not taken much time to replenish." He gave the great dragon body before him a look-over. "Appears to me that you've only replenished once since you last saw him, saw your friend Fornaign." The wizard spun around twice more and continued. "In order to help him the way you've planned -- and yes, we know all of that too. You're not very good at concealing your emotional decisions, you know."

He spun around again and when he came to a stop, he moved over to Meteranke's shoulder and gave it a few pats. "Don't worry about that though, you're *very* good at other things -- we've seen."

THE ELDER WAS RIGHT. THEY WOULD NEVER BE THE SAME.

The wizard took a deep breath and was ready to continue when a torn section of gossamer came into view as Meteranke settled his great body.

"Here!" The wizard motioned to the wizards on that side of the dragon's body. "Attend to that wing! It's quite injured."

He looked back to Meteranke's waiting gaze. "The truth is, you can't help Fornaign until you're fully repaired. Can't do it." He felt Meteranke's hopes for his friend begin to fall. "Now, now, don't give up! We'll have you fixed up in no time. Just give us a few wizard hours and you'll be back to your fine self once again!" The wizard beamed and then added, "Maybe better!"

It was quite true. Meteranke had pushed himself further than he ever had. The wizards lulled him into a deep sleep where there were no thoughts, no concerns, no Time-Stream, no raging walls of fire, and no injured friend. Only sleep. It was what he needed.

Fornaign sensed a presence. It lifted his spirit and slightly, ever so slightly, activated his life force. The wizards noticed it all. There was more than hope. First the healing of Meteranke; then the healing of Fornaign. And then the two dragons could decide. The wizards weren't attached to any decision the dragons would make. They had simply been called to rescue and create a healing realm, and that was exactly what they were doing.

CHAPTER NINETEEN

THE TIME IS NOW!

Within the ever changing Dream State, those awakening dragons who naturally chose the familiarity of their own wisdom, carried a vibration around themselves. They were strong and, once again, sure of their steppings upon the land. Their surety affected not only those dragons who were just beginning to shake the thick cloud from their thoughts, but also affected the very land itself. The land began to hold the imprints and vibrations of the awakened state.

It couldn't be said that the dragons were returning to their previous selves, as they had been residing in the lulling sleep and were now awakened. They had changed and consequently were able to express more. Their awakening brought forth a new acquaintance with previously unrecognized strengths and awarenesses within their own great dragon selves. The land, too, was not returning to its previous lush expression, but was thriving in a new vibrancy.

Such fullness in both the land and the dragons caused the protective walls of the once Dream State to totally dissolve and be nonexistent, as did also the Dream State itself. Each dragon's projected self — the self that had been lulled and held in the protections of the Dream

State — began to return to itself in the very alive present moment.

Each gloriously awakened projection, filled with new strength and more deeply accessed wisdom, returned to its dragon body as it sat, frozen, in the Kloan gathering — the gathering where Zoanna had been speaking to them of their leader's second future travel. The *Moment in Stretched Time* slowly, but with certainty, began to unstretch itself. One moment atop another, it returned to the land and its dragons that called their seeming regular rhythm of time.

The Ancient Ones watched with renewed hope rising in the hearts of their golden radiance. The interweaving of Truth within activities of so many dragons who were fully capable of knowing the Truth of themselves and who they really were, and of knowing their histories resting within the Time-Stream, opened the possibility for the Ancient Ones to fulfill the purposes set in motion at the completing of the very first era with the very first Neekontuk.

The golden essence comprising the Ancient Ones shone brighter as each event carried their journey's end; brighter, that is, except for one. As the *Moment in Stretched Time* released itself, Zog's essence began to wane. Even as Zoanna continued their merging, she could feel him slipping away. Only the whispered words of those Golden Dragons surrounding their chamber gave her the thread of a chance of promise. *"More is at work than you know. You and your beloved are not alone. One you would never suspect will turn events. It is nearly certain."*

Zoanna could have attached her concern for Zog to the words *nearly certain*, but she did not. She drew strength from *the one who would turn events*. All her efforts rested within the maintaining of a merging with a beloved who barely existed. She held onto all of Zog that she could find and filled him with memories of his greatness, his life's journeys, and the love of his inglets. She would not let go.

· · · · ·

Winjut, Plienze, and Clorfothian felt the waning of Zog's very existence. Without his existence, the realm they had created — and been forced to maintain *because* of Zog's presence — would naturally vanish, as did all wizard-created realms when the wizards were through with their play.

Initially the three wizards had felt a little persnickety at having to maintain one of their created realms; but as their relationship with the then inglet-Zog had grown, they had developed a fondness for the realm. They had often visited the realm to give themselves a small sip of the enthusiastic innocence the inglet had deposited there.

Only Zog knew, however, that he had, with his last breath of a future journey, created within that realm a portal for his dragons. As long as Zog existed, the realm *and* its portal to the land of the dragons remained. That a created wizard's realm had been connected to the Time-Stream was not recognized by any — except, of course, the Oldest Dragon. Such connecting, he observed, caused the realm to be of the Time-Stream, yet separate from its cause and effects. He had admitted to himself that the results of Zog's extreme efforts to save his dragons could never have been foretold — even by the Oldest Dragon. The admitting to himself of such a fact gave him great pleasure and brought forth a soft laugh only he could hear.

• • • • •

"Now." Clorfothian's spray of light and sparks surprised Mentard. Such an action was unlike his wizard friend.

Winjut stood exactly beside Clorfothian, with Plienze also stepping into line. All three together said, "Now."

"Now?" asked Mentard.

It was Plienze who stepped up to the dragon he'd come to love. "Mentard, the time is now. You must do what you've been practicing — **right now!**"

None of the three wanted to alert Mentard to Zog's waning existence. It was imperative that Mentard remain focused on removing Zog from one location in the Time-Stream and depositing him in another. The idea of *saving* Zog remained unspoken, even in their thoughts.

Mentard stood in the center of their realm. He felt the urgency in their call for him to take action. With fully expanded wings, he summoned the fireball. It grew greater and greater, rumbling within his chest, and then rose up his long, outstretched neck. Mentard bellow his own call to action, opening his great dragon mouth, and breathing his fiery breath into his own healing realm. His fans flashed open. Balls of white light charged out, rapidly, one after the other. It seemed to the three wizards that Mentard grew in size before their eyes. His piercing yellow eyes blazed with Truth as he spoke it, "NOW, my dear wizard friends, is the time!" They could only watch, wait, and hope.

Mentard called forth his blue structure. Little did he know that upon this journey rested the hope of many and the very existence of his beloved leader. Blue lines raced upon themselves and formed the familiar vessel that would hold Mentard as he stretched his life force toward the great fiery wall.

Mentard's determined intent situated itself within every cell of his dragon body. Before he could recall the vision, his life force began to gather within the upper portion of his heart. Just as he had practiced, he summoned it forth. The white flowed from his heart and gathered before him.

He didn't know why; he hadn't planned it. Yet instead of directing it, he was thought-merging with the white. *Brilliant!* he flashed. He knew the Ancient Ones were with him. Instead of sending his white life force forth, this was better. He was along for the ride while his body was maintained within the blue lines.

Mentard determined himself down the Time-Stream. The white stretched and flowed itself, carrying Mentard's consciousness with it. It seemed that a journey down the Time-Stream should prove to be instantaneous. But it was not.

Lights flashed at different locations, inviting Mentard's life force to enter. He neither inspected them nor made a record of their location; he ignored them. The white followed his intent.

The closer he came to the moment, the location most familiar to him, the slower the white stretched itself.

"What's going on? What can I do?" He sent out a call.

The three wizards knew. It was Winjut who answered. "Stay focused, Mentard. You're slowing momentum because you're nearing the Time-Stream where you were anchoring. But Mentard, you want to go past that time."

"Seems like I'm stuck here, barely moving," said Mentard.

"Old Boy," said Plienze, "remember this is the Time-Stream. All this has already happened... er, well most of it anyway."

Clorfothian completed his guidance with, "It's natural to feel the pull to your own self, Mentard. You know how to do this! I know you do! Trust your own instincts, Mentard."

It was just what he needed to hear. Clarity returned. He had actually begun to feel the doubt and inability to be in control of his own actions -- the same doubt he had felt during his last anchoring for Zog. He looked down into the Time-Stream, bracing himself for a possible shock. It was a good move.

There, he saw himself anchoring, struggling to maintain. He felt the emotions of that time radiate outward. His next action was as automatic as breathing fire. He thought-merged with the Mentard who was anchoring. *"You can do it,"* he told himself. *"You are more than you think you are."*

In the next moment he had released his brief merge and was speeding along the same avenue as had Zog -- toward the great wall of consuming fire. Toward the Neekontuk.

Mentard saw his homeland below. *Beautiful, it was beautiful*, he thought. Past Mutchiat where the Kloan gathering was meeting, Mentard stretched his white life force. At the edge of the mountain range, the wall of fire held itself high. It raged and spit its flames. Mentard was momentarily in awe of the force before him.

Plienze nudged. "Zog. Mentard, locate Zog! Remember, you are stretched into the past!"

Mentard knew that when this was over he would kiss that wizard right atop his wizard head. The nudge was all he needed. He stretched and scanned, dipping his life force closer and deeper into the flames. The roar was deafening.

In the blue structure, Mentard's body began to drop great waves of liquid — first blue, then green, and finally white. His life force spilled forth out of every pattern, out of his fans, and flowed down his long neck. The white swirled about the dragon body and at last began to form itself, flowing along the already stretched life force. Nothing stopped it. Nothing slowed it. Quickly, solidly, it reached its destination: that white carrying Mentard's consciousness. The white merged with its own self, augmenting Mentard's clarity and abilities.

Through the fury of the licking, biting flames, Mentard heard the words so familiar to his heart. Zog's words, his patterns, *"Gather here where I gather."*

Mentard raised his life force, and quicker than lightening, flashed it like a speared bolt into the flames toward the words. But the flames spit his speared attempt back out. Again and again he slit though the flames, intending to attach to Zog. Again and again he was refused entry.

A wisp of a vision slipped through his thoughts. "That's what I'll do!" He knew it would work. Lifting his life force out of the Time-Stream, Mentard flowed himself just a little further back in time. His vision peered through the Time-Stream until he saw the battle Zog was fighting against the raging wall of fire. Mentard held his presence, watching Zog as he charged into the flames and back out. Then it happened. Mentard heard Zog's words, "You are no more. Only I am!" The fire paused and in one movement folded back into itself. Mentard brought his life force to the very edge of the Time-Stream. He knew what would happen next. It did. Zog charged himself into the flames.

"Now!" Mentard commanded his life force. It's laser point stretched and raced, plunging itself into the flames, through the exact entry Zog had used. Mentard determined that he would not feel the effects of the flames. He determined his life force to follow Zog's patterns. He heard the words again, *"Gather here where I am...."* They echoed again and again, first in one location and then in another.

Mentard determined his life force to gather the echoes, to gather Zog's patterns. The white raced unscathed through the flames. A little pattern here, latched on and gathered. The echo over there, under the fold called, *"Gather here...."* The white stretched itself further, latching on again.

Twenty, then thirty-two times did Mentard's life force stretch and gather Zog's scattered patterns until there was no call remaining. Mentard had collected all of Zog's patterning, all of his battered dragon body. He had succeeded. Now to unstretch his life force a little and deposit Zog into his own blue structure, where Mentard himself was anchoring in his own past, in the past of all dragons.

Mentard felt the pain and anguish of Zog's body flow through the white. He wanted to absorb it, to lift it from Zog. It would be so easy. Zog would live and he, Mentard, would give up his life for his beloved leader.

Winjut's voice pierced the thought-merge, "Mentard! Zog needs his pain! Needs his suffering!"

It was Clorfothian's words, however, that caused Mentard to let go of what he was considering. Clorfothian didn't yell or speak with any force. He whispered the truth. *"All* dragons need you to do this, Mentard. Be their leader. Do it." Mentard inserted his own barrier into the white — a barrier against Zog's pain. He heard Zog yell out. Mentard placed a barrier against the sound of Zog's suffering.

The white unstretched itself just enough to hover over Zog's blue structure. Zog's patterns formed and unformed themselves. The white released the charred body into its last holding place. Mentard saw himself, as the primary anchor, sicken at the sight of Zog and then lose consciousness.

Unexpected. The sight was unexpected. A saving gift. Mentard's life force remained stretched over the scene in the anchoring chamber just long enough to see it. Zoanna took form before his eyes and without hesitation merged with the tattered, wasted body of Zog. It was private, very private, yet Mentard's life force remained to see. The spirit of Zog, a Golden Dragon, lifted from the used body and merged with Zoanna. Two as one. Mentard wanted to turn away, yet his gaze remained.

Before his eyes appeared two Golden Dragons, merging and unmerging, two then one. They turned toward the white, the life force of Mentard. Mentard saw one of them step from the gold. It was Zog. An Ancient One. Zog spoke to the white, spoke directly into all that was Mentard.

> *"You are a great dragon, Mentard. We have*
> *journeyed together throughout many realms.*
> *Now you have created a future for our dragons.*
> *Trust your knowing.*
> *You always have the Truth within you."*

Mentard drank in the words, the love, and the essence of the leader he loved deep in his heart.

The Ancient One began to dissolve. Mentard watched Zog's familiar features release form and flow toward Zoanna. Zog's last words softly surrounded and caressed the white, *"Mentard... you are my hero."*

The two merged once again and the golden light swirled around once, twice, and then disappeared.

"Come back now...." Mentard heard Winjut's voice as if it were echoing from the far distance of the furthest peak of Mutchiat. *"Come back now,"* it said again. All three wizards stood around the blue structure as the white life force continued to unstretch itself and return to Mentard's still-standing body. Most of the white restored itself directly into his heart, while the remainder flowed softly, slowly, spinning around his body. The last to return was the river of white to Mentard's fans. They opened to receive it; and when the very last of Mentard's life force had settled within him, the fans gently but certainly closed.

Mentard determined his journey to be complete. The blue lines traveled upon themselves until they too had dissolved.

The three wizards heard his request. It was easy. They waved their arms and together created the largest lush green meadow they could muster. There, Mentard laid himself down to rest, to replenish, and to remember... everything.

Along the Time-Stream, the created wizard realm of old remained as it always had — a paradise, beautiful and glowing.

• • • • •

The depositing of Zog within his own story within the Time-Stream brought the realignment of possibilities to actuality. The dragons attending the Kloan Gathering where Zoanna had been speaking, became also aligned within their present moment. It was as if they caught up with themselves.

The dissolving of Zoanna in the midst of her speaking alerted the Representatives to possible unexpected results within Zog's future-travel. Yet her beseeching for unity had filled them with her tremendous love and had also inspired them to thought-merge within their deepest capabilities.

Unknown to the Representatives or to any dragons, the realignment and settling within their rhythm caused the Time-Stream to relax and relieve itself of the unnatural fold — the Moment in Stretched Time — that had resided in one of its streams. Such relaxed condition allowed the residue of the experiences within the Dream State to integrate into the entirety of its own Stream, like the waves of the Great Lac returning to the depths of its own body.

Then, as the Representatives remained within the thought-merge of their Kloan gathering, the remembrance of another gathering filled them. In a vision, they saw and heard the youngest dragon speak through his own innocence. Held within their expanded merging, they saw the Oldest Dragon swoop into their cavern and stand before them. This time, however, when they heard his words, *all* of the Representatives remained awake. There was no need to try to figure out what his words meant. They knew instinctively, just as the encodings within their wedge wings activated automatically. The dragons were almost ready for the giant step they would be asked to make as the Neekontuk, too, began to settle back into its natural momentum. For the moment, they were complete until the next call to gather would bring them together to fulfill their destiny. The Ancient Ones could only watch and wait.

CHAPTER TWENTY

ONE YOU WILL NEVER SUSPECT WILL TURN EVENTS!

The Kloan's knowing radiated outward toward their homes. Each Representative had united with the openhearted female Receiver within his individual Floggen. The knowing held within the Kloan easily and fully filled not only the Receivers but also, then, each dragon. All dragons felt the uplift of Truth within themselves.

The newly accessed Truth bloomed and vibrated within them, and the encodings they had been carrying within the fabric of their wedge wings also awakened and activated. As the Truth continued to expand within their thought-merging, all dragons began to feel the integration of the contents of the encodings within their consciousness. It was a soft feeling, one that gently relieved them of the need to worry; yet at the same time, their thinking and discerning sharpened. It seemed that the more intensely the Truth flowed through them, the easier their lives became. What was the known for one dragon became the seeds of knowing for all dragons.

· · · · ·

It was during Brianna, Mothan, and Meteranke's flight toward the early histories that Brianna felt the gentle opening of her personal holding place of the known. She felt the Truth of dragon history and heritage wanting to join the wholeness of the activated encodings. The avenue for such joining tapped on the shoulders of Mothan, and Meteranke.

Meteranke was the first to speak. What he had previously doubted now was raised to an urgency to know. "Bri, release the full information of the eras." He paused in mid-flight and, in response, Brianna and Mothan also paused. "The first hundred eras," Meteranke spoke clearly as he felt the seeds of Truth surge through him, "let us have it all! Now!" He was hungry for it, as all dragons were. The Truth begged to be known.

Without hesitation Brianna activated the visions she had experienced with the Old One, her discovery of the eras, and the counting of three hundred and sixty-two in all.

Meteranke and Mothan absorbed her discoveries. She felt the Old One encouraging her to release the entirety of the journey she had made while her body had lain replenishing itself. She did. The pictures and feelings unreeled themselves like a love story a mother might speak to her inglet before his or her Beginning Speaking. Brianna's love for the dragons of the first hundred eras filled her and spilled over and into Meteranke and Mothan. They easily stepped into her vision and, again, they drank in the Truth as if it were the thirst-quenching, cool water they had gulped down after their first inglet Metaclores Match.

The histories resting within the first hundred eras felt the call to be revealed and absorbed into the rhythm of all histories. Meteranke and Mothan felt the same wondering that had pulled Brianna to take form beside the one-hundred-era dragons. Through her taking form and within her shared vision, they too were easily able to discern the absence of thought-merging within the dragons of old.

Their journey of Truth followed her explorations' steppings, and again Meteranke and Mothan found themselves craving an answer to the questions that were once Brianna's but had now become theirs. They saw the entire one-hundred-era dragon population raise themselves and fly in a circle over their Great Lac. And they also saw them plunge themselves, one after the other, into the great waters.

ONE YOU WILL NEVER SUSPECT WILL TURN EVENTS!

Meteranke and Mothan felt Brianna's determining to follow the dragons into the waters. In their experience of her vision, they too followed the dragons into the water. Brianna's delight in her discovery of the one-hundred-era dragons' thought-merging while in water became their delight. And more so, as Brianna had merged with the one-hundred-era dragons, so now did Meteranke and Mothan. The great revelation was released. The one-hundred-era dragons were water dragons who merged as they flew within the waters of their Great Lac. They had no knowledge or awareness of fire! Neither did they breathe fire!

Meteranke and Mothan allowed the Truth to live and flow through them. Their wedge wings raised themselves in celebration. Throughout the three hundred and sixty-third era, the knowing of their own heritage — though but a seed of such Truth — entered the consciousness of all dragons. And all dragons' wedge wings also lifted –- again and again.

The rhythm and momentum of the beginnings and endings of the dragon eras found itself within the three hundred and sixty-third era as the flames of the Neekontuk raised themselves and once again voraciously devoured all within its path. The three dragons felt the immediacy of the moment and turned from their intended destination. For the first time in a very long time, Brianna, Meteranke, and Mothan determined their presence to be home. They hadn't expected to feel excited; yet as they flew toward the location of home on the Time-Stream, their speed increased until they were looking down at the light they knew so well to be home. They could hardly wait to be there!

One glance at each other was all the three needed to agree. As they flew into the Stream and to their land, they were thrilled to see it, feel it, smell it, and be within it. Home. The air was clear and the thought-merging complete. The wholeness they felt there was more than refreshing. It was necessary. The beginning of the possible solution to the plight of their entire dragon world was already ongoing! Brianna, Mothan, and Meteranke were ready for action.

The call for a Glarian Gathering echoed through them all. Not only the Representatives, but also all dragons of all Floggen flew to the great mountain of Mutchiat. Never before had Mutchiat opened itself so wide to accommodate so many dragons. The mountain loved them and allowed itself to expand its great cavern to include their vast numbers, even the youngest inglets.

The fairies hovered atop the great cavern watching the inglets arrive. This gathering was different from times in the past when the fairies cared for and protected inglet innocence from the intensity of a Kloan Gathering. Now their inglets could not be — would not be — shielded from this gathering, from decisions as they would be called forth, nor from the Truth as it grew even within their glowing inglet innocence. Still, the fairies loved their inglet dragons and continued to hold the sweetness of their young curiosity within the flutter of gossamer fairy wings.

Brianna searched the gathering for Treiga, Kleeana, and Karthentonen. Though she felt their presence with her and with the gathering, she knew they would remain located somewhere else. Brianna's scan located Karthentonen in a healing realm separate from the Time-Stream, and she thought she also recognized Fornaign's patterns in the same location.

Brianna further scanned for the remaining two of their group, which surprisingly led her to their Neecha. She easily merged with the expanded Truth, as her extended presence was welcomed into the cavern. Treiga and Kleeana radiated white light to their beloved Brianna, knowing that her journey would be one of intensity, determining, and, at last, the fulfillment she had sought within their histories.

The six compatriots had never spoken of it among themselves. Yet each had intrinsically known that their Brianna would adventure onward from their gatherings, that she was destined for greatness. What they were not aware of was that, in a like manner, Brianna knew that each of them, too, would journey beyond any adventure they could possibly plan. Now, she liked that she knew where they all were and the feeling of that satisfaction filled her as she turned her attention toward the gathering.

As the Glarian Gathering formed, a silent expectation filled the cavern. An unspoken whisper filled them. *The Neekontuk is here! What are we going to do?* One Representative stood and, although the reason for their gathering was a crisis they had never before faced, he began speaking unhurriedly, as of old.

"Great Dragons, we gather here in the union of who we are.

"Great Dragons, our families and Floggen..." he paused and looked around at the entirety of their numbers, "are here with us!"

Another Representative stood and, nodding to the first, continued with the speaking.

"Great Dragons, we have before us...." As he spoke, the awareness of the closeness of the Neekontuk filled them. He felt his own and their shudder and began again. "Great Dragons, we have before us...." Again, as he spoke, they became alert to the closeness of the Neekontuk. In their quickened state, all dragons remembered Zoanna's empowering words and the reason they had last assembled to hear her words.

Before the second Representative could speak again, the entire gathering was filled with the realization of the death of Zog and the resulting releasing from physicality of both of their leaders. Many of them had never known a dragon breath without Zog and Zoanna.

Mothan knew very well what the absenting of Zog and Zoanna felt like. He knew the aching within himself and felt that same aching within the heart of the gathering. Before their mourning could intensify, Mothan boldly stepped into the center of the gathering and further, into the very center of their aching for the loss of Zog and Zoanna. Strangely, it was there that his yearning to be with both Zog and Zoanna was fulfilled.

As if it were her great dragon arms surrounding him, Zoanna's embrace and the essence of her love flowed around Mothan and lifted his awareness to her ever-lasting presence. Oblivious to any other occurrence, he basked in her love. A remembrance of his own words floated into his thought-merge. *Perhaps I am but an inglet wanting his mother's loving embrace once again.*

It was within Zoanna's loving embrace that Mothan's final unspoken wish was granted as Zog's strength filled him. Zog released to his now mature dragon inglet, a different kind of love — a love that was filled with the strength and fortitude necessary to step into the unknown and make it known. It was what had been missing in Mothan's passing from inglet to Nacta. Zog's gift filled him to the brim and overflowing.

Though the fulfillment of Mothan's yearning occurred within one dragon breath, he knew Zog and Zoanna's true gift was their eternal presence. Now Mothan was ready for his own adventures, the first of which lay before him in the immediacy of the moment. His readiness held him standing in the center of their gathering while the transforming force of his full Nacta radiated outward. He began to speak.

"I am Mothan. I am not your leader. Yet I stand before you. I am Nacta of Zog and Zoanna. My Nacta sister is Kleeana. Though she is not here at this gathering, she is, in this very moment, accomplishing another purpose for us, for all."

The Truth filled him; and where courage would once have urged him onward, now surety filled his every word. "The great fire of old, the Neekontuk, is upon us! It bites at our hills. It licks at our mountain. Soon it will be here, where we gather!

"I alone do not hold the answer to our approaching demise." He looked to them all, even into the eyes of their inglets. "It is *together* that we have the answer to our question, *what can we do?* **Together!**"

They were more accustomed to Zog leading them in a direction his visioning had foretold. They were more accustomed to Zoanna singing her songs to place their thought-merging within the timelessness of her radiant love. Before they could conclude that they couldn't possibly know the answer, Mothan continued.

"Listen to me! I have learned many of the teachings that your leaders -- both of my parents -- proposed for you." He beseeched them, "Hear my words! **YOU** have the answer!"

The great hall of Mutchiat became filled with a bright, golden light as the Ancient Ones gathered in the hope of their dragons' abilities to transform, in the hope that their dragons' awakening would continue instead of pulsing back into sleep.

One inglet spoke out, his little voice easily heard in the silence. "Let's do it!" As he stood, the other inglets also stood. Again and again they repeated, "Let's do it! Let's do it!"

ONE YOU WILL NEVER SUSPECT WILL TURN EVENTS!

Mothan looked up to the fairies. They sang the Song of Rejoicing[45], a song only they could sing. The children heard the sweet sounds and looked around at the entire dragon population. Mothan didn't hesitate for a moment. Ancient Wisdom burst into his knowing and in the next breath became his spoken words.

"Great dragons, let our thought-merging be total. We are all present here." He sent a message to Kleeana even though he knew that she was aware of all that was happening. "When we unite, let us determine that the answer not only lives within us. Let us also determine that we hear it, see it, and know it — together as one!"

In the histories of their gatherings, never before had all dragons gathered within the great cavern of Mutchiat. The intensity of the moment brought their awareness into full focus. It sizzled and cracked along the edges of their wedge wings. They knew. They were being called to enter the unknown with more than a hope that it would bring salvation from their impending doom. They were being called to enter the unknown with a determination not only to discover the nature of that salvation, but to grab onto it and squeeze the Truth from it!

One Representative thought-whispered and the others heard, *He said that together we have the answer.*

We must have the answer, another declared. *There is no other alternative!*

Let's do it, echoed the inglets.

Mothan's fierce determination spoken within the splendor of the fairies' sweet sounds and their inglets' call to action became the final ingredient to transform the dragons' frantic question. *What can we do?* changed to *Do! DO THIS!*

Their unanimous decision initiated the swirling, as one hint of Truth merged with another. The unknown surrendered itself to the moment. With the initial flames of the great wall of fire singeing their homes, they united as one. With the devouring of the caverns where they had rested their wings and had sung

---

45 Song of Rejoicing: only sung by the fairies, a song in celebration of the action of choice by an inglet, such choice being one that has grown from an inner awareness to an external action.

songs to their inglets, they united as one. Though fear called them into itself, the memories of the futility of panic as it had resided within the projected Dream State filled them. They refused fear.

They felt a trickling of Truth. It flowed forth not only from Mothan, but also from others and then from themselves. The trickling became a story and the story became a vision. The vision gifted them with what they called *the answer*. They were certain of it. That is, they were all certain of it except for one. Except for Brianna.

Before she could speak, before she could tell them that their answer was a vision from their histories, before she could ask them to seek another answer, a different answer, the entirety of the dragons began to vacate the cavern. Without hesitation they lifted their wings and flew toward their Great Lac. The vision had shown them what to do. They were certain of it.

Mothan looked to Brianna and then to Meteranke. It was in that moment that Meteranke heard the echoing words. It was Karthentonen's voice. It seemed that Karthentonen was speaking directly to him, to them. *"I don't know where we go from here. I only know this is the next part of this journey."*

Meteranke believed the words and looked directly into Mothan's concerned dragon eyes. "You asked for a union. You asked for the answer. It came! Trust it. Trust it, Mothan!"

Mothan was already moving. "Let's fly!" he called out. "Let's fly like we did with the Old One!"

Three grand dragons flew among their Glarian, weaving designs in and out as they all soared toward their Great Lac. The Old One felt the now familiar swelling of pride within his old dragon chest. *They are doing quite well,* he repeated to himself. The Ancient Ones continued to watch. The entirety of the three hundred and sixty-third era in the history of all dragons waited to be experienced.

The dragons approached their Great Lac and, with strength and courage within their hearts and with determined focus within their merging. Around they flew, forming their large circle and then, as the vision had so clearly demonstrated, they increased

ONE YOU WILL NEVER SUSPECT WILL TURN EVENTS!

their momentum and flew faster and faster. They brought themselves closer to each other while the three — Brianna, Meteranke, and Mothan — wove patterns around them.

It was Meteranke who knew. It was time. The wall of fire reared itself over their mountain range, over their beloved Mutchiat. The Neekontuk roared its presence at them like a great beast hovering over its prey.

Meteranke knew that he could not allow them to feel the fear that would diffuse their unity into confusion. "NOW!" he shouted, darting into the center of their circle. "FOLLOW ME! NOW!" Meteranke folded back his wings the way the Old One had taught them. Without wavering, he dove straight toward the waters of the Grand Lac. He knew none had done what he was showing them to do. In fact, Meteranke had never deliberately plummeted himself into these or any other waters. They saw. Meteranke entered the waters just as their vision had shown.

Then Mothan flew within their moving circle. He looked at them with his yellow, piercing eyes. He called forth courage from their hearts. "Come!" His voice boomed across their circle. "You have the answer! Follow me!" Mothan too bent his wings behind him and dove toward the water. He hoped they would follow him. What else could they do? They saw Mothan plunge himself into the center of their Great Lac.

Brianna too had heard Karthentonen's words. It was true that she neither knew if this step was actually the right one, the answer; nor did she know for certain if they weren't leading the entire dragon population to their end. She only knew that this was the next action — seemingly the *only* action — for her to take.

Brianna determined her purpose. As the circle of dragons flew above their Great Lac, Brianna sped around and around them at nearly twice their speed. Then, she breathed into them her knowing of their ancestors. She breathed into them again and again the vision of the one-hundred-era dragons as they flew into their Great Lac. When she knew they were filled, she flew once more around their circle. She released colors and sounds, raising their spirits in the face of the raging wall of fire as it hungered for their dragon hides.

She felt them become more than brave. She felt them become the dragons they had longed to be. And it was in that becoming that she gathered the strands of the magnificent dragons that they really were and pulled them toward their Great Lac.

It was as if they were flying in a dream, yet their flying was real. They were real. The entire grand population of empowered dragons flew once more around their Great Lac. Then, like Meteranke and Mothan had, they bent back their great wings and dove toward the center of the waters. One after the other, like the dragons in their heritage, in union they determined their flight. Unlike the dragons of their early heritage, they saw and felt the Neekontuk. The flames licked at their bent wings as they plunged into the waters.

Brianna was waiting for them. She moved her great, graceful wings as she had in the histories of long ago, and showed her dragon family how to fly in the waters of their Great Lac. Following her lead, they flew and soared. The inglets discovered the ease of using their still-developing wings and effortlessly followed the gliding of the others. Together they formed a circle as Brianna called them to maintain their thought-merging.

Mothan and Meteranke saw the graceful flowing within Brianna's wings. It was true. She had been there, just as her vision had demonstrated. She had flown in the Great Lac of the one-hundred-era dragons. She had merged with them.

Something else began to fill the dragon's knowing. Mothan and Meteranke recognized it. Brianna recognized it. The knowing of the history of the first hundred-era dragons flowed into all dragons.

The first hundred-era dragons knew nothing of fire! They had flow in their Great Lac and the Neekontuk had laid itself down upon the waters! All dragons had perished — era after era! The Truth was known. The next question quickly rose. "WHAT DO WE DO NOW???"

Brianna heard the question and kept flying. They all followed her lead. What else could they do? She sent an encoded message to Mothan and Meteranke. They had no answer. She

ONE YOU WILL NEVER SUSPECT WILL TURN EVENTS!

sent an encoded message to the Old One. She did not hear a response. Instead, she heard the echoing of already spoken words. She believed they were new, spoken for her, for them all.

"More is at work than you know. You and your beloved are not alone. One you would never suspect will turn events. It is nearly certain."

Brianna had no way of knowing that those words had been spoken to Zoanna. She had no way of knowing that she was hearing the echoing of words already fulfilled in their purpose. Brianna didn't care who spoke the words. She believed they were spoken just for her and she breathed them into her heart.

With renewed intent Brianna raised her wings and called all dragons to fly within the dancing myriad of colors she placed about them in the Lac's waters. She enticed them, played with them, and loved them until they surrendered the knowing of histories to her. She gathered it all like strands of Truth waving in the currents they created with their water flying. Opening the door to her personal knowing, like a magnet she pulled it to herself until she had collected it all. Then, with the softness of less than a sigh, she closed the door.

They flew with her and around her, suspended in the seeming timelessness she had created by gathering the knowing of their histories. Brianna knew one would come. The speaking had reassured her. Mothan and Meteranke dared not venture their thoughts to any manner or time except the present moment. They shielded their curiosities from themselves and they shielded their concerns from the others, including Brianna.

CHAPTER TWENTY-ONE

WE MUST DRINK THE MORE-OF-THAT-WHICH-WE-ARE!

The crisis of the very existence of his dragons brushed at Mentard's sleeping. He moved his dragon shoulder as if to shy away from any would-be arousal from his replenishing. Again, the emergency racing through the impending devouring by the Neekontuk brushed against Mentard's resting, begging him toward consciousness. He raised his great dragon arm and, with his clawed hand, brushed the air around him, as if brushing a pesky nuisance that had come to disturb his sleep.

It wasn't the crisis that pulled him to awaken, but his own amusement at the fact that he had brushed away nothing, just like his wizard friend, Clorfothian, did. His laughter called the three wizards to his side. It was, however, the encoded call that had been sent by a very adept female dragon that quickly alerted him into a fully awakened state. And it was the content of the encoded call and the description of the emergency that bolted Mentard's body upright and ready for action.

"Who is she?" he asked. "Who could be sending out such an intricately encoded call?"

Winjut, Plienze, and Clorfothian looked to each other for the answer. None could be found.

WE MUST DRINK THE MORE-OF-THAT-WHICH-WE-ARE!

It was Plienze who answered Mentard's question. "Ah... Mentard, it appears that you are the only one who is hearing a call."

"It's true," confessed Clorfothian, "I don't hear a thing either!"

Winjut stepped up to Mentard's sitting dragon body. "If you determine the call to me, Mentard, I'll be able to check for patterns of the sender."

Without much effort at all, Mentard sent the contents of the encoded call to all three wizards.

"Brianna," said Winjut, after his less-than-a-wink-in-time scan. "The sender is Brianna." Winjut checked his scan again. "And Mentard," he added, "the contents are accurate."

"Oh boy," recited Clorfothian. "OH BOY!" His refined ability to pull out a visual picture from a message had led him to the exact moment in the Time-Stream that the dragon named Brianna had sent her sophisticatedly encoded call.

"What!" said Mentard to Clorfothian's muttered comments.

"Take a look at this," said Clorfothian, as he flashed his visual picture for all of them to see.

At first they saw the surprising fact that the dragons were actually flying in the waters of their Great Lac. But then, it was Mentard who recognized the reason for Brianna's call.

"There!" Mentard pointed a clawed finger. "There! The fire wall!" He growled out a fierce breath. "I would know that fire anywhere! THAT, my dear wizards, is the NEEKONTUK!"

Together, the wizards knew that he would go, go to his dragons. Together, they knew that he would try to save them. What they didn't know was whether Mentard would succeed, or if they would ever see him again. He had become himself. They agreed within their own familiar thought-merge, *He has become the dragon he was meant to be.*

Clorfothian's visual of the Neekontuk's wall of fire activated Mentard's memory of his recent bout with that same wall of fire. In the next moment, he had leaped to his feet and bellowed loudly, just as he had before his rescue of Zog.

Mentard felt his life force race through his body, felt his life force become ready to be projected again. "Oh no, not this time," he commanded the intense white essence as it continued to build in its own power. "This time I'm coming along!"

He lifted his great wings, clicked open his fans, and encircled the wizard's meadow in one quick flash. He swooped down toward them, placed a huge dragon kiss on the top of Plienze's head, and loudly boasted, **"I love you guys!"**

One waft of his fully expanded wings carried him to the portal of their created realm. Just before he disappeared, they heard his great dragon bellow, **"THIS IS ONE BATTLE I'M NOT GOING TO MISS!!!"**

Mentard sped away from the wizard's realm and when the Time-Stream came into his laser vision, he directed his force to carry him to the moment before Brianna had sent her encoded call. It was there that he placed his gaze and ascertained exactly what had transpired.

There was so much going on with everything happening all at once: the dissolving of the boundaries of the Dream State, the unfolding of the Moment in Stretched Time, the awakening of dragons.... Mentard skipped his viewing to the moment of the encoded call. There they were. Everyone was holding on. Everyone was maintaining a focus on what they were doing; especially that one called Brianna. He saw the light emanating from Brianna's wings and from her heart. *She's holding it all together!* Mentard exclaimed to himself. *She's waiting... waiting for help.*

Perhaps the Mentard of long ago would have swooped down into the moment and raged the greatest fiery battle that he could call forth to sway the Neekontuk. And it is quite true that the Mentard of long ago would have perished in his attempts to save his dragons.

However, transformed into the fullness of who he was, Mentard took different action. He called upon the Ancient Ones, beseeching them to guide him, to tell him what to do. He listened. No words. He asked again. "Ancient Ones!" he called out, "Golden Ones! Tell me! What should I do?"

WE MUST DRINK THE MORE-OF-THAT-WHICH-WE-ARE!

Mentard's answer came within the words that rose from his great heart.

*You are a great dragon, Mentard. We have
journeyed together throughout many realms.
Now you have created a future for our dragons.
Trust your knowing.
You always have the Truth within you.*

Mentard's memory of his gathering of Zog played itself before him. He quickly scanned his own actions. Everything flowed — except for one moment. Even now Mentard remained confused. Again and again he looked back in time at his leader's movements. *Why?* he asked the pictures. *Why did he do it? After the wall of fire had lain back upon itself, why did Zog fly into the flames? Why didn't he fly safely home?*

The moment called him to action, and still Mentard didn't have his answer. Without it, he knew he would be lost. He knew that they all would be lost. One glance in the Time-Stream showed him the entire dragon population spreading their wings, flying in the waters of the Great Lac. One glance showed him Brianna, leading their dragons, and waiting, waiting for help to arrive.

Mentard heard the words again. *Trust your knowing. You always have the Truth within you.* His thoughts raced back and forth between the repeated words and the also repeating vision of Zog dashing himself into the flames.

More words came to him. He didn't know who spoke them. The speaking was filled with surety. Mentard gazed again at the Time-Stream and saw that the same words had echoed themselves to Brianna. He determined to listen to them. *"I don't know where we go from here. I only know this is the next part of this journey."* They didn't repeat themselves, but remained suspended before him. The realization flashed through him.

"Then I'll do it!" Mentard determined. "Then we'll all do it!"

The decision was made, the course of action determined. Mentard knew exactly what he must do. He knew exactly where he must lead his dragons. He opened his great dragon wings, expanded his gossamers, and activated the encodings within his wedge wings. His fans clicked open on command. The white essence, Mentard's life force, gathered itself, waiting for his direction. Everything was ready — except for one detail. Mentard softened his gathering force and whispered one encoded message. *"I am here. You are not alone. Together, we can do this."* He sent the message to the one they called Brianna.

Mentard swooped down, aiming his force directly at the Neekontuk as it prepared to cover the Great Lac. The mammoth wall of fire raised itself to its full height and raced its deadly flames around the edges of the Great Lac. Sizzling, singeing, and blistering, the flames remained until they had consumed all that they had laid themselves upon. When the flames returned to the wall of fire, everything that had lived and breathed a breath at the edge of the Great Lac was no more. Blackness. Smoke. That was all that remained.

As the flames returned to the great wall, Mentard made his move. His life force filled him and increased his size to be nearly the height of the wall. His fans prepared to charge. When the last bit of fire had returned to the wall, he called it to battle, just as Zog had.

Mentard's fans fired white balls of crackling, scorching light into the center of the wall. Ten, twenty, forty balls fired into its wall! The great wall of fire paused only for a moment, paused to see what was challenging it.

In that moment, Mentard summoned his own fire. It was ready, had been ready and waiting for the call. With the speed of dragon's breath, it swelled and built within him, forming its furnace of fire. He leaned his great dragon head back and felt the furnace race up his long, thick neck. His hot breath told him it was time, and without hesitation he opened his great dragon mouth and breathed his furnace of fire into the Neekontuk. Mentard's furnace of fire continued to build and be breathed forth. It swelled and cracked and scorched while the great wall received the flames, received the substance of that which it was.

WE MUST DRINK THE MORE-OF-THAT-WHICH-WE-ARE!

The Neekontuk absorbed into itself all of Mentard's fire, as it continued to plunge and rage into its wall.

It was then that Mentard spewed forth his intent, forcing it along the blazing pathway to the Neekontuk. With the fullness of all that he was, Mentard bellowed the words, "YOU ARE NO MORE! ONLY I AM!" Once, twice, three times he bellowed the words. Three times he ordered his intent into the Neekontuk.

The great wall of fire raised upward, ready to crash itself upon its challenger. And when it did, the battle it had waged with Zog began to replay itself. The patterns of that past time raced into action. Readying itself to smash down, the great wall of fire leaned its huge self back and back and back, until — just as it had once before — it folded in upon itself. The Neekontuk paused in its own flowing.

Mentard knew it was a brief pause. He reinforced his challenge and again charged the words into the wall, "YOU ARE NO MORE! ONLY I AM!" Then, in one swift move, he pivoted around, turning from the building furnace and toward the Great Lac. He folded his raised wings back and, with all the determination he could call forth, plunged himself into the Great Lac.

He felt the waters catch him, embrace him, love him. Mentard's dive brought his great dragon body and presence directly into the center of the entire population of circling, water-soaring dragons. He wasted no time. It was as if the answer to his wondering of what to do next were born in the moment.

Mentard scanned the group for the one called Brianna. She flew to his side. All dragons, including Mothan and Meteranke, stopped flying and watched the two dragons in the center of their circle.

"You are the one," Brianna said. "You're the one who sent me the message... aren't you?"

Mentard looked down at the courageous dragon before him, the dragon who had held the entire population in wholeness and in union, until... until he could arrive.

"Yes," he said. "I am the one."

"What do we do now?" she asked. Brianna turned her thought-speaking to a partial encoding so that the dragons could hear some of what was being communicated, but would also maintain their union against the panic and fear that wanted to rise to the surface. They felt the placing of the encoding and also felt the reason for Brianna's deciding to encode. It had been a loving choice, and that was exactly how the dragons received her gift.

Mentard nodded to Brianna and then quickly continued. "You probably won't believe what I'm going to tell you."

"Oh, I think you can give it a try."

"Actually, I can hardly believe it myself," Mentard confessed.

"These are extreme times." Brianna encouraged the great dragon before her. Never before had she so freely communicated within encoded thought-merging. *This is easy,* she thought to herself and at the same time felt the fondness of the Old One radiate toward her. "So far, these times have called for extreme choices. Here we are, after all, IN our Great Lac!"

"Well, here it is," said Mentard. "We don't have much time."

"It seems that we never do!" inserted Brianna's thought-merge. She braced herself for the plan this dragon was about to divulge.

"We have to get them flying again -- flying as fast as they can -- and then, together we're going to lift out of the Lac...."

"But the fire! The Neekontuk!" Brianna exclaimed.

"There's more," Mentard continued. "We will have to lift out of the Lac as One Dragon. We will have to be totally united in purpose and intent."

"But... what is our purpose? And, what will our intent be?"

"That's easy," smiled Mentard. "To make it out of this!"

"But...."

"We don't have time to go over this, you know. You'll just have to trust me," said Mentard, and then added, "Just like I'm having to trust that what I'm doing is right."

"Well, that's exactly what I've been doing, of course," Brianna agreed. "So, let's get on with it. What's the rest?"

"Once we are flying in total union and lift out of the Lac, then we will -- one after the other, like a long line of dragons -- fly directly into the Neekontuk." He waited for what he said to settle in to the dragon before him.

"What???"

"That's what we have to do."

"Then what? We perish in the fire?? Like all dragons have perished? Era after era?"

"No. Of course not."

"Then what??" Brianna repeated.

"I don't know."

Brianna looked up into the yellow eyes of this dragon. She saw the Truth, felt the certainty, felt Mentard's honesty.

"Look," he said, "I have some experience with the fire...."

"You don't have to say another word," she interrupted. "I trust you. I trust that you'll know what to do when that moment comes."

"You do?" Mentard felt relief melt though his body, through his on-alert consciousness. It was a gift, he knew.

"Yes. Now trust yourself," she said and added, "and trust me."

It was all that Mentard needed to hear. She was with him. Brianna was with him. Now to lead their dragons through a journey they had been running from for eras. Would they do it? Would they follow?

The first thing Brianna did was send the entire uncoded communication to Mothan and Meteranke so that they would be prepared for the plan. She felt their wave of disbelief and then their mutual recognizing that the choices were few... and that this dragon had come with the intent of helping them. The three nodded to each other and then to Mentard, who had observed the quick exchange. *Now there are four of us,* Mentard thought to himself.

Again it was Mothan who stepped into the center to speak. He knew what he had to do. "The time is upon us," he began, "the time for action." He looked to them all. "We have all been wondering what we will do, and we have all bravely continued to keep ourselves in union. Even now we are still in union — as One." Mothan glanced at Mentard, who nodded for him to continue.

"Long ago our leader, Zog, spoke words to you all. At that gathering, the words sounded strange to you. Some of you have forgotten the words," Mothan's scan around the gathering led him to another awareness, "and some of you have remembered those words.

"Now is the time of which Zog spoke," Mothan continued. "I will speak those words to you," he assured them, "so that you will remember clearly."

The dragons were ready — ready to hear and ready for action. Their energies, too, had been building. The force of who they were becoming begged to be expressed.

"Yet," Mothan continued, "as I speak these words to you, remember that these words are *your* words. Remember that all the words spoken here are *your* words."

He called them to gather and merge in a deeper manner, just as his father had long ago. Mothan felt the surge of golden light fill him, and he felt not only Zog's presence, but many Ancient Ones uniting with him as he spoke. *It IS true,* he thought to himself, *these ARE all dragons' words!*

"Merge your thoughts, your knowing. Open your great dragon hearts!" Mothan knew he spoke the exact words Zog had. Then the feeling shifted within him and the speaking changed. "We are all together here! This has never happened before! This is more than a Glarian Gathering! This is a Gathering of One — one entire population of dragons. All of us!"

Mothan knew there were four dragons who were residing elsewhere, but he also knew that their presence was merged with all dragons. It could be no other way! He felt the words continue to flow forth.

"As the Gathering of One, your words form and are spoken through me. It is actually *you* who are speaking."

Then the words of long ago — the words of the Kloan that were spoken through Zog — began. *"We are great dragon beings. We are more than who we have been. We are more than the Ancient Ones to whom we look for guidance."*

The speaking through Mothan changed. The ones who remembered recognized the change. *"This is the day that each one*

WE MUST DRINK THE MORE-OF-THAT-WHICH-WE-ARE!

of us will be called upon to demonstrate the Truth that we are more than dragons."

Heightened awareness filled the dragons as they listened and absorbed what was flowing forth from Mothan's speaking.

"We have left everything that is familiar. In truth we are residing within our Great Lac for the first time!"

Mothan felt the urgency to complete the speaking, yet it continued without notice of his urgency. *"The greatness of who we have been, the stories of our adventures, and the fulfilling of our hopes and dreams called us to remain as we were. But we did change. We have changed!*

"Now, in this moment, we are again being asked to change. Our love for each other and our love for who we are will plead with us to remain. Yet we cannot -- and survive!"

Mothan had spoken the word *survive*; yet fear did not fill them nor did they answer its invitation to participate in its nuances.

"Today is the day, this moment is the moment that each one of us must drink of the more-of-that-which-we-are! And it is true, we don't know what that is. We won't know until we have done all that we are called to do today. In this moment, then, we must together turn from all that we have been. We must turn from our stories. And we must face where we are going. We must step into our One Adventure together!"

Mothan paused and allowed the words to fill them, to integrate within their knowing. He looked up at the towering dragon beside him. He had never seen such a large dragon. Mentard nodded that he was ready.

"And," continued Mothan, "what is that adventure?" He looked up to Mentard. "This great dragon has heard our call! He has come here to help us. He has come here to lead us into what we must do -- to live, to survive, to exist beyond the Era of the Neekontuk."

Mentard didn't let them think it over or reflect upon the intimating of what was being asked of them. He stepped into their full merging and spoke. "I am Mentard. What I will speak with you about, I have already done. What I will speak with you about another has already done. The other was Zog.

"And I will be honest with you...." Mentard felt Brianna's nudge, yet he continued. "I only know for certain what we are to do next. I don't know what else we will be called to do until that moment. It has been the nature of my life ever since... well, ever since I chose to do what I am called to do." Mentard added, "Just as you are called to do what you must do."

Mentard looked around at the great, full circle of dragons. He looked into the wide-open eyes of the inglets, and he looked above to the fairies. "Today is the ending of one way of living, of residing upon our land, and the beginning of another way. I don't know what the new way will be."

He surprised even Brianna with his next words. "I have seen a place that is... is more beautiful than any. It is even more beautiful than our lands that the Neekontuk has already devoured. I don't know if that is our new home. I only know that I have seen it and that it exists. I don't know where it exists. And, in this moment, I don't know how to get there. I only know what I am to do in this moment."

Without a pause, Mentard dove right into their next call to action. "What are we called to do in this moment? Perhaps you will not believe what I am about to say. But, hear my words! It is the only choice we have. And, we ALL must agree. We ALL must choose. We must enter this adventure together as One.

"Ask yourselves," he placed the choice to them even before they knew what they were choosing, "if you are willing to remain in union. Ask yourselves if you will choose to go forth together into... into the unknown and make it your known. Ask yourselves now!"

He felt their decision. They would, of course, remain as One. Some thought it useless to even ask such a question. *Of course we will remain merged and go forth together!* they thought-merged to Mentard.

"Great dragons! You have decided! Then, now! I will tell you of our next adventure together."

WE MUST DRINK THE MORE-OF-THAT-WHICH-WE-ARE!

Brianna sent forth her love and embracing. Mothan sent forth his strength and the eternal presence of Zog and Zoanna. Meteranke sent forth his surety of action. Treiga, Kleeana, and the Elder breathed their breath of white essence upon the entire gathering. Karthentonen and Fornaign united, two dragons as one, and flowed forth the essence of their union. The Ancient Ones watched. The Oldest Dragon knew.

"This is what we will do — together," began Mentard. "We will fly, as you have been in your merged circle. We will fly faster and faster until it feels as though we are spinning." Mentard didn't know where the plan was coming from. He was just as anxious as the others to hear what he would say next.

"We will be spinning together, around in this, our Great Lac. Our inglets will automatically rise up and rest at our sides. Our fairies will care for them.

"When we have reached a momentum greater than the force of old that knocks at our door, we will fly with all our strength -- out of our Lac and, one after the other, we will plunge ourselves right into the leaned back wave of the Neekontuk." He didn't leave them one moment for fear. "When we dive into the Neekontuk, we will say together, YOU ARE NO MORE! ONLY I AM!"

Then the words came that he had hoped would come. "On the other side of the Neekontuk is our new way. On the other side of the Neekontuk we are saved from its onslaught. On the other side of the Neekontuk, it can devour us no more. On the other side of the Neekontuk, the Ancient Ones will weep at our splendor! On the other side of the Neekontuk, we will be all that we are and the unknown will be known."

He felt Brianna at his side. She beamed her thought-merge to him, *BRAVO!*

The answer had come. The journey unfolded itself for them. Now all that was left was for them to step into it -- together as One.

CHAPTER TWENTY-TWO

FOLLOW MEEEEE!

The choice before them was immense. Also before them stood Mentard, emanating strength and courage. They were stunned. First one and then another thought-spoke their disbelief. As hard as they tried to discover a different solution to their plight, only one conclusion surfaced.

It was Freena, Receiver for the Floggen located in what used to be their closest mountain range, Frainakta, who spoke their conclusion. "It seems we have but two choices." She looked to the gathering for confirmation of their unanimous decision. All dragons released the force of their united strength to Freena.

"One choice," she continued, "is to remain here in our Lac. That choice, however, brings with it the inevitable smothering of the Neekontuk upon us until we are no more." Freena snorted a small, dark stream of smoke.

"The other choice is to follow the plan given to us by Mentard, who came here to help us! Though many of us feel the possibility of our perishing with Mentard's plan, we have decided that it is better to take action than to cower here in our Lac, waiting for our own demise!"

Freena slowly looked around the circle of her family of dragons, and then turned her gaze upward to Mentard. "Brave dragon," she

FOLLOW MEEEEE!

began with their unanimous words, "it is our decision, as dragons gathered together in union and choice, to go forth with your plan." She raised her voice to its fullest volume, **"We have decided to make your plan, our plan!"**

They cheered their own decision. They cheered their own bravery and the bravery of the great dragon who stood before them. They cheered like those who prepare for battle, not knowing if they would only growl their battle cry and then quickly perish; not knowing if they would rage their life force toward its intended target and then still perish. And they cheered like those who prepare for battle and dive into the center of its blaze, without thought of where it will lead them.

Mentard bellowed his cry! At once he began flying in the waters of their Great Lac. Around and around he flew. Mothan and Meteranke joined behind him. It was all that was needed to begin the momentum. All dragons lifted their great wings and soared together. Brianna felt the force of their intent and when the last dragon had entered the circling mass, she flew with them.

Around and around they flew until their momentum grew to such a pitch that they felt as though they were each spinning around separately and yet together. But Mentard only increased his speed, pulling them to greater speeds than they believed possible! The fairies swooped into their circle and held their inglets within the spinning, racing river of dragon-determined courage.

"Now," they thought, "it must be now that we are ready!"

Yet again Mentard increased his speed, wafting his great wings and pulling them onward to do all that they could do. He called their strength and they responded. Their wings stretched and grew. Their long necks extended and they soared like the dragons of old. They soared like the Oldest Dragon did in his first flight.

"Now!" commanded Mentard. It wasn't that he was commanding them, but more than he was commanding their power and force as it had melded into One Force. "Now!" he bellowed, "FOLLOW ME!"

247

Mentard knew they would follow because they were now not only part of him; they were him and he was them. It was with a gigantic effort and with seemingly no effort at all that Mentard crashed through the surface of their Lac and rose up into the smoke-filled air.

"AH-HA!" he growled and breathed the smoke deep into his chest. The blackness mixed with Mentard's smoke; and when he breathed it back out, it filled the air with blacker force and power. Flames flicked out from both sides of his mouth.

His dragons followed, emerging from the Lac, breathing and spewing smoke and flames. Their united growl became the sound of a battle that had never been waged. Their united sound rang though the smoke and fire. Their united sound resounded throughout all eras and all realms.

Treiga, Kleeana, and the Elder heard the ringing. Karthentonen and Fornaign felt the call resonate through them. The Oldest Dragon heard and recognized it: The Call to Return to One. They flew toward the battle. They would be waiting.

Mentard swelled with pride at Brianna — the last dragon to burst forth from the waters.

It wasn't something Brianna had planned. Nothing was. Mentard felt her turn toward the expanse of the Time-Stream. He remembered her words, *and trust me*.

Just as the Neekontuk began to release its paused leaning back, Brianna stretched her life force down the Time-Stream further and further, back past the eras she hadn't yet entered, back to the end of the first hundred eras. Her impeccable ability to locate and enter, unleashed her stretched life force into that moment just as the Neekontuk of that long-ago time was prepared to lay itself upon the Lac of unsuspecting water dragons.

She laced her life force around their innocence and called them, loved them, enticed them to remember her, to remember their merging. They did. In their elation, again they merged with Brianna's life force.

Mentard saw exactly what Brianna was doing. Without hesitation, he joined his life force with Brianna's and together they lifted the first hundred era dragons from their plight. Their joined life force unstretched itself and carried with it those wondrous dragons. Mentard and Brianna easily and completely deposited the water dragons into the wholeness of all dragons. The water dragons found themselves swimming within a union grander than any they had ever known, found themselves resting within the entirety of the One gathering.

Even though the wall of fire loomed and determined its crashing movement, Brianna continued to hold her purpose and reached into her place of knowing. There she found the gathered known histories of the water dragons. Quietly and softly, she released those memories back into the entirety of the dragons of the land.

The dragons of the present, three hundred sixty-third era, remembered their belief that the answer to their plight was to flee to their Great Lac. They had done just that! They remembered the fear they had felt in realizing the inevitable devouring of the raging fire.

When the three hundred sixty third-era dragons felt their new family of water dragons awaken to what had been their continued plight, the three hundred sixty third-era dragons laid their remembrance — of Brianna's gathering of their fear — upon the awakening of the water dragons. Where the water dragons' fear was, the three hundred sixty third-era dragons placed the resounding call to union — their call to One. The water dragons readily embraced the call.

Mentard was proud of them. They had remained in the moment and automatically knew what to do! *Now,* he thought, *we have more to do — together!* Brianna heard his thought and readied herself for action.

Mentard reared himself above his dragons, united in force and purpose. He bellowed his call to charge into their adventure. "NOW! GREAT DRAGONS! NOW WE GO FORTH!!!" He flew around them and between them, gathering their courage and strength. He breathed his determined intent upon their unanimous choice and he summoned the dragons that he knew they were.

The Neekontuk raised and stretched its licking, fiery wall and prepared to devour the force before it, the Great Lac, and any remnants of what had resided upon and within the dragon land. The Neekontuk sputtered and crackled as if it were daring any to enter the battle. The dragons more than dared.

Mentard's growl rumbled against the furnace. "REMEMBER, DRAGONS! REMEMBER THE WORDS!" His great dragon mouth opened as he shouted over the deafening roar of the hovering blaze. "REMEMBER! YOU ARE NO MORE! ONLY I AM!" They remembered. United as one dragon, they began to chant the words. Louder and louder their chant grew.

The Neekontuk also remembered the words. It breathed into itself all of its own power, all of its own devouring force and prepared to consume... everything.

"Now! The time is now!" Mentard heard the words whispered... from somewhere, from someone. *"Now, Mentard. Lead them home. Now."*

Mentard called them forth. It was not a battle after all. It was a choice they had made. Together. Together as One. He called them to their destiny.

"NOW! NOW WE ENTER OUR FREEDOM! NOW, GREAT DRAGONS, WE BECOME WHO WE REALLY ARE!" He felt their building force ready to burst. Mentard glanced once at Brianna and toward the surging furnace of flames. "FOLLOW MEEEEEEE!"

Mentard leaned back his expanded wings and plunged himself into the Neekontuk. "YOU ARE NO MORE! ONLY I AM!!" The great river of dragons fulfilled their choice. All stretched wings, leaned back to their fullest capacity, flew and carried their dragons directly into the center of the wall of flames. All fairies plunged themselves and their inglets into the flames.

One after the other, like a giant river of courage and strength, of determined choice, the dragons flew into the flames while simultaneously growling, "YOU ARE NO MORE! ONLY I AM!" The entirety of all that they had been individually and together plunged into the flames.

Brianna saw her water dragons, filled with the knowing of their own histories and united with determined intent, plunge themselves into the flames that they had previously and

FOLLOW MEEEEE!

Brianna saw her water dragons. Each one plunged into the flames, challenging, "You are no more! Only I am!"

unknowingly perished in. Their charge was filled with the power of their newfound Truth. Each one in turn plunged into the flames and changed the nature of their histories with their cry: "YOU ARE NO MORE! ONLY I AM!"

Brianna was the last dragon to enter the flames. *Come, my dear, we are waiting for you.* It was the voice of the Old One. The time of one breath remained.

She opened her wings further and further, commanded her fans, and deliberately activated the encodings within her wedge wings. Alive! It was the most alive she had ever felt herself to be! In one swift flight, Brianna flew across the Neekontuk's wall, charging great white balls of light from her fans into its blaze. In one swift flight, she placed herself in the direct path of the crashing wall. She knew what she was to do. She did it.

The great Neekontuk of the three hundred sixty-third era crashed itself, as it always had, upon all that was before it. In this crashing, however, it was relieved of its own existence. In this crashing, just at its own moment of fulfillment, it heard the words echo throughout its entire raging, fiery, licking, spewing self. The words were strong. The words were powerful. The words were definite. The words changed the nature of the history of the Neekontuk. The words completed its journey.

It was Brianna who growled the last words:

"YOU ARE NO MORE!!!!"

• • • • •

She had flown through the flames and — as if nothing could ever again be a surprise — then into the white light. There had been no burning, no singeing, no biting, no licking of flames upon any part of her dragon body. The roar was gone. The smoke was gone. The furnace was gone. The Neekontuk was gone.

White light surrounded her as if she had flown into the side of a cloud. She heard their laughter and then their call. "We're over here. Keep coming!" It wasn't that she flew to them, but more that she decided to be there — and there she was.

The light sparkled and swirled; and when she entered it, Brianna felt their laughter move through her. She felt their love move through her. When she laughed, they laughed. Her delight in all that she was, became their delight.

In one breath she wondered where she was and in the next moment she knew. They were all one dragon, just as they had determined themselves to be. She was herself and she was all dragons. They were each themselves, they were each other, and they were one dragon. The white sparkled and flowed around them and through them.

They were all there — Mothan, Meteranke, Treiga, Kleeana, Karthentonen, and Fornaign — she felt their presence. She could see them, yet they had no dragon body. She could speak with them, as in times of old, but the speaking was... *not really necessary*, she thought. The feeling was more than familiar. It was home.

The Old One appeared and Brianna quickly spanned the seeming distance between them. "We did it, didn't we?" She couldn't contain her knowing and then her overflowing joy.

He loved her. Had always loved her from the moment she had taken form upon the land. There had always been something about Brianna that engendered in his old dragon being the hope that the era might complete itself differently, that perhaps there would be the Return to One at long last.

It wasn't that he was tired of his long journey upon the land, and it wasn't that the adventures didn't still delight him as each one of his dragons explored more and more of their own capabilities. He supposed it was the Neekontuk that tired him and then again, he knew. It was the disheartening presence of sleep that had lingered within his wondrous dragons. And at times he had heard himself wonder if it would ever end. Had he actually created an eternal, unending cycle? A cycle that would continue again and again to return to itself, only to birth and repeat the journey? Had he actually breathed into existence his own demise?

It had been hundreds and hundreds of eras, after all. And each era had ended with the rage of the Neekontuk. *Yes, it's true*, he had spoken to himself countless times, *that the Ancient Ones did remain in the hopes that one day the patterns of Truth would be known and the creation — my breathing forth of my own dragon self — would be released to return to... to the Nothingness at last.*

Brianna repeated her words, "We did it. Didn't we, Old One?" He felt as soft as he ever did, as loving as he ever had been. She knew that he was the Oldest Dragon, the First Dragon. But to her, he would always be her *Old One*.

"Yes," he said. "Yes, you did, my dear."

Brianna felt her Old One's love. "Is this really what home feels like?" she asked.

"Partly," he said.

"Oh."

"There's more, you know," the Old One breathed into her.

"Oh?"

"This is not quite the journey's end," he said softly.

It wasn't that she was tired of her own journey, but more, it was that she just wanted this to be the end — the end of it all. "What else do we have to do?" she sighed.

The Old One's laughter tickled at her sigh and pulled at her innocence. "Why, my dear, you don't *have* to do anything!"

"Oh, I know. I... well, I want something different, if you really must know," she admitted to the Old One and to herself. "I don't know exactly what it would be... can't even think of what it could be."

Brianna felt another tickle. It placed itself around her heart at the same moment she heard herself say, "It's like Mentard said...." She remembered his words exactly, *I only know what I am to do in this moment.* "Do you know what I mean, Old One?"

Just as he guided her once before, again he said, "Keep going. You're almost there."

His all-knowing thrilled her and comforted her all in the same breath. "Well," she continued, "I feel as though I've been part of this journey for a very long time... and, truthfully, I'd like a different one! That's it! I'd like a different one."

"Bravo!" the Old One cheered her honest discovery.

"Soooo, what's next?" she smiled through his celebrating.

"As I said, there's more." He felt her curiosity peak, as it had in the past. "This is called the Return to One."

"Well, Old One! Don't you think we've already done that?"

"My dear, as I said, there's more. This is not the destination. In fact, didn't you yourself say that you wanted a different journey?"

"Well, yes, that's what I said, but...."

He interrupted her continued questioning with something she never expected.

CHAPTER TWENTY-THREE

THE OLDEST DRAGON CALLED

"Long ago, there was one dragon who stepped from the Nothingness and took form."

"What do you mean *stepped from the Nothingness?*"

"Well, that's what I'm getting to," he smiled at the intensity of her focused attention. "But since you asked, I'll speak of that first.

"The Nothingness is just that. It is the essence of everything that has ever been or ever will be –- without form. Just essence."

"Is it something like this white, sparkling... whatever this is... that's..." Brianna searched for the words. "Well, it seems like this white is holding us all together. Seems like it IS all of us."

"The Nothingness is something like this," the Oldest Dragon said, "but without design, without character."

"Oh! Without the 'us' in it!"

Brianna's journey through the Truth brought a chuckle to his old dragon being, and as he felt it ripple through him, he wondered if it would indeed be his last chuckle.

"In a sense," he continued, "you're right. Yet there's just a little more. You see, here there is white, sparkling essence — as you call it. And that's just it, the essence is here for us to call it something, for us to identify in some manner."

He paused to allow the speaking to settle into her knowing.

"And?"

She was ready for more in less than a pause. It pleased him.

"Well, in the Nothingness, there is nothing. There is no white, sparkling essence. It simply is."

"All Right. I think I have that part of it. Thank you, Old One." It took her less than a moment to ask, "Will you continue now? And, was the one dragon who took form you?" She realized the depth of her question and added, "...Sir?"

"Yes, that first dragon was and is me. I am the First Dragon."

She liked that. The Truth felt grand and simple all in one.

The Oldest Dragon continued, "When I stepped into form and upon the Land, I realized that there was so much to experience, so many journeys within which to adventure, that I would never be able to enjoy them all.

"So, my dear, I breathed my dragon breath forth and determined to create dragons -- many dragons -- who would journey and adventure forth, who would experience all there was to experience."

"You did?" Brianna whispered. "You really did that?"

"Yes, my dear. That's exactly what I did. What I didn't realize was that in my breathing forth, I also breathed forth part of the pattern that lived in the *taking form*."

"I don't understand that, Old One," she readily admitted. "Would you explain it more?"

"Well, let's see how I can put it." The Oldest Dragon knew that he was speaking the Truth to Brianna AND as he did, he was also speaking the Truth to all dragons, united as One. *It was a fine realization* he had decided.

"When I breathed my breath forth to take form, I breathed the *pattern of dragon*." He looked to see if she understood.

"All right... I understand that.... And they did take form, right?"

"Yes, exactly. However, what I didn't realize was that I also breathed forth the pattern called *taking form*."

"Oh I see!" she exclaimed excitedly. "You breathed forth the pattern of dragon. But it couldn't actually take form unless you also breathed forth the pattern called *taking form*! I see," she repeated. "It's kind of like this white essence we're in. You needed to breathe... to create a way that the dragon pattern *could* take form!"

"Very good!" the Oldest Dragon cheered, "I don't think I could have translated it better myself."

"So, then what happened... that is, after you realized that you had breathed the *pattern of taking form*?"

"Well, within the *pattern of taking form,* there was something else that also flowed forth and took form. The something else was a necessary part of taking form. In truth, no dragons could have taken form without it. Yet... it flowed forth and became a form also."

"Well, what was it????" She couldn't wait a moment longer.

"It was fire. And, it became what has been called the Neekontuk." He waited. She didn't disappoint him.

"FIRE!? THE NEEKONTUK?? Yikes! So THAT's what's been going on!! How amazing! How absolutely amazing!" She let the knowing of Truth surge through her. She knew there was more. She knew by the way the Old One was waiting. The more came.

"I have it! Wow! I mean, WOW!!" She allowed her excited awareness to settle, and then she continued with, "It all fits into place, doesn't it?"

"Keep going," the Oldest Dragon urged her.

"Everything fits exactly into its right place. We may never know that's what's going on in the moment, but it is.

"We all entered the Neekontuk and said the words *You are no more. Only I am.* WE were completing the journey, weren't we? We were turning the Neekontuk back toward you, weren't we? We were bringing that part of the *pattern of taking form* back to you... so that... so that you could gather us all together... and bring us back to the Nothingness. ...So that YOU could go back to the Nothingness! That's right! Isn't it, Sir?"

"Exactly, my dear. Exactly." The Oldest Dragon continued, "You see, the Neekontuk had lived within its own eras for so long that it was beginning to take on its own character and purpose. It was time. It was time for it to be relieved... so that it, too, could return to One, could return home."

"Oh."

"And, my dear, that's the remainder of this journey, the Return to One. Now we all simply let go of all that we have been and... step into the Nothingness!" He laughed at the relief of it all.

"But, sir!" Brianna had to know. She had to know right now. "If we step into the Nothingness, then we are nothing... right?" She didn't allow him time to answer, but continued with, "Then how do we take form again? Do you, will you step forth and be the First Dragon again? Will you breathe us forth? Again? And, if not, then... how do I — how do we — have a way to... well, to have the other journey that I'd like to have? Sir, I have to know!"

"So many questions!"

"Sir!"

"To begin with, my dear, no, I will not step forth and again be the First Dragon." He staved off her racing questions with a wave of pure love. It softened her and it brought her peace, the peace that she was aching for. She'd thought that the answers to her questions would have brought her peace, but she still had those questions AND she had this delicious peace.

"Another will be the First Dragon. It will be another time, another... *era*, if that's what it's named. And that dragon will breathe forth his form — this time without the pattern of taking form."

"But how? How will we take form?"

"Everything will be different the next time, my dear. My time was the first time, the first time dragons had ever taken form. Now my time is nearly complete.

"All that we have learned, all that you have learned and experienced will be part of your taking form, part of the next First Dragon's taking form."

"But what about the Neekontuk? Will that happen again?"

"The Neekontuk is part of my era, my dear. It was part of my creating. The next Dragon will know, just as you know. There will be no need... well, I suppose there will be no need for the *pattern of taking form!*" He knew he was racing ahead of her ability to absorb all that he was saying.

"Sir?"

"I suppose that within the breath there will be simply taking form... in the moment.... I believe that the next First Dragon will simply breathe his breath and, if you have decided that you would like to take form again — and it seems that you have decided that in your wanting of a new journey — then you will simply take form!" He thought upon it and added, "How absolutely simple! How wonderful!"

"Sir, do you mean that before we step into the Nothingness if we decide we want to... well, to have another journey, to take form again, all we need to do is decide?"

"That's exactly correct."

"But, sir, who will be the next First Dragon??"

"My dear, that's only for the next First Dragon to know."

"Oh."

Both Brianna and the Oldest Dragon felt the swirling and celebrating of all dragons as the Truth radiated outward and became part of all dragons' knowing. The sparkling white essence flowed around them as dancing and twirling, spinning and flying. The freedom of Truth filled them to the brim and overflowed, only to swirl around them and fill them again.

It was Mentard who was next at her side. "So, sweet Brianna, you've decided to take form again?"

"Yes, Mentard, I have. The next journey promises to be a grand one, don't you think?"

"I do. In fact," he continued, "I've also decided to take form. I... well, I know that I'm the next leader." *There, I've said it*, thought Mentard to himself. *But I know it's the Truth!*

"I know it's the Truth, too, Mentard," she responded to his whole statement, even to the thoughts to himself. "I know that you are the next leader. It's obvious!"

Again the recognition filled Mentard with relief. He was about to thank her when she said, "I... I know that I'm to speak before the Kloan — if that's what we will call the gatherings — yet a female hasn't just stepped up there and... well, spoken!"

"That's what the past eras were like, Brianna," Mentard assured her. "This time everything's bound to be different."

"Well, I wouldn't be too sure about the *everything* part," she said. "Some ways are bound to be the same, or at least similar."

"In that case," smiled Mentard as he surrounded her with his great dragon strength, "then a previous manner will have to take precedent."

"Oh? And what would that precedent be?" She liked the feeling of his presence about her. It brought a sigh to her heart.

"You'll just have to be the partner of the leader." He smiled a big smile, the biggest he'd ever had, he supposed.

"Why Mentard, that would be just fine," she said. Her heart overflowed. "That would be just fine."

The Oldest Dragon called them all to come forth, to return to One, to release their journeys and return to their home, to him, and to the Nothingness.

"Sweet dragons, wondrous dragons, brave dragons, united dragons! Bring yourselves here. Bring yourselves to me. It is time to rest.

"Great dragons, your journeys have been full of adventures and discoveries.

"Great dragons, you have fulfilled your hearts' desires in so many wondrous ways,

"And in so doing, you have fulfilled my heart's desire in so many wondrous ways.

"Brave dragons, you have captured the sleep of your journey and transformed it into this moment,

"You have gathered all of yourselves together, and in so doing, you have gathered together all of that which is me.

"You are more than my children. You ARE me. And I am you. We are the same dragon. We always have been.

"Prepare yourselves, dear ones, to Return to One!"

He called them forth to return to him. The Oldest Dragon breathed his breath upon all dragons, loving them, caressing them, and gathering them to himself.

They not only heard the call to One, they felt it within the very core of their heart, within the very core of themselves. They felt his great love and wanted more. They were supposed to want more of his love. It was the avenue through which they would return to him.

The Oldest Dragon, the First Dragon, opened his great heart and called them to return.

Brianna and Mentard were the first to respond to the call. Together, they appeared before their Old One and received his love. It surrounded them and filled them and in that filling they stepped through the entry to the Nothingness.

The Oldest Dragon called them again to return to him. They did. All dragons, one after the other, flowed past him and into the Nothingness just as their leaders had.

"Kar," said Fornaign, "while my body was healing, I had the opportunity to travel. And when I say *travel* I mean beyond anything we've ever known."

Karthentonen had always enjoyed Fornaign's spirit of adventure. "And?"

"Well, I don't think I want to take form again, Kar. I want to travel to those realms the same way I did before — that is, without my body."

"Ohhh." Karthentonen should have been accustomed to being surprised by Fornaign's plans, yet here he was, at the entryway to the Nothingness, and he was again surprised. "That's quite a plan, For. Sounds exciting."

"So, do you want to come?" Fornaign asked his long-time friend.

"For... it sounds great, but I don't think it's for me. I just have to have a taste of the new way. I've some ideas of my own and... well, I have to follow them." He was about to say more when a familiar voice chimed in.

It was Meteranke. "Boy am I glad to see the two of you... er, that is, before we step in!" He turned to Fornaign, "I had a plan to get you..."

"I know," said Fornaign. "I know everything."

"Oh. Sure, that's right. I forgot!" Meteranke smiled at the very thought of forgetting. It was a new freedom for him and he enjoyed the letting go of what had been. It was part of the process of the entryway, in which the three of them had paused. "Anyway, For, I'd like to join you! You know, without a physical body. I think that's a great plan! Why we could..."

It was then that the three stepped through the entryway and into the Nothingness.

· · · · ·

Mothan whispered to Kleeana, "What have you decided?"

"I'm not sure. I'm... I'm waiting for someone, she said, looking around for Treiga.

"Oh."

"How about you, Mothan, have you decided?"

"Yep! I'm going to enter The Sectors of Learning — without a body. I have a plan..."

"Oh Mothan, that sounds exciting!"

"As I said," he continued, "I have a plan. I think that within The Sectors of Learning there must be a way to take form and then release form. You know, like Zoanna did — only more so." He beamed a flash of light toward Kleeana and without a further word, stepped into the Nothingness.

Kleeana hadn't planned on waiting. She hadn't planned on anything. In fact, there were only two other dragons left to enter the Nothingness and she knew one of them had to be Treiga. She was right.

Treiga and the Oldest Dragon met at the entryway.

"Sir," said Treiga, "I heard that you won't be coming back. That is, you won't be taking form as the First Dragon again."

"That's correct, Treiga. My journey is done. This Oldest Dragon has fulfilled his intended purpose."

Kleeana heard them talking and brought her presence to theirs. "Hello, you two!"

Both Treiga and the Oldest Dragon delighted in her presence. Treiga moved closer to Kleeana. The Oldest Dragon liked the two of them and further enjoyed they way they merged together without effort.

"I guess we're the last ones," said Kleeana. "Feels a little strange, don't you think?"

Treiga answered, "Feels a little like the Neecha to me — only augmented. Doesn't it?"

"Well, now that you mention it, Trei, it does."

"What's your hesitation, Kleeana?"

"I'm not sure what to decide," she admitted. "And I feel like an inglet because of it."

Treiga loved her innocence, loved her. "Why don't you simply decide to take form with me? And however that happens, it'll be right."

"Why of course!" Kleeana felt the relief she'd been waiting for. "Of course, Trei, I'll take form with you! What could be better?"

"I can't think of anything," he said, spreading his love around her.

"Are you coming?" she asked. "I mean, are you coming into the Nothingness?"

"I will," Treiga assured her. "I just want to ask the Old One a last question."

"Oh. A last question for the Last Dragon?"

"I suppose you could say it that way," he smiled.

"Well... I'll see you in form!" and with that Kleeana stepped into the Nothingness as the others had before her.

Treiga turned to the Oldest Dragon. "Sir, if you're not going to return and take form as the First Dragon... well, who will, Sir?"

"Why Treiga," said the Oldest Dragon, "don't you know?"

"Know what, Sir?"

The Oldest Dragon loved Treiga's clarity, but most of all he loved his innocence. "Treiga," he said to the last of his dragons, "here we are together. I am the Oldest Dragon. I was the First Dragon and now I will be the Last Dragon. And you... why, it's you, Treiga."

"Sir?"

"You, Treiga, you'll be the First Dragon."

"But…"

"As it looks now," said the Oldest Dragon, "You and Kleeana will be the First Dragons! Now that's something new — right from the start." The Old One liked that and thought to himself, *I suppose they'll breathe them into existence together! Ha! That's how it will happen! The two will breathe their breaths together — and there won't be a need for the pattern of taking form. They will be it. Ha! Great plan! I like it!*

"Well, young one," the Oldest Dragon said to Treiga, "you'd best be letting me be. I've been waiting for this journey for a very long time."

"Thank you, Sir. Thank you for everything." Treiga felt a slight humor in the speaking of the word *everything* as it did refer to the fact that the Oldest Dragon had created everything.

Of course the Oldest Dragon also felt the slight humor; and as Treiga stepped through and into the Nothingness, his slight chuckle echoed to where there was just one dragon. The Last Dragon.

He gathered to him all the stories, all the adventures, all the causes and effects, all the eras and the birthing of the eras. He gathered to him all the names of all the dragons and all the characters of the many Kloans. He gathered to him the green of the Land and the violet of the Great Lac. He gathered to him all the peaks and all the ranges of mountains as they had laid upon the Land. Lastly, he gathered to him the great Mutchiat as it has stood though the many eras and realms.

The Last Dragon breathed his loving breath toward the realms of the Wizards and released them to their own decidings. It was then that the Golden Ancient Ones appeared before him.

Your time is now, they said.

The Last Dragon looked to them. "You are free now. You are free, free to return to the Nothingness." The Last Dragon couldn't help saying the words aloud, "They awakened! Imagine that! They did it — at long last." He was filled with the finality of his journey. "What will you do?" he asked them. It was his last question.

"We will remain." It had been their decision long ago. Some would remain and some would return to the Nothingness. All had returned now. That is, except for the Last Dragon.

"Ahhh," sighed the Last Dragon. "This has been an amazing journey! Who would have known…" he shook his great, old dragon head. "Who would have known." With those words, the Last Dragon stepped his great old dragon being through the entryway and into the Nothingness.

EPILOGUE

In the breathing of the first breath from the Nothingness, two flowed forth. They were known as Treiga and Kleeana: The First Dragons. Together they knew that the many journeys and adventures upon the land would be more than what they could possibly experience. Together they decided to breathe one breath — two breaths as one — and create from themselves, those who would reside upon the lands: Dragons. And that is exactly what they did.

• • • • •

The dragons took form upon the beautiful and lush land. It's green meadows laid themselves wide and soft and its majestic mountains rose to such a height that the simple viewing of them tugged at the dragons' wings to open and explore the many adventures that waited, nestled in the peaks.

Waterfalls spilled forth from the mountains, and rivulets curved and wound their way down past the meadows and into the Grand Lac. There, the cool waters sparkled and spread themselves invitingly wide. The land was more than perfect; it was Paradise. And the entryway to Paradise held itself ready for its dragons to step through.

The dragons didn't know who had created their homeland or why. They did know that it lived separate from the Time-Stream, yet inserted within it. The facts about their homeland seemed to be the only facts they couldn't, as yet, access. In a casual way — as the land lent itself to a natural rhythm of living — the dragons wondered about such facts.

After all, they had mused, there was a deep familiarity within the patterns that were imbedded in the entryway. They had all agreed that, upon stepping through the entryway, they each had heard the words *Gather here where I am!* And, they further agreed that even before their first step touched the land, they had felt a breath of great peace shower upon them. It was as if they were being assured that they would be cared for, beyond what their magnificent capabilities could imagine.

The facts didn't beg to be known, and the dragons didn't pursue their discovery. It was more that every once in a while they chatted about it all and, in the end, continued to feel quite comfortable in their ability to let the mystery remain – just for a little while longer.

And, it was as if they knew the name of their land, even as they breathed their first fiery breaths into the clear air. The name rode forth upon those fires and rumbled around the great mountains. They liked it, they had agreed:

Kah-na Tro-Linaht, The New Beginning.

・・・・・

Mentard, asked Brianna, *when we take form like this, do the histories of other times remain the same? Can we enter the Time-Stream of the last time?* She added, *I had planned to do a study of the second hundred eras.*

I suppose the other times are always a little changed, Mentard answered, enjoying the casual nature of their thought-merge.

Oh? Why is that?

Seems as though there's always some dragon dipping herself into an era and merging with the dragons there. Heard she was the type that just can't stop herself.

Brianna paused in mid-flight. *Oh? And why would that be?*

EPILOGUE

Mentard's gaze caressed her slightly agitated exterior. *I heard that her heart was so big and that she loved all dragons so completely that she simply had to merge with them.* He paused and then added, *I happen to think that she's making major changes in the Streams themselves — because she's here to unite all dragons in all eras.*

Brianna felt it coming.

...And what better way, said Mentard, *than to merge. I think she's brilliant!*

It came. It was the first time in this time that Brianna blushed from the tip of her fiery nose to the end of her long tail.

Nice, said Mentard. *Very becoming.*

· · · · ·

It had been the beginning of a mating. The entire Glarian had felt it: two dragons joined in flight by their celebrated union. Because it had thus far lasted over sixty of their dragon years, the dragons on the land rejoiced in the knowing that they would be gifted with two great leaders. What they did not know — yet — was that the journey they would be led through, would give to all dragons in all Time-Streams the complete history of their wondrous dragon selves. But that, of course, is another story.

GLOSSARY

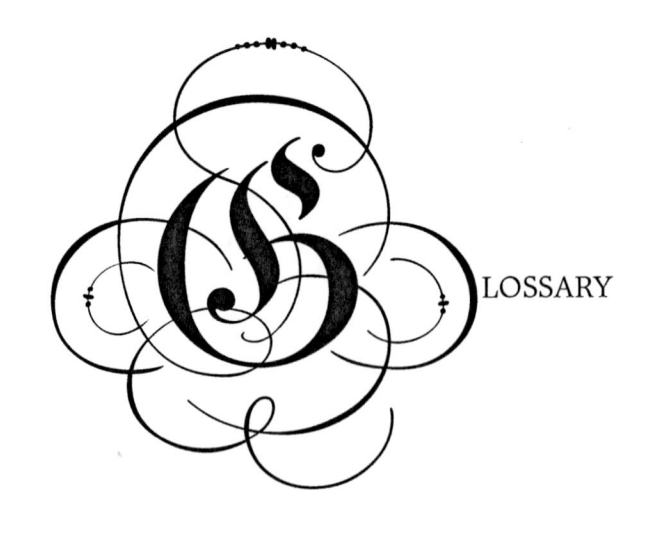

GLOSSARY

Ala-kleeha: Chosen during the Mehentuk, a new life and return to a physical dragon body. Ala-kleeha is a process for male dragons. Within the process, the male dragon — having released his previous life and physical body — returns to be birthed within a new family and a new life.

Beginning Visionings: When inglets are brought to the Great Lac for the first time, their parents take the responsibility of thought-merging and form a link between themselves, their inglet, and the population of dragons present at the Lac. During the first visit, the inglet feels and experiences the effects of this also first thought-merging with more than his family. Within the thought-merge, the inglet calls forth from the patterns within his still-forming wedge wings. The patterns release the great gift of a vision and the inglet celebrates a knowing of the nature of the possibility of his adventures during the next phase of his maturing. Because the vision occurs within a mind-merge, the population of all dragons joyfully carry within their knowing, the first visionings of all inglets. When any dragon, inglet, or elder, refers to his or her Beginning Visioning at the Great Lac, those patterns are called forth within the dragon population. The effect of such calling forth establishes a deeper merging, which can be used to enhance whatever is currently occurring.

Blue Structure: See Structure, Blue.

Cantoon: The time of year when summer's end brings the harvest and falling of leaves from the trees.

Cavern of Learning and Forming: An invitation to enter the Cavern of Learning and Forming has been extended to few dragons who continued to remain in physical form. In truth, Zoanna was the second; her great-grandmother, during the end times of the first great dragon existence, had been the first. The cavern itself resides within a realm that contains the encodings of both physical and nonphysical. It is necessary for any who enter to have the ability to maintain a knowing that, although they appear to be residing in physical form, in truth their form is not staid but is a pulsebeat of form and non-form. Within that knowing then, those who enter this particular chamber would necessarily also be aware that their physical nature was the smallest — though not insignificant by any means – part of who they were. Zoanna, as well as her great-grandmother, questioned what comprised the totality of all that she was, even when she was an inglet. Few could speak with her upon the topic and it was then her great-grandmother, in nonphysical form, who whispered to her within her inglet wonderings. Her speakings with her great-grandmother had begun her search into the realms beyond physical while she was still considered an inglet. The Cavern of Learning and Forming pulsates itself into many different forms and patterns, demonstrating the lessons and adventures that can be experienced within its vast boundaries.

Chamber of Replenishment: Once adult dragons have become mates, their merging together creates patterns of wholeness, love, and the celebration of their union. From that time forward, any merging automatically creates a chamber comprised of the patterns, and functions to re-establish those patterns within both dragons. Within the merging, each dragon can then release into the wholeness, experiences and adventures, discoveries and beauty. All that is released is merged to become part of both dragons.

Circle of Fairies: An enveloping circle of love created by the fairies who attended inglets. The purpose of the circle was primarily to protect the innocence of inglets from any expanded vibrations from Kloan Gatherings; from non-physical exploration, as inglets continued to take form and develop; and from any physical, non-physical, or vibrational threat that might prematurely end inglet innocence.

Decision of Mature Females: In the instances where non fully-developed maturity resides within a female who wishes to cocoon, another adult female – often the mother or mentor – will

GLOSSARY

merge with the young female and together they will form a cocoon. Such formings began within the embracings of loving adults. Though not encouraged, within recent histories young females have successfully cocooned and transformed, giving birth to themselves. Some young females have questioned procedures, as young ones do, and have suggested that both male and female dragons have the capabilities to rebirth in their own and each other's manner. Recent could be defined as within the previous 500 years.

Dragon Eyes: Yellow in color, as the golden essence of all Ancient Ones, dragon eyes contain in their very center, a mirror image of the encodings of the Living Word residing within the portal to the Nothingness.

Dragon Wings: Dragons have **four sets of wings**, the largest being **the middle pair** attached at the middle of their back. These wings, as do the other three sets, contain a communication system. Unique to the middle wings, across the top edge runs an energy within which resides the DNA, cellular patterning. The **smallest set of wings** has been misinterpreted in some histories as gills, but they are not. Set right at the throat, directly under the jaw, they fan outward upon command. Signaling dragon presence, such fanning sends vibrations and frequencies from the face of the fan, catapulting forth a flash of light with force similar to that of a bolt of lightening. The **third set of wings** is located under the large middle wings and is set forward so that the middle wings overlap a little. The top part of these seemingly small wings is exposed of themselves. Very thin and translucent and at times the palest of light blue or green, they have the capabilities of activating crystalline structures. The **fourth set of wings** is seemingly part of the very large ones in the center of the body, but shaped differently. They reside only on the edge of the center wings and are about one-fourth or one-fifth the size of the large wings. Like a very slick wedge, the large part is attached and then shapes itself to a point. Such wings enable their large bodies to be extremely capable of refined, determined movement.

Dream State: Or sleep state, both referring to that consciousness which resides within the Moment in Stretched Time, the Kah-na Tro-Linaht. The Dream State changed when time folded in upon itself and the Moment slowed to near stop.

Fairy Circle: An enveloping circle of love created by the fairies who attend inglets. The purpose of the circle is primarily to protect the innocence of inglets from any expanded vibrations from Kloan Gatherings; from non-physical exploration, as inglets continued to take form and develop; and from any physical, non-physical, or vibrational threat that might prematurely end inglet innocence.

Farthem: One thousand miles.

Fleecia: Section or block of time outside the realms of cause and effect.

Floggen: Family and community.

Glarian: The entire population of dragons residing physically in One Realm, even though they might journey to and participate within other realms not designated as their home.

The Grand Truth: One Dragon did flow forth and step upon the land. His experiences were so plentiful that he breathed himself forth in forms of himself, dragons, so that all possible journeys might be explored. The last journey would then be the realizing of their dragon identity: all dragons are the breath of One Dragon. And thusly would be concluded that they were only One, One Dragon. Completing such a journey and Return to One, the One Dragon would then also return to the Portal to the Nothingness to release his form and all that had been created and experienced. The Nothingness then breathes itself into being again and another dragon becomes the One. Although all journeys and experiences appear to cover eras upon eras of dragon existence, within an illusionary time and its created Time-Streams, all that had been created from the One Dragon did and does occur in one breath, one moment. Such a Truth has not as yet been held within the physical nature. Neither has it been held within the vehicle for such knowing, thought-merging.

Great Lac: A body of water used by the elders for traveling to those realms wherein the gatherings of Floggen Elders from other mountain ranges meet. Also a body of water used by parents and their young during times of seasonal transformation and the shedding of the previous journey's experiences, a merging experience for the young, similar to the adult replenishment merging chamber.

Illusionary Peaks around Mutchiat: The gnomes, it was supposed –- as not many had built an intimate relationship with the gnomes –- were of the land itself and could, at their own deciding, summon the land to rise and take a particular form. In a like manner, they also could summon the image of a form, such as the illusionary peaks around Mutchiat.

It was assumed that the illusionary peaks were created to protect Mutchiat from curiosity-seekers, and would therefore only allow those who were ready for the other-realm adventures accessible only through the portals at the peak. Some also believed that the gnomes simply did not enjoy a lot of traffic near one of their favorite spots.

Illusionary, time & concepts of beginning and ending: See Oo-Nah.

Inglets: Newly birthed and young dragons.

Kah-na Tro-Linaht: The New Beginning; the name given by the Ancient Ones to the manner in which the dragons resided within the Moment in Stretched Time.

Kilchek: A leader of his own Floggen who perished in the onslaught of the Great Fire.

Kloan Gathering: A gathering during which a Floggen introduces their young and where the elders demonstrate practices integrated from other realms not accessible to the entire Floggen; also, when within the Cavern of Mutchiat, a decision-making gathering of the Elders and Representatives of each dragon Floggen.

Known Histories: Actually, the dissolving of all that is by the Neekontuk had occurred in the number of three hundred and sixty-two times. However, the development of dragon consciousness had not reached a level that could either contain the truth or understand its implications until the three hundred and sixty-first time.

Maintain structure for future-travel: It had been discovered that some could maintain (Zog's blue structure) for what seemed like an unlimited number of future-journeys, while others were limited to as few as two. For this reason, the training program had been developed. As a secondary purpose though not lesser, those who trained also became quite familiar with the patternings involved in future-travel.

Manifesting of Being within Merging: learned within the Cavern of Learning and Forming. See Cavern of Learning and Forming.

Mehentuk: At the time of passing from physical the dragon sends forth a call and in response to the call, waves of memories and the causes and effects of the now ending dragon life rise to the surface of the consciousness. The rising forth of the richness of the events and the viewing is called Mehentuk.

Mehentuknen: A guide, one who assists the dragon involved in the Mehentuk to maintain a balanced viewing.

Meran: Floggen elder, leader, and father of Zog.

GLOSSARY

Metaclores: The highest measurements of dragon fire.

Moment in Stretched Time: A seeming moment within which the causes and effects reside outside of the ongoing timeline, as if in a timeless realm. See Kah-na Tro-Linaht.

Music at the Opening of Gossamer Wings: Light, delicate, flowing melody. The sound of gossamer wings opening were a gift from the fairies to soften the apparent need.

Mutchiat: The largest mountain range and location of Floggen and Glarian Gatherings.

Myo-Neechanen: Birthing dragons, a group of six female dragons plus the elder or Myo-Neelanen, who are adept at reading and understanding the patterns emanated from the wedge wings during the time of Myo-Neela.

Myo-Neela: Although they may, females do not necessarily release their physical bodies and can choose an entirely different process. In the moment before releasing their physical bodies, female dragons can choose Myo-Neela, a cocooned reforming and self-birthing process. Female dragons have the ability to form a cocoon of tissue (similar to the fabric some adept dragons use in creating of their personal chamber — as in the oldest dragon's chamber) which begins to flow from the glands located under their light gossamer wings. A female's deciding to form a cocoon rests upon her maturity* and abilities to mind-merge with an elder female dragon (**Myo-Neelanen**), who assists by participating in the aligning of new purposes while incorporating abilities developed within the current ending life. When such a choice is made, the forming of the cocoon requires approximately four days of focused thought-merging. Once completed, the cocoon (each female dragon's cocoon varies in color and design) displays the pulsating patterns within the female's wedge wing, and serves as a transformation and replenishment chamber for the following twelve years. **

During this time, not only the cellular structure of her physical body, but also the spontaneity of youthful joy and innocence is restored to their full capacity, giving the female the choice of exactly what abilities she would like to have available for developing when she is ready to birth herself.

After the time of twelve dragon years, the female then begins to release from the tip of her wedge wings, an essence which begins to dissolve the seven-foot thick cocoon walls from the inside to the outside. Such dissolving radiates outward colors and sounds which alert the **Myo-Neechanen** or birthing dragons*** to gather, thus relieving the Mylo-Neelanen from her mind-merge. Each Mylo-Neechanen incorporates the patterns from the wedge wings of the birthing dragon within a white smoke, which she breathes forth. It is into the white smoke, which contains the chosen patterns of her own forming, that the transformed female births herself. The Mylo-Neechanen maintain the patterned breathing and smoke for three days. At the end of three days, they step aside and the female stands before them with her glistening white body. As she sings her own song of birth, her body takes on the colors of her choices and the color of the land. Most female dragons bear the color similar to the male's green hide. The female's gossamer wings, however, maintain the colors of her birthing song.

Na-Hotep: When a female dragon does not choose Myo-Neela, she then chooses to remain in nonphysical form. That residing is called Na-Hotep and continues until the female dragon is called to enter physical residing by a new mother. As the bond between the female dragon and the mother requires merged encodings and patterns, a female dragon cannot simply choose to enter a new physical life and consequently must wait for the call of the new mother.

***Decision of Mature Females** – In the instances where non fully-developed maturity resides within a female who wishes to cocoon, another adult female – often the mother or mentor – will merge with the young female and together they will form a cocoon. Such formings began within the embracings of loving adults.

Though not encouraged, within recent histories young females have successfully cocooned and transformed, giving birth to themselves. Some young females have questioned procedures, as young ones do, and have suggested that both male and female dragons have the capabilities to rebirth in their own and each other's manner. Recent could be defined as within the previous 500 years.

**Twelve Years within the Cocoon – Some female dragons, who have mastered traveling beyond the timeline, have been known to collapse the twelve years into a lesser time. A few have actually collapsed the time to be but a breath. It was rumored, but not documented, that Zoanna had actually birthed herself more times than any and did so within a breath of time.

***Myo-Neechanen: Birthing dragons, a group of six female dragons plus the elder or Myo-Neelanen, who are adept at reading and understanding the patterns emanated from the wedge wings during the time of Myo-Neela.

<u>Nacha</u>: A mountain range two distances from their home.

<u>Nacta</u>: Adult dragon living.

<u>Na-Hotep</u>: When a female dragon does not choose Myo-Neela, she then chooses to remain in nonphysical form. That residing is called Na-Hotep and continues until the female dragon is called to enter physical residing by a new mother. As the bond between the female dragon and the mother requires merged encodings and patterns, a female dragon cannot simply choose to enter a new physical life and consequently must wait for the call of the new mother.

<u>Neecha</u>: An inner sanctum between two major mountain ranges, wherein dragons entered alone or together to explore without the automatic merging with their Floggen or with the Glarian.

<u>Neekontuk</u>: Written of in Glarian histories as an onslaught of raging fire and power, which disintegrates everything in its path.

In known histories, the Neekontuk has thus far endured through three endings and beginnings of Dragon existence.

Oldest Dragon: Literally the oldest dragon. That fact unknown to the seven, they refer to him as Old One, Sir, or Mehentuknen.

Oo-Nah: A consciousness describing the all-knowing of the Ancient Ones and any being who could maintain the expanded knowing of One; i.e., continual flowing, taking form and releasing form; while also taking form themselves and residing within the physical rhythms upon the land. Until the Great Change, only one could and has maintained Oo-Nah, that being the Oldest Dragon, or The One. There are others, the wizards in particular, who can maintain the consciousness of All Knowing; yet, they have not been able to maintain a physical presence upon the land. They have been able to create realms wherein a semblance of residing upon the land might occur. However, within those realms, they have never been able to create the cause and effect as it does naturally occur within physical form upon the land and within the belief-created boundaries of time. Consequently, the wizards are aware of the illusion of time, but have not been able to incarnate that knowing, or enjoy Oo-Nah.

Partnering with the land: The land of itself fulfilled its own needs within its rhythm of flourishing and completing that flourishing to dissolve back into its own self. Through partnership, the dragons lived within the natural cycles of the land and that which grew from and returned to it.

Representatives of Floggen are always male: Each Representative had been chosen by his own Floggen for his ability to thought-merge. Even a dragon who attends a Kloan for the first time, thought-merges and having done so, activates the patterning within wing encodings, allowing him to participate with their sophisticated communicating as one entire unit.
The females, who are the balancers of the energies and thought-formings of their Floggen, remain in their home location while

the male Representative attends each Kloan Gathering. Each female dragon also receives the transmittings of the Representative concerning the topics of the Kloan Gathering. From her, the families access such transmissions for full integration and understanding of the entire dragon population.

Return to One: In the histories of dragons residing upon the land, there had always been an experience that had led them to a type of union that would intimate the Grand Truth. See the **Grand Truth**.

Sleecha: The first breath of spring.

Sleep State: See Dream State.

Song of Rejoicing: Only sung by the fairies, a song in celebration of the action of choice by an inglet, such choice being one that has grown from an inner awareness to an external action.

Structure, Blue: Created by the wizards, blue lines racing upon themselves to form an energetic structure in the shape of the two of Mutchiat's peaks, one upright and one inverted, each residing within the other. Created for Zog the first time he, as an inglet, began to phase out of the wizard's realm. As Winzoarian, Zog continued to use the blue structure for future-travel purposes.

Timeless Realm: The Moment in Stretched Time was a seeming moment within which the causes and effects resided outside of the ongoing timeline, as if in a timeless realm.

Treiga: The deepest of winter.

Twelve Years within the Cocoon: Some female dragons, who have mastered traveling beyond the timeline, have been known to collapse the twelve years into a lesser time. A few have actually collapsed the time to be but a breath. It was rumored, but not documented, that Zoanna had actually birthed herself more times than any and did so within a breath of time.

Winzoarian: One who is adept at producing abilities written of only in the histories and carried in the encoded symbols each dragon contains within the portal of his or her heart. Among such abilities are included changing form while in mid-flight, entering the encoded portals of the wizards and, not only communicating with them but studying their wizardry — including the ability to take physical form from one realm to another.

Zoanna's Love: Being Grand Damme and the oldest of all female dragons, she has loved them all for the length of their lives, and that love has provided the platform upon which she has stood many times, calling them to be all that they can be.

AUTHOR'S BIOGRAPHY

Internationally known as one of the clearest channels on the planet, author, lecturer, and deep level channeler Miriandra Rota has been working in the field of spiritual exploration for over twenty-five years.

Her experiences as a psychic child were explored in the magazine *Venture Inward* published by the Association of Research and Enlightenment. Her channeling story is told at length in Henry Leo Bolduc's book, Journey Within: Past Life Regression and Channeling. Dr. Henry Reed also explores Miriandra's work in two books: Edgar Cayce on Channeling Your Higher Self and Developing Your Psychic Ability. Her expanded consciousness journeys are described in Michael L. Schuster's latest book, Masters of Shambala. Miriandra's channeling is a longtime favorite in the magazine, *Sedona Journal of Emergence!*

Of her first book, Welcome Home – A Time for Uniting, Sir George Trevelyan states, "...a fine example of channeling at its best...

of profound significance for the spiritual awakening of our time." Her second book, <u>The Story of the People</u>, is a compelling vision of current and upcoming changes, our choices and the New Earth.

Sought after around the world for her workshops and full-day intensives, Miriandra is a dynamic speaker and her workshops are alive, interactive and inspiring.

Contact Miriandra at Dragons@direcway.com or by writing to Visionary Works, P. O. Box 81, Troutdale, VA 24378.

ALSO BY E. MIRIANDRA ROTA

BOOKS

Welcome Home – A Time for Uniting
The Story of the People
Pretty Flower's 51 Delightful Stories on the Path

TAPES

From Mere Survival to Really Living
Peace: Your New Way to Total Fulfillment
Nourishment of Being
Your Expanded Consciousness!
Oh Beings of Home!
Stories on the Path

KAHLIL GIBRAN, THREE VOLUMES

Healing of the Heart
To Carry You Away
Indeed, Death and Beyond